スケバンターボ

PROUD ST

EST. 2012

IDW
PRESENTS

COLLECTION EDITS
JUSTIN EISINGER & ALONZO SIMON

ISBN: 978-1-68405-481-7   22 21 20 19   1 2 3 4

Special thanks to **Olivier Jalabert** of **Glénat Editions** for his invaluable assistance.

Chris Ryall, President & Publisher/CCO • **John Barber**, Editor-in-Chief • **Robbie Robbins**, EVP/Sr. Art Director • **Cara Morrison**, Chief Financial Officer • **Matthew Ruzicka**, Chief Accounting Officer • **David Hedgecock**, Associate Publisher • **Jerry Bennington**, VP of New Product Development • **Lorelei Bunjes**, VP of Digital Services • **Justin Eisinger**, Editorial Director, Graphic novels and Collections • **Eric Moss**, Sr. Director, Licensing & Business Development

Ted Adams, IDW Founder

www.IDWPUBLISHING.com
For international rights, contact
licensing@idwpublishing.com

Facebook: **facebook.com/idwpublishing**
Twitter: **@idwpublishing**
YouTube: **youtube.com/idwpublishing**
Tumblr: **tumblr.idwpublishing.com**
Instagram: **instagram.com/idwpublishing**

 You Tube

WRITTEN BY
SYLVAIN RUNBERG

ART BY
VICTOR SANTOS

LETTERS & COLLECTION DESIGN BY
SHAWN LEE

SERIES EDITOR
ELIZABETH BREI

GROUP EDITOR
DENTON J. TIPTON

VICTOR SANTOS

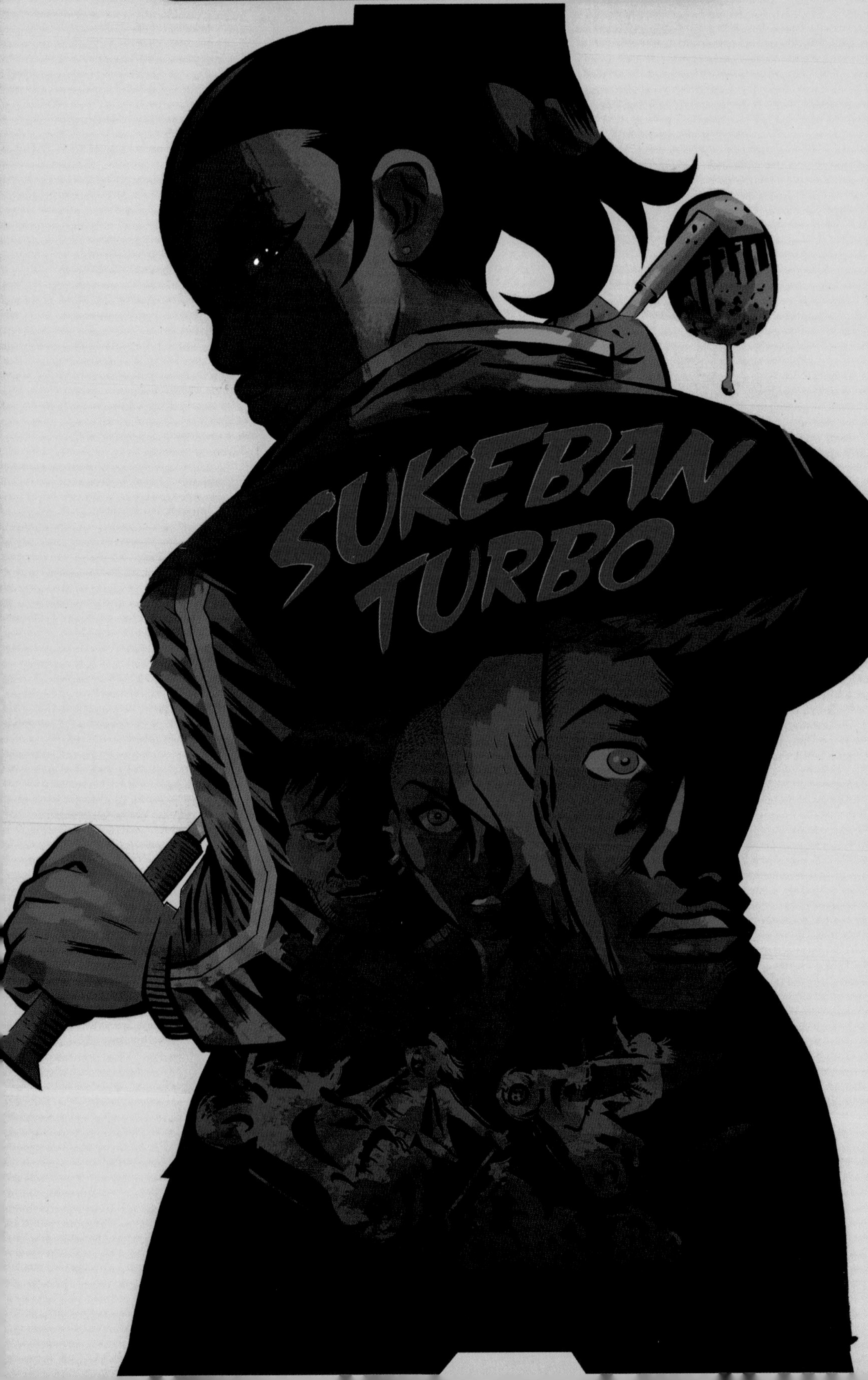
SUKEBAN
TURBO

New York.
Spring 2012.

OLIVER'S PARADISE
MOVIES \ VIDEOS \
DVD \ RENTALS

NEW RELEASES

OLIVER'S PARADISE
MOVIES/ VIDEOS/
DVD/RENTALS

election

2X1 OFFERS!

SCI FI

THE AMERICAN

NOIR

$5

URRGGHHH!

H-H-
HELP!

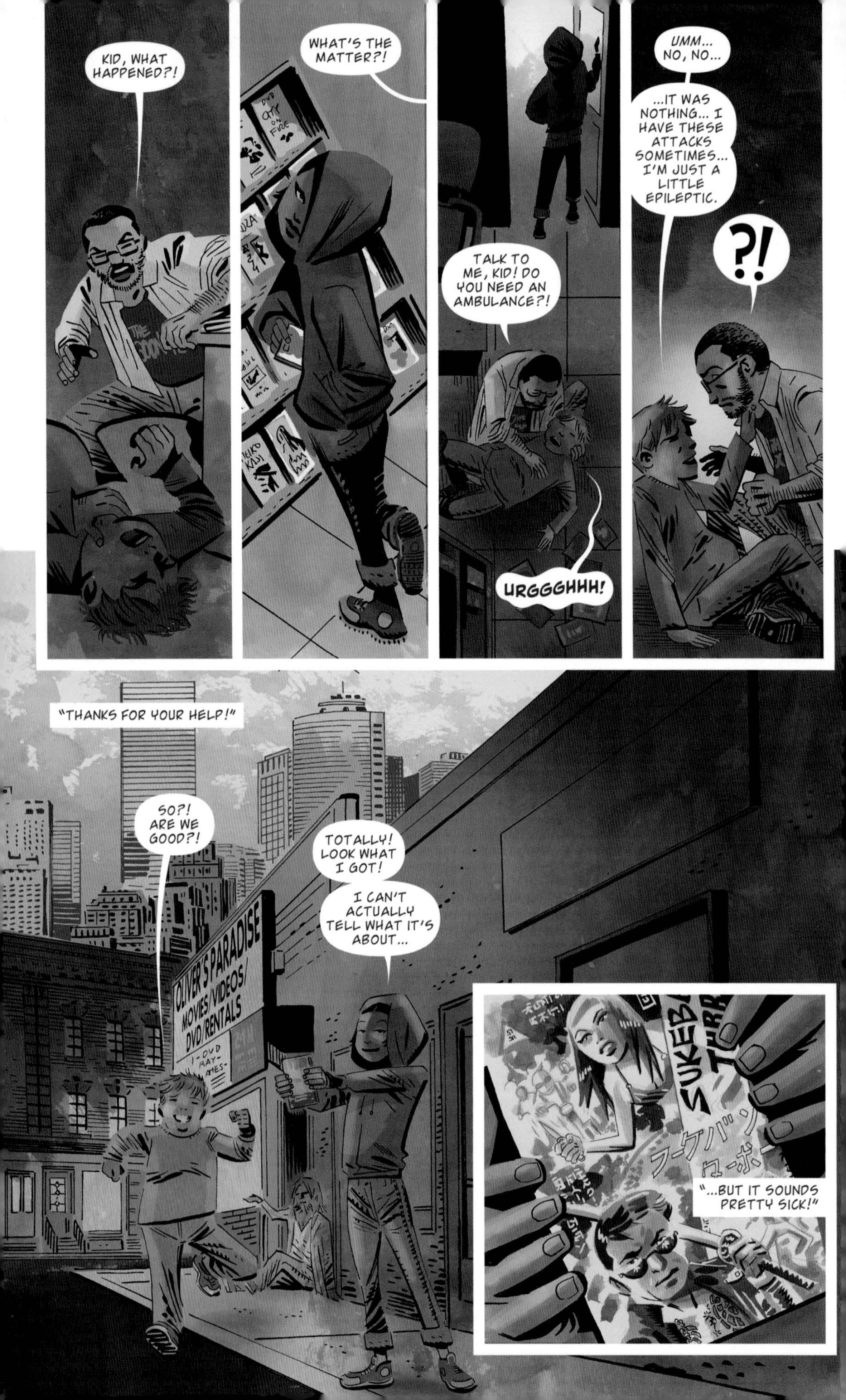
KID, WHAT HAPPENED?!
WHAT'S THE MATTER?!
TALK TO ME, KID! DO YOU NEED AN AMBULANCE?!
URGGGHHH!
UMM... NO, NO...
...IT WAS NOTHING... I HAVE THESE ATTACKS SOMETIMES... I'M JUST A LITTLE EPILEPTIC.
?!
"THANKS FOR YOUR HELP!"
SO?! ARE WE GOOD?!
TOTALLY! LOOK WHAT I GOT!
I CAN'T ACTUALLY TELL WHAT IT'S ABOUT...
OLIVER'S PARADISE
MOVIES/VIDEOS/
DVD/RENTALS
"...BUT IT SOUNDS PRETTY SICK!"

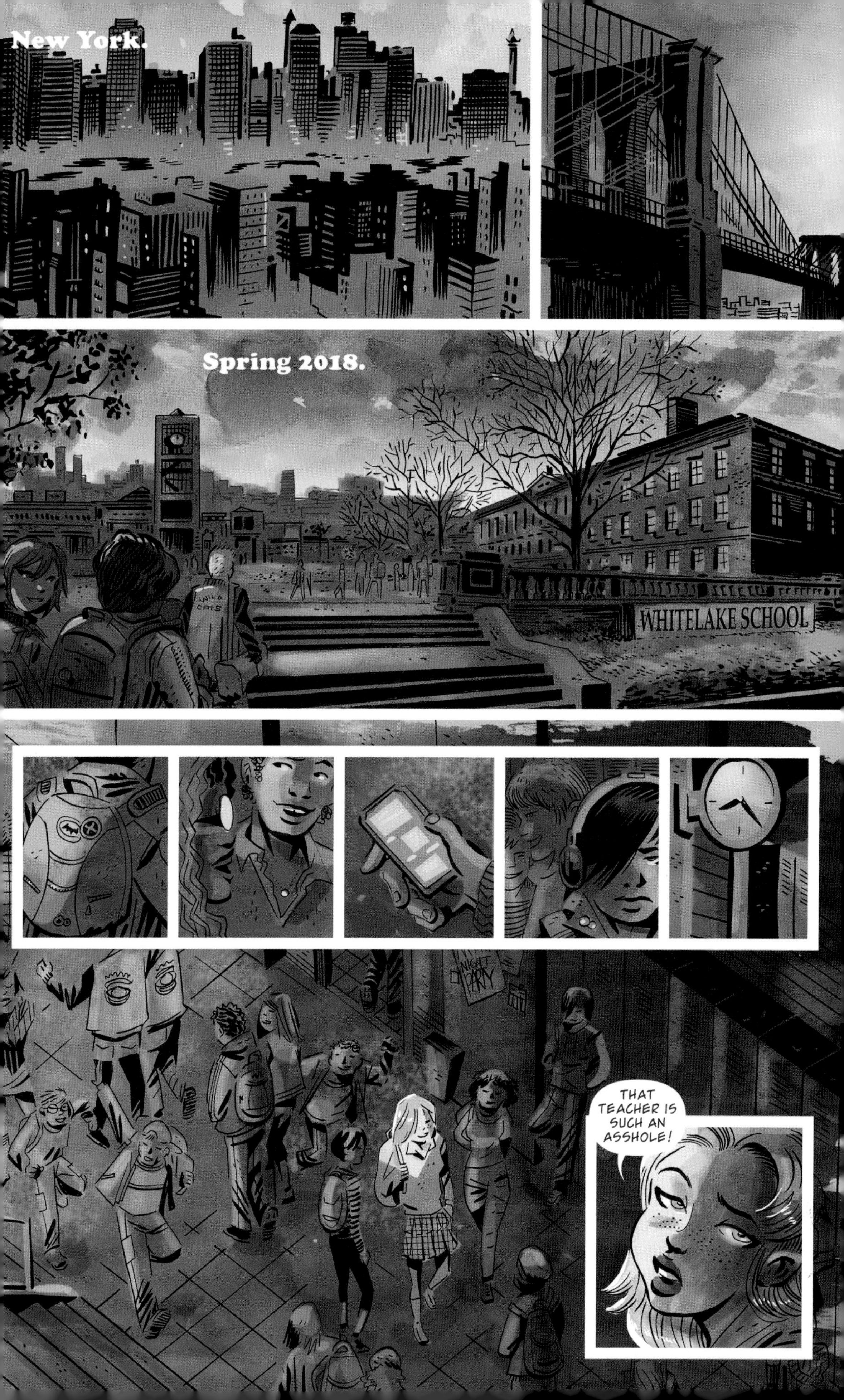
New York.
Spring 2018.
WILD CATS
WHITELAKE SCHOOL
NIGHT PARTY
THAT TEACHER IS SUCH AN ASSHOLE!

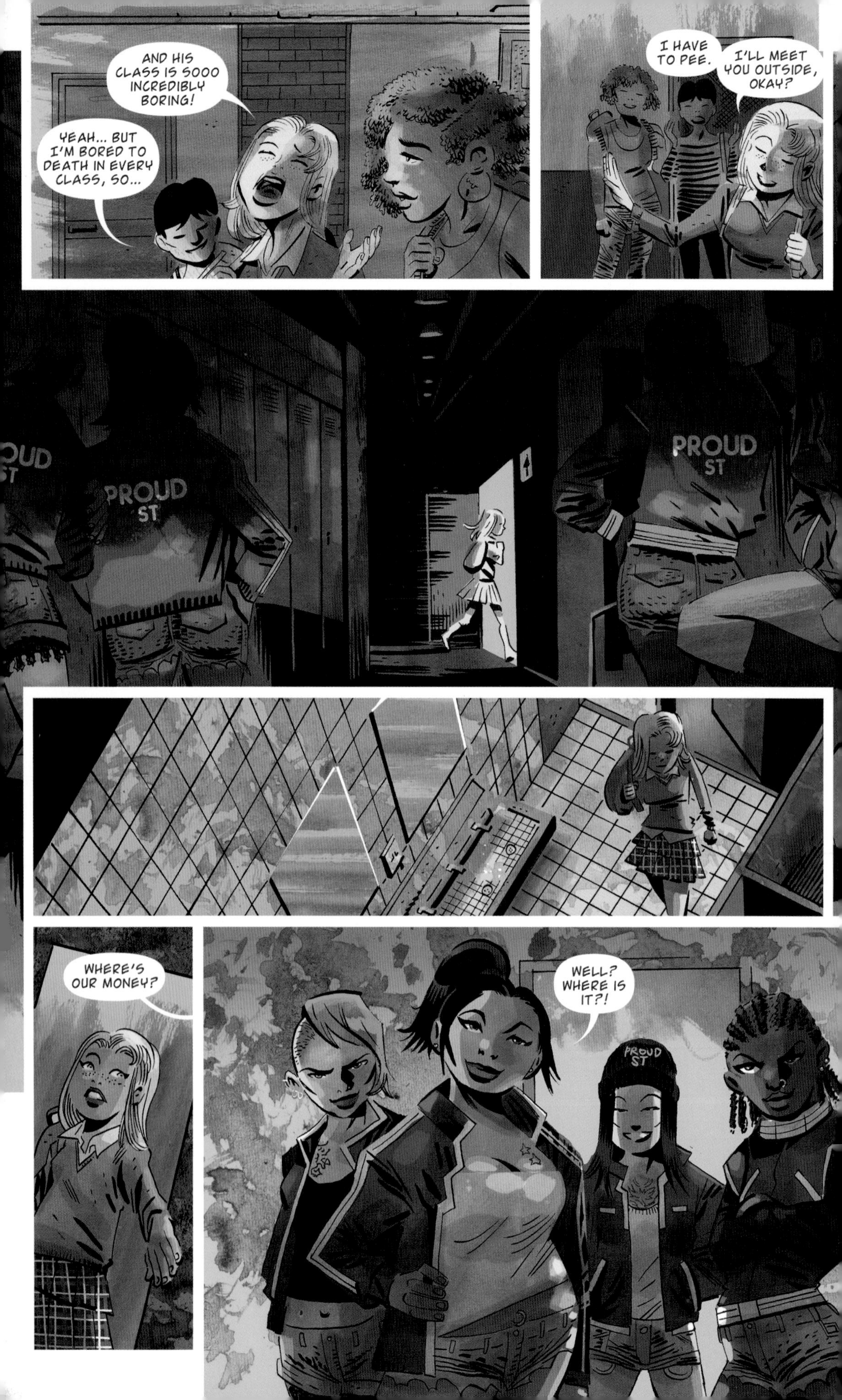
AND HIS CLASS IS SOOO INCREDIBLY BORING!
YEAH... BUT I'M BORED TO DEATH IN EVERY CLASS, SO...
I HAVE TO PEE.
I'LL MEET YOU OUTSIDE, OKAY?
PROUD ST
PROUD ST
WHERE'S OUR MONEY?
WELL? WHERE IS IT?!
PROUD ST

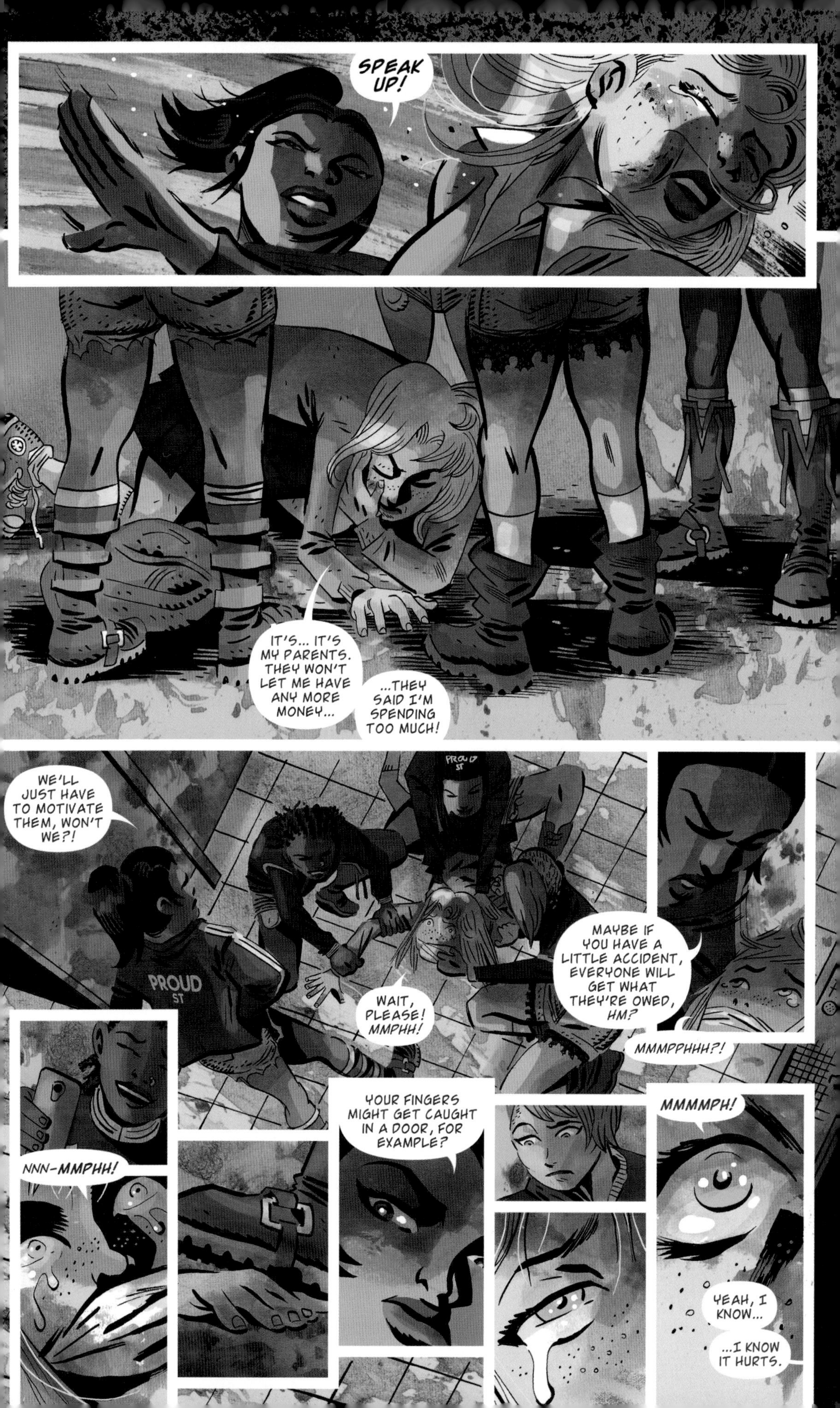
SPEAK UP!
IT'S... IT'S MY PARENTS. THEY WON'T LET ME HAVE ANY MORE MONEY...
...THEY SAID I'M SPENDING TOO MUCH!
WE'LL JUST HAVE TO MOTIVATE THEM, WON'T WE?!
PROUD ST
PROUD ST
WAIT, PLEASE! MMPHH!
MAYBE IF YOU HAVE A LITTLE ACCIDENT, EVERYONE WILL GET WHAT THEY'RE OWED, HM?
MMMPPHHH?!
NNN-MMPHH!
YOUR FINGERS MIGHT GET CAUGHT IN A DOOR, FOR EXAMPLE?
MMMMPH!
YEAH, I KNOW...
...I KNOW IT HURTS.

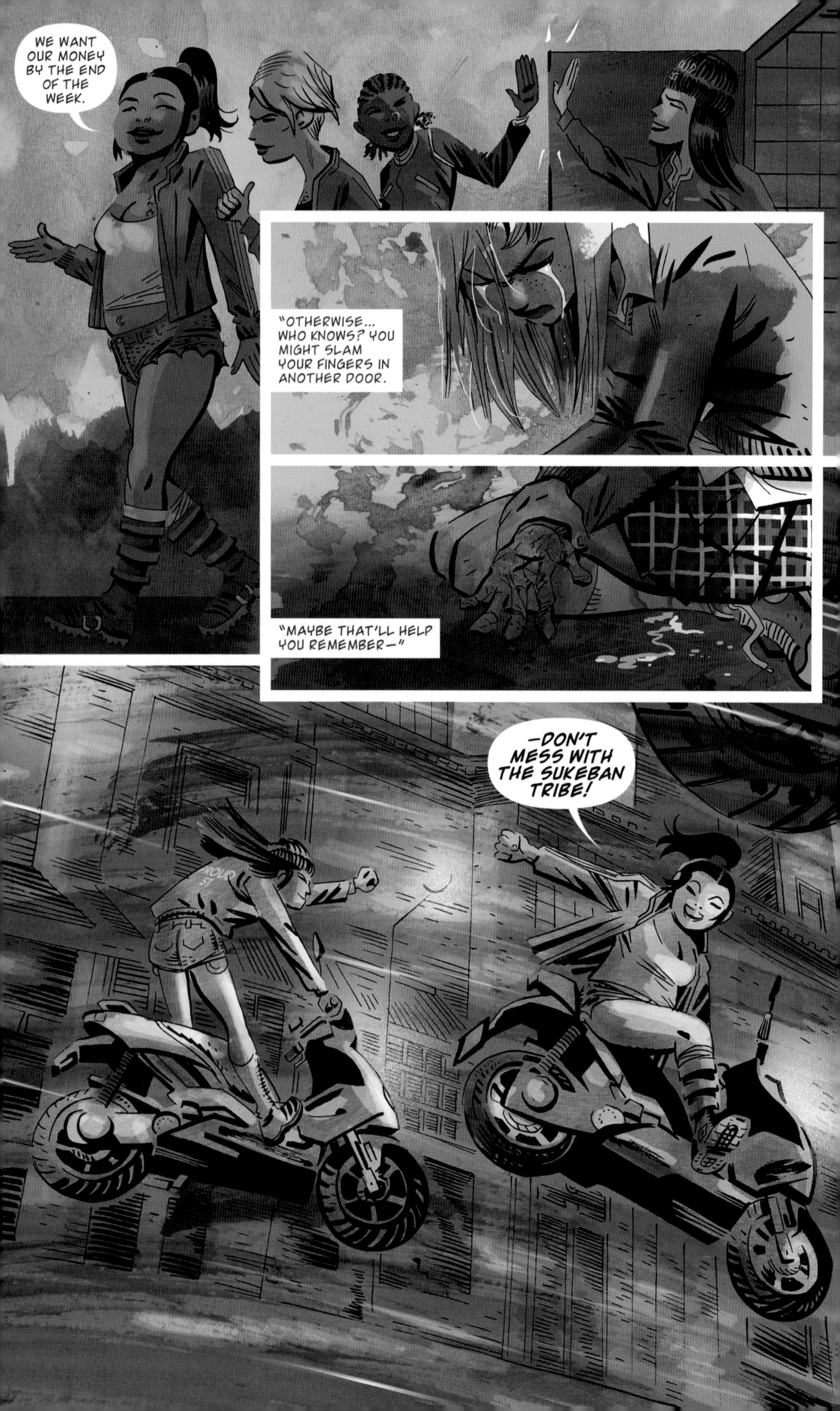
WE WANT OUR MONEY BY THE END OF THE WEEK.
"OTHERWISE... WHO KNOWS? YOU MIGHT SLAM YOUR FINGERS IN ANOTHER DOOR.
"MAYBE THAT'LL HELP YOU REMEMBER—"
—DON'T MESS WITH THE SUKEBAN TRIBE!

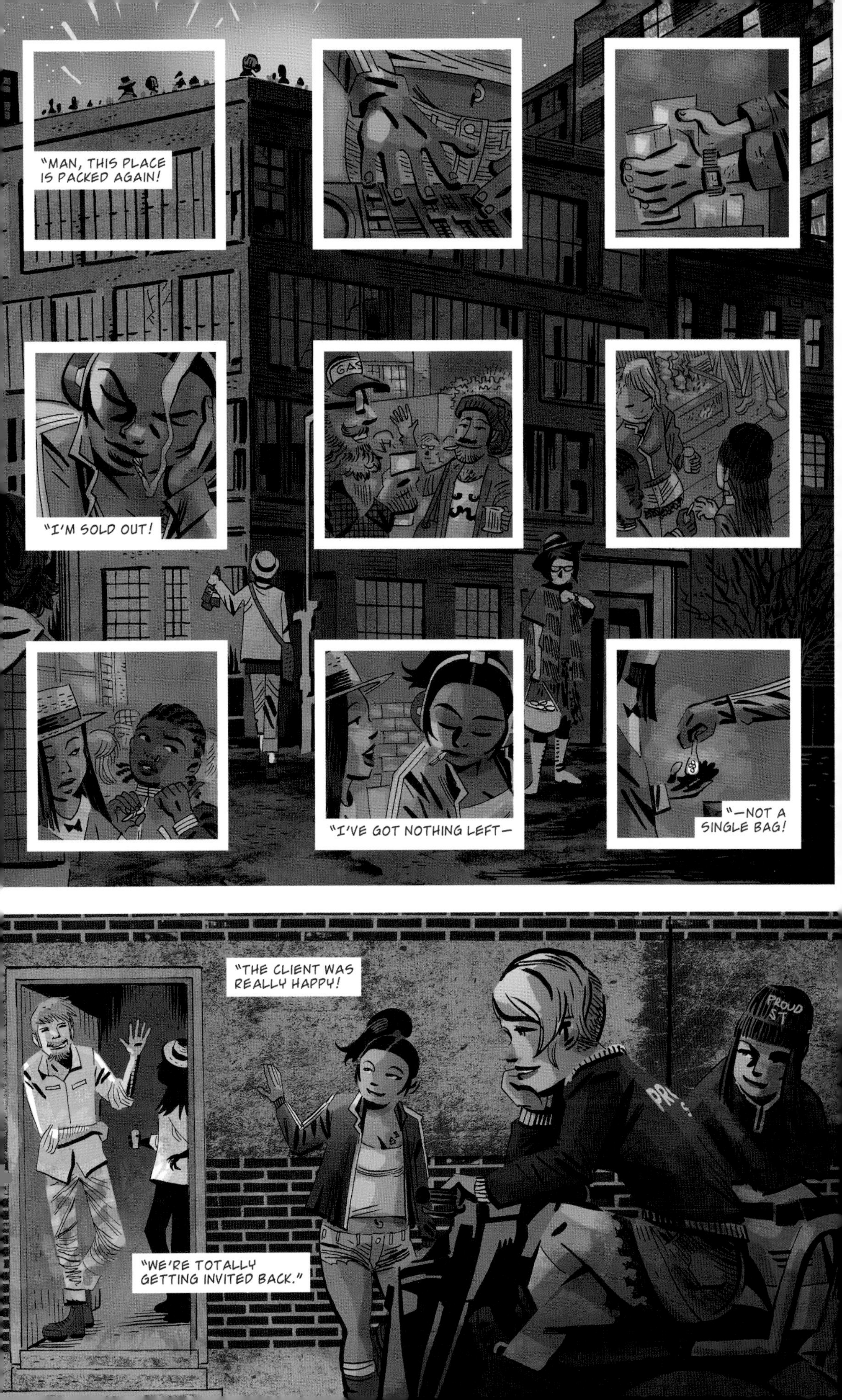
"MAN, THIS PLACE IS PACKED AGAIN!
GAS
"I'M SOLD OUT!
"I'VE GOT NOTHING LEFT—
"—NOT A SINGLE BAG!
"THE CLIENT WAS REALLY HAPPY!
PROUD ST
"WE'RE TOTALLY GETTING INVITED BACK."

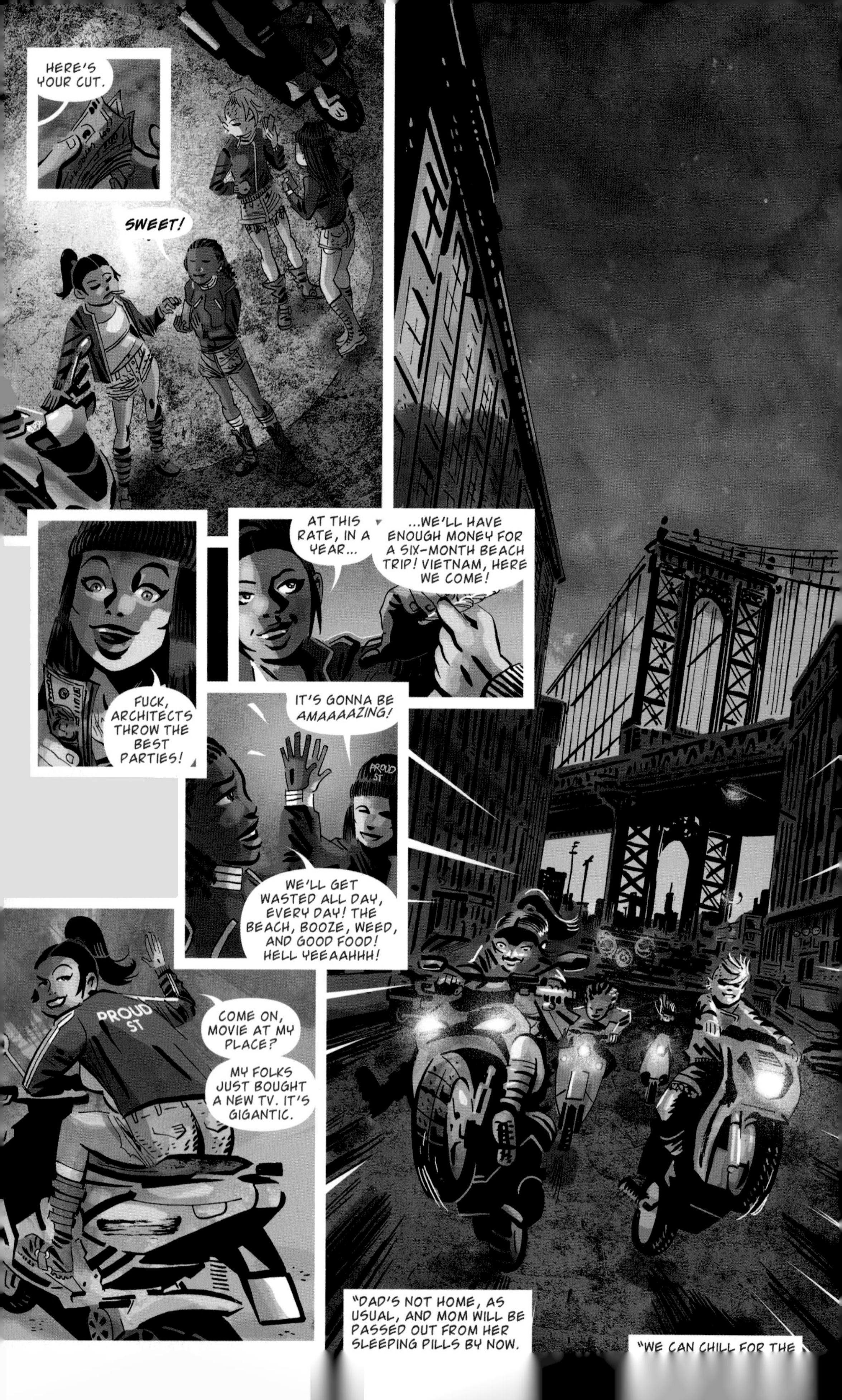
HERE'S YOUR CUT.
SWEET!
AT THIS RATE, IN A YEAR...
...WE'LL HAVE ENOUGH MONEY FOR A SIX-MONTH BEACH TRIP! VIETNAM, HERE WE COME!
FUCK, ARCHITECTS THROW THE BEST PARTIES!
IT'S GONNA BE AMAAAAZING!
PROUD ST
WE'LL GET WASTED ALL DAY, EVERY DAY! THE BEACH, BOOZE, WEED, AND GOOD FOOD! HELL YEEAAHHH!
PROUD ST
COME ON, MOVIE AT MY PLACE?
MY FOLKS JUST BOUGHT A NEW TV. IT'S GIGANTIC.
"DAD'S NOT HOME, AS USUAL, AND MOM WILL BE PASSED OUT FROM HER SLEEPING PILLS BY NOW.
"WE CAN CHILL FOR THE

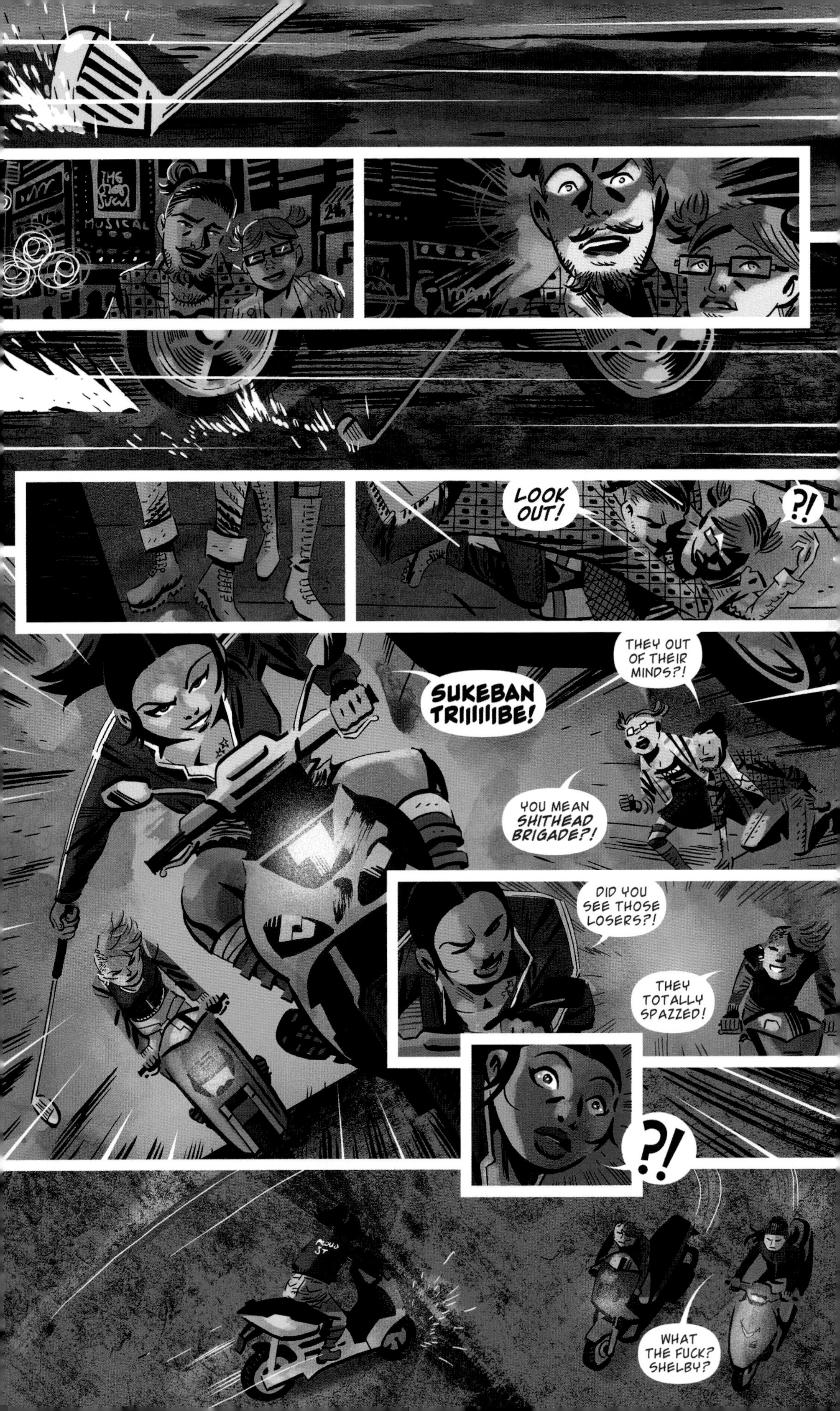
LOOK OUT!
?!
SUKEBAN TRIIIIIIBE!
THEY OUT OF THEIR MINDS?!
YOU MEAN SHITHEAD BRIGADE?!
DID YOU SEE THOSE LOSERS?!
THEY TOTALLY SPAZZED!
?!
WHAT THE FUCK? SHELBY?

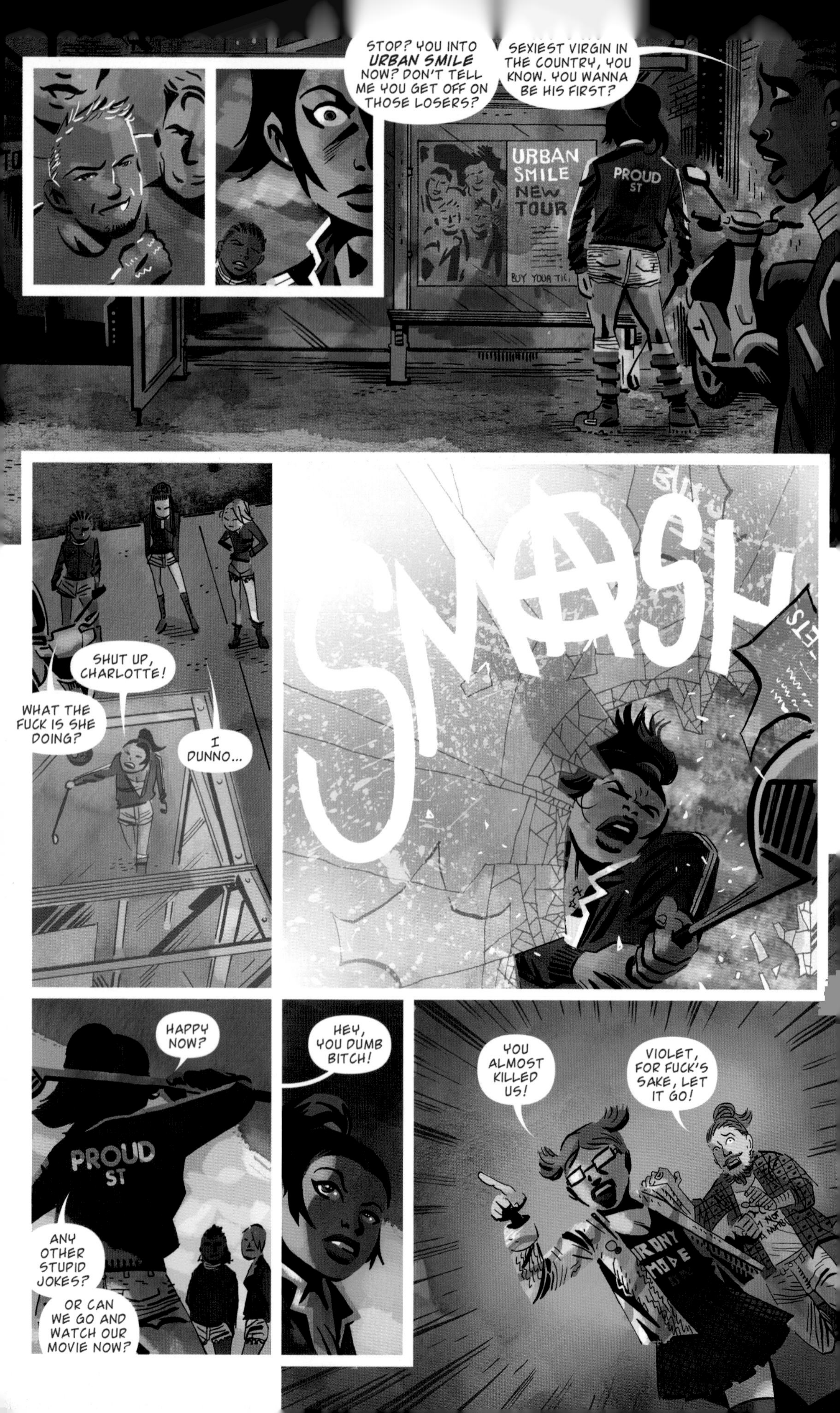
STOP? YOU INTO URBAN SMILE NOW? DON'T TELL ME YOU GET OFF ON THOSE LOSERS?
SEXIEST VIRGIN IN THE COUNTRY, YOU KNOW. YOU WANNA BE HIS FIRST?
URBAN SMILE NEW TOUR
BUY YOUR TI
PROUD ST
WHAT THE FUCK IS SHE DOING?
SHUT UP, CHARLOTTE!
I DUNNO...
SMASH
HAPPY NOW?
ANY OTHER STUPID JOKES?
OR CAN WE GO AND WATCH OUR MOVIE NOW?
PROUD ST
HEY, YOU DUMB BITCH!
YOU ALMOST KILLED US!
VIOLET, FOR FUCK'S SAKE, LET IT GO!

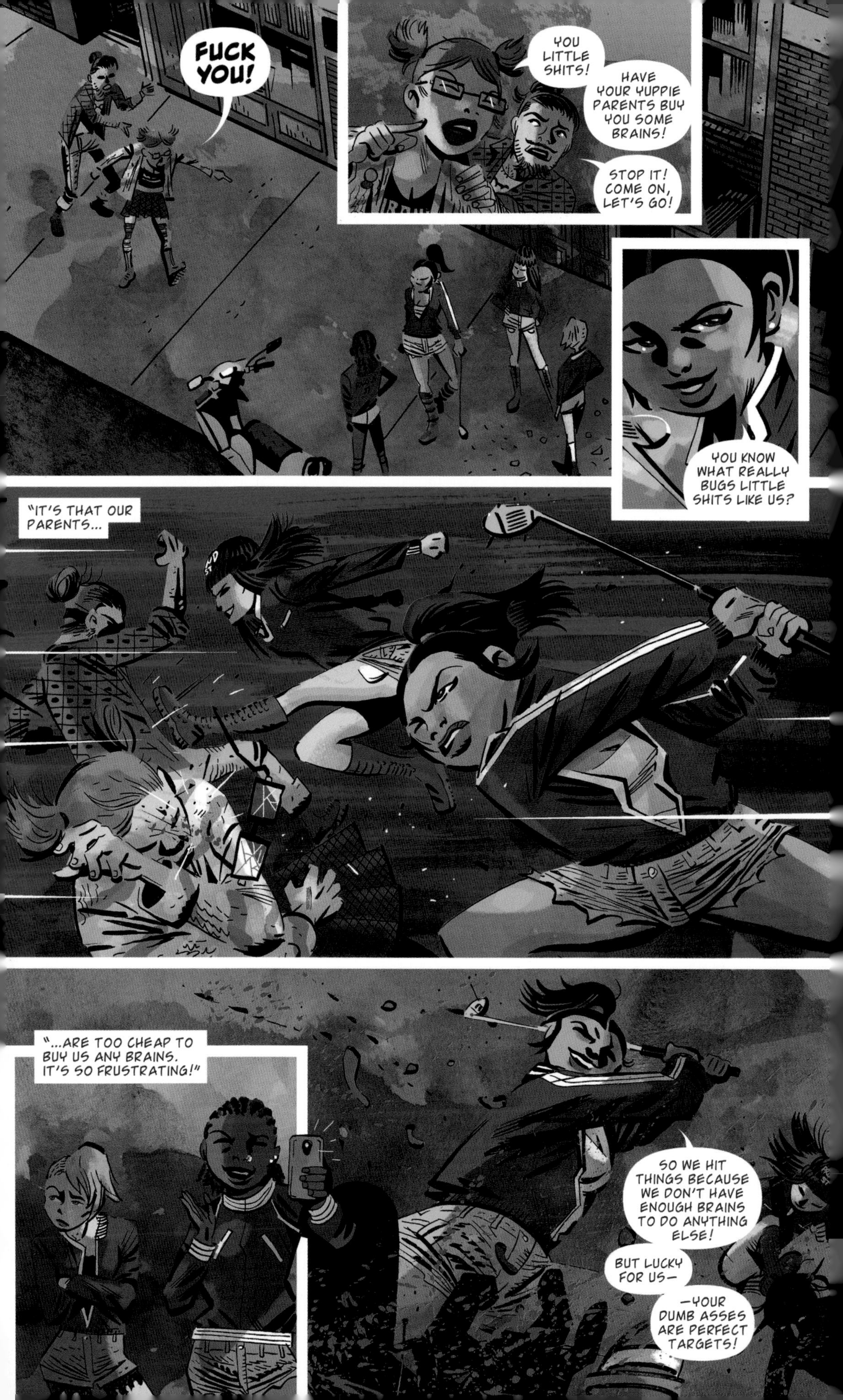
FUCK YOU!
YOU LITTLE SHITS!
HAVE YOUR YUPPIE PARENTS BUY YOU SOME BRAINS!
STOP IT! COME ON, LET'S GO!
YOU KNOW WHAT REALLY BUGS LITTLE SHITS LIKE US?
"IT'S THAT OUR PARENTS...
"...ARE TOO CHEAP TO BUY US ANY BRAINS. IT'S SO FRUSTRATING!"
SO WE HIT THINGS BECAUSE WE DON'T HAVE ENOUGH BRAINS TO DO ANYTHING ELSE!
BUT LUCKY FOR US—
—YOUR DUMB ASSES ARE PERFECT TARGETS!

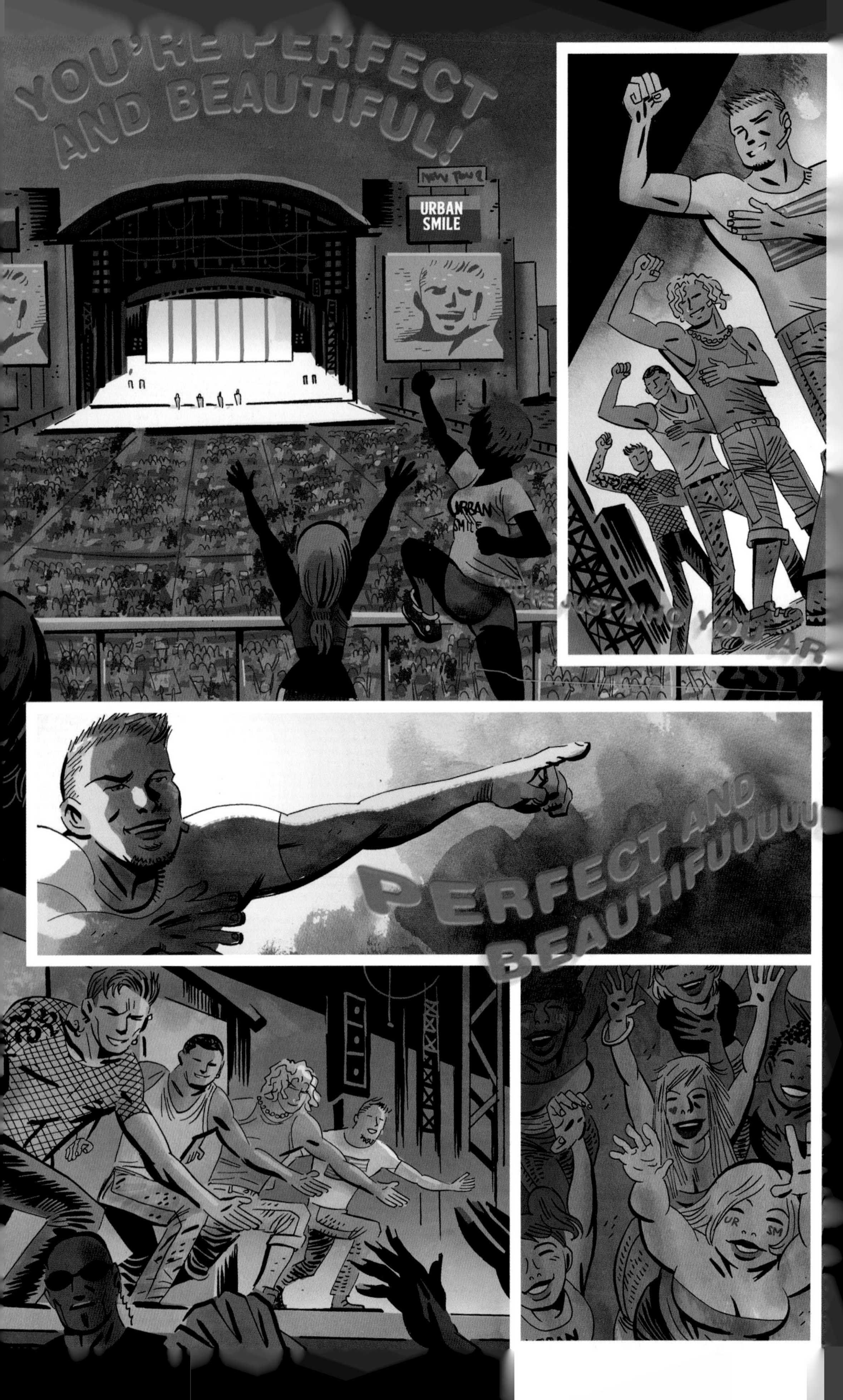

YOU'RE PERFECT AND BEAUTIFUL!
NEW TOUR
URBAN SMILE
URBAN SMILE
YOU'RE JUST WHO YOU AR
PERFECT AND BEAUTIFUUUUU
UR SM

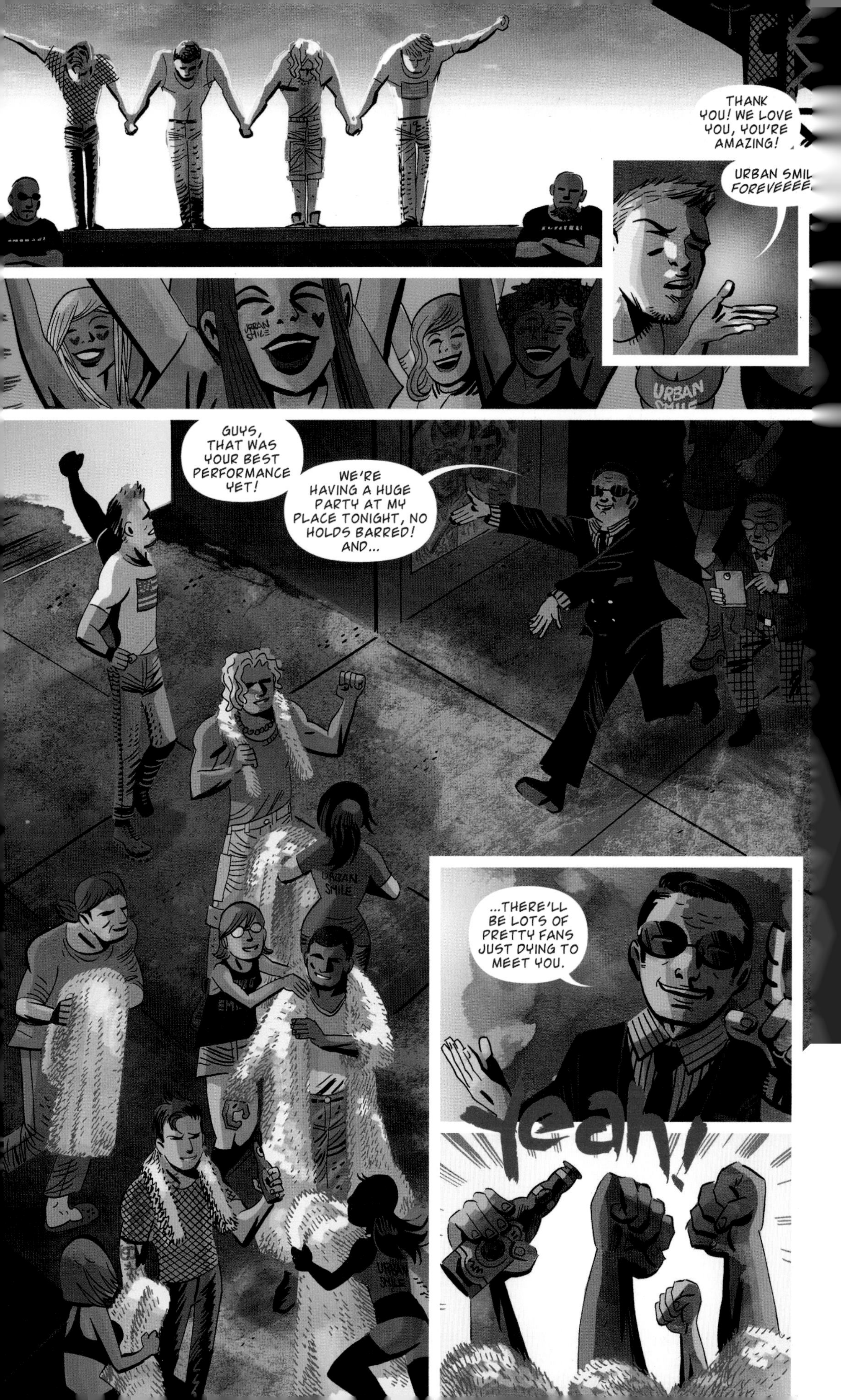
THANK YOU! WE LOVE YOU, YOU'RE AMAZING!
URBAN SMIL FOREVEEEEE
URBAN SMILE
GUYS, THAT WAS YOUR BEST PERFORMANCE YET!
WE'RE HAVING A HUGE PARTY AT MY PLACE TONIGHT, NO HOLDS BARRED! AND...
...THERE'LL BE LOTS OF PRETTY FANS JUST DYING TO MEET YOU.
YEAH!

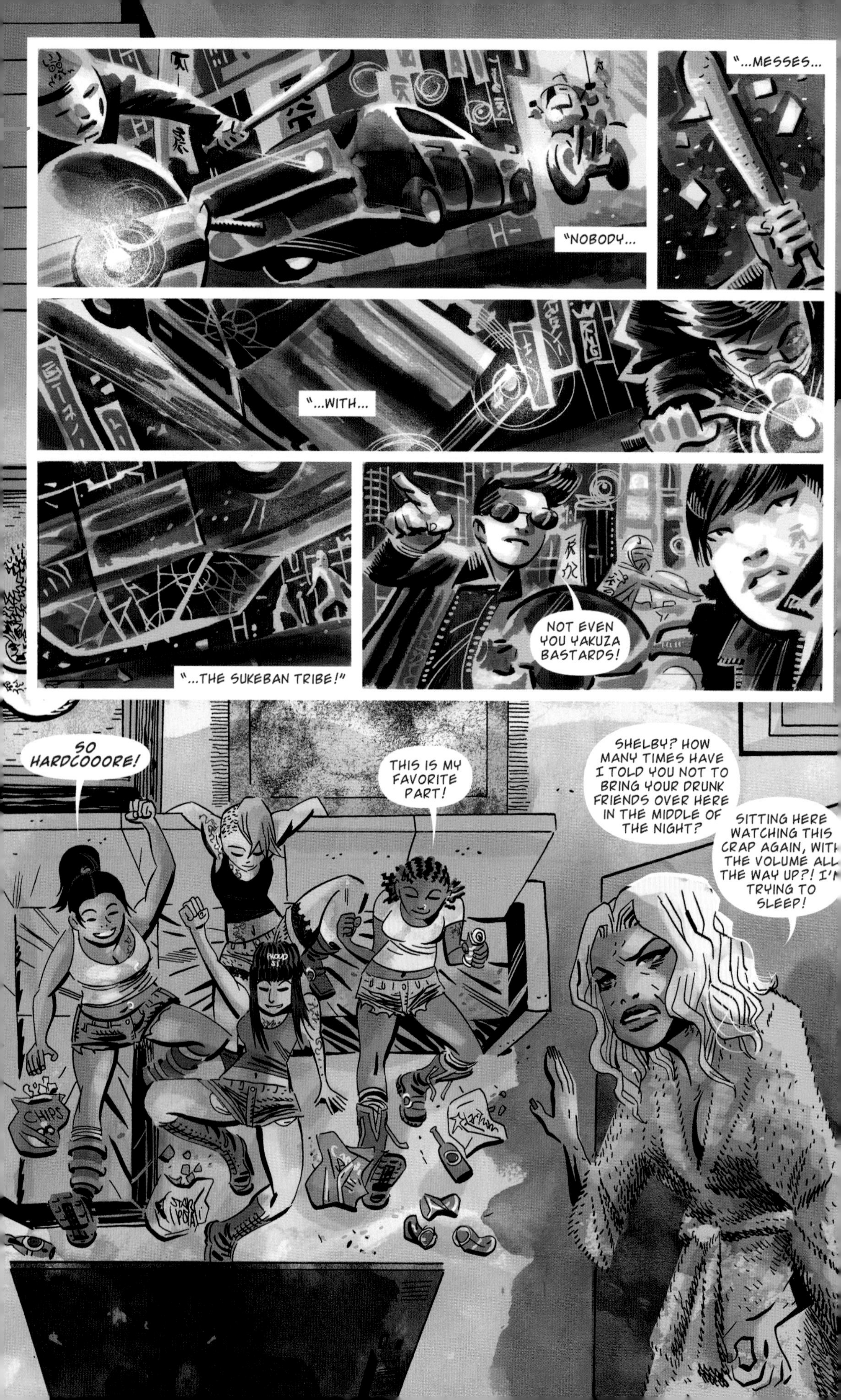
"NOBODY...
"...MESSES...
"...WITH...
"...THE SUKEBAN TRIBE!"
NOT EVEN YOU YAKUZA BASTARDS!
SO HARDCOOORE!
THIS IS MY FAVORITE PART!
SHELBY? HOW MANY TIMES HAVE I TOLD YOU NOT TO BRING YOUR DRUNK FRIENDS OVER HERE IN THE MIDDLE OF THE NIGHT?
SITTING HERE WATCHING THIS CRAP AGAIN, WITH THE VOLUME ALL THE WAY UP?! I'M TRYING TO SLEEP!
CHIPS

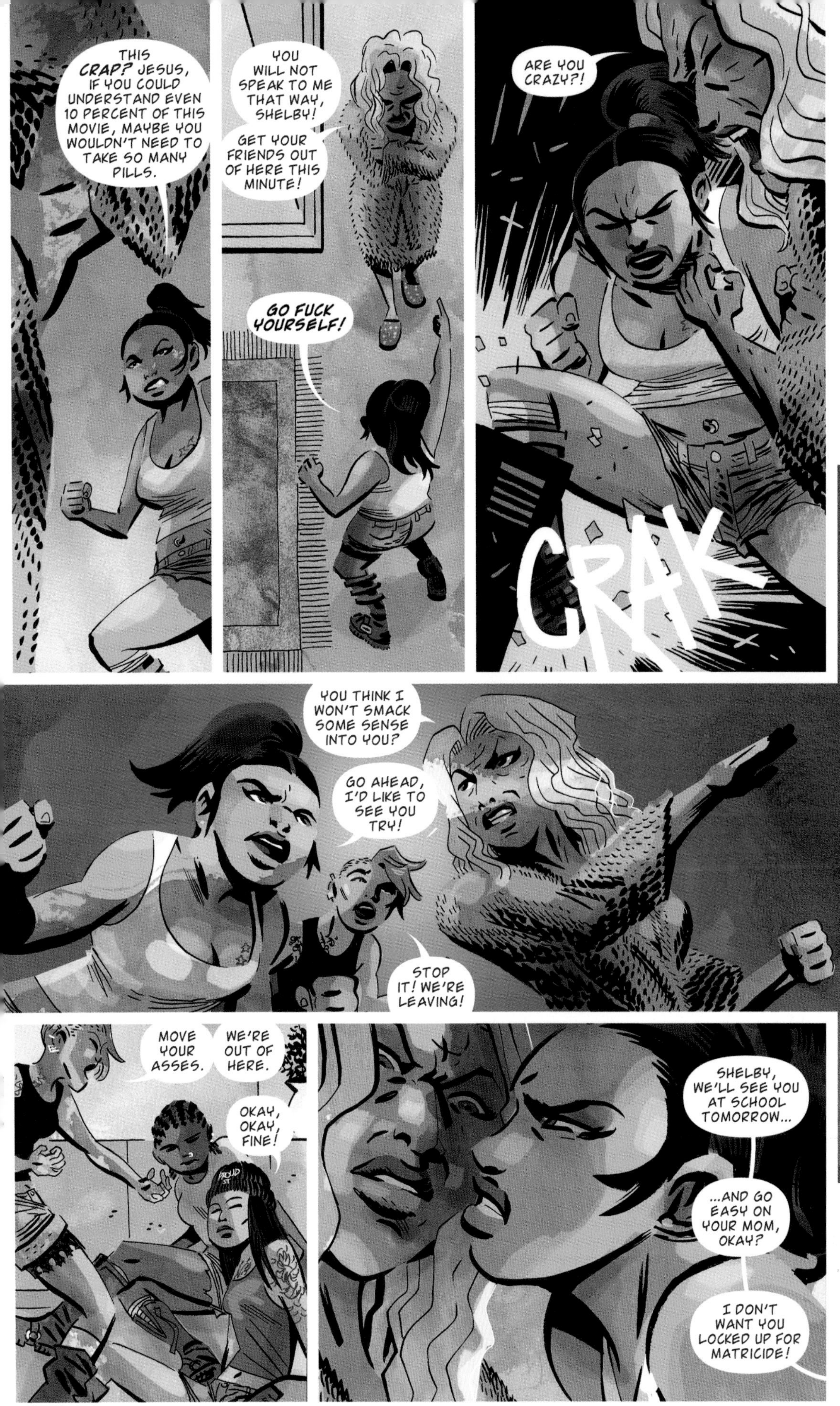

THIS CRAP? JESUS, IF YOU COULD UNDERSTAND EVEN 10 PERCENT OF THIS MOVIE, MAYBE YOU WOULDN'T NEED TO TAKE SO MANY PILLS.
YOU WILL NOT SPEAK TO ME THAT WAY, SHELBY!
GET YOUR FRIENDS OUT OF HERE THIS MINUTE!
GO FUCK YOURSELF!
ARE YOU CRAZY?!
CRAK
YOU THINK I WON'T SMACK SOME SENSE INTO YOU?
GO AHEAD, I'D LIKE TO SEE YOU TRY!
STOP IT! WE'RE LEAVING!
MOVE YOUR ASSES.
WE'RE OUT OF HERE.
OKAY, OKAY, FINE!
SHELBY, WE'LL SEE YOU AT SCHOOL TOMORROW...
...AND GO EASY ON YOUR MOM, OKAY?
I DON'T WANT YOU LOCKED UP FOR MATRICIDE!

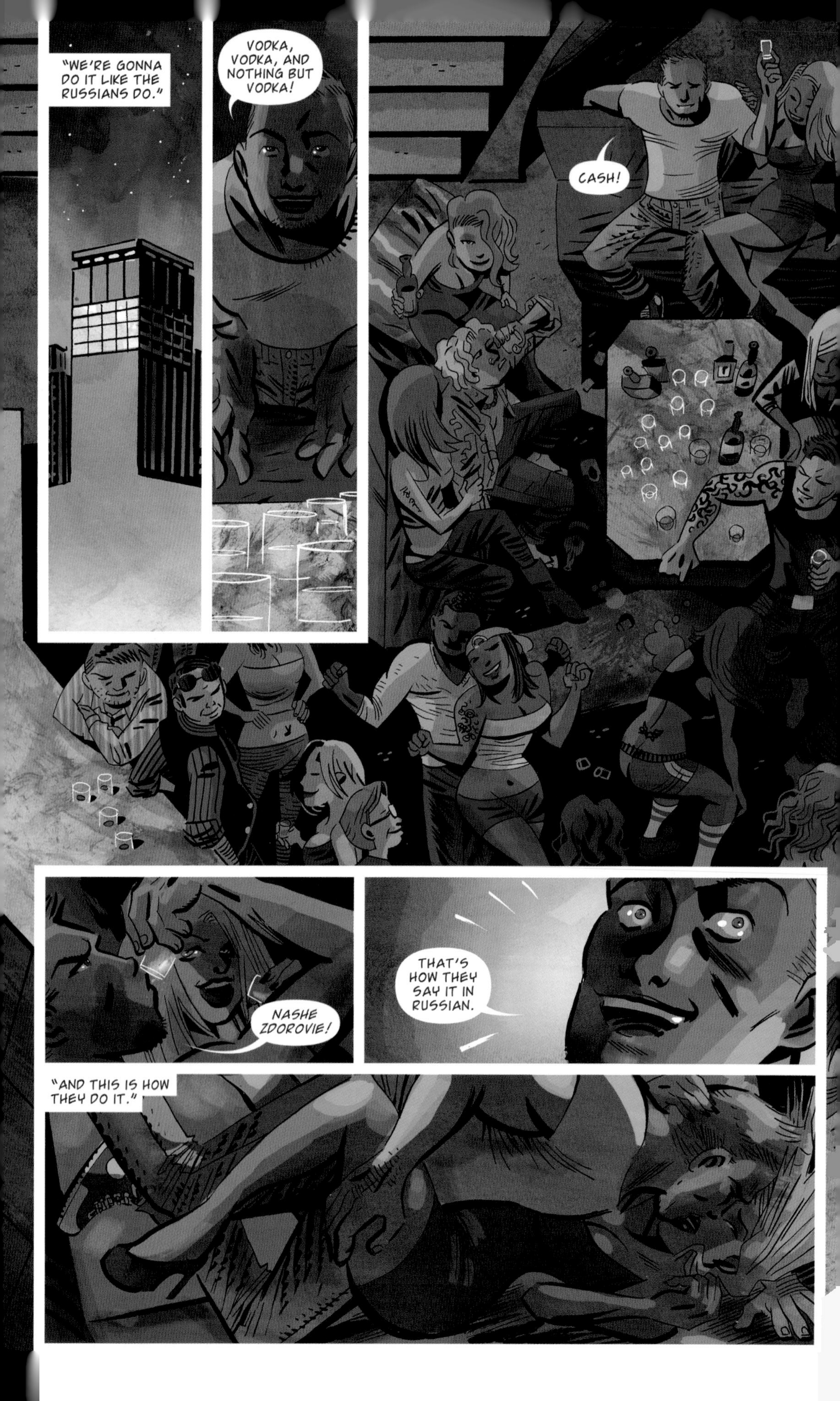
"WE'RE GONNA DO IT LIKE THE RUSSIANS DO."
VODKA, VODKA, AND NOTHING BUT VODKA!
CASH!
NASHE ZDOROVIE!
THAT'S HOW THEY SAY IT IN RUSSIAN.
"AND THIS IS HOW THEY DO IT."

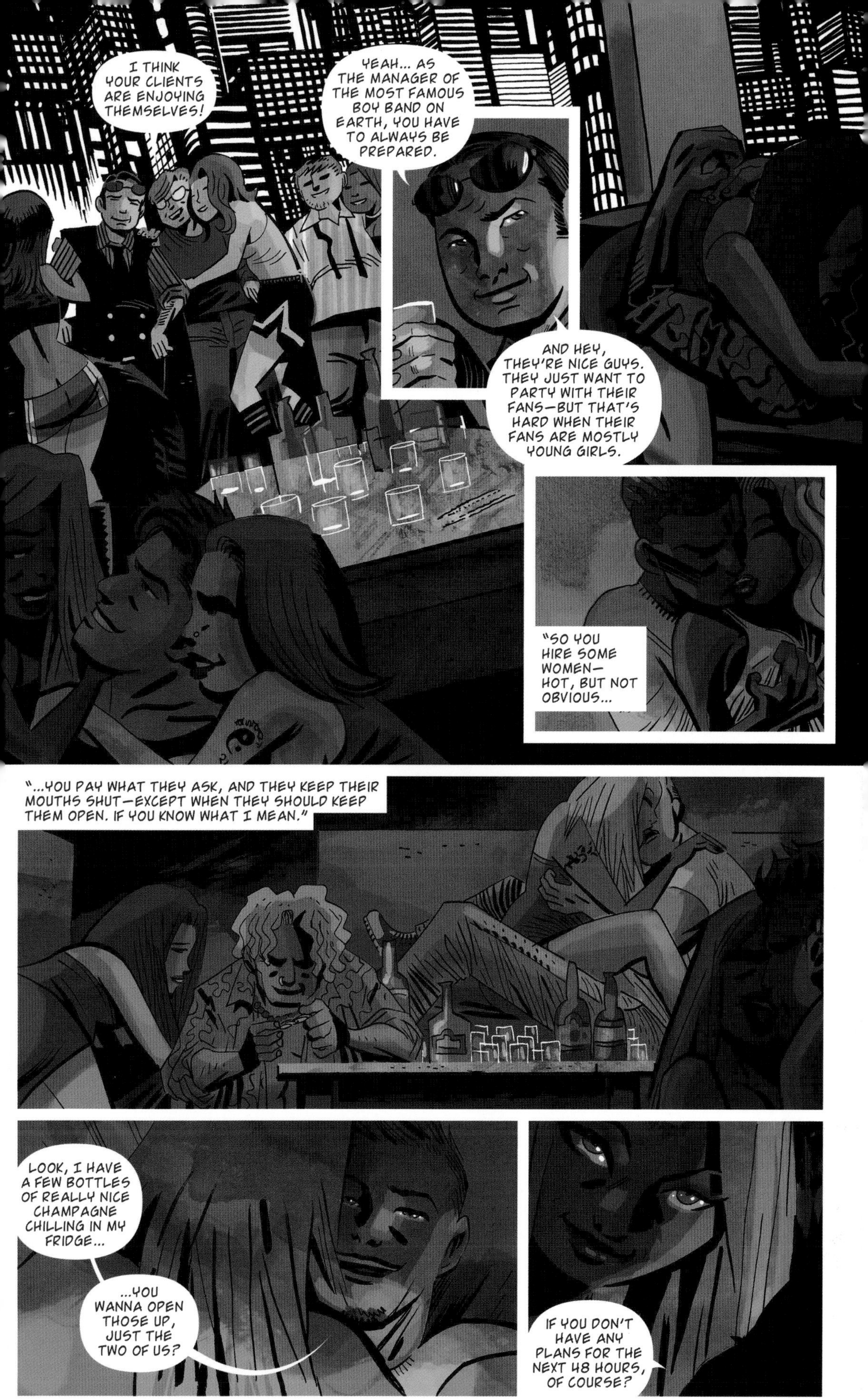

I THINK YOUR CLIENTS ARE ENJOYING THEMSELVES!
YEAH... AS THE MANAGER OF THE MOST FAMOUS BOY BAND ON EARTH, YOU HAVE TO ALWAYS BE PREPARED.
AND HEY, THEY'RE NICE GUYS. THEY JUST WANT TO PARTY WITH THEIR FANS—BUT THAT'S HARD WHEN THEIR FANS ARE MOSTLY YOUNG GIRLS.
"SO YOU HIRE SOME WOMEN—HOT, BUT NOT OBVIOUS...
"...YOU PAY WHAT THEY ASK, AND THEY KEEP THEIR MOUTHS SHUT—EXCEPT WHEN THEY SHOULD KEEP THEM OPEN. IF YOU KNOW WHAT I MEAN."
LOOK, I HAVE A FEW BOTTLES OF REALLY NICE CHAMPAGNE CHILLING IN MY FRIDGE...
...YOU WANNA OPEN THOSE UP, JUST THE TWO OF US?
IF YOU DON'T HAVE ANY PLANS FOR THE NEXT 48 HOURS, OF COURSE?

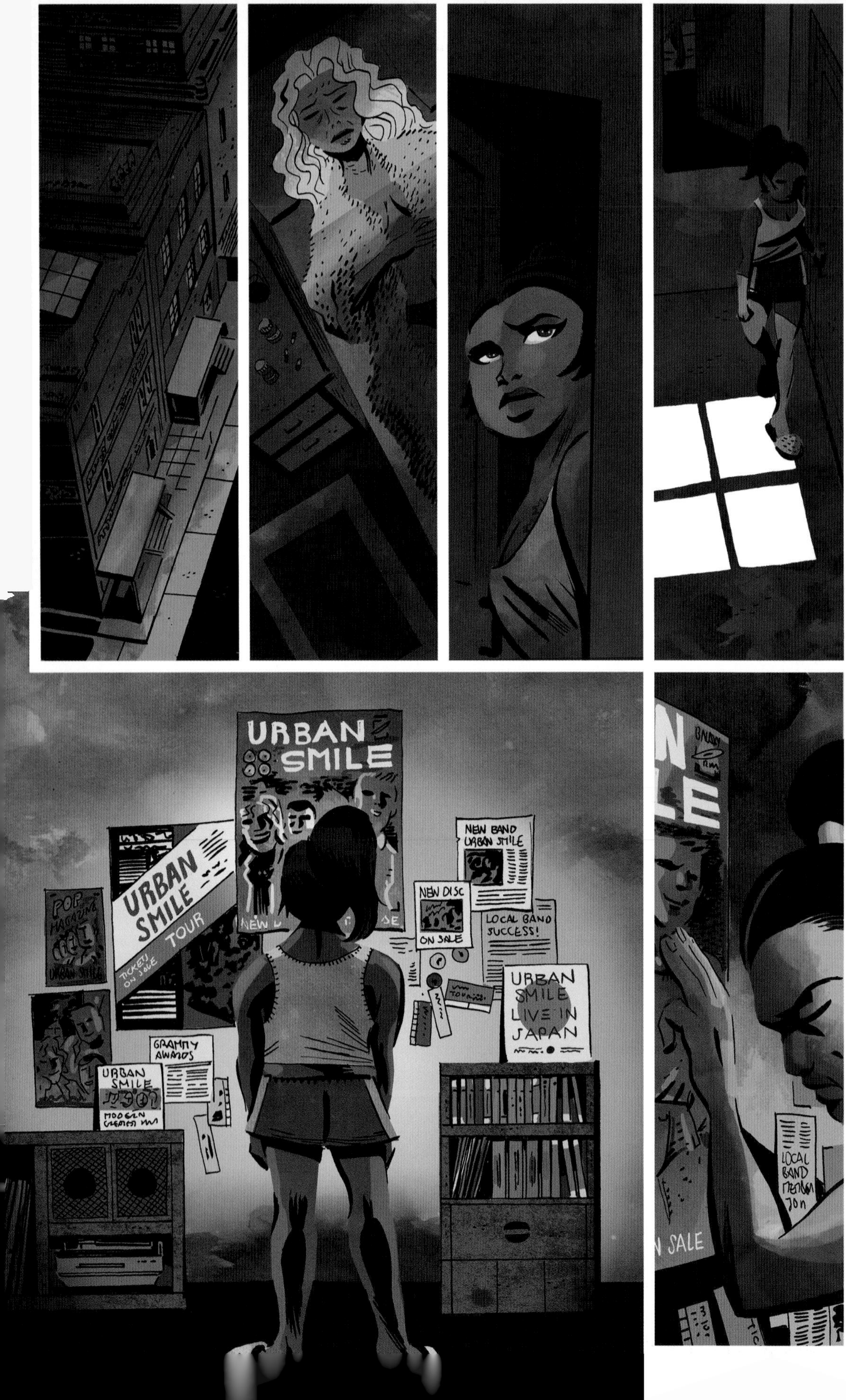
URBAN SMILE
URBAN SMILE TOUR
POP MAGAZINE
NEW BAND URBAN SMILE
NEW DISC ON SALE
LOCAL BAND SUCCESS!
URBAN SMILE LIVE IN JAPAN
GRAMMY AWARDS
URBAN SMILE
LOCAL BAND
ON SALE

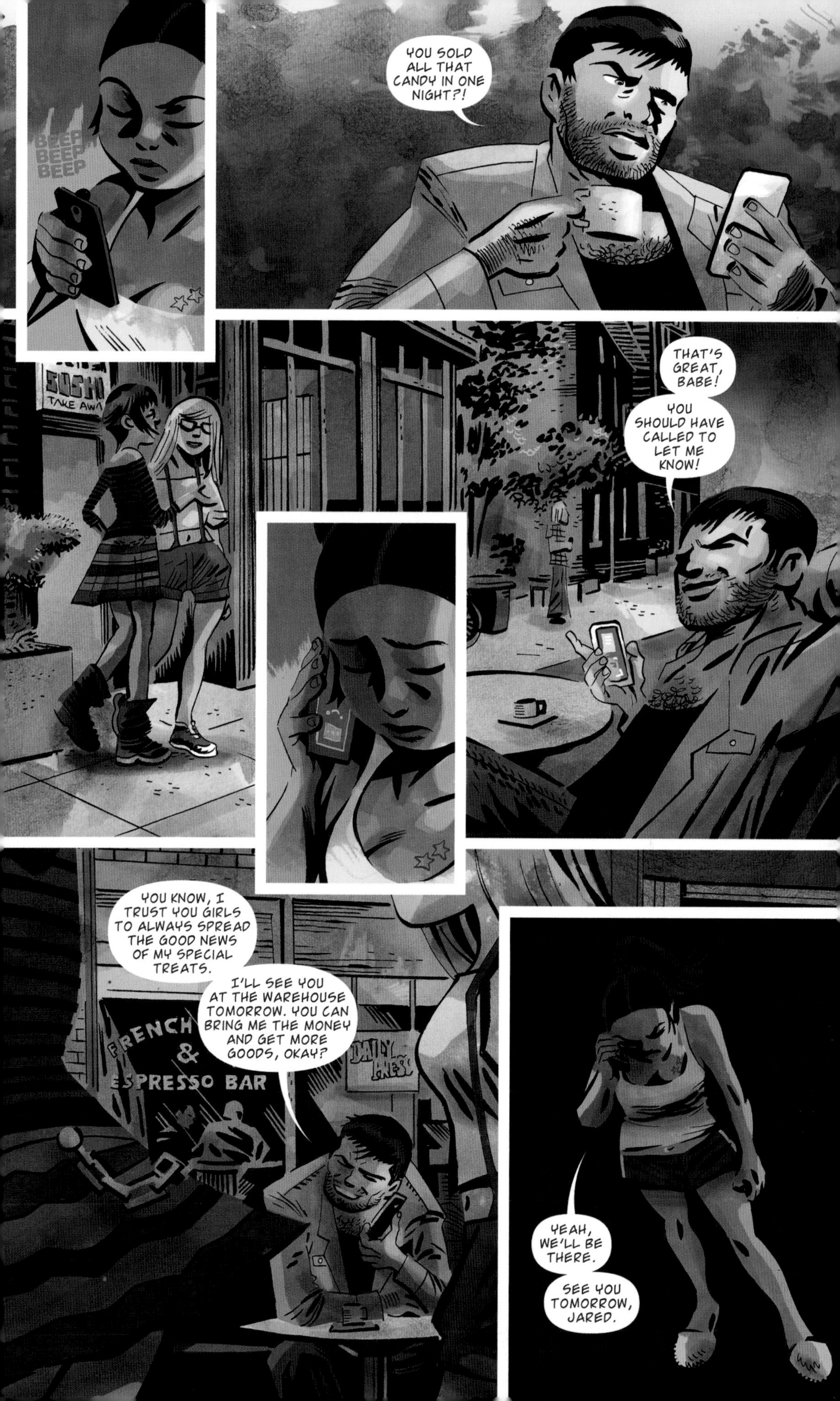
BEEP BEEP BEEP
YOU SOLD ALL THAT CANDY IN ONE NIGHT?!
SUSHI TAKE AWA
THAT'S GREAT, BABE!
YOU SHOULD HAVE CALLED TO LET ME KNOW!
YOU KNOW, I TRUST YOU GIRLS TO ALWAYS SPREAD THE GOOD NEWS OF MY SPECIAL TREATS.
I'LL SEE YOU AT THE WAREHOUSE TOMORROW. YOU CAN BRING ME THE MONEY AND GET MORE GOODS, OKAY?
FRENCH & ESPRESSO BAR
YEAH, WE'LL BE THERE.
SEE YOU TOMORROW, JARED.

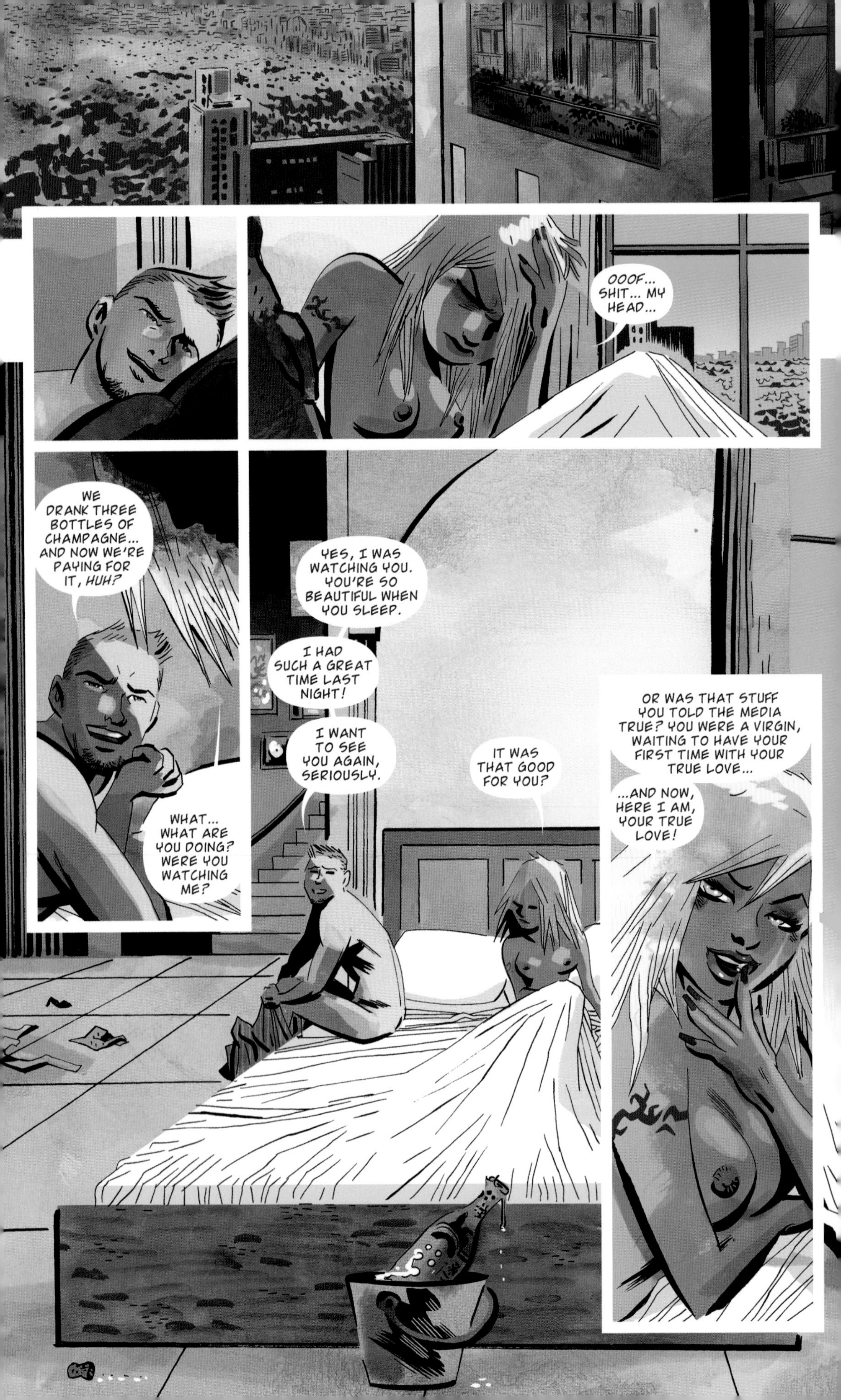

OOOF... SHIT... MY HEAD...
WE DRANK THREE BOTTLES OF CHAMPAGNE... AND NOW WE'RE PAYING FOR IT, *HUH?*
WHAT... WHAT ARE YOU DOING? WERE YOU WATCHING ME?
YES, I WAS WATCHING YOU. YOU'RE SO BEAUTIFUL WHEN YOU SLEEP.
I HAD SUCH A GREAT TIME LAST NIGHT!
I WANT TO SEE YOU AGAIN, SERIOUSLY.
IT WAS THAT GOOD FOR YOU?
OR WAS THAT STUFF YOU TOLD THE MEDIA TRUE? YOU WERE A VIRGIN, WAITING TO HAVE YOUR FIRST TIME WITH YOUR TRUE LOVE...
...AND NOW, HERE I AM, YOUR TRUE LOVE!

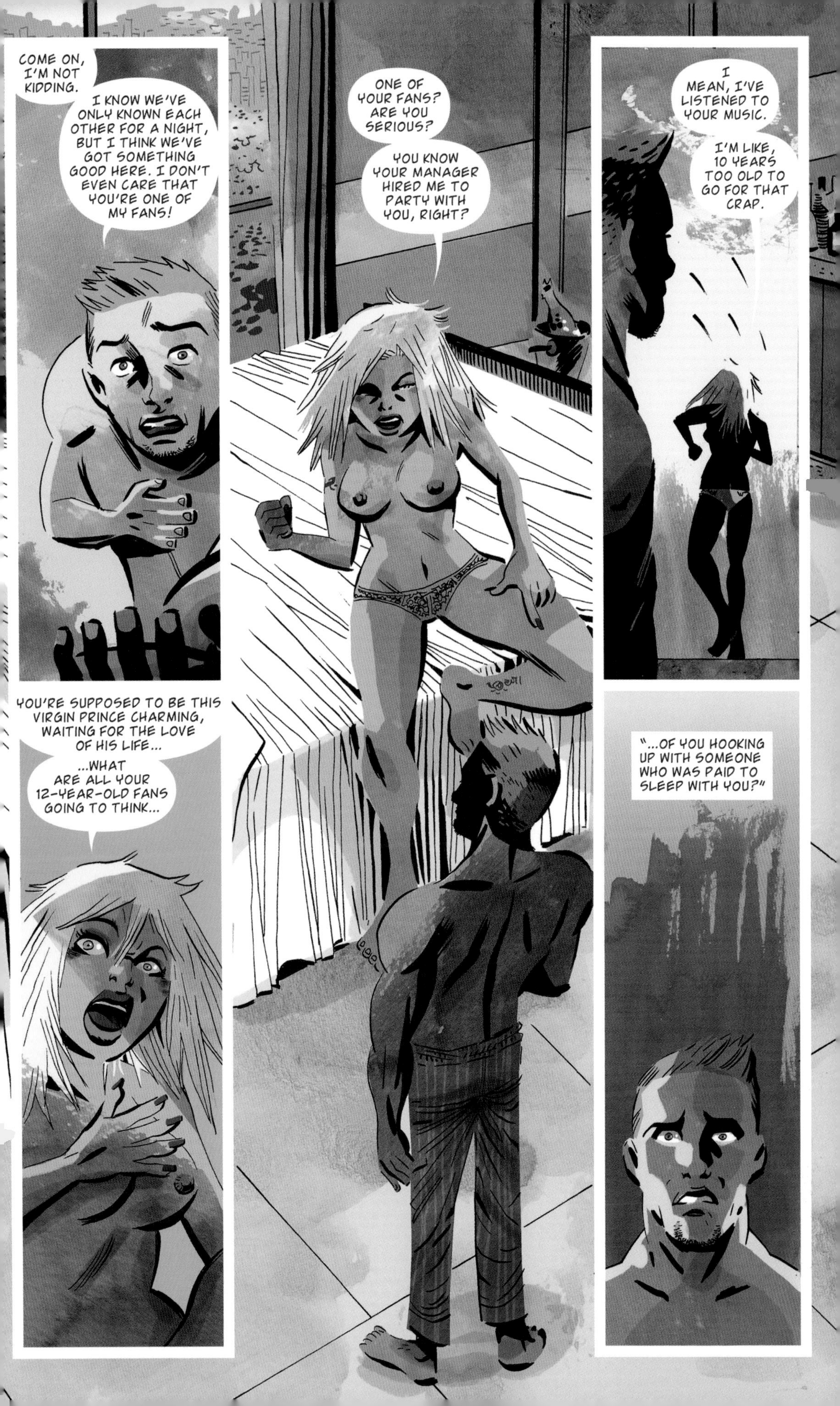
COME ON, I'M NOT KIDDING.
I KNOW WE'VE ONLY KNOWN EACH OTHER FOR A NIGHT, BUT I THINK WE'VE GOT SOMETHING GOOD HERE. I DON'T EVEN CARE THAT YOU'RE ONE OF MY FANS!
ONE OF YOUR FANS? ARE YOU SERIOUS?
YOU KNOW YOUR MANAGER HIRED ME TO PARTY WITH YOU, RIGHT?
I MEAN, I'VE LISTENED TO YOUR MUSIC.
I'M LIKE, 10 YEARS TOO OLD TO GO FOR THAT CRAP.
YOU'RE SUPPOSED TO BE THIS VIRGIN PRINCE CHARMING, WAITING FOR THE LOVE OF HIS LIFE...
...WHAT ARE ALL YOUR 12-YEAR-OLD FANS GOING TO THINK...
"...OF YOU HOOKING UP WITH SOMEONE WHO WAS PAID TO SLEEP WITH YOU?"

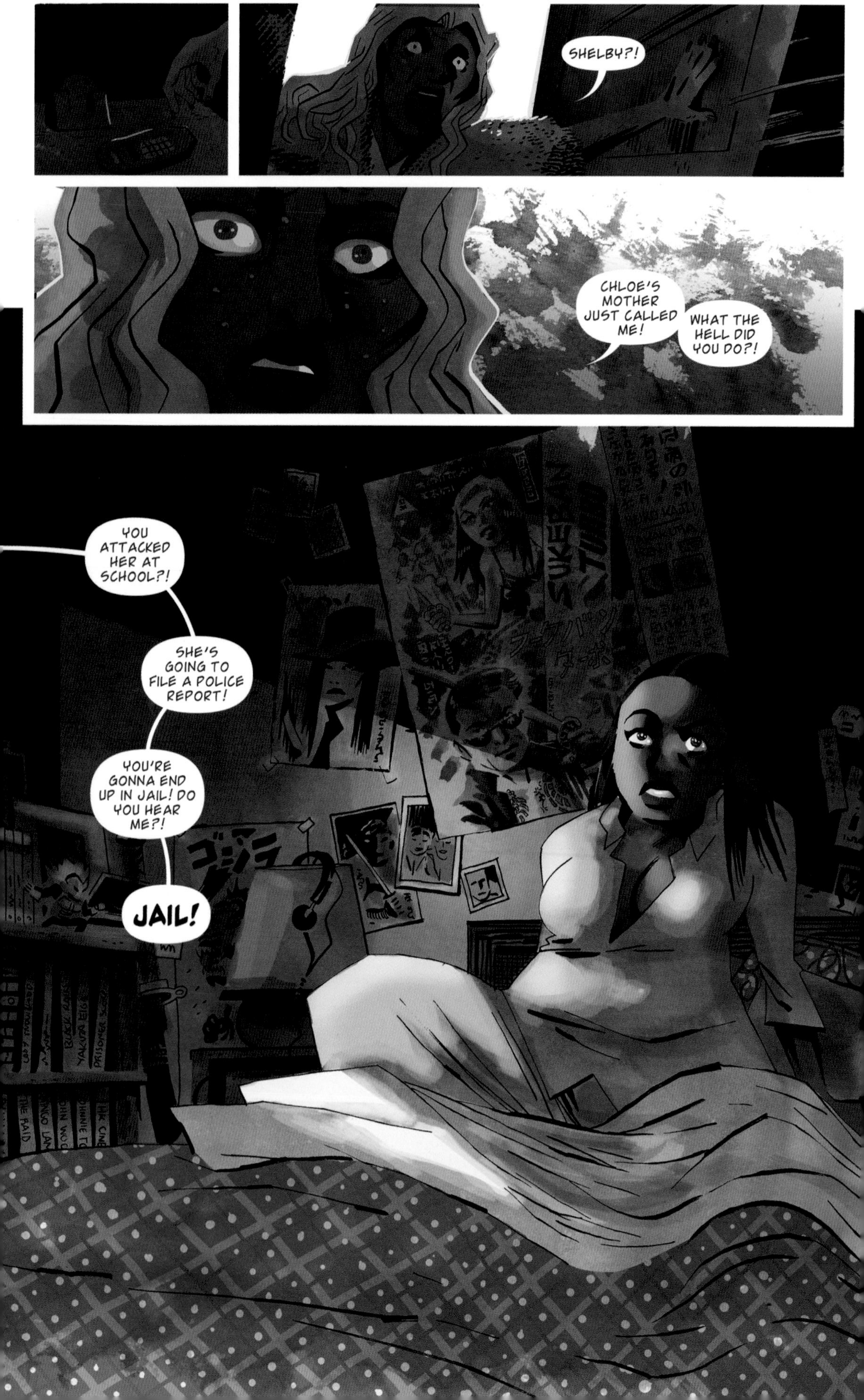
SHELBY?!
CHLOE'S MOTHER JUST CALLED ME!
WHAT THE HELL DID YOU DO?!
YOU ATTACKED HER AT SCHOOL?!
SHE'S GOING TO FILE A POLICE REPORT!
YOU'RE GONNA END UP IN JAIL! DO YOU HEAR ME?!
JAIL!

VICTOR SANTOS

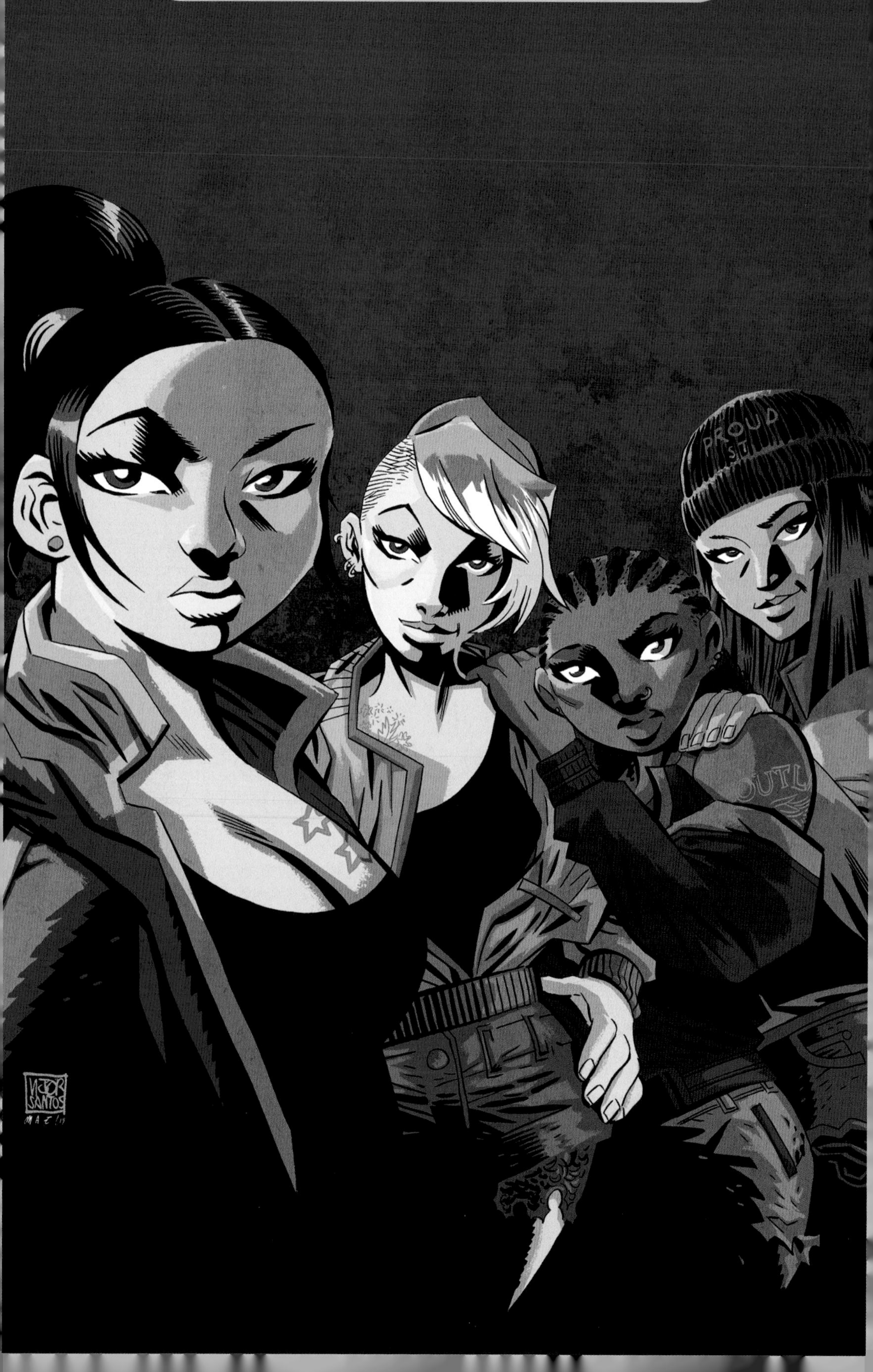
PROUD

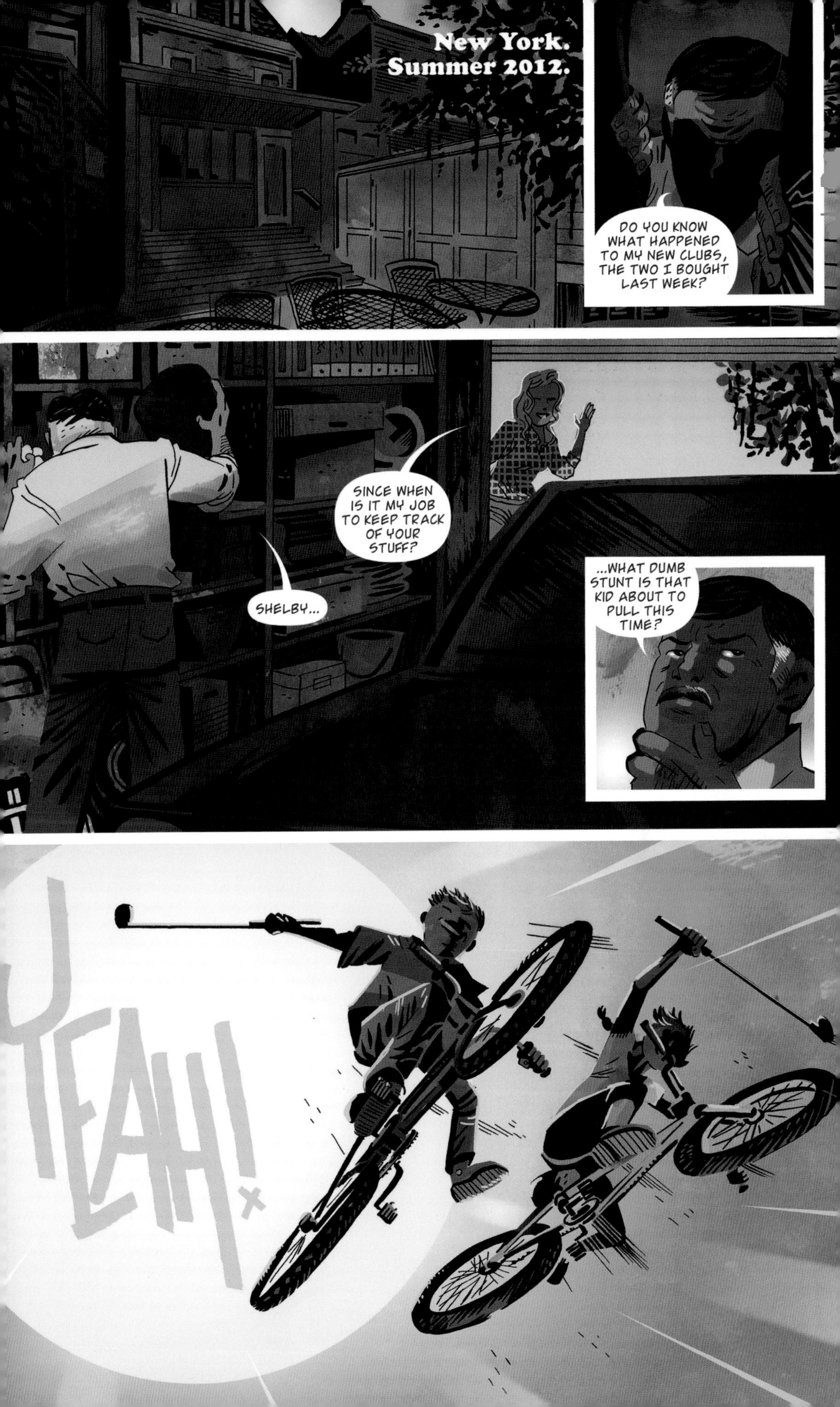
New York.
Summer 2012.
DO YOU KNOW WHAT HAPPENED TO MY NEW CLUBS, THE TWO I BOUGHT LAST WEEK?
SINCE WHEN IS IT MY JOB TO KEEP TRACK OF YOUR STUFF?
SHELBY...
...WHAT DUMB STUNT IS THAT KID ABOUT TO PULL THIS TIME?
YEAH!

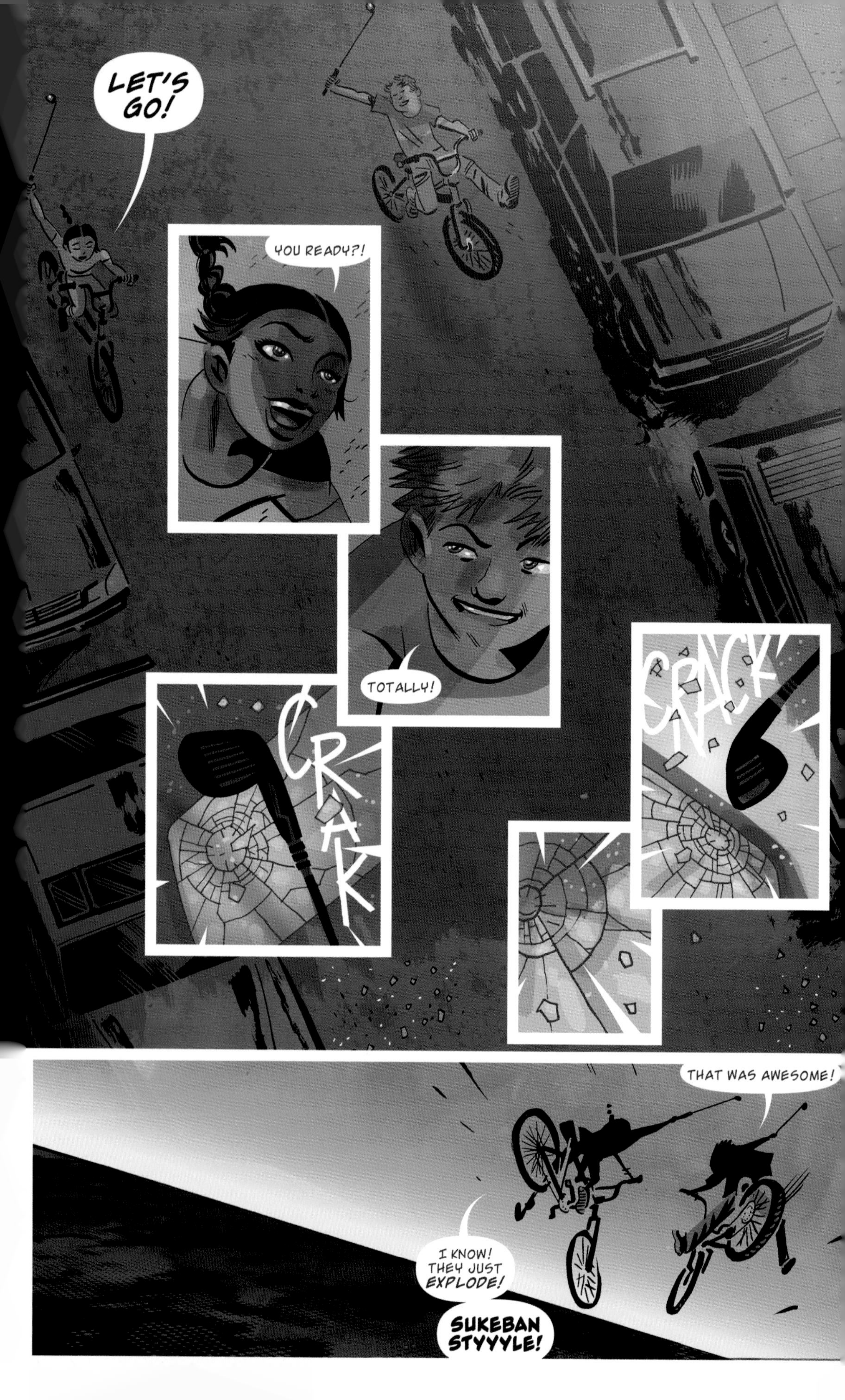
LET'S GO!
YOU READY?!
TOTALLY!
CRAK
CRACK
THAT WAS AWESOME!
I KNOW! THEY JUST EXPLODE!
SUKEBAN STYYYLE!

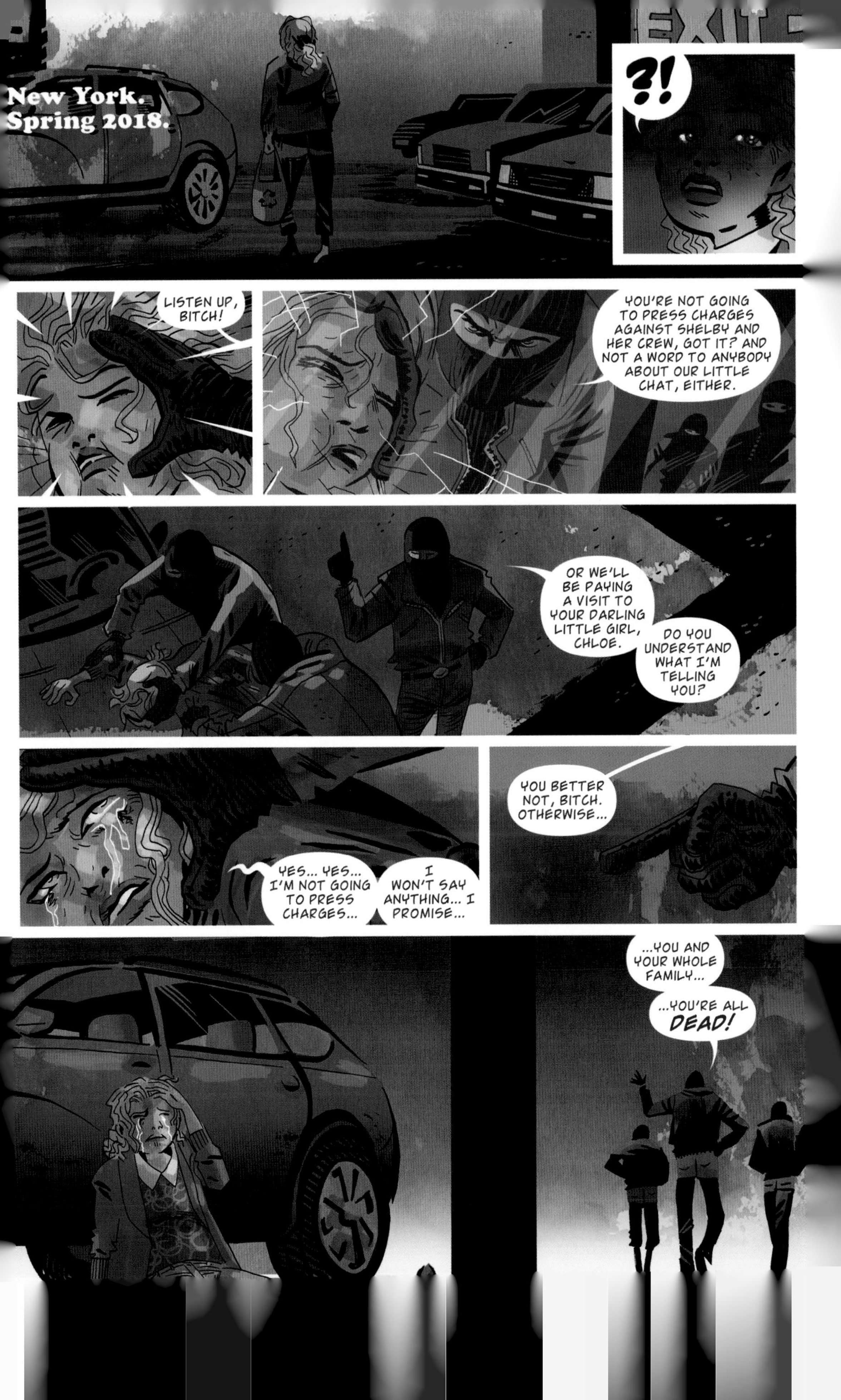
New York.
Spring 2018.
EXIT
?!
LISTEN UP, BITCH!
YOU'RE NOT GOING TO PRESS CHARGES AGAINST SHELBY AND HER CREW, GOT IT? AND NOT A WORD TO ANYBODY ABOUT OUR LITTLE CHAT, EITHER.
OR WE'LL BE PAYING A VISIT TO YOUR DARLING LITTLE GIRL, CHLOE.
DO YOU UNDERSTAND WHAT I'M TELLING YOU?
YES... YES... I'M NOT GOING TO PRESS CHARGES...
I WON'T SAY ANYTHING... I PROMISE...
YOU BETTER NOT, BITCH. OTHERWISE...
...YOU AND YOUR WHOLE FAMILY...
...YOU'RE ALL DEAD!

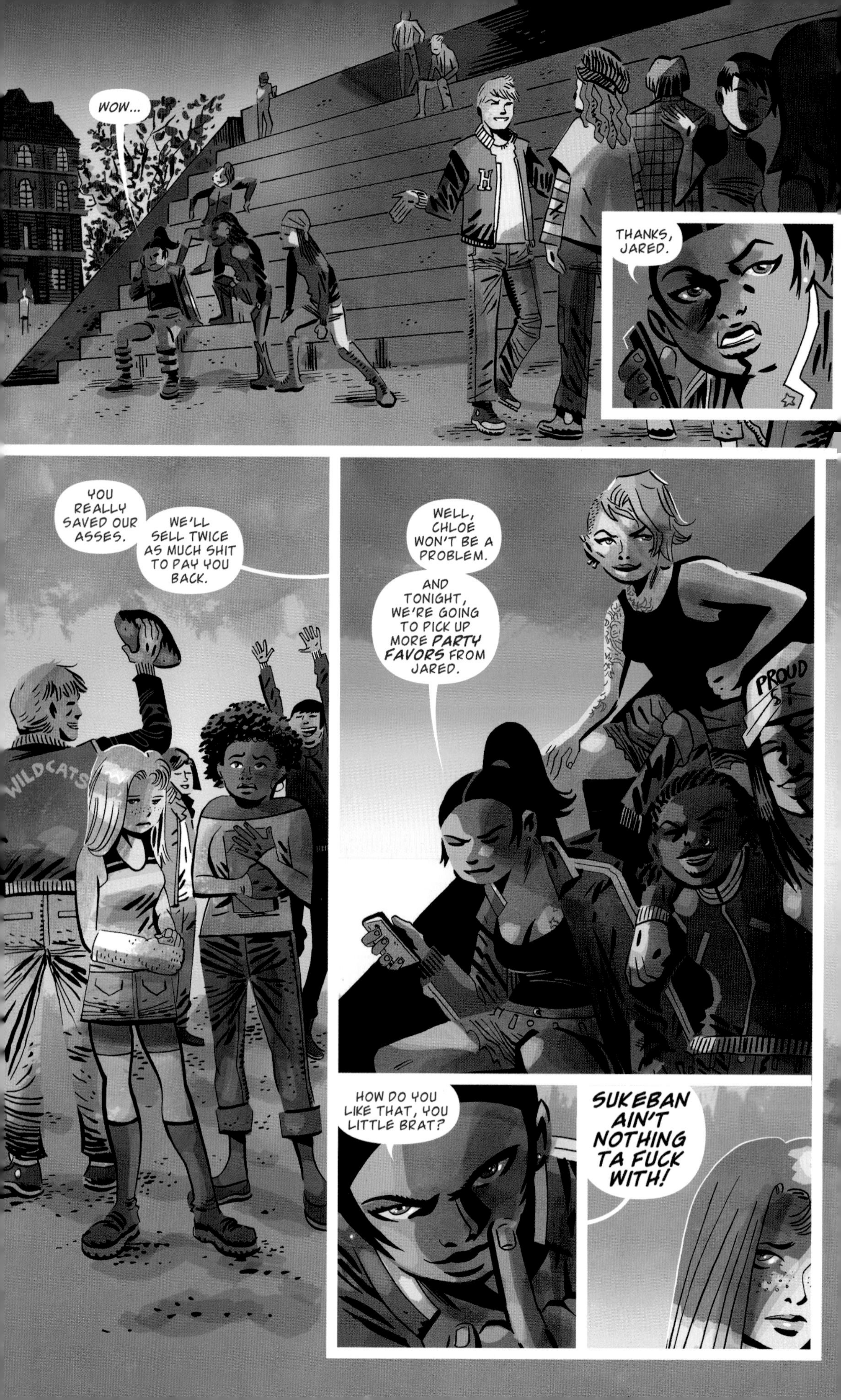

WOW...
THANKS, JARED.
YOU REALLY SAVED OUR ASSES.
WE'LL SELL TWICE AS MUCH SHIT TO PAY YOU BACK.
WELL, CHLOE WON'T BE A PROBLEM.
AND TONIGHT, WE'RE GOING TO PICK UP MORE PARTY FAVORS FROM JARED.
PROUD
HOW DO YOU LIKE THAT, YOU LITTLE BRAT?
SUKEBAN AIN'T NOTHING TA FUCK WITH!

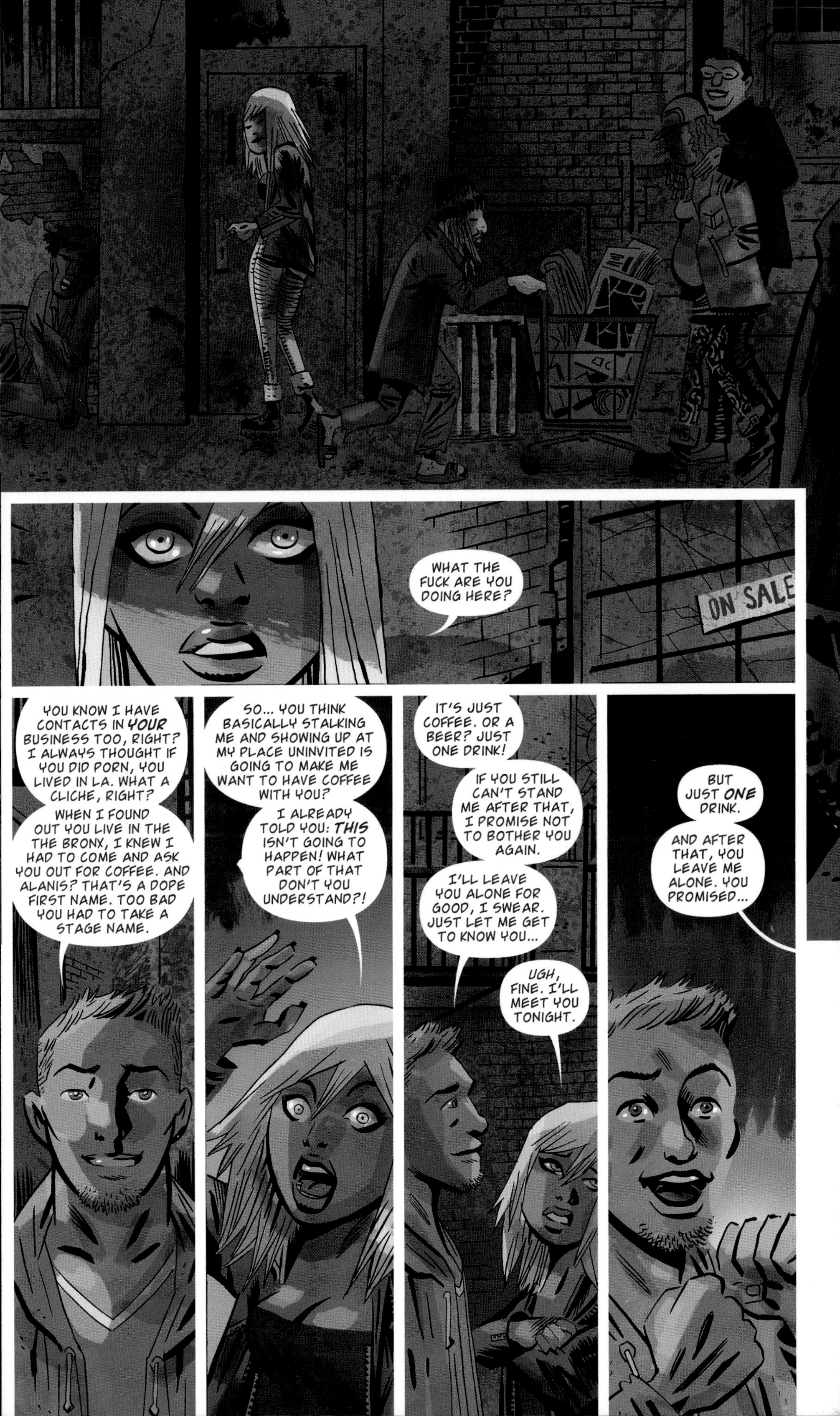
WHAT THE FUCK ARE YOU DOING HERE?
ON SALE
YOU KNOW I HAVE CONTACTS IN YOUR BUSINESS TOO, RIGHT? I ALWAYS THOUGHT IF YOU DID PORN, YOU LIVED IN LA. WHAT A CLICHE, RIGHT?
WHEN I FOUND OUT YOU LIVE IN THE THE BRONX, I KNEW I HAD TO COME AND ASK YOU OUT FOR COFFEE. AND ALANIS? THAT'S A DOPE FIRST NAME. TOO BAD YOU HAD TO TAKE A STAGE NAME.
SO... YOU THINK BASICALLY STALKING ME AND SHOWING UP AT MY PLACE UNINVITED IS GOING TO MAKE ME WANT TO HAVE COFFEE WITH YOU?
I ALREADY TOLD YOU: THIS ISN'T GOING TO HAPPEN! WHAT PART OF THAT DON'T YOU UNDERSTAND?!
IT'S JUST COFFEE. OR A BEER? JUST ONE DRINK!
IF YOU STILL CAN'T STAND ME AFTER THAT, I PROMISE NOT TO BOTHER YOU AGAIN.
I'LL LEAVE YOU ALONE FOR GOOD, I SWEAR. JUST LET ME GET TO KNOW YOU...
UGH, FINE. I'LL MEET YOU TONIGHT.
BUT JUST ONE DRINK.
AND AFTER THAT, YOU LEAVE ME ALONE. YOU PROMISED...

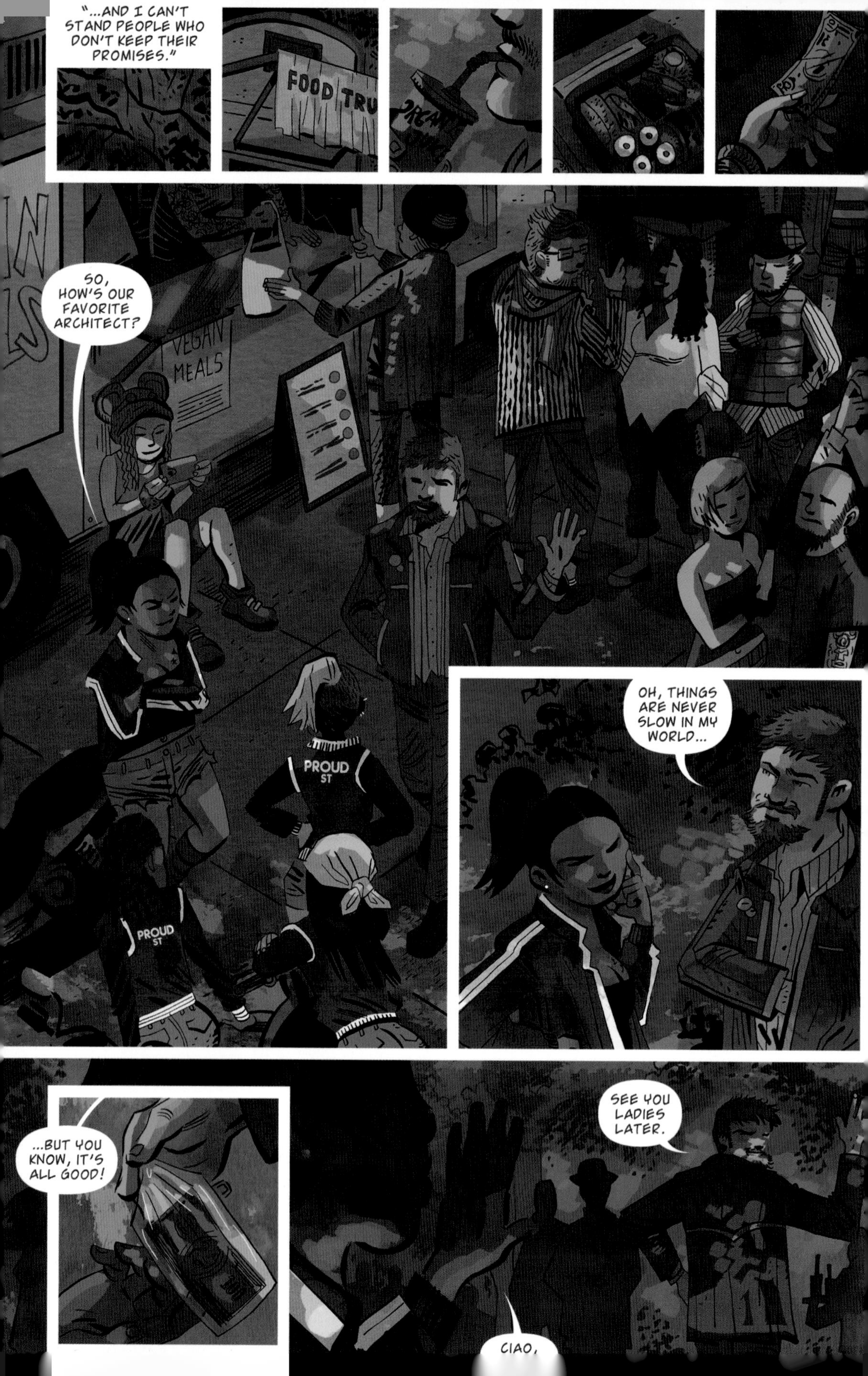
"...AND I CAN'T STAND PEOPLE WHO DON'T KEEP THEIR PROMISES."
FOOD TRU
SO, HOW'S OUR FAVORITE ARCHITECT?
VEGAN MEALS
PROUD ST
OH, THINGS ARE NEVER SLOW IN MY WORLD...
PROUD ST
...BUT YOU KNOW, IT'S ALL GOOD!
SEE YOU LADIES LATER.
CIAO,

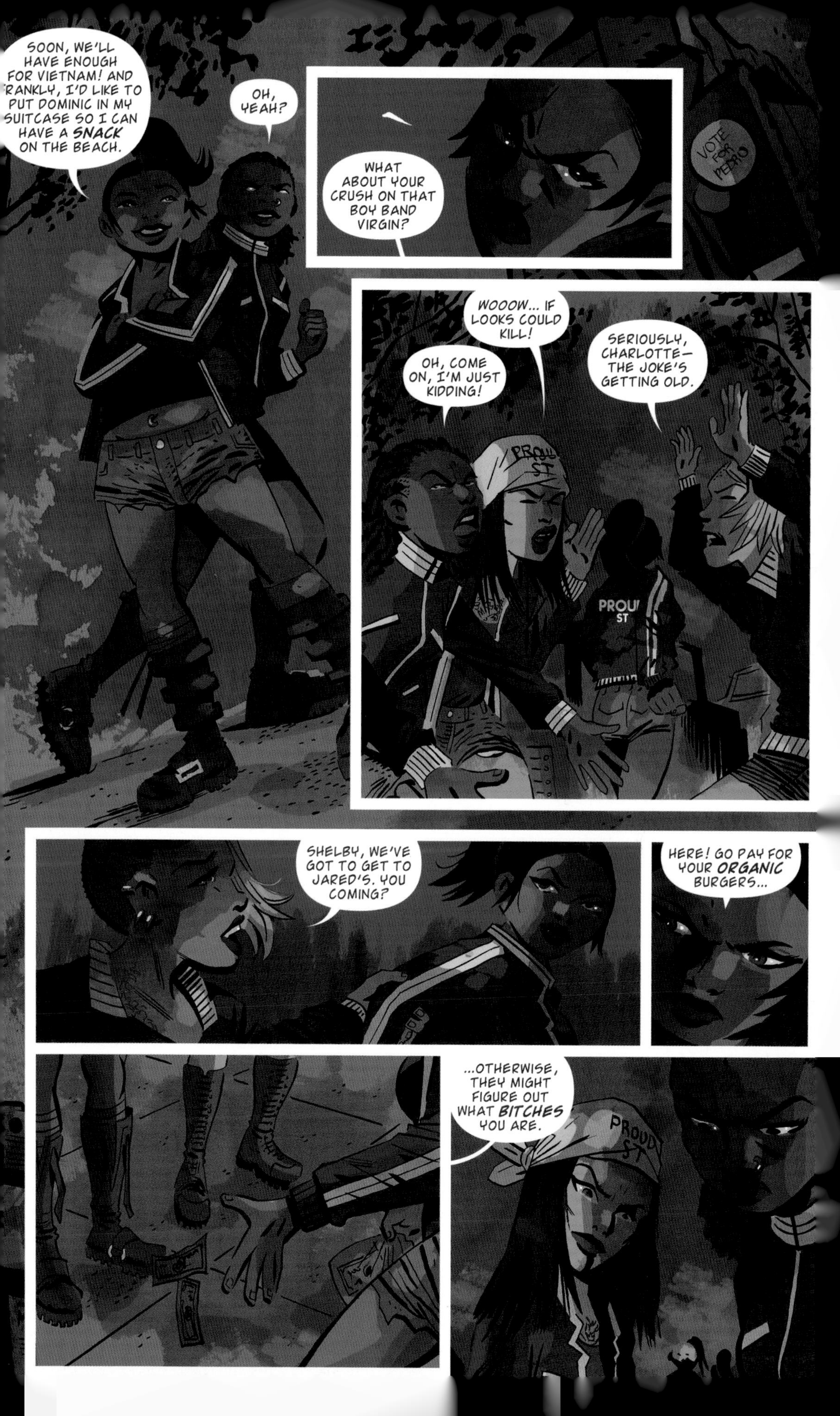
SOON, WE'LL HAVE ENOUGH FOR VIETNAM! AND FRANKLY, I'D LIKE TO PUT DOMINIC IN MY SUITCASE SO I CAN HAVE A SNACK ON THE BEACH.
OH, YEAH?
WHAT ABOUT YOUR CRUSH ON THAT BOY BAND VIRGIN?
VOTE FOR PEDRO
WOOOW... IF LOOKS COULD KILL!
OH, COME ON, I'M JUST KIDDING!
SERIOUSLY, CHARLOTTE— THE JOKE'S GETTING OLD.
PROUD ST
SHELBY, WE'VE GOT TO GET TO JARED'S. YOU COMING?
HERE! GO PAY FOR YOUR ORGANIC BURGERS...
...OTHERWISE, THEY MIGHT FIGURE OUT WHAT BITCHES YOU ARE.

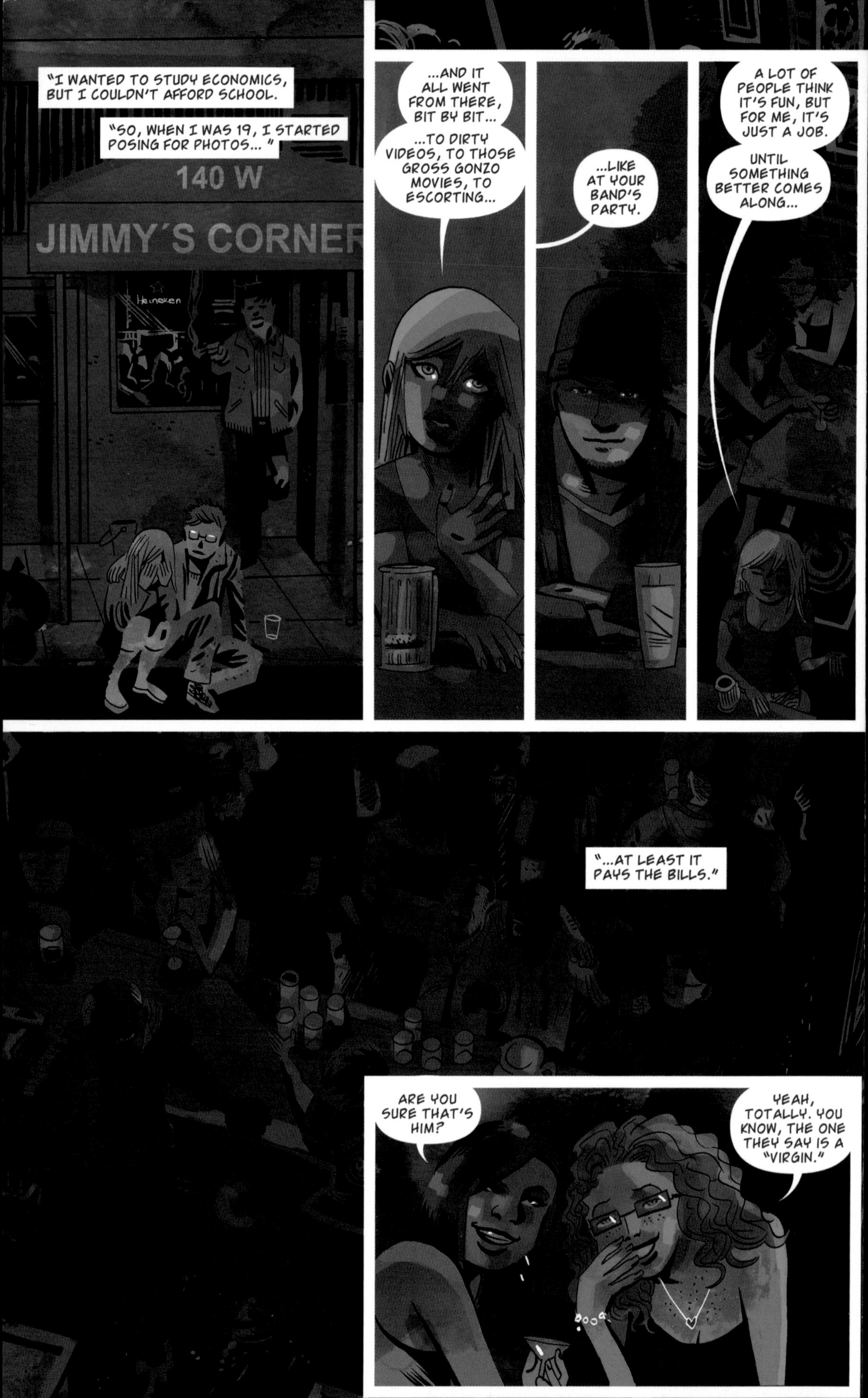
"I WANTED TO STUDY ECONOMICS, BUT I COULDN'T AFFORD SCHOOL.
"SO, WHEN I WAS 19, I STARTED POSING FOR PHOTOS..."
140 W
JIMMY´S CORNER
Heineken
...AND IT ALL WENT FROM THERE, BIT BY BIT...
...TO DIRTY VIDEOS, TO THOSE GROSS GONZO MOVIES, TO ESCORTING...
...LIKE AT YOUR BAND'S PARTY.
A LOT OF PEOPLE THINK IT'S FUN, BUT FOR ME, IT'S JUST A JOB.
UNTIL SOMETHING BETTER COMES ALONG...
"...AT LEAST IT PAYS THE BILLS."
ARE YOU SURE THAT'S HIM?
YEAH, TOTALLY. YOU KNOW, THE ONE THEY SAY IS A "VIRGIN."

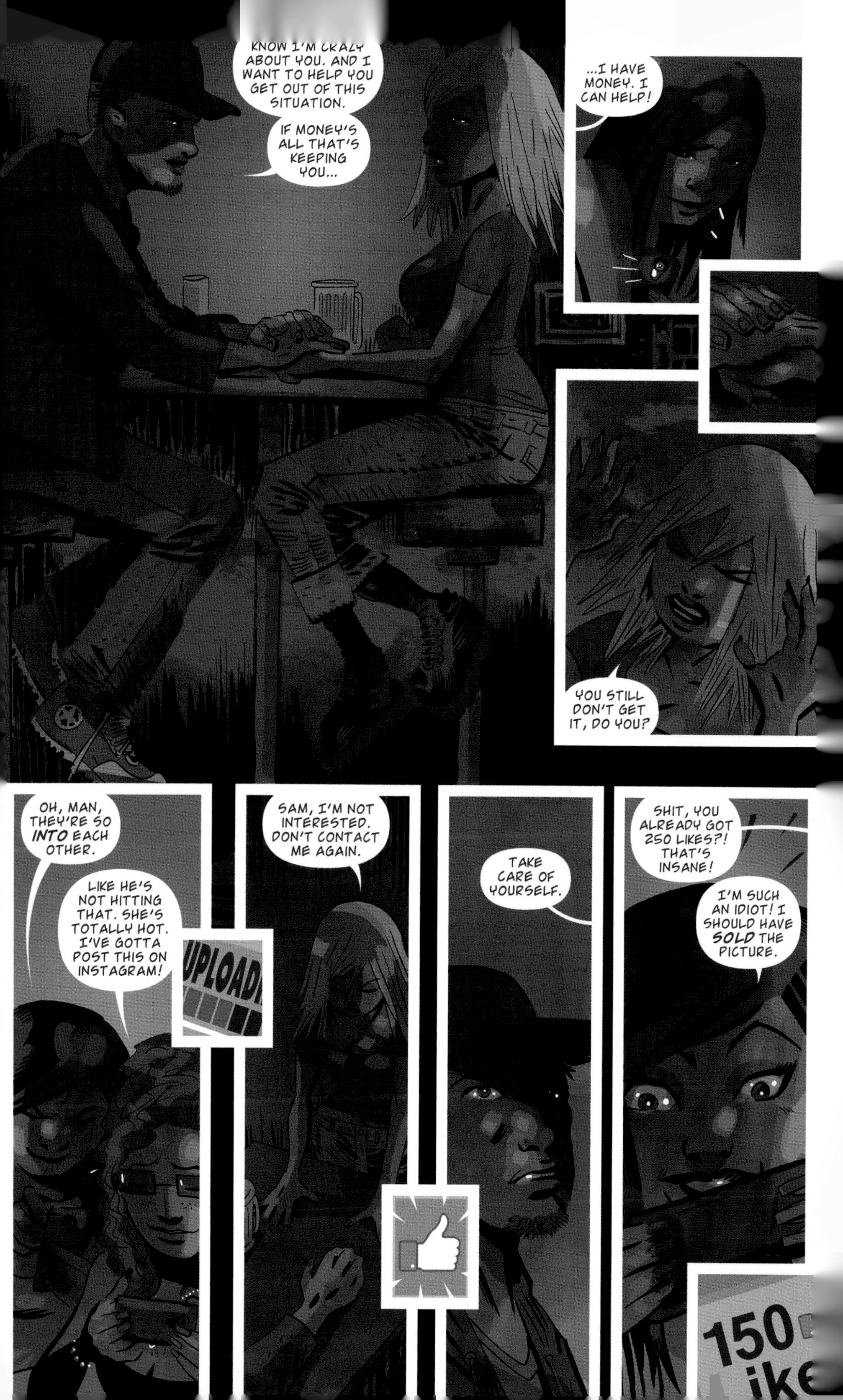
KNOW I'M CRAZY ABOUT YOU. AND I WANT TO HELP YOU GET OUT OF THIS SITUATION.
IF MONEY'S ALL THAT'S KEEPING YOU...
...I HAVE MONEY. I CAN HELP!
YOU STILL DON'T GET IT, DO YOU?
OH, MAN, THEY'RE SO INTO EACH OTHER.
LIKE HE'S NOT HITTING THAT. SHE'S TOTALLY HOT. I'VE GOTTA POST THIS ON INSTAGRAM!
UPLOADI
SAM, I'M NOT INTERESTED. DON'T CONTACT ME AGAIN.
TAKE CARE OF YOURSELF.
SHIT, YOU ALREADY GOT 250 LIKES?! THAT'S INSANE!
I'M SUCH AN IDIOT! I SHOULD HAVE SOLD THE PICTURE.
150
ike

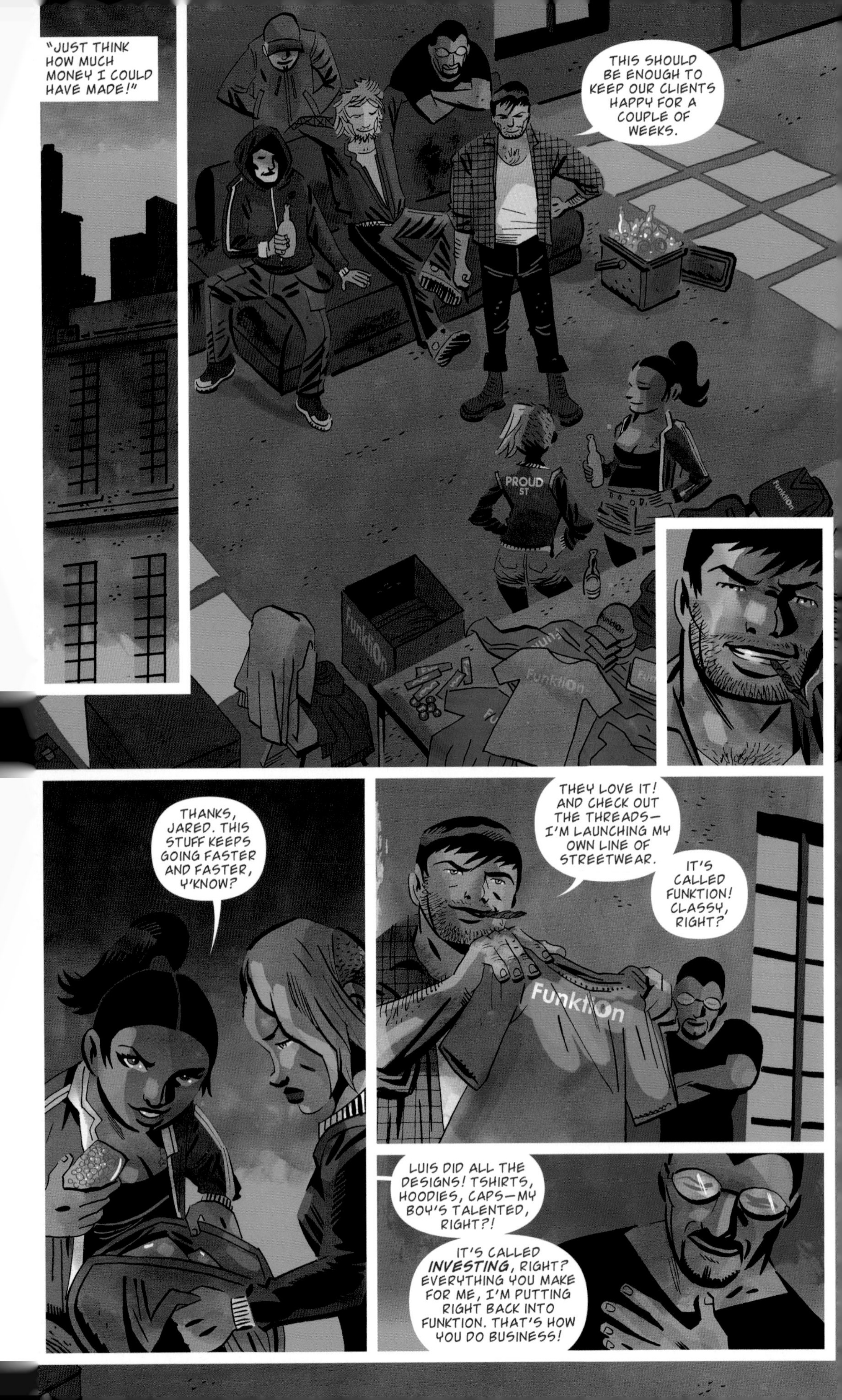

"JUST THINK HOW MUCH MONEY I COULD HAVE MADE!"
THIS SHOULD BE ENOUGH TO KEEP OUR CLIENTS HAPPY FOR A COUPLE OF WEEKS.
PROUD ST
Funktion
THANKS, JARED. THIS STUFF KEEPS GOING FASTER AND FASTER, Y'KNOW?
THEY LOVE IT! AND CHECK OUT THE THREADS—I'M LAUNCHING MY OWN LINE OF STREETWEAR.
IT'S CALLED FUNKTION! CLASSY, RIGHT?
Funktion
LUIS DID ALL THE DESIGNS! TSHIRTS, HOODIES, CAPS—MY BOY'S TALENTED, RIGHT?!
IT'S CALLED *INVESTING*, RIGHT? EVERYTHING YOU MAKE FOR ME, I'M PUTTING RIGHT BACK INTO FUNKTION. THAT'S HOW YOU DO BUSINESS!

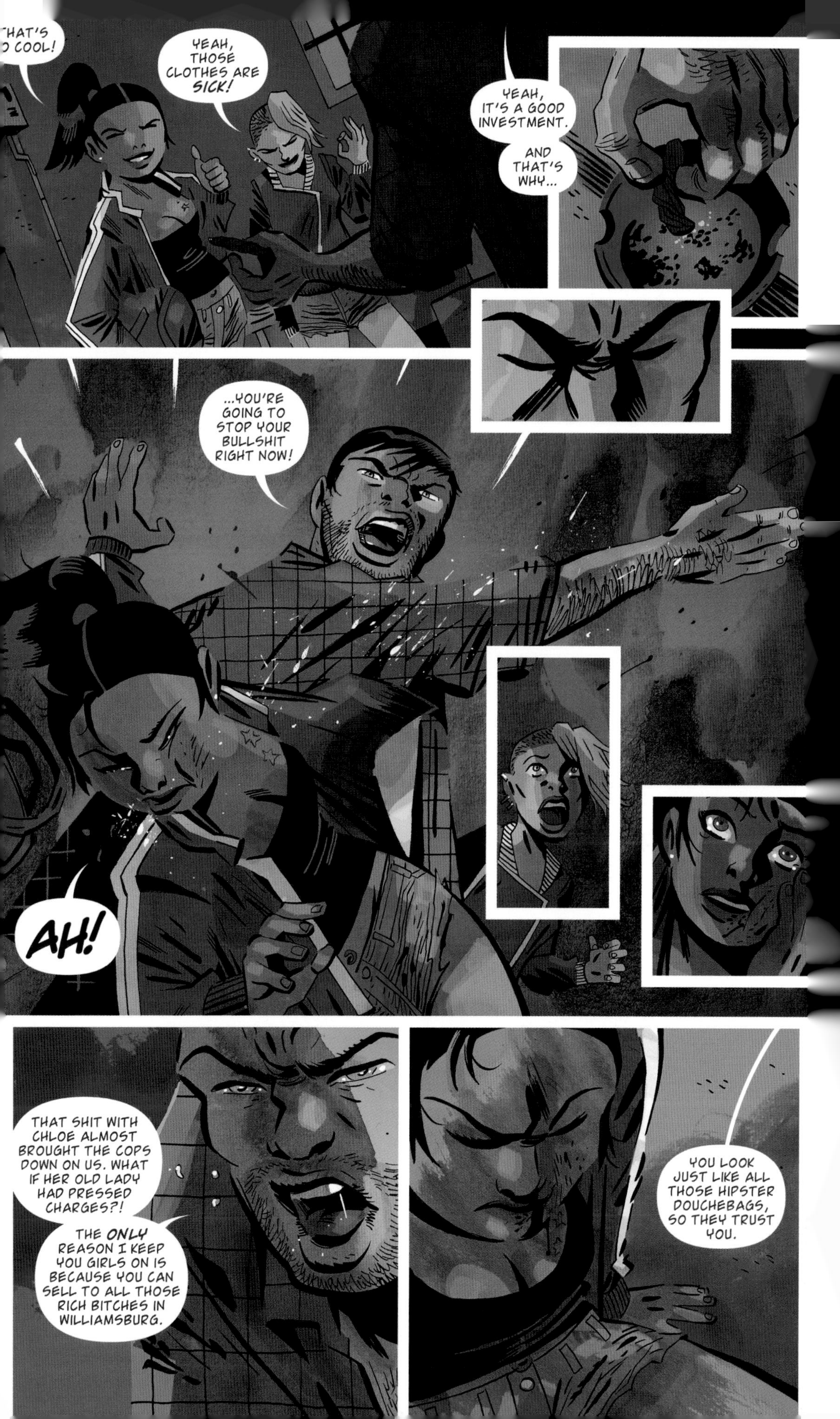

THAT'S SO COOL!
YEAH, THOSE CLOTHES ARE SICK!
YEAH, IT'S A GOOD INVESTMENT.
AND THAT'S WHY...
...YOU'RE GOING TO STOP YOUR BULLSHIT RIGHT NOW!
AH!
THAT SHIT WITH CHLOE ALMOST BROUGHT THE COPS DOWN ON US. WHAT IF HER OLD LADY HAD PRESSED CHARGES?!
THE ONLY REASON I KEEP YOU GIRLS ON IS BECAUSE YOU CAN SELL TO ALL THOSE RICH BITCHES IN WILLIAMSBURG.
YOU LOOK JUST LIKE ALL THOSE HIPSTER DOUCHEBAGS, SO THEY TRUST YOU.

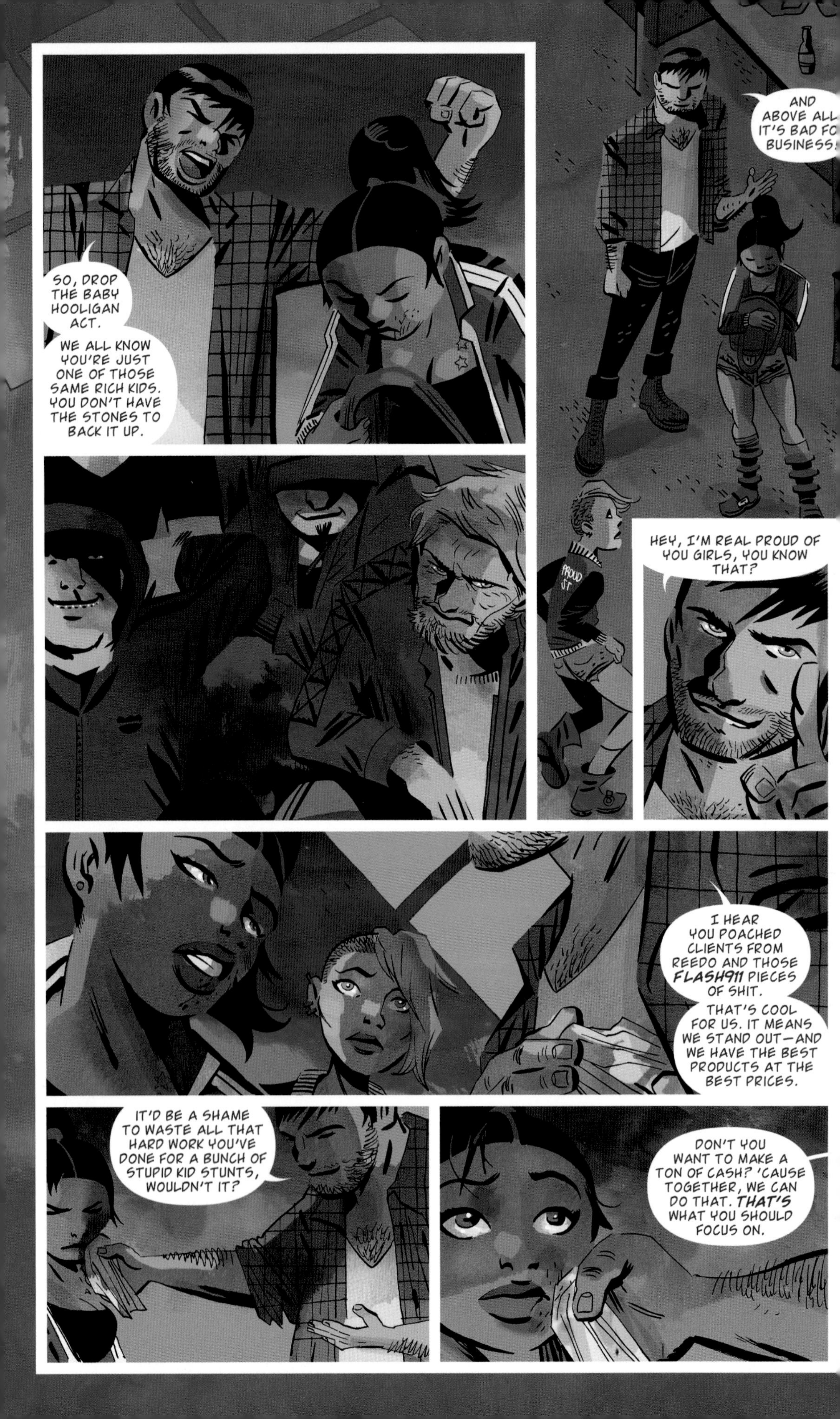
SO, DROP THE BABY HOOLIGAN ACT.
WE ALL KNOW YOU'RE JUST ONE OF THOSE SAME RICH KIDS. YOU DON'T HAVE THE STONES TO BACK IT UP.
AND ABOVE ALL IT'S BAD FO BUSINESS.
PROUD ST
HEY, I'M REAL PROUD OF YOU GIRLS, YOU KNOW THAT?
I HEAR YOU POACHED CLIENTS FROM REEDO AND THOSE FLASH911 PIECES OF SHIT.
THAT'S COOL FOR US. IT MEANS WE STAND OUT—AND WE HAVE THE BEST PRODUCTS AT THE BEST PRICES.
IT'D BE A SHAME TO WASTE ALL THAT HARD WORK YOU'VE DONE FOR A BUNCH OF STUPID KID STUNTS, WOULDN'T IT?
DON'T YOU WANT TO MAKE A TON OF CASH? 'CAUSE TOGETHER, WE CAN DO THAT. THAT'S WHAT YOU SHOULD FOCUS ON.

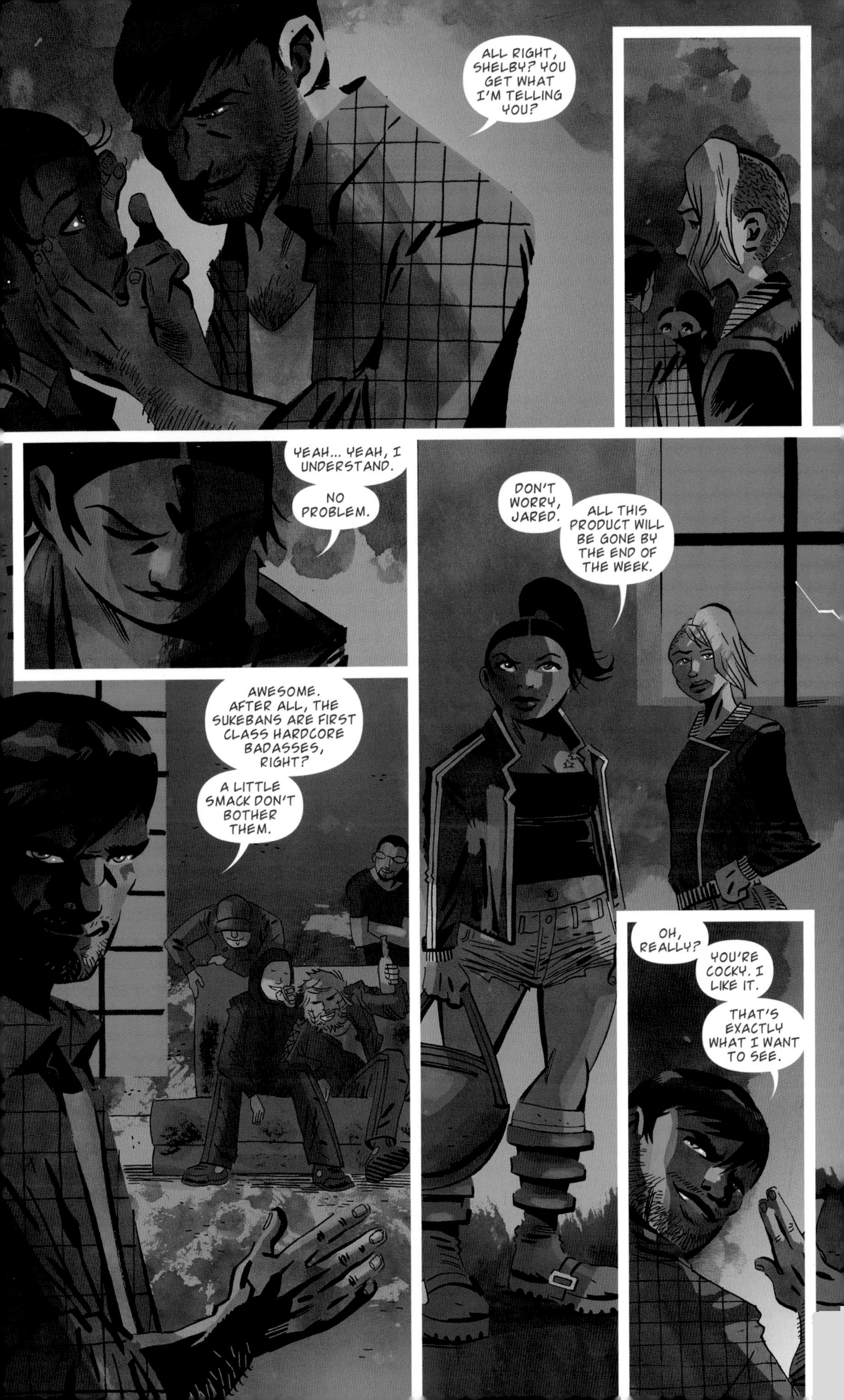
ALL RIGHT, SHELBY? YOU GET WHAT I'M TELLING YOU?
YEAH... YEAH, I UNDERSTAND.
NO PROBLEM.
AWESOME. AFTER ALL, THE SUKEBANS ARE FIRST CLASS HARDCORE BADASSES, RIGHT?
A LITTLE SMACK DON'T BOTHER THEM.
DON'T WORRY, JARED.
ALL THIS PRODUCT WILL BE GONE BY THE END OF THE WEEK.
OH, REALLY?
YOU'RE COCKY. I LIKE IT.
THAT'S EXACTLY WHAT I WANT TO SEE.

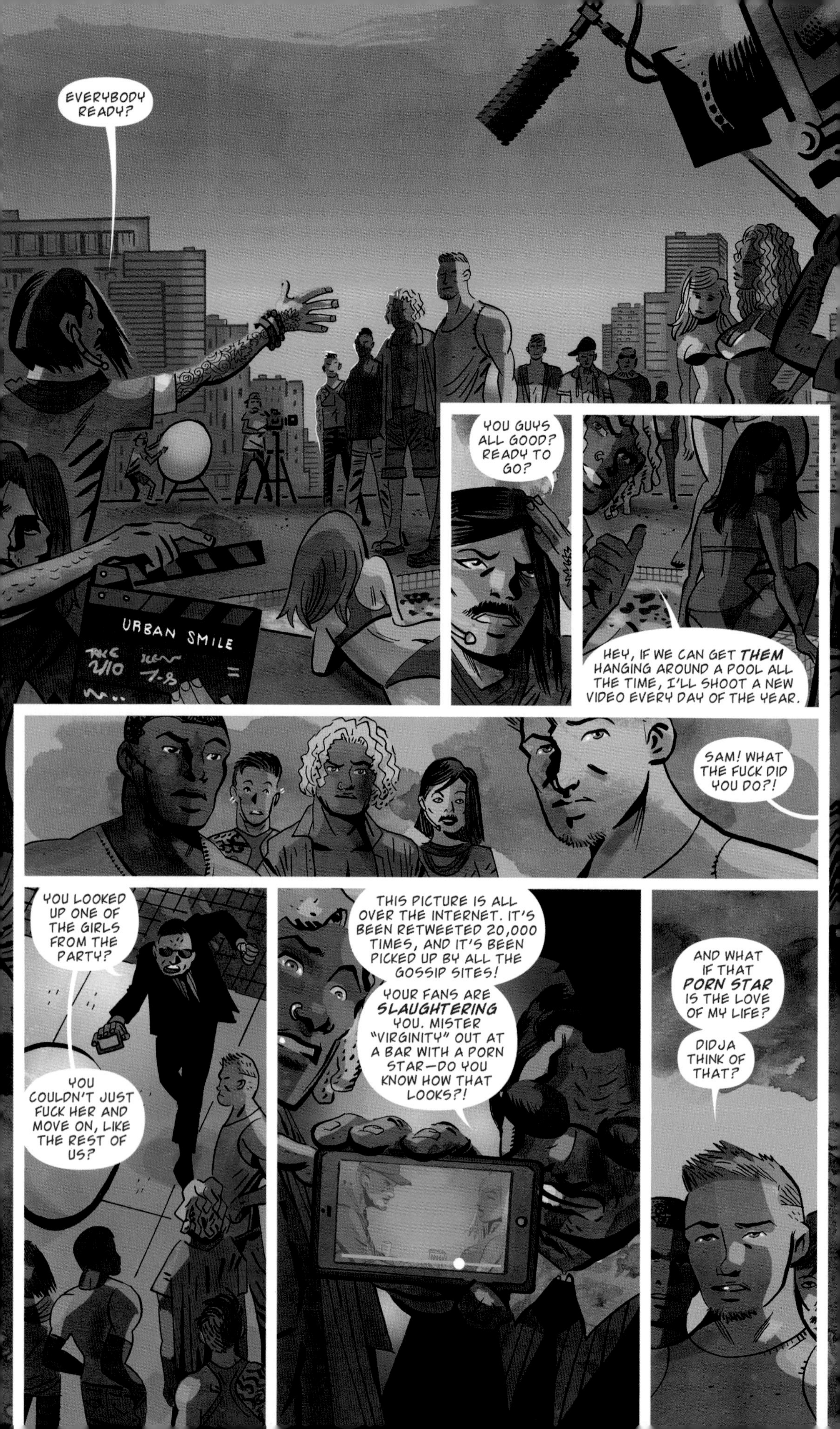
EVERYBODY READY?
URBAN SMILE
YOU GUYS ALL GOOD? READY TO GO?
HEY, IF WE CAN GET THEM HANGING AROUND A POOL ALL THE TIME, I'LL SHOOT A NEW VIDEO EVERY DAY OF THE YEAR.
SAM! WHAT THE FUCK DID YOU DO?!
YOU LOOKED UP ONE OF THE GIRLS FROM THE PARTY?
YOU COULDN'T JUST FUCK HER AND MOVE ON, LIKE THE REST OF US?
THIS PICTURE IS ALL OVER THE INTERNET. IT'S BEEN RETWEETED 20,000 TIMES, AND IT'S BEEN PICKED UP BY ALL THE GOSSIP SITES!
YOUR FANS ARE SLAUGHTERING YOU. MISTER "VIRGINITY" OUT AT A BAR WITH A PORN STAR—DO YOU KNOW HOW THAT LOOKS?!
AND WHAT IF THAT PORN STAR IS THE LOVE OF MY LIFE?
DIDJA THINK OF THAT?

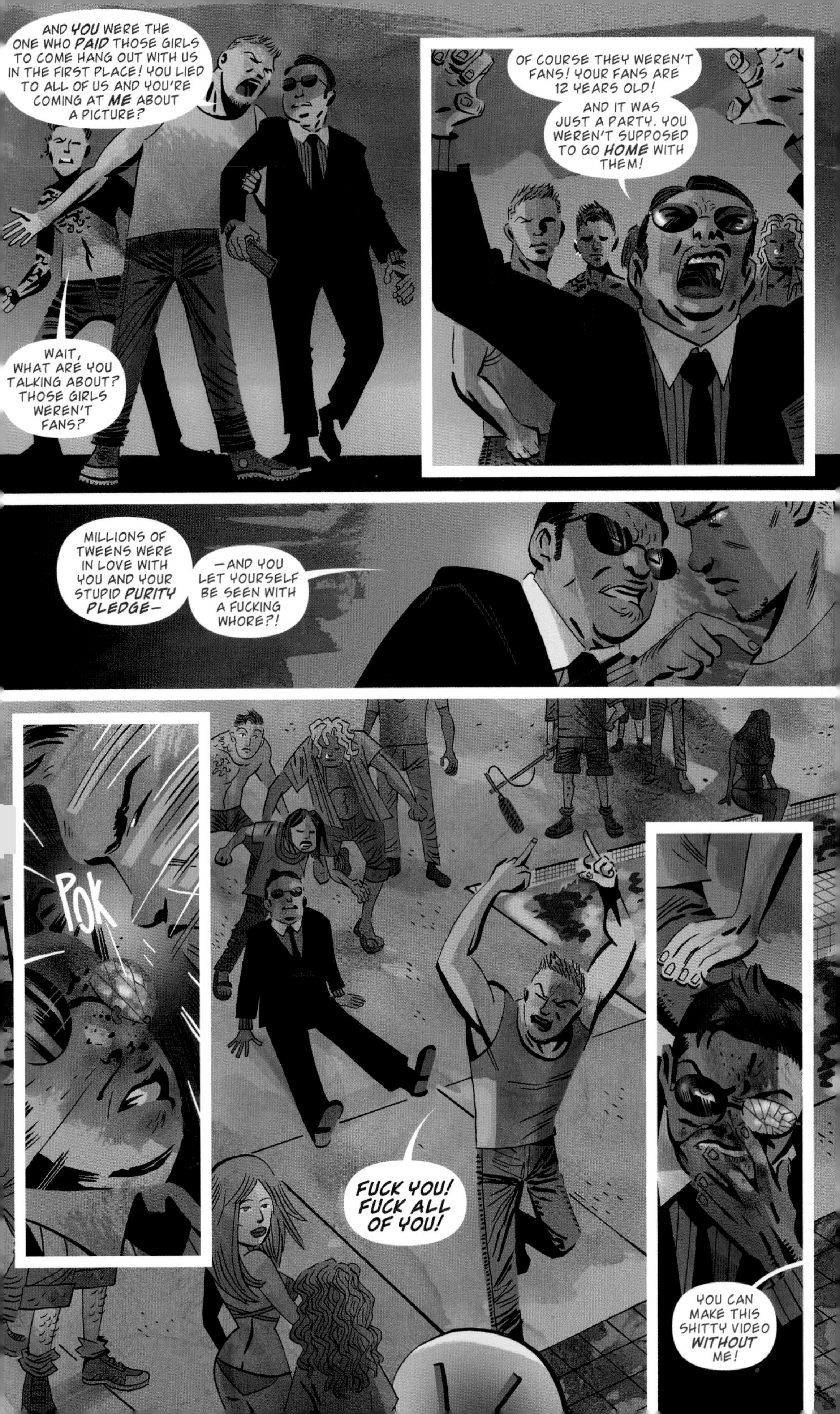
AND YOU WERE THE ONE WHO PAID THOSE GIRLS TO COME HANG OUT WITH US IN THE FIRST PLACE! YOU LIED TO ALL OF US AND YOU'RE COMING AT ME ABOUT A PICTURE?
WAIT, WHAT ARE YOU TALKING ABOUT? THOSE GIRLS WEREN'T FANS?
OF COURSE THEY WEREN'T FANS! YOUR FANS ARE 12 YEARS OLD!
AND IT WAS JUST A PARTY. YOU WEREN'T SUPPOSED TO GO HOME WITH THEM!
MILLIONS OF TWEENS WERE IN LOVE WITH YOU AND YOUR STUPID PURITY PLEDGE—
—AND YOU LET YOURSELF BE SEEN WITH A FUCKING WHORE?!
POK
FUCK YOU! FUCK ALL OF YOU!
YOU CAN MAKE THIS SHITTY VIDEO WITHOUT ME!

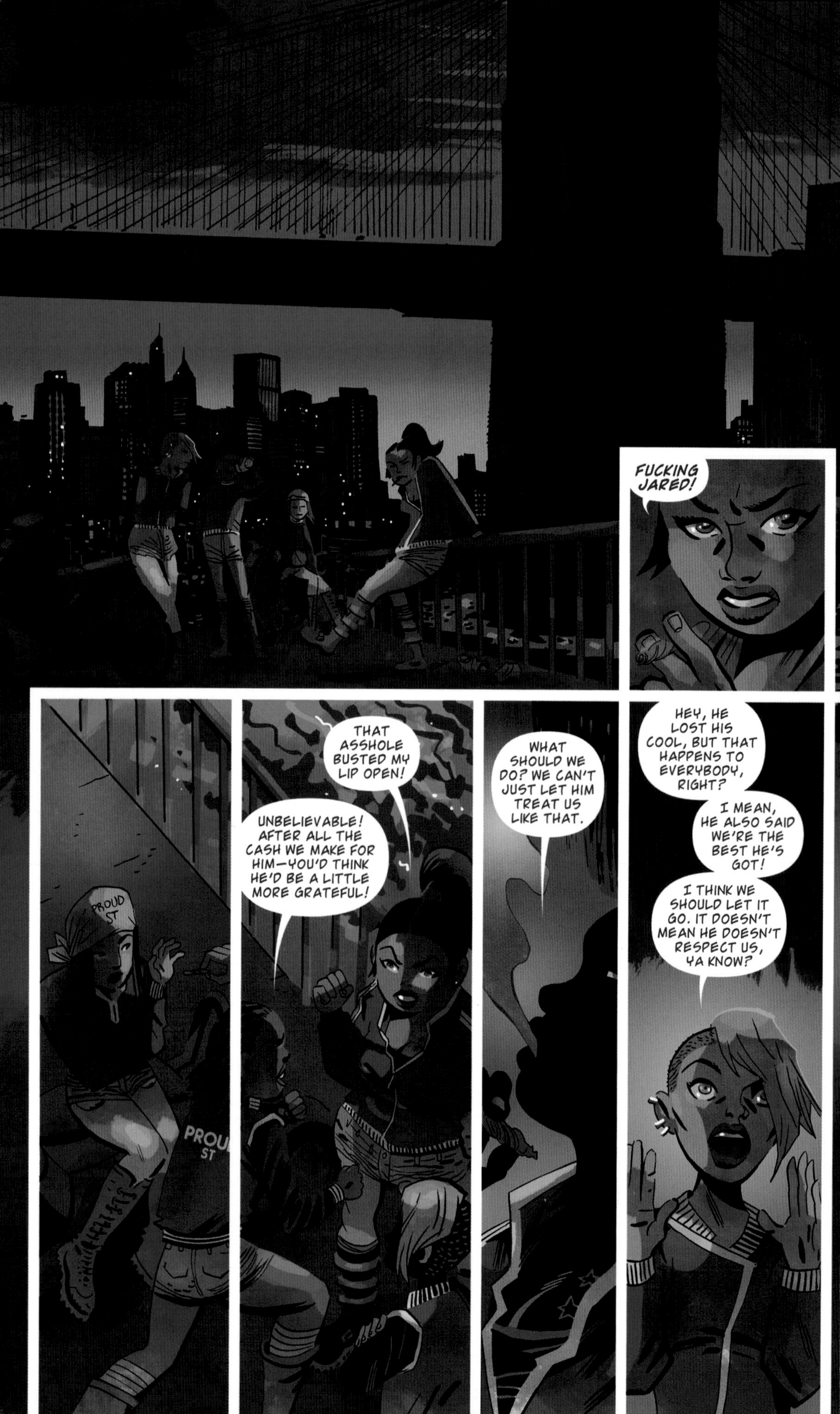
FUCKING JARED!
UNBELIEVABLE! AFTER ALL THE CASH WE MAKE FOR HIM—YOU'D THINK HE'D BE A LITTLE MORE GRATEFUL!
THAT ASSHOLE BUSTED MY LIP OPEN!
WHAT SHOULD WE DO? WE CAN'T JUST LET HIM TREAT US LIKE THAT.
HEY, HE LOST HIS COOL, BUT THAT HAPPENS TO EVERYBODY, RIGHT?
I MEAN, HE ALSO SAID WE'RE THE BEST HE'S GOT!
I THINK WE SHOULD LET IT GO. IT DOESN'T MEAN HE DOESN'T RESPECT US, YA KNOW?
PROUD ST
PROUD ST

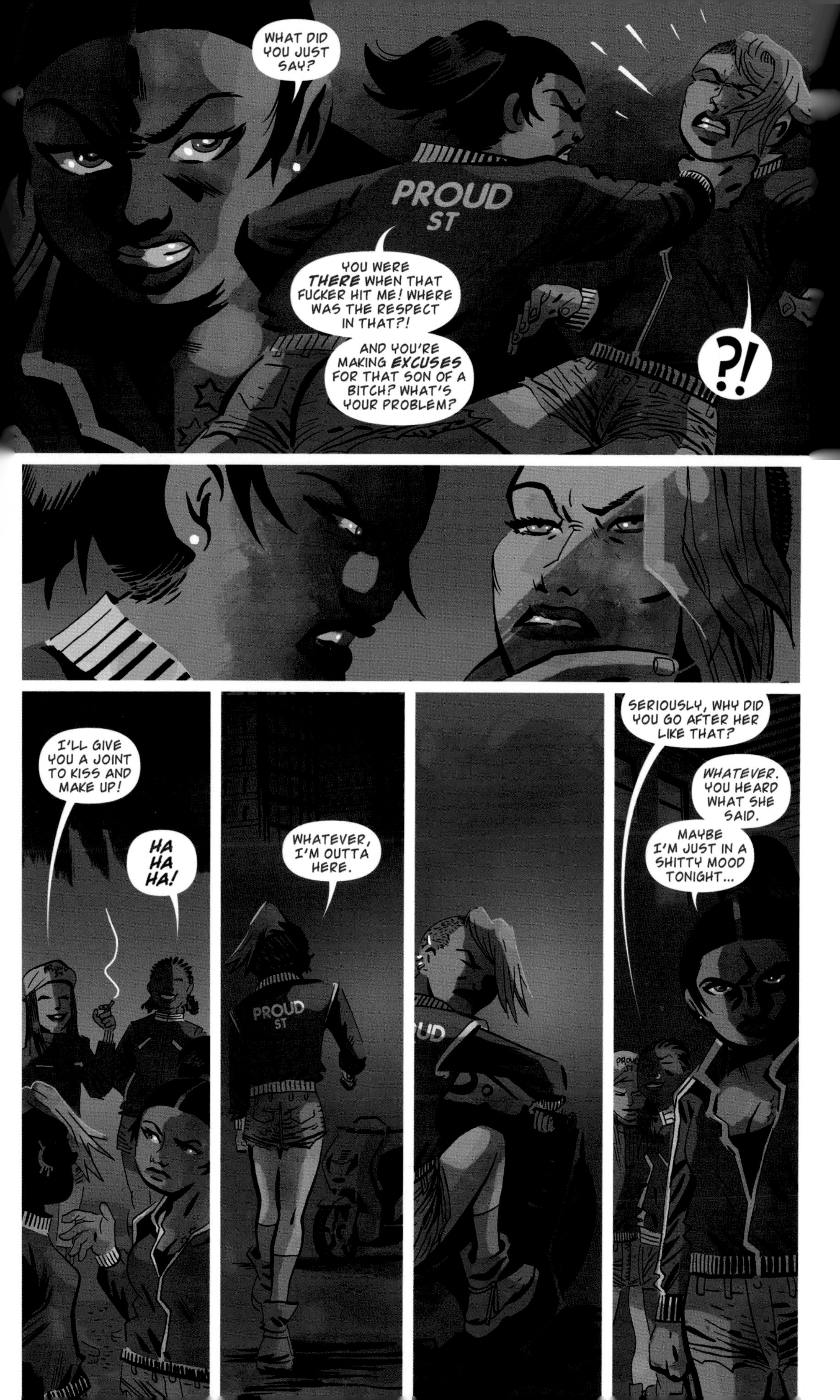

WHAT DID YOU JUST SAY?
?!
YOU WERE THERE WHEN THAT FUCKER HIT ME! WHERE WAS THE RESPECT IN THAT?!
AND YOU'RE MAKING EXCUSES FOR THAT SON OF A BITCH? WHAT'S YOUR PROBLEM?
PROUD ST
I'LL GIVE YOU A JOINT TO KISS AND MAKE UP!
HA HA HA!
WHATEVER, I'M OUTTA HERE.
PROUD ST
SERIOUSLY, WHY DID YOU GO AFTER HER LIKE THAT?
WHATEVER. YOU HEARD WHAT SHE SAID.
MAYBE I'M JUST IN A SHITTY MOOD TONIGHT...

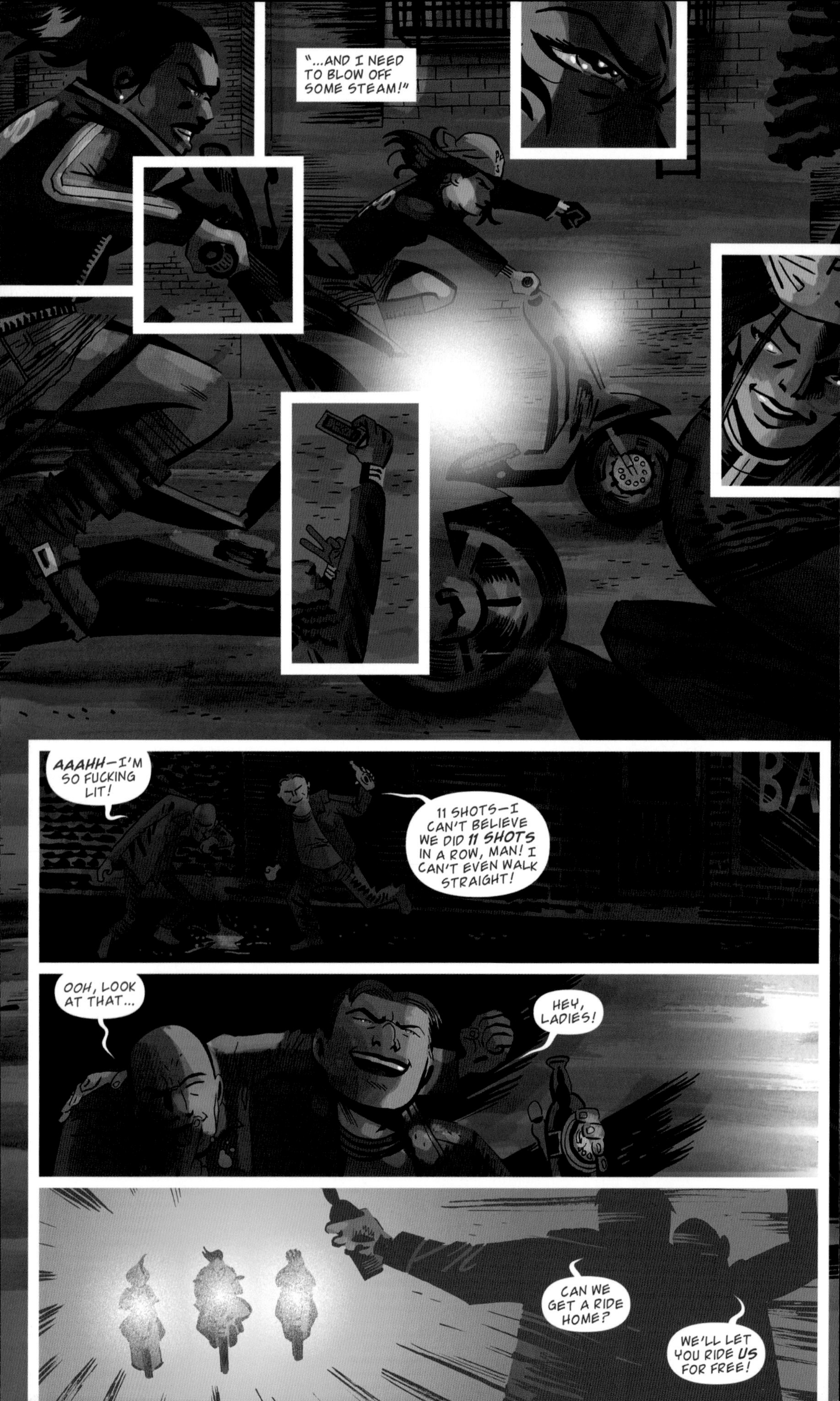

"...AND I NEED TO BLOW OFF SOME STEAM!"
AAAHH—I'M SO FUCKING LIT!
11 SHOTS—I CAN'T BELIEVE WE DID 11 SHOTS IN A ROW, MAN! I CAN'T EVEN WALK STRAIGHT!
OOH, LOOK AT THAT...
HEY, LADIES!
CAN WE GET A RIDE HOME?
WE'LL LET YOU RIDE US FOR FREE!

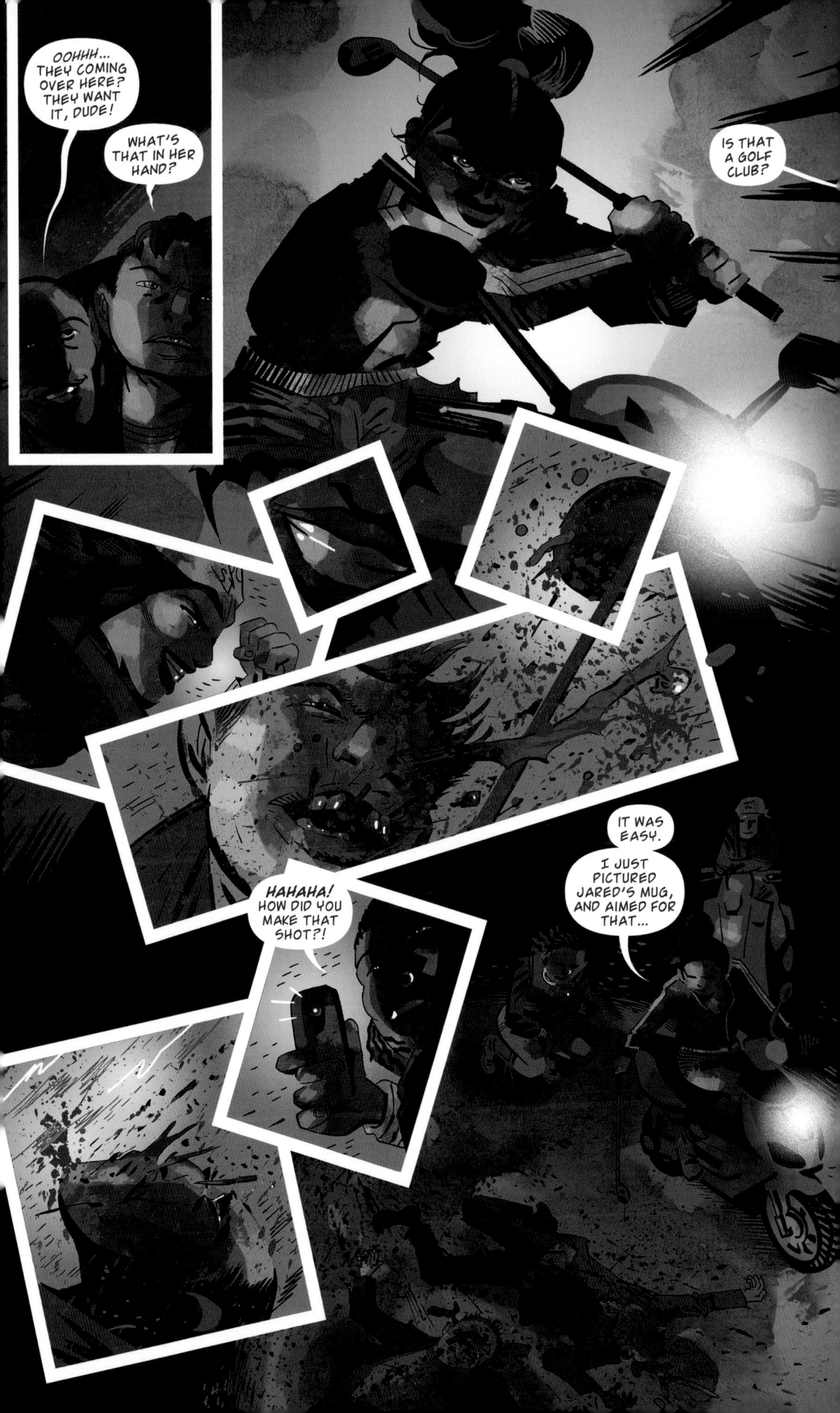
OOHHH... THEY COMING OVER HERE? THEY WANT IT, DUDE!
WHAT'S THAT IN HER HAND?
IS THAT A GOLF CLUB?
HAHAHA! HOW DID YOU MAKE THAT SHOT?!
IT WAS EASY.
I JUST PICTURED JARED'S MUG, AND AIMED FOR THAT...

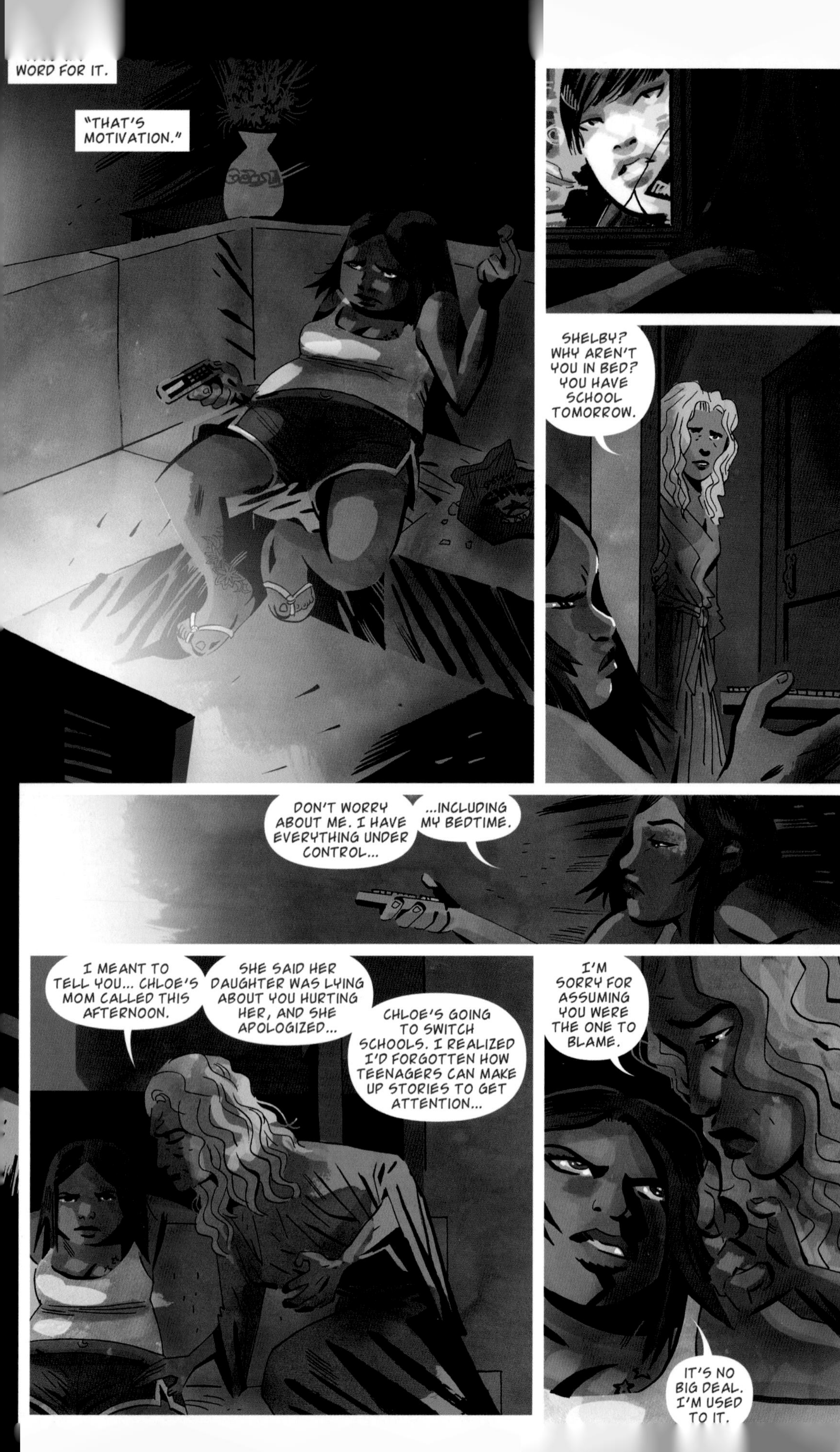
WORD FOR IT.
"THAT'S MOTIVATION."
SHELBY? WHY AREN'T YOU IN BED? YOU HAVE SCHOOL TOMORROW.
DON'T WORRY ABOUT ME. I HAVE EVERYTHING UNDER CONTROL...
...INCLUDING MY BEDTIME.
I MEANT TO TELL YOU... CHLOE'S MOM CALLED THIS AFTERNOON.
SHE SAID HER DAUGHTER WAS LYING ABOUT YOU HURTING HER, AND SHE APOLOGIZED...
CHLOE'S GOING TO SWITCH SCHOOLS. I REALIZED I'D FORGOTTEN HOW TEENAGERS CAN MAKE UP STORIES TO GET ATTENTION...
I'M SORRY FOR ASSUMING YOU WERE THE ONE TO BLAME.
IT'S NO BIG DEAL. I'M USED TO IT.

BY THE WAY, I NEVER TALKED TO YOUR FATHER ABOUT IT.

I COULDN'T REACH HIM—IT'S SO HARD WHEN HE'S AWAY.

BUT EVEN YOU HAVE TO ADMIT, SHELBY, CONSIDERING EVERYTHING YOU'VE PUT US THROUGH THE PAST FEW YEARS...

...I HAD TO TAKE IT SERIOUSLY, DIDN'T I?

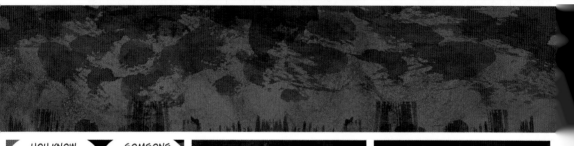

YOU KNOW WHAT? WE NEED SOMEONE FAMOUS TO REALLY GET PEOPLE TALKING ABOUT FUNKTION...

...SOMEONE THE CLIENTELE WOULD LIKE—KANYE, JUSTIN TIMBERLAKE, SOMEBODY LIKE THAT, RIGHT?

HAVE YOU HEARD OF URBAN SMILE?

THEY'RE HUGE RIGHT NOW—ESPECIALLY WITH GIRLS.

I KNOW SOMEONE WHO COULD PUT YOU IN TOUCH WITH THEIR FRONT MAN, THE MOST POPULAR GUY IN THE GROUP...

...SAM.

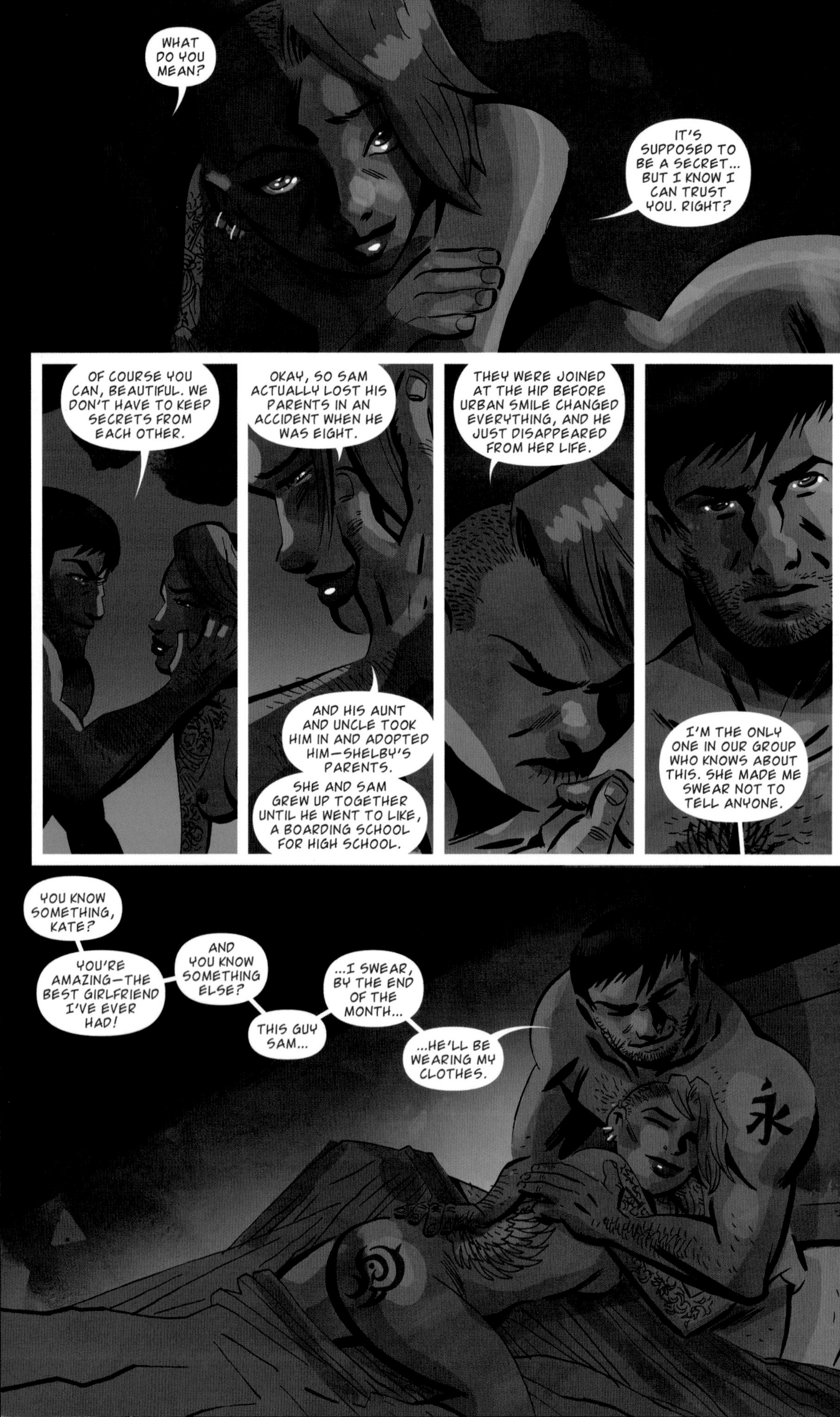
WHAT DO YOU MEAN?
IT'S SUPPOSED TO BE A SECRET... BUT I KNOW I CAN TRUST YOU. RIGHT?
OF COURSE YOU CAN, BEAUTIFUL. WE DON'T HAVE TO KEEP SECRETS FROM EACH OTHER.
OKAY, SO SAM ACTUALLY LOST HIS PARENTS IN AN ACCIDENT WHEN HE WAS EIGHT.
AND HIS AUNT AND UNCLE TOOK HIM IN AND ADOPTED HIM—SHELBY'S PARENTS.
SHE AND SAM GREW UP TOGETHER UNTIL HE WENT TO LIKE, A BOARDING SCHOOL FOR HIGH SCHOOL.
THEY WERE JOINED AT THE HIP BEFORE URBAN SMILE CHANGED EVERYTHING, AND HE JUST DISAPPEARED FROM HER LIFE.
I'M THE ONLY ONE IN OUR GROUP WHO KNOWS ABOUT THIS. SHE MADE ME SWEAR NOT TO TELL ANYONE.
YOU KNOW SOMETHING, KATE?
YOU'RE AMAZING—THE BEST GIRLFRIEND I'VE EVER HAD!
AND YOU KNOW SOMETHING ELSE?
THIS GUY SAM...
...I SWEAR, BY THE END OF THE MONTH...
...HE'LL BE WEARING MY CLOTHES.

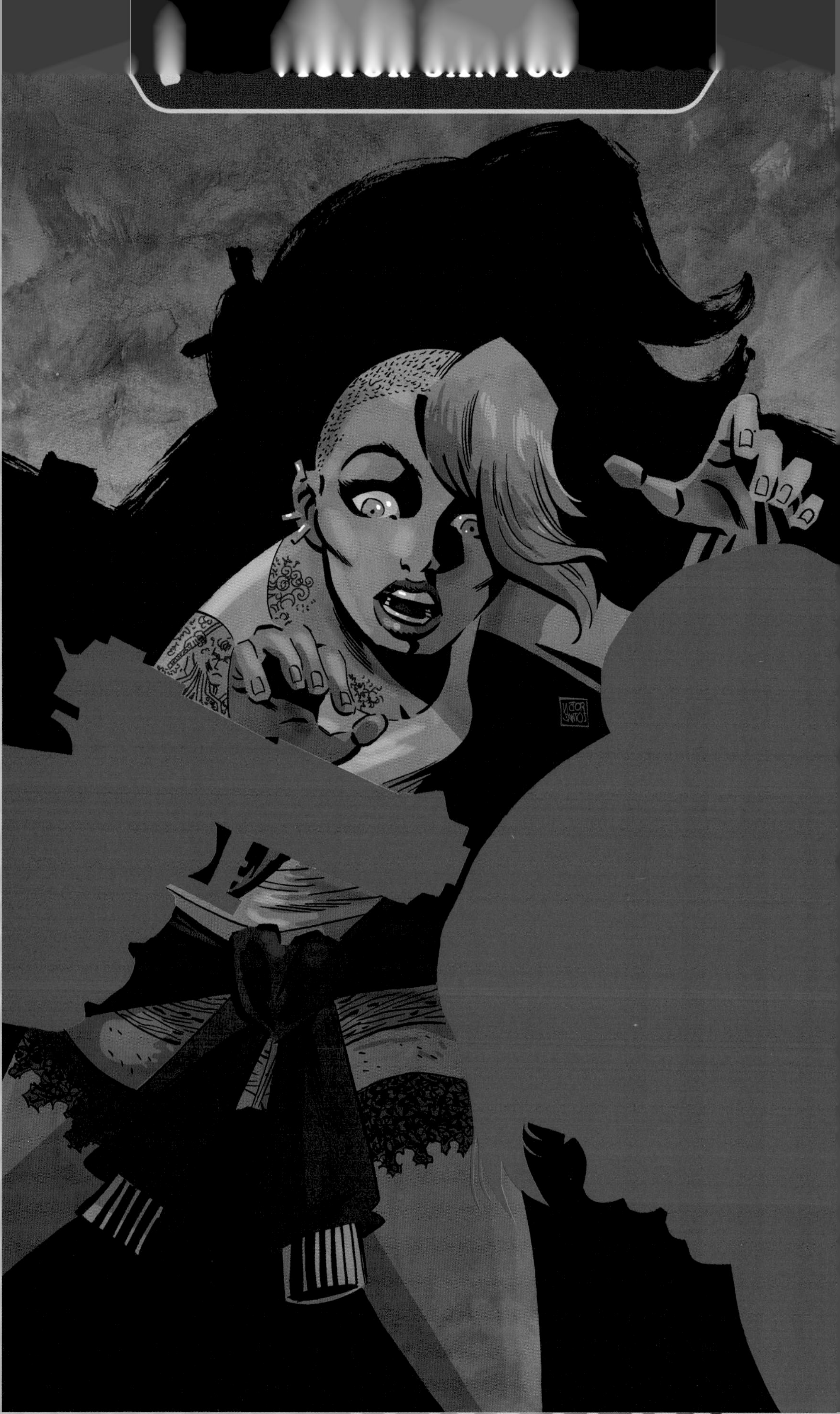

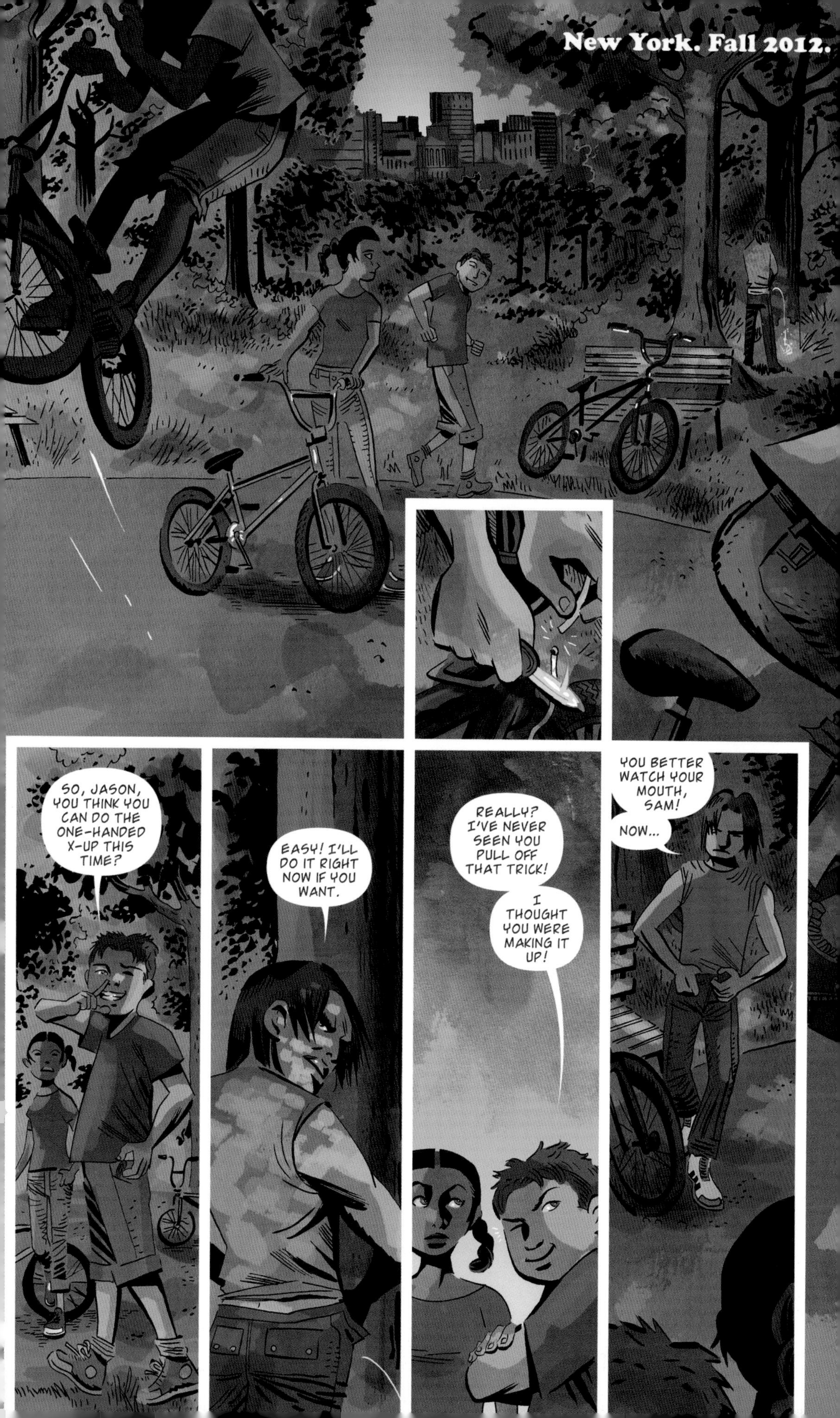

New York. Fall 2012.
SO, JASON, YOU THINK YOU CAN DO THE ONE-HANDED X-UP THIS TIME?
EASY! I'LL DO IT RIGHT NOW IF YOU WANT.
REALLY? I'VE NEVER SEEN YOU PULL OFF THAT TRICK!
I THOUGHT YOU WERE MAKING IT UP!
YOU BETTER WATCH YOUR MOUTH, SAM!
NOW...

...WATCH AND LEARN!

HERE WE GO*OO!

YEAH...

...LET'S SEE HOW FAR YOU GO!

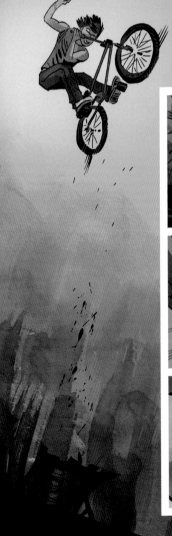

I CAN'T SLOW DOWN!

BEEEEEP

BLAM

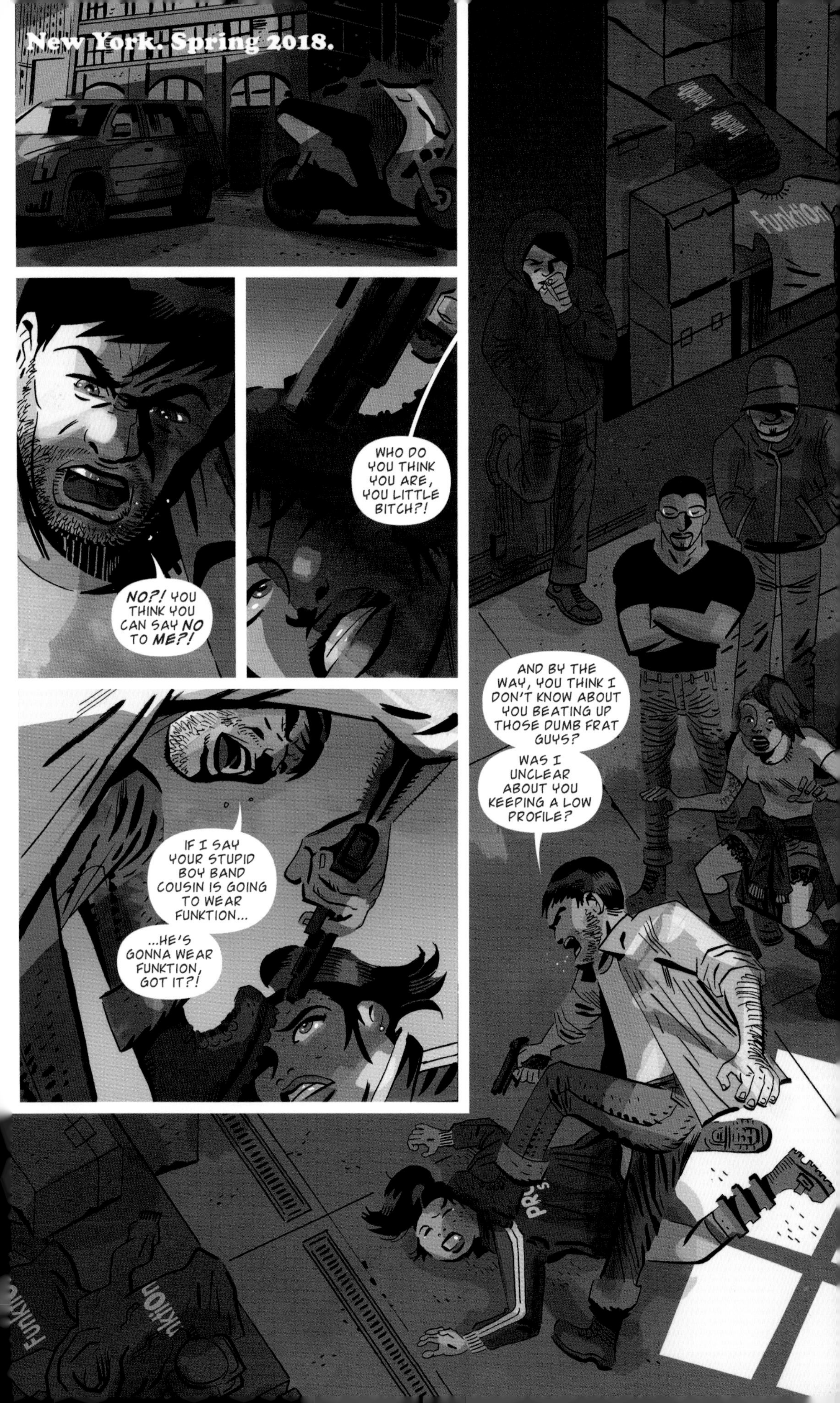
New York. Spring 2018.
NO?! YOU THINK YOU CAN SAY NO TO ME?!
WHO DO YOU THINK YOU ARE, YOU LITTLE BITCH?!
IF I SAY YOUR STUPID BOY BAND COUSIN IS GOING TO WEAR FUNKTION...
...HE'S GONNA WEAR FUNKTION, GOT IT?!
AND BY THE WAY, YOU THINK I DON'T KNOW ABOUT YOU BEATING UP THOSE DUMB FRAT GUYS?
WAS I UNCLEAR ABOUT YOU KEEPING A LOW PROFILE?
Funktion

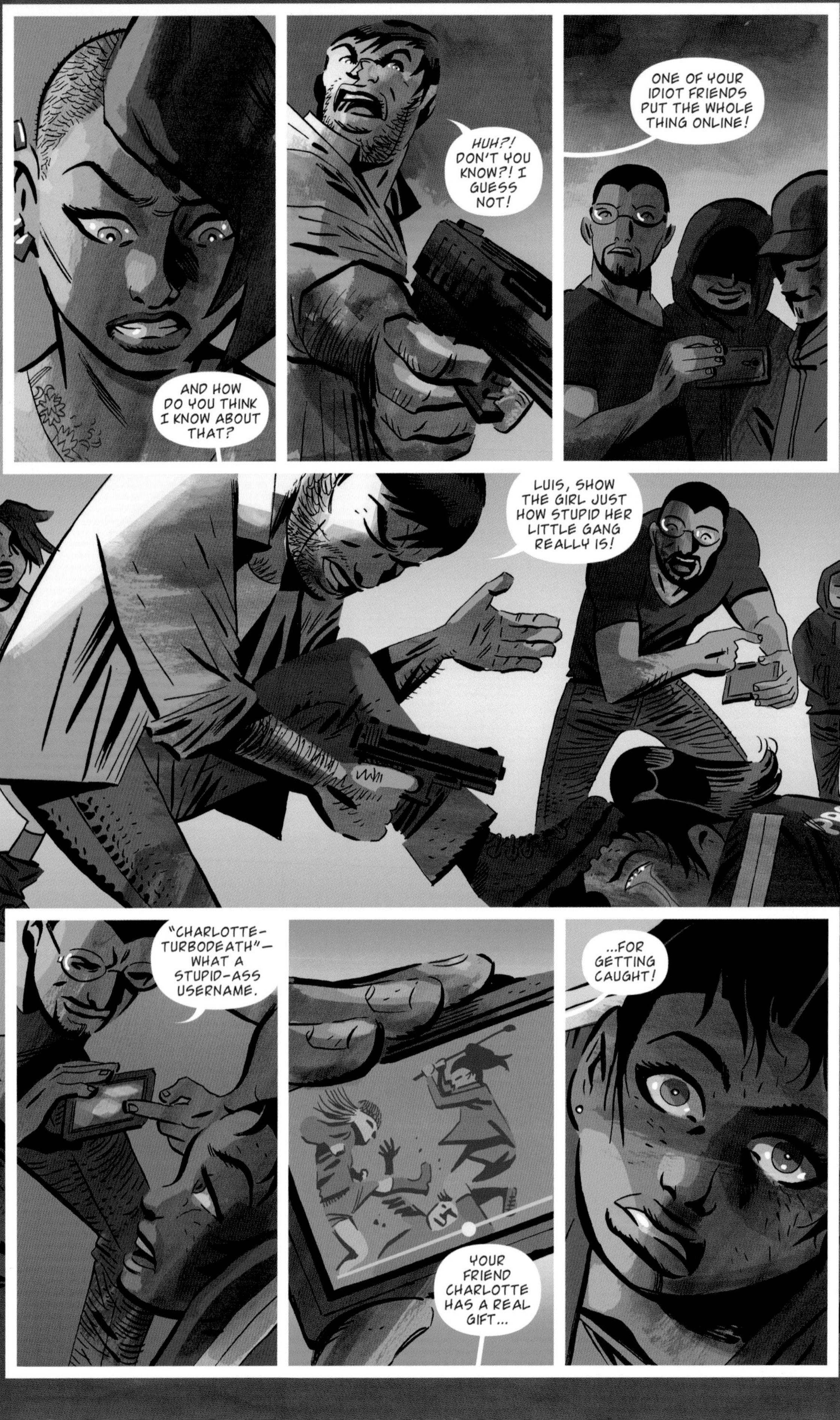
AND HOW DO YOU THINK I KNOW ABOUT THAT?
HUH?! DON'T YOU KNOW?! I GUESS NOT!
ONE OF YOUR IDIOT FRIENDS PUT THE WHOLE THING ONLINE!
LUIS, SHOW THE GIRL JUST HOW STUPID HER LITTLE GANG REALLY IS!
"CHARLOTTE-TURBODEATH"—WHAT A STUPID-ASS USERNAME.
YOUR FRIEND CHARLOTTE HAS A REAL GIFT...
...FOR GETTING CAUGHT!

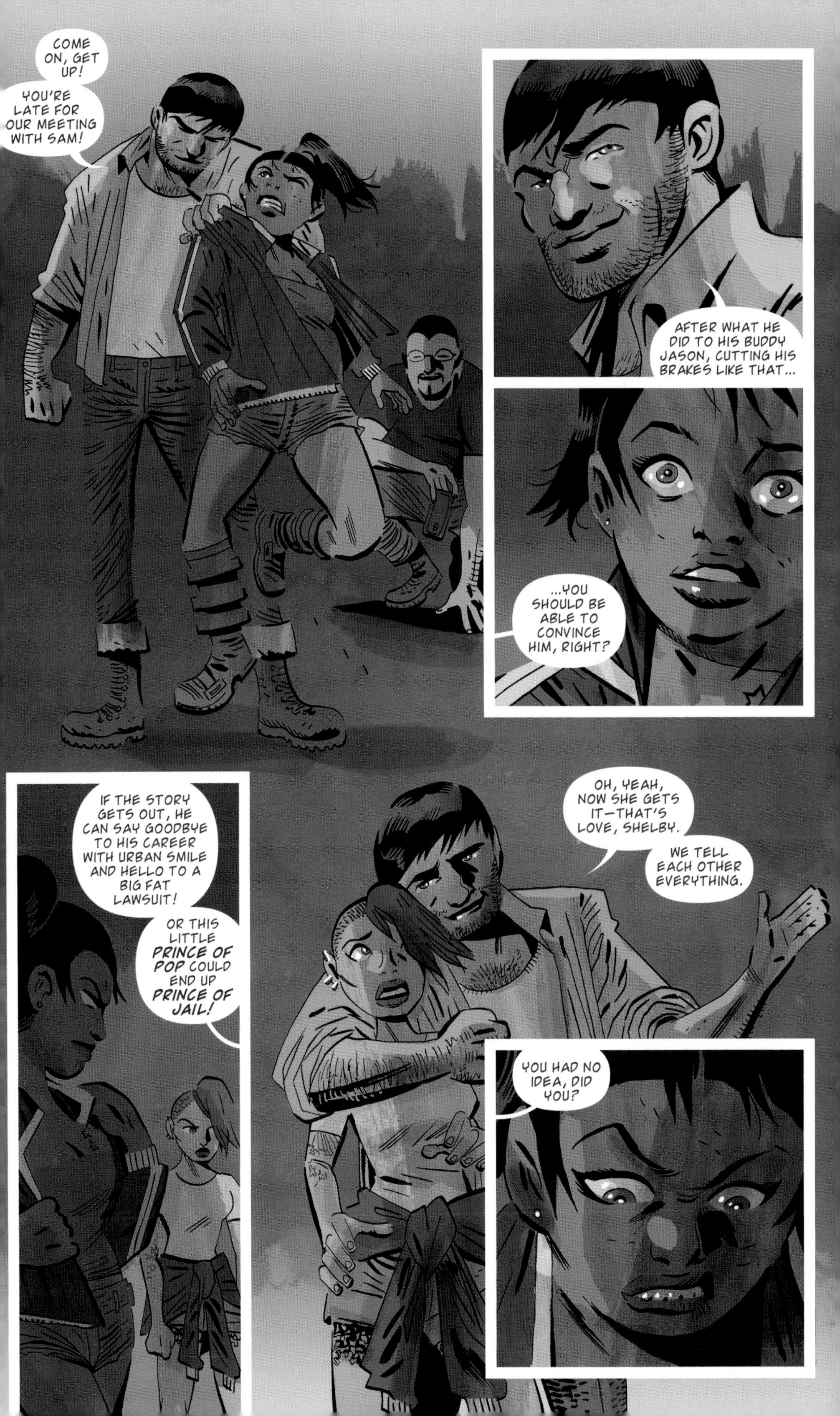
COME ON, GET UP!
YOU'RE LATE FOR OUR MEETING WITH SAM!
AFTER WHAT HE DID TO HIS BUDDY JASON, CUTTING HIS BRAKES LIKE THAT...
...YOU SHOULD BE ABLE TO CONVINCE HIM, RIGHT?
IF THE STORY GETS OUT, HE CAN SAY GOODBYE TO HIS CAREER WITH URBAN SMILE AND HELLO TO A BIG FAT LAWSUIT!
OR THIS LITTLE PRINCE OF POP COULD END UP PRINCE OF JAIL!
OH, YEAH, NOW SHE GETS IT—THAT'S LOVE, SHELBY.
WE TELL EACH OTHER EVERYTHING.
YOU HAD NO IDEA, DID YOU?

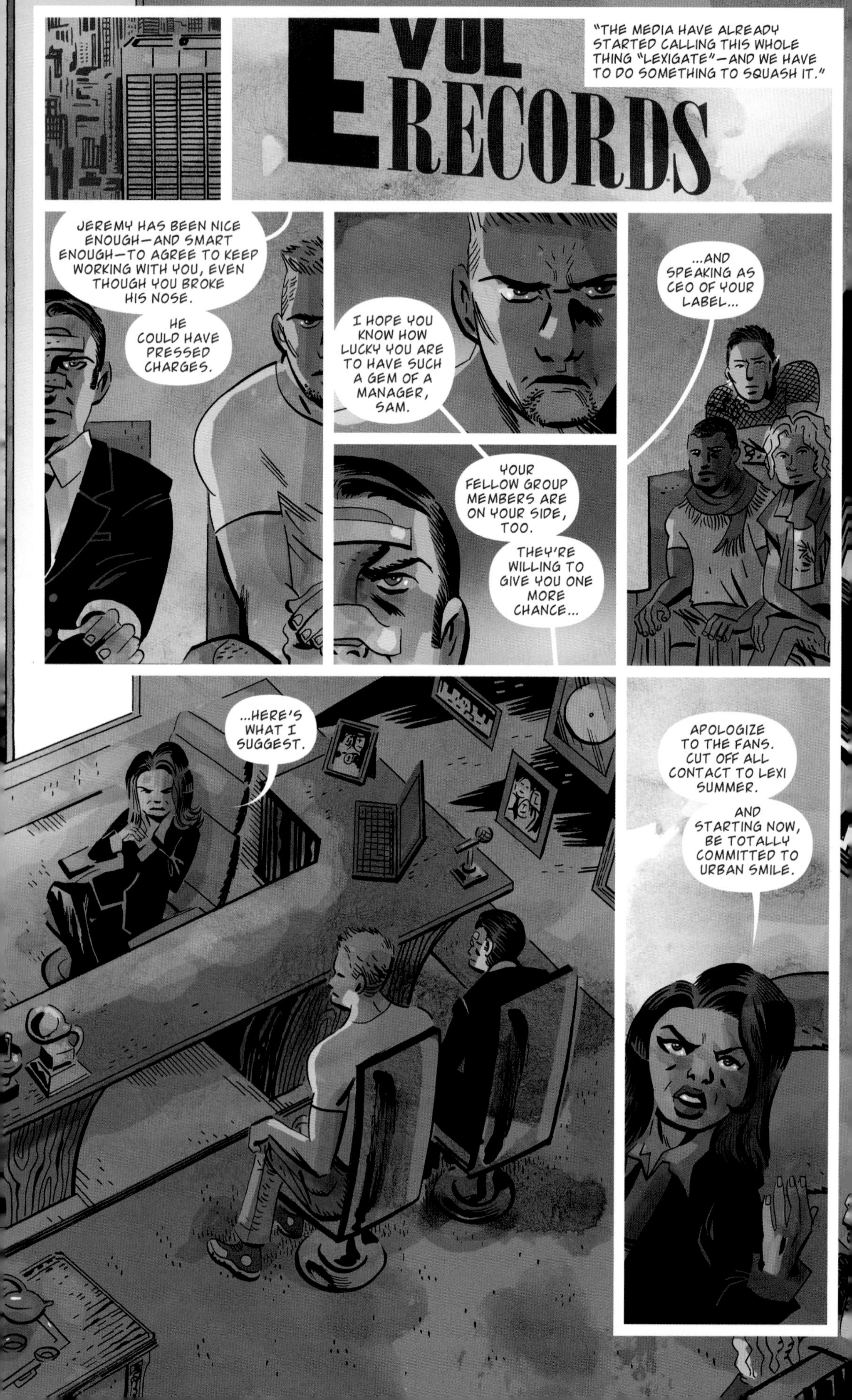
EVOL RECORDS
"THE MEDIA HAVE ALREADY STARTED CALLING THIS WHOLE THING "LEXIGATE"—AND WE HAVE TO DO SOMETHING TO SQUASH IT."
JEREMY HAS BEEN NICE ENOUGH—AND SMART ENOUGH—TO AGREE TO KEEP WORKING WITH YOU, EVEN THOUGH YOU BROKE HIS NOSE.
HE COULD HAVE PRESSED CHARGES.
I HOPE YOU KNOW HOW LUCKY YOU ARE TO HAVE SUCH A GEM OF A MANAGER, SAM.
YOUR FELLOW GROUP MEMBERS ARE ON YOUR SIDE, TOO.
THEY'RE WILLING TO GIVE YOU ONE MORE CHANCE...
...AND SPEAKING AS CEO OF YOUR LABEL...
...HERE'S WHAT I SUGGEST.
APOLOGIZE TO THE FANS. CUT OFF ALL CONTACT TO LEXI SUMMER.
AND STARTING NOW, BE TOTALLY COMMITTED TO URBAN SMILE.

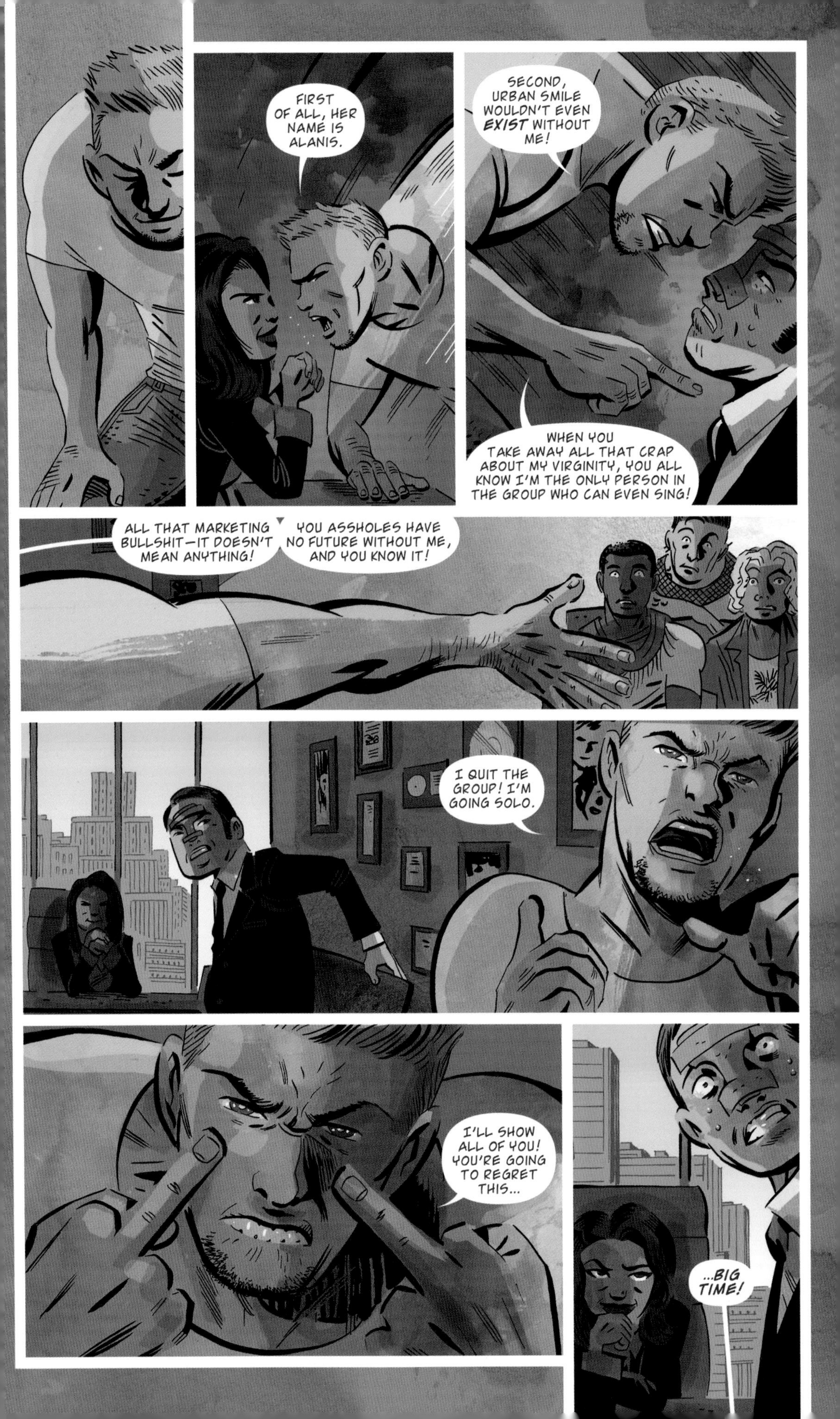
FIRST OF ALL, HER NAME IS ALANIS.
SECOND, URBAN SMILE WOULDN'T EVEN EXIST WITHOUT ME!
WHEN YOU TAKE AWAY ALL THAT CRAP ABOUT MY VIRGINITY, YOU ALL KNOW I'M THE ONLY PERSON IN THE GROUP WHO CAN EVEN SING!
ALL THAT MARKETING BULLSHIT—IT DOESN'T MEAN ANYTHING!
YOU ASSHOLES HAVE NO FUTURE WITHOUT ME, AND YOU KNOW IT!
I QUIT THE GROUP! I'M GOING SOLO.
I'LL SHOW ALL OF YOU! YOU'RE GOING TO REGRET THIS...
...BIG TIME!

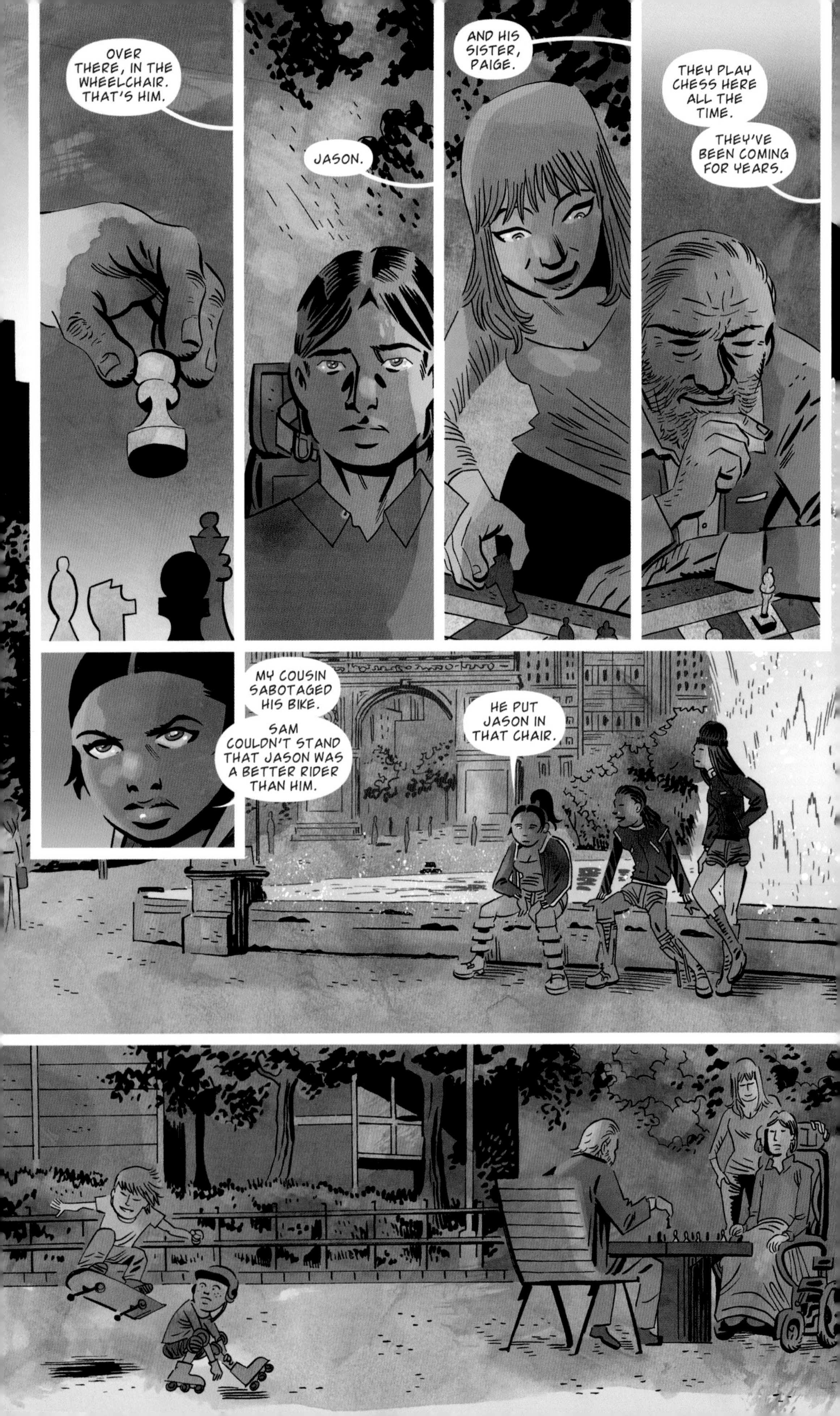

OVER THERE, IN THE WHEELCHAIR. THAT'S HIM.
JASON.
AND HIS SISTER, PAIGE.
THEY PLAY CHESS HERE ALL THE TIME.
THEY'VE BEEN COMING FOR YEARS.
MY COUSIN SABOTAGED HIS BIKE.
SAM COULDN'T STAND THAT JASON WAS A BETTER RIDER THAN HIM.
HE PUT JASON IN THAT CHAIR.

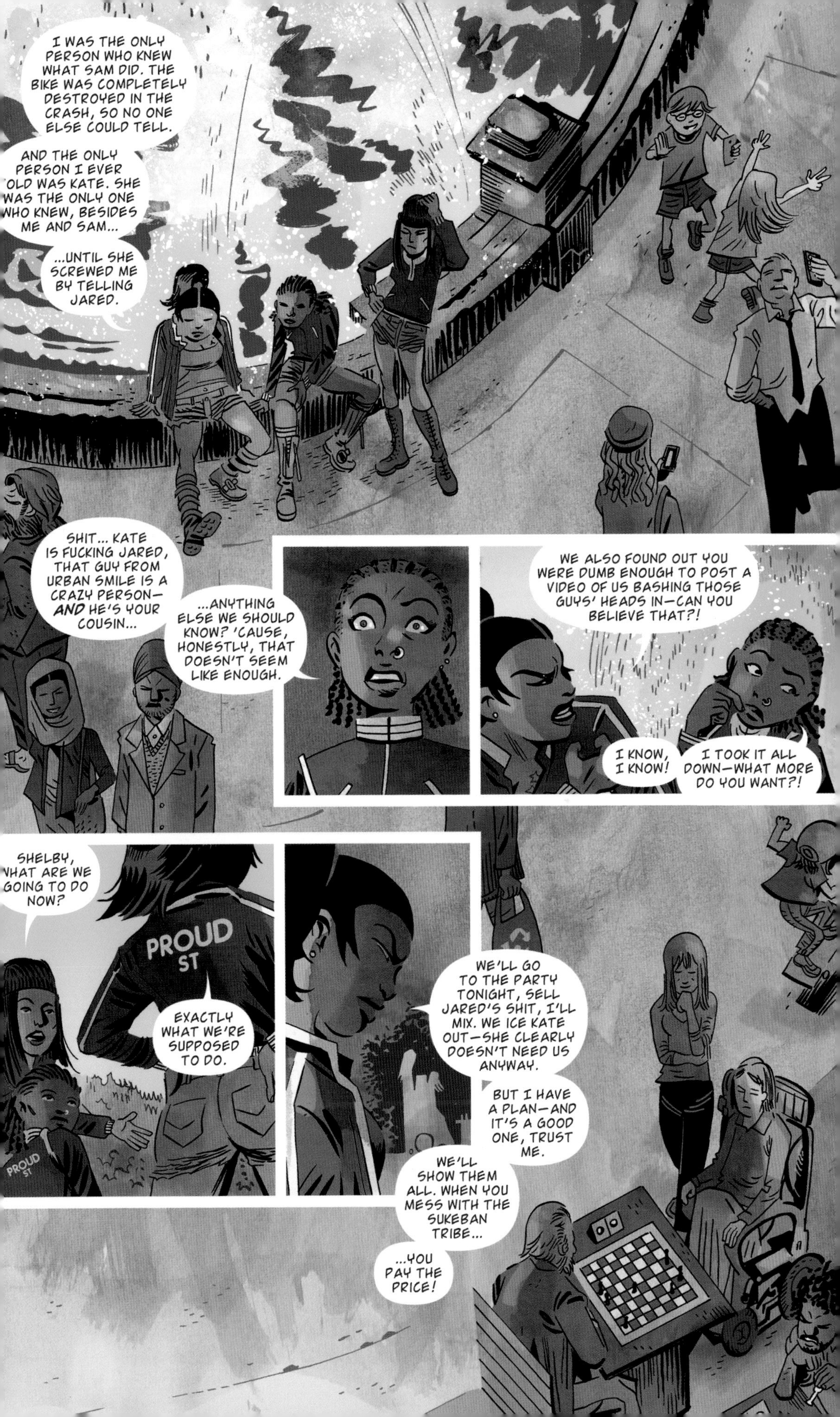
I WAS THE ONLY PERSON WHO KNEW WHAT SAM DID. THE BIKE WAS COMPLETELY DESTROYED IN THE CRASH, SO NO ONE ELSE COULD TELL.
AND THE ONLY PERSON I EVER TOLD WAS KATE. SHE WAS THE ONLY ONE WHO KNEW, BESIDES ME AND SAM...
...UNTIL SHE SCREWED ME BY TELLING JARED.
SHIT... KATE IS FUCKING JARED, THAT GUY FROM URBAN SMILE IS A CRAZY PERSON—AND HE'S YOUR COUSIN...
...ANYTHING ELSE WE SHOULD KNOW? 'CAUSE, HONESTLY, THAT DOESN'T SEEM LIKE ENOUGH.
WE ALSO FOUND OUT YOU WERE DUMB ENOUGH TO POST A VIDEO OF US BASHING THOSE GUYS' HEADS IN—CAN YOU BELIEVE THAT?!
I KNOW, I KNOW!
I TOOK IT ALL DOWN—WHAT MORE DO YOU WANT?!
SHELBY, WHAT ARE WE GOING TO DO NOW?
PROUD ST
EXACTLY WHAT WE'RE SUPPOSED TO DO.
PROUD ST
WE'LL GO TO THE PARTY TONIGHT, SELL JARED'S SHIT, I'LL MIX. WE ICE KATE OUT—SHE CLEARLY DOESN'T NEED US ANYWAY.
BUT I HAVE A PLAN—AND IT'S A GOOD ONE, TRUST ME.
WE'LL SHOW THEM ALL. WHEN YOU MESS WITH THE SUKEBAN TRIBE...
...YOU PAY THE PRICE!

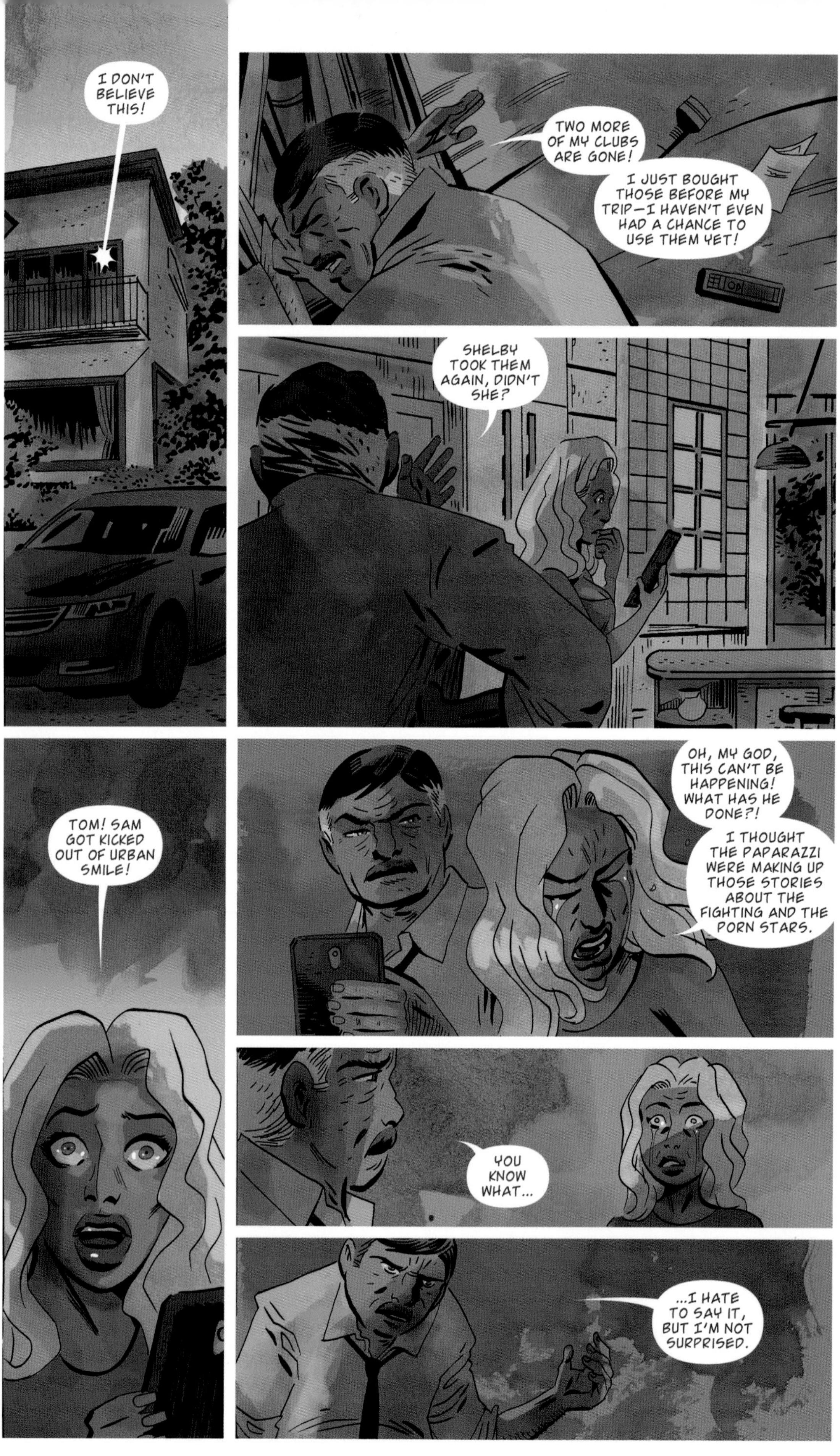
I DON'T BELIEVE THIS!
TWO MORE OF MY CLUBS ARE GONE!
I JUST BOUGHT THOSE BEFORE MY TRIP—I HAVEN'T EVEN HAD A CHANCE TO USE THEM YET!
SHELBY TOOK THEM AGAIN, DIDN'T SHE?
TOM! SAM GOT KICKED OUT OF URBAN SMILE!
OH, MY GOD, THIS CAN'T BE HAPPENING! WHAT HAS HE DONE?!
I THOUGHT THE PAPARAZZI WERE MAKING UP THOSE STORIES ABOUT THE FIGHTING AND THE PORN STARS.
YOU KNOW WHAT...
...I HATE TO SAY IT, BUT I'M NOT SURPRISED.

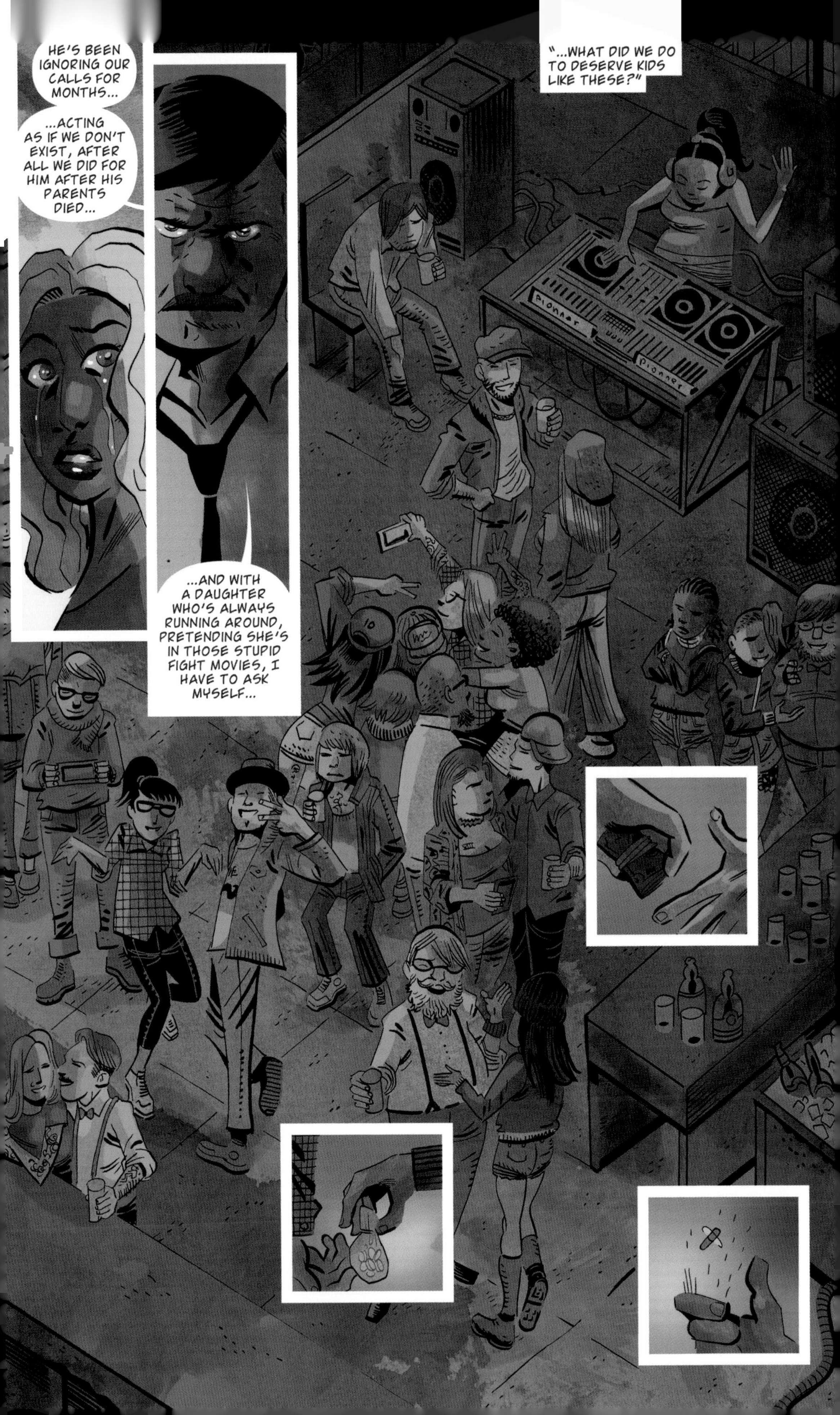
HE'S BEEN IGNORING OUR CALLS FOR MONTHS...
...ACTING AS IF WE DON'T EXIST, AFTER ALL WE DID FOR HIM AFTER HIS PARENTS DIED...
...AND WITH A DAUGHTER WHO'S ALWAYS RUNNING AROUND, PRETENDING SHE'S IN THOSE STUPID FIGHT MOVIES, I HAVE TO ASK MYSELF...
"...WHAT DID WE DO TO DESERVE KIDS LIKE THESE?"

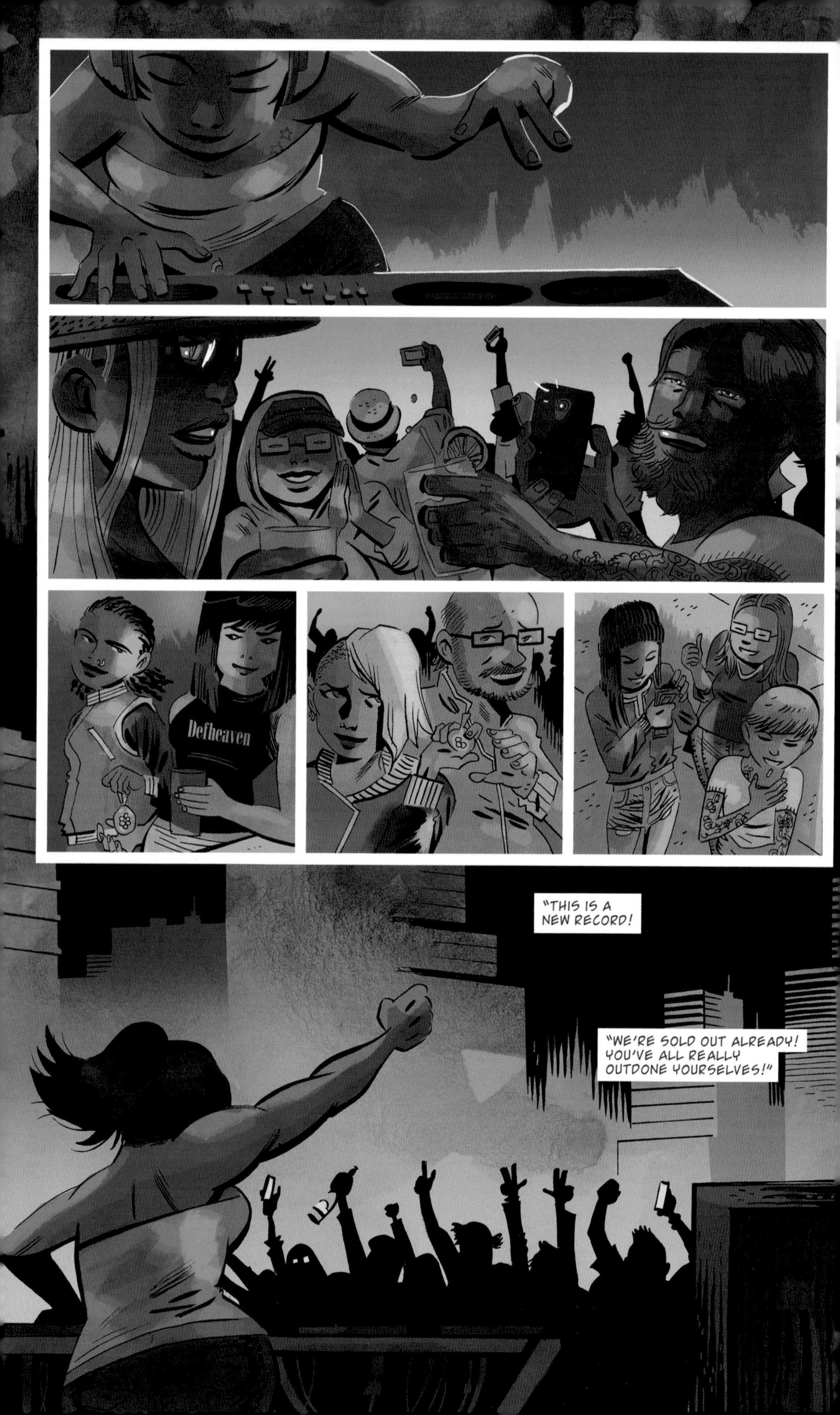
Defheaven
"THIS IS A NEW RECORD!
"WE'RE SOLD OUT ALREADY! YOU'VE ALL REALLY OUTDONE YOURSELVES!"

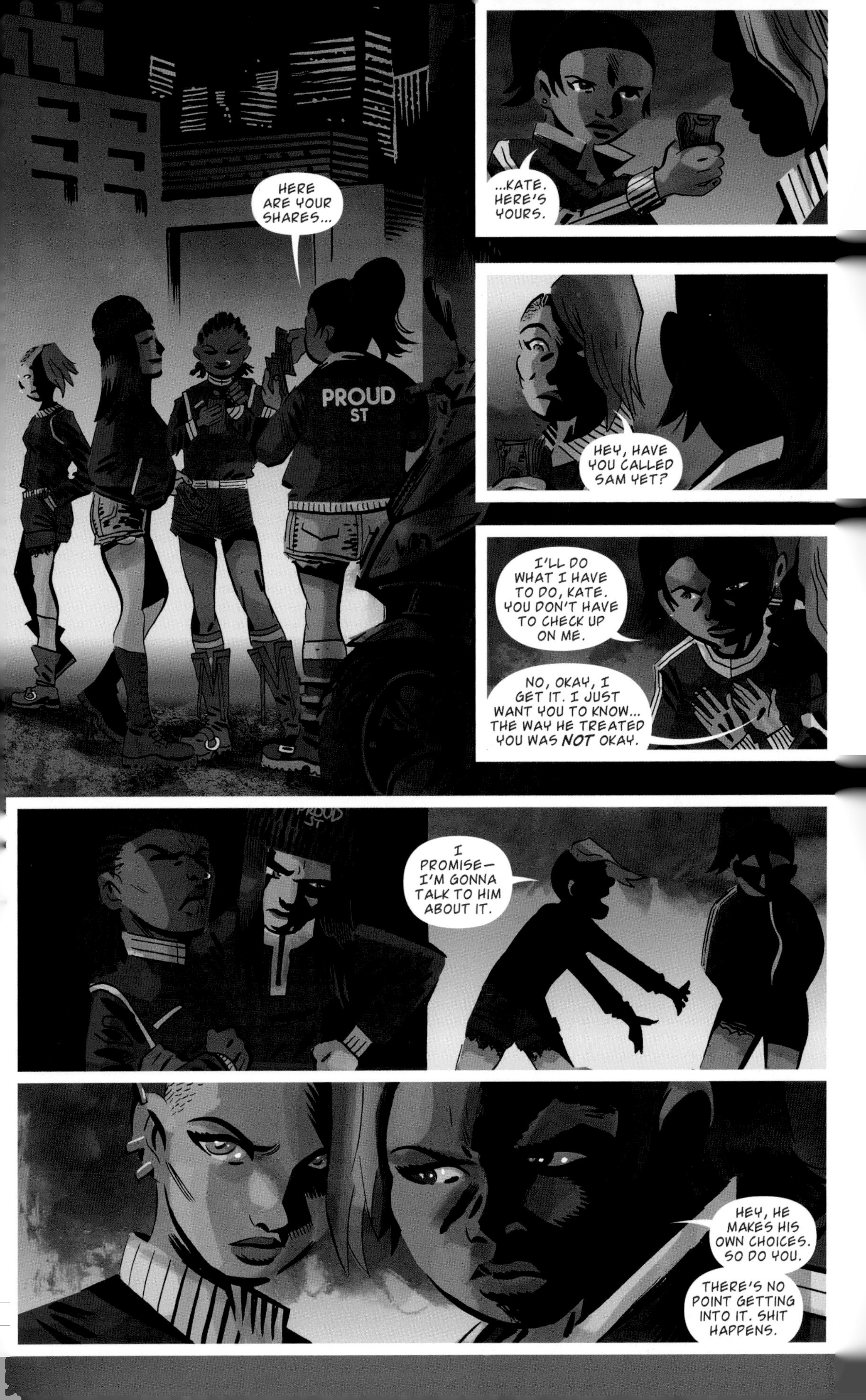
HERE ARE YOUR SHARES...
PROUD ST
...KATE. HERE'S YOURS.
HEY, HAVE YOU CALLED SAM YET?
I'LL DO WHAT I HAVE TO DO, KATE. YOU DON'T HAVE TO CHECK UP ON ME.
NO, OKAY, I GET IT. I JUST WANT YOU TO KNOW... THE WAY HE TREATED YOU WAS NOT OKAY.
I PROMISE— I'M GONNA TALK TO HIM ABOUT IT.
HEY, HE MAKES HIS OWN CHOICES. SO DO YOU.
THERE'S NO POINT GETTING INTO IT. SHIT HAPPENS.

I'M GONNA GO FOR A RIDE—CLEAR MY HEAD.

CATCH YOU LATER!

UM... I'VE GOT SOME WEED.

YOU WANNA GO SMOKE DOWN BY THE BRIDGE?

NAH, I'M GOOD.

TAKE CARE, KATE.

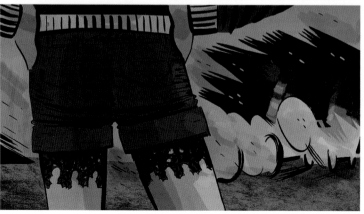

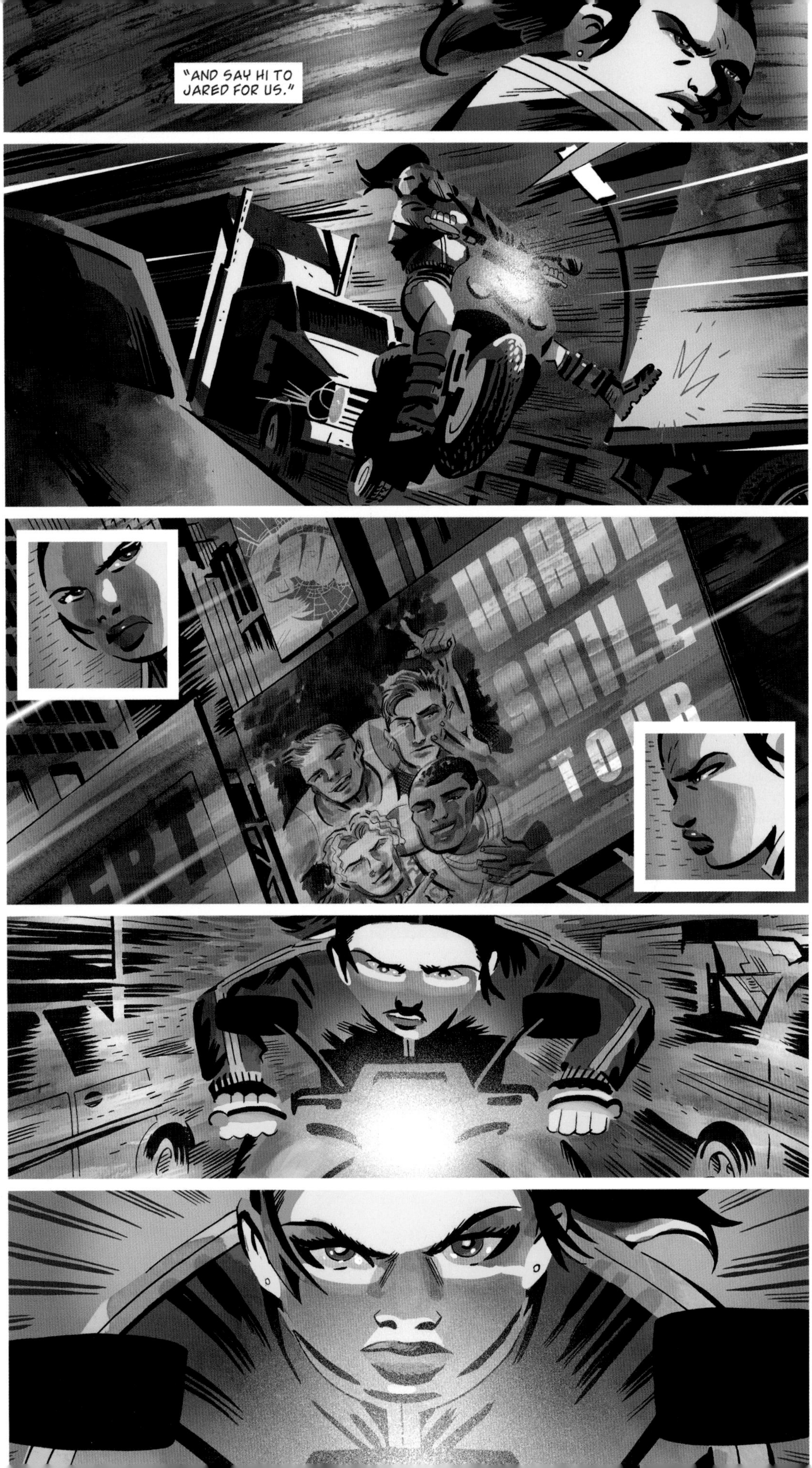
"AND SAY HI TO JARED FOR US."
SMILE

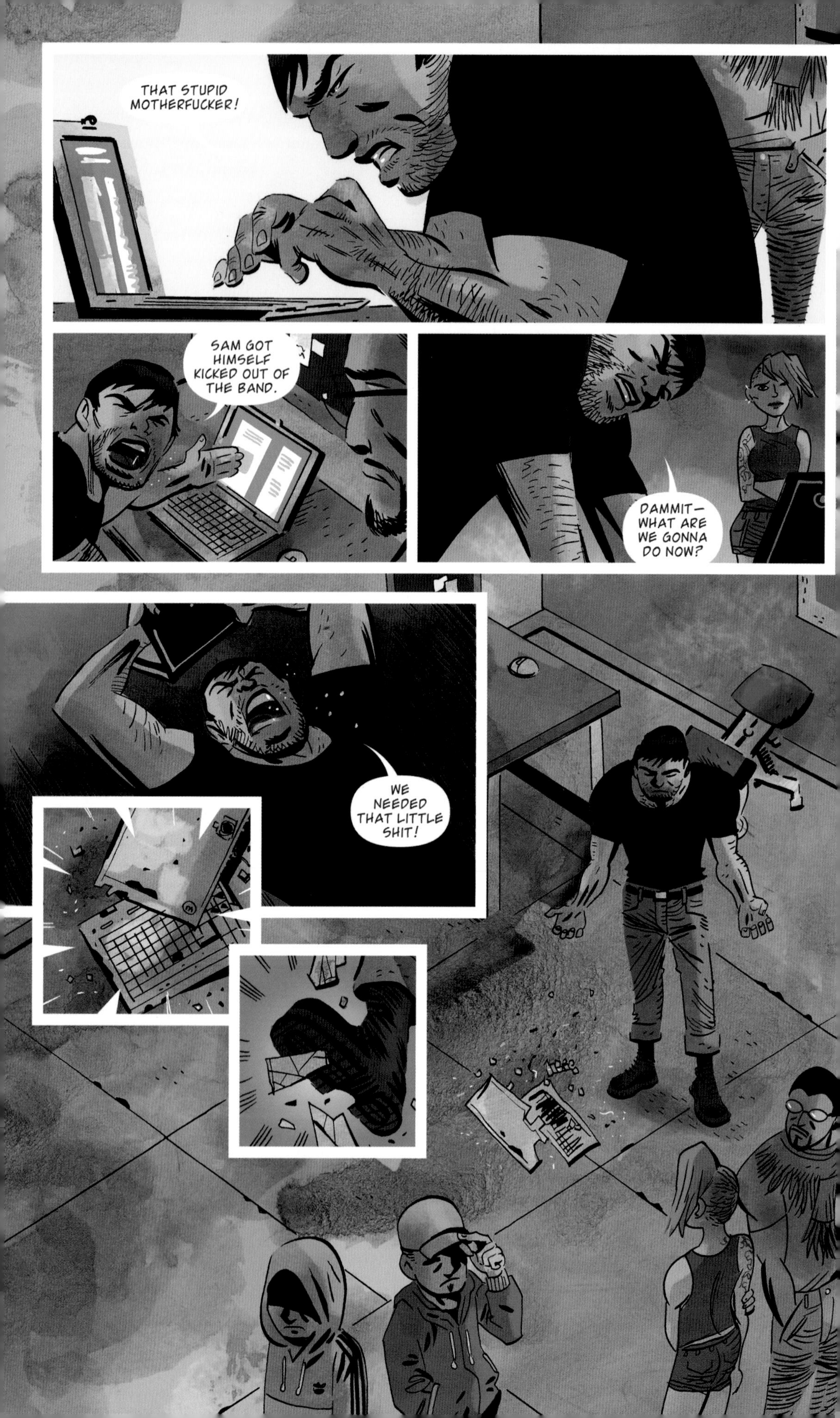
THAT STUPID MOTHERFUCKER!
SAM GOT HIMSELF KICKED OUT OF THE BAND.
DAMMIT— WHAT ARE WE GONNA DO NOW?
WE NEEDED THAT LITTLE SHIT!

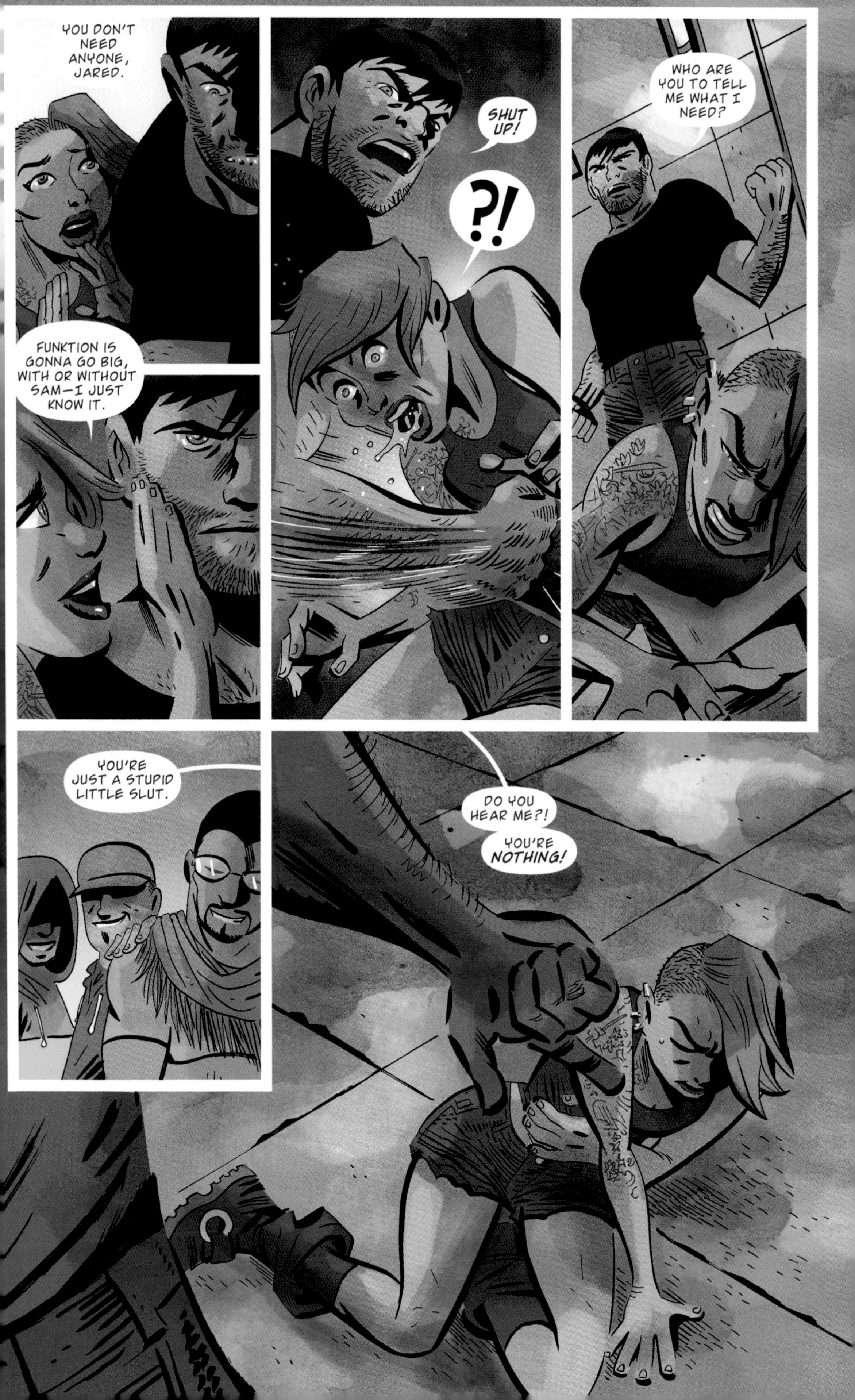
YOU DON'T NEED ANYONE, JARED.
FUNKTION IS GONNA GO BIG, WITH OR WITHOUT SAM—I JUST KNOW IT.
SHUT UP!
?!
WHO ARE YOU TO TELL ME WHAT I NEED?
YOU'RE JUST A STUPID LITTLE SLUT.
DO YOU HEAR ME?!
YOU'RE NOTHING!

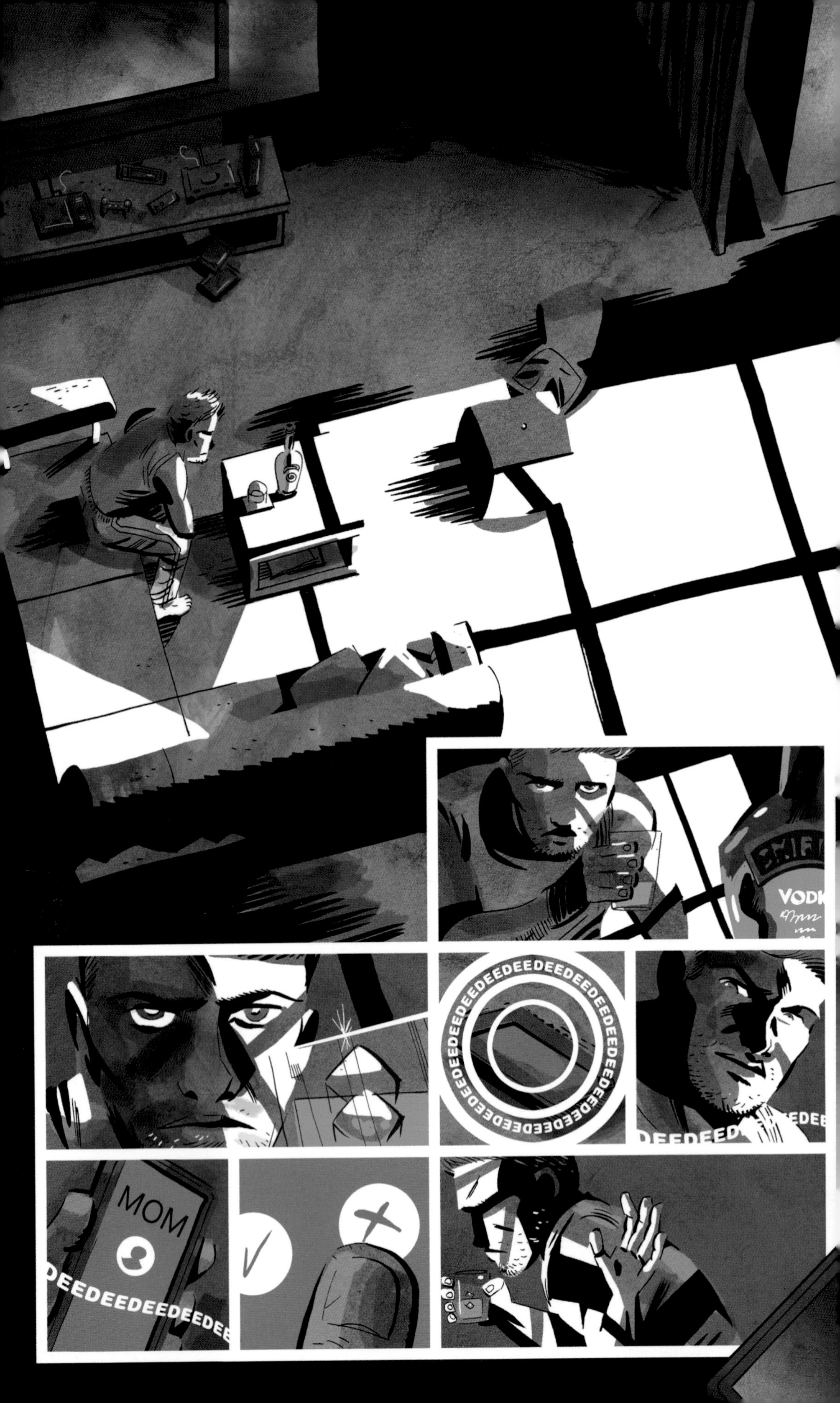
VODK
DEEDEEDEEDEEDEEDEEDEEDEE
DEEDEEDEE
MOM
DEEDEEDEEDEEDEE

URBAN SMILE

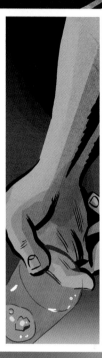

Search

Lexi Summer + porn + best video|

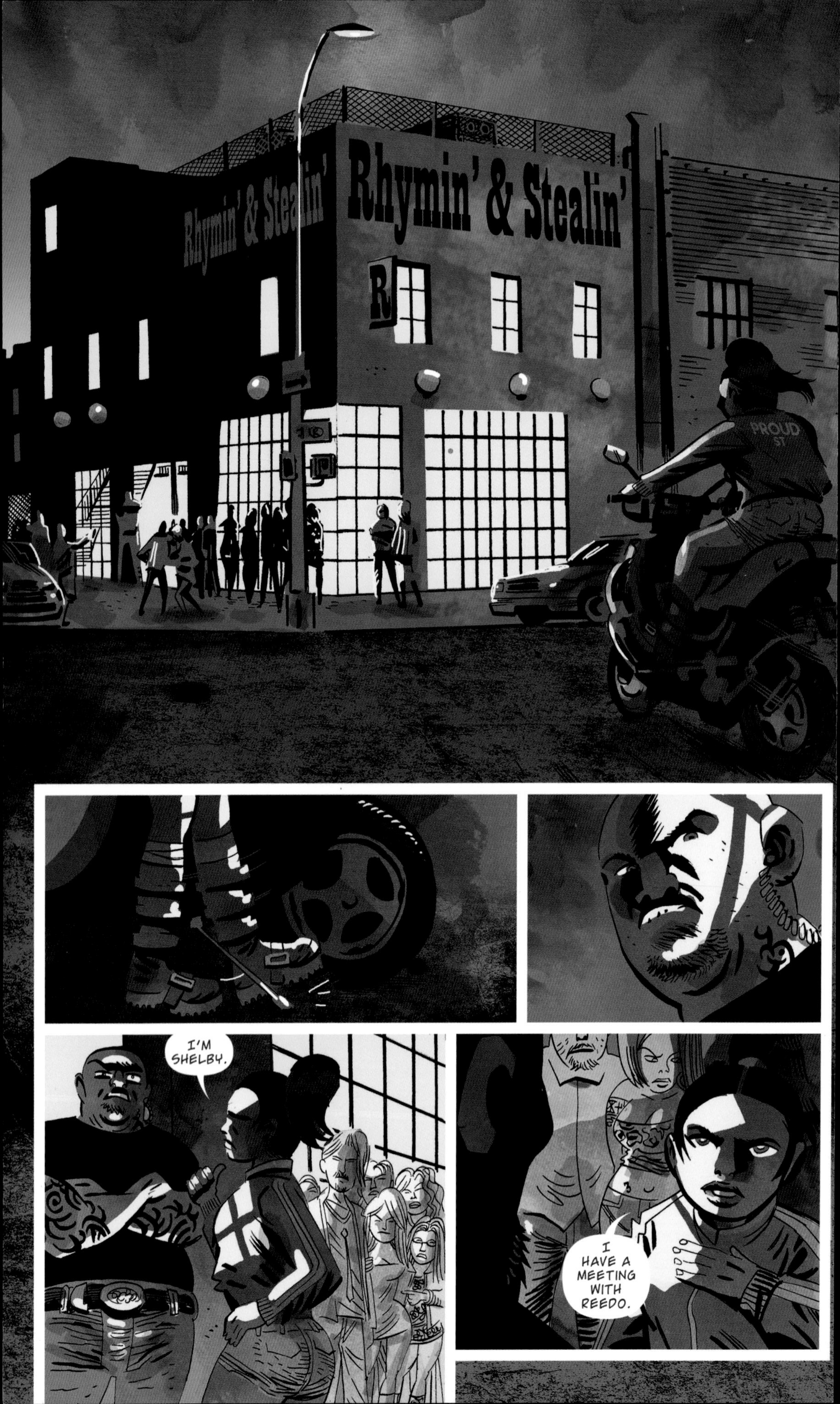
Rhymin' & Stealin'
Rhymin' & Stealin'
R
PROUD ST
I'M SHELBY.
I HAVE A MEETING WITH REEDO.

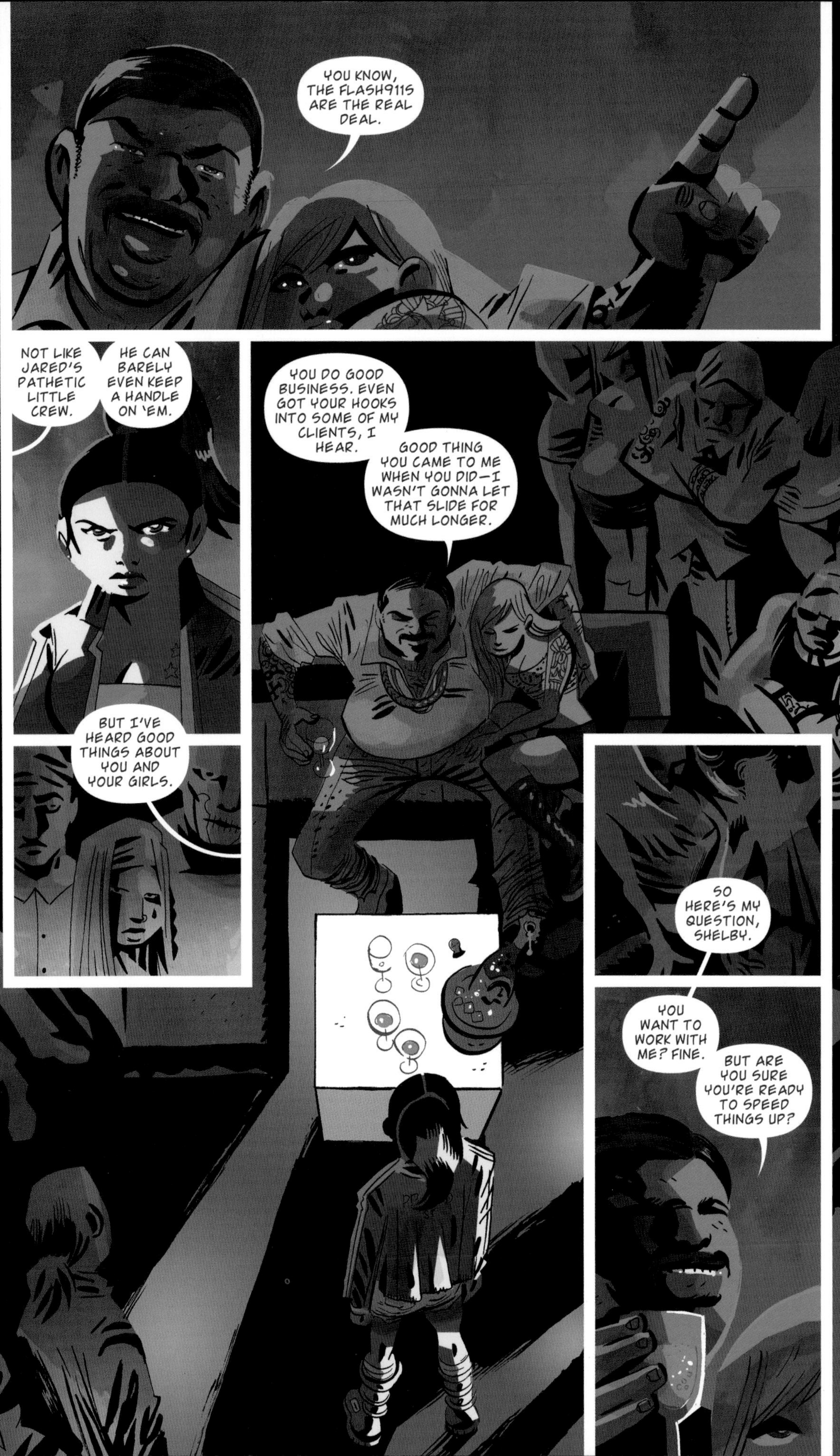
YOU KNOW, THE FLASH911S ARE THE REAL DEAL.
NOT LIKE JARED'S PATHETIC LITTLE CREW.
HE CAN BARELY EVEN KEEP A HANDLE ON 'EM.
BUT I'VE HEARD GOOD THINGS ABOUT YOU AND YOUR GIRLS.
YOU DO GOOD BUSINESS. EVEN GOT YOUR HOOKS INTO SOME OF MY CLIENTS, I HEAR.
GOOD THING YOU CAME TO ME WHEN YOU DID—I WASN'T GONNA LET THAT SLIDE FOR MUCH LONGER.
SO HERE'S MY QUESTION, SHELBY.
YOU WANT TO WORK WITH ME? FINE.
BUT ARE YOU SURE YOU'RE READY TO SPEED THINGS UP?

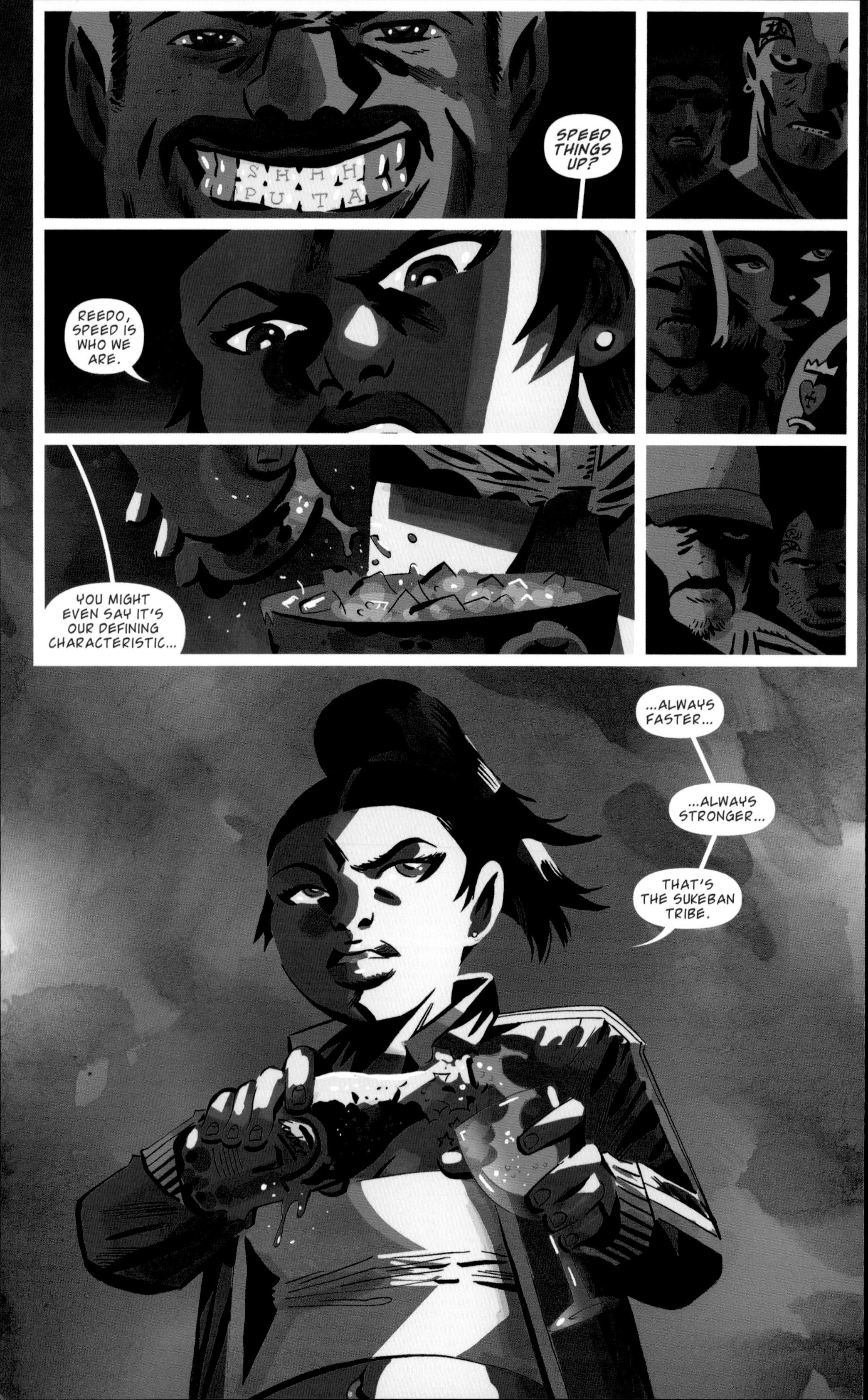
SHHH PUTA
SPEED THINGS UP?
REEDO, SPEED IS WHO WE ARE.
YOU MIGHT EVEN SAY IT'S OUR DEFINING CHARACTERISTIC...
...ALWAYS FASTER...
...ALWAYS STRONGER...
THAT'S THE SUKEBAN TRIBE.

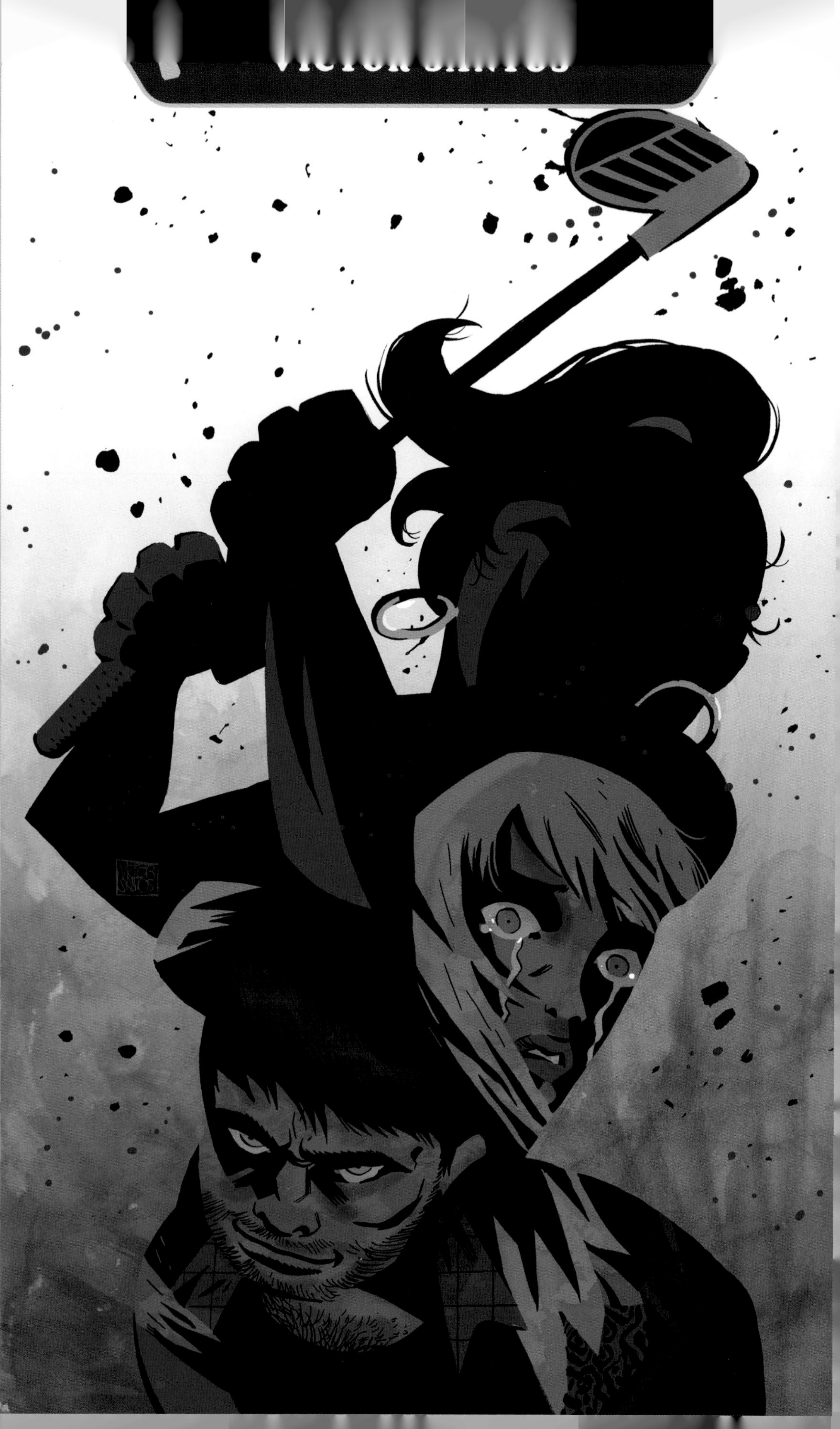

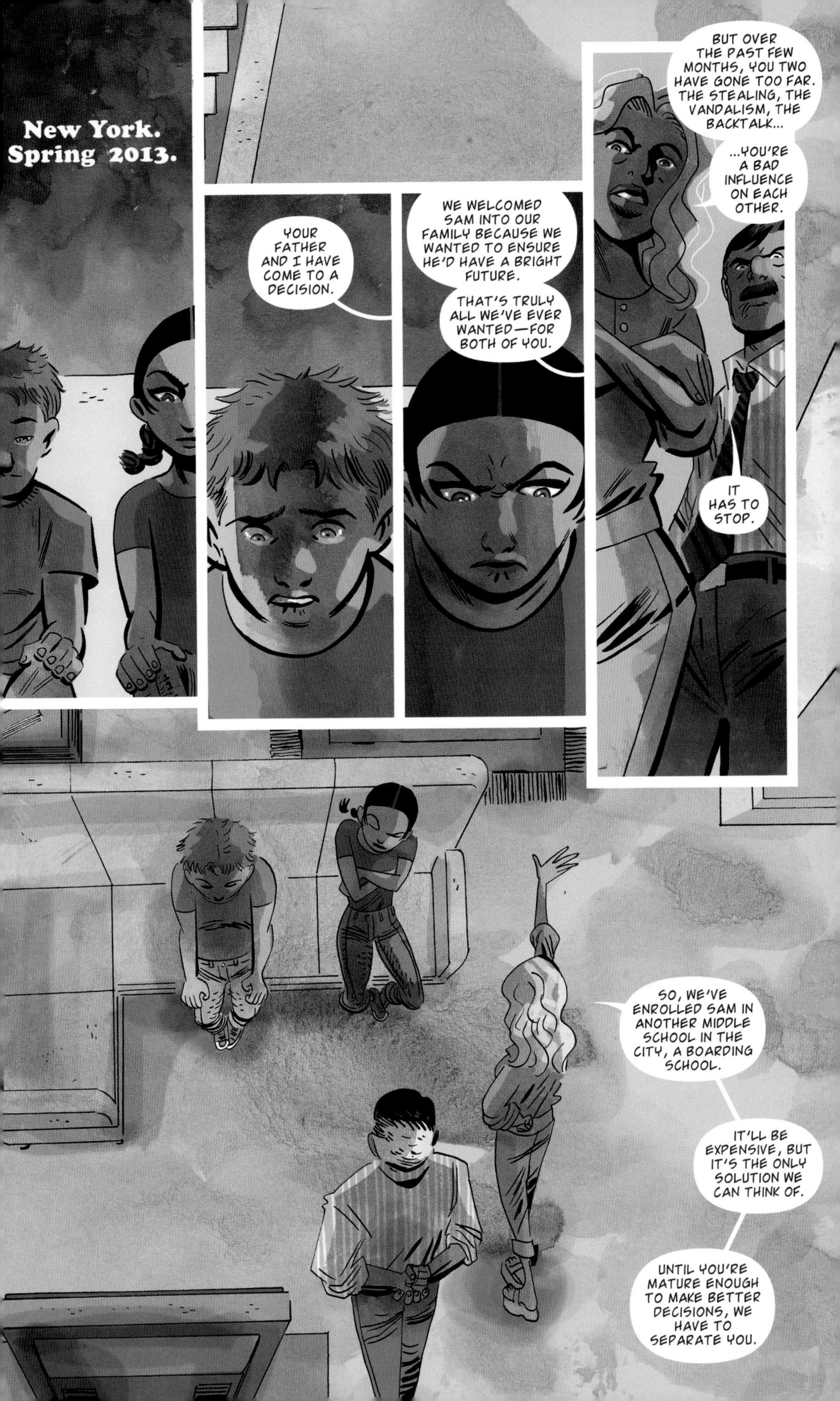
New York.
Spring 2013.
YOUR FATHER AND I HAVE COME TO A DECISION.
WE WELCOMED SAM INTO OUR FAMILY BECAUSE WE WANTED TO ENSURE HE'D HAVE A BRIGHT FUTURE.
THAT'S TRULY ALL WE'VE EVER WANTED—FOR BOTH OF YOU.
BUT OVER THE PAST FEW MONTHS, YOU TWO HAVE GONE TOO FAR. THE STEALING, THE VANDALISM, THE BACKTALK...
...YOU'RE A BAD INFLUENCE ON EACH OTHER.
IT HAS TO STOP.
SO, WE'VE ENROLLED SAM IN ANOTHER MIDDLE SCHOOL IN THE CITY, A BOARDING SCHOOL.
IT'LL BE EXPENSIVE, BUT IT'S THE ONLY SOLUTION WE CAN THINK OF.
UNTIL YOU'RE MATURE ENOUGH TO MAKE BETTER DECISIONS, WE HAVE TO SEPARATE YOU.

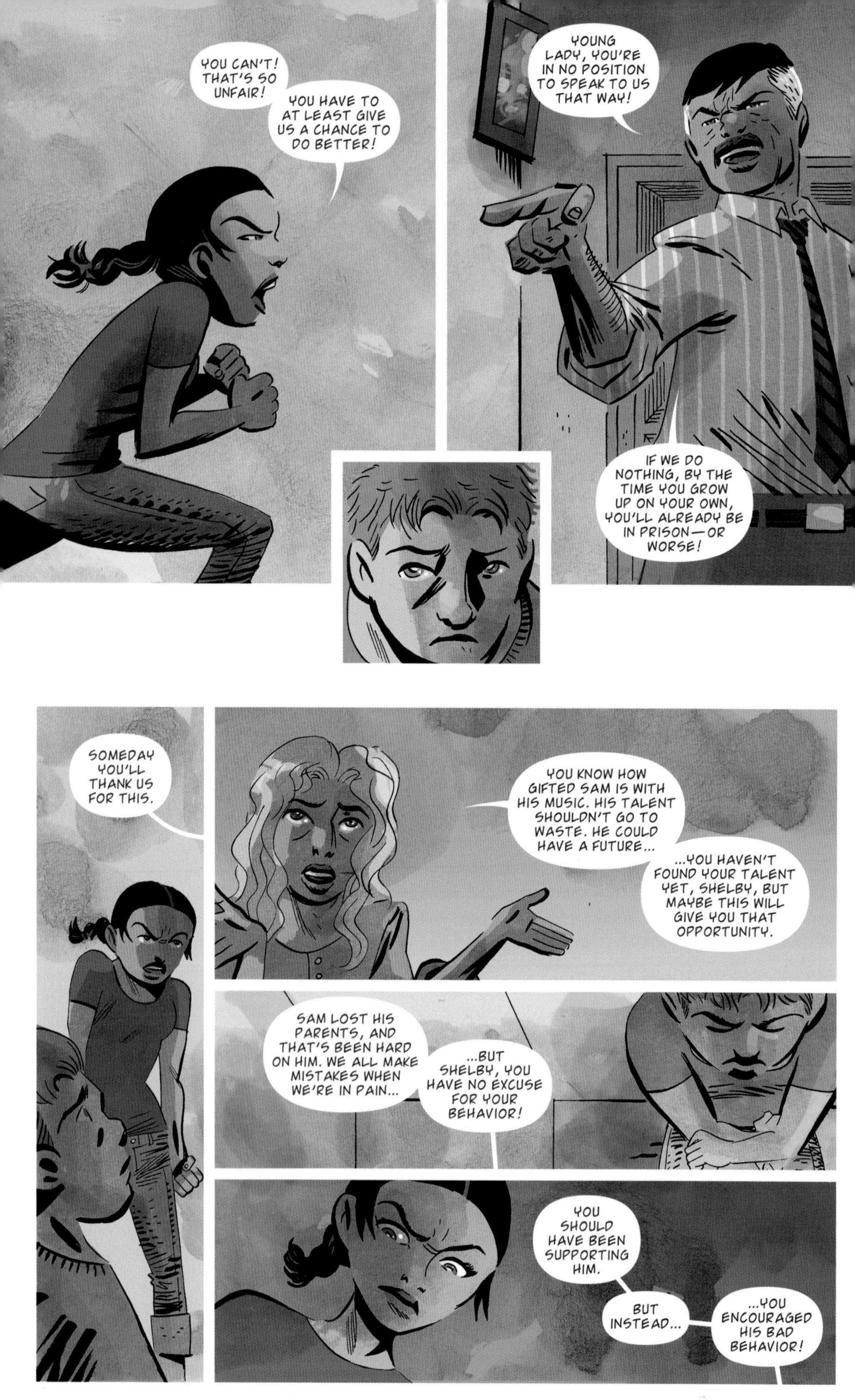

YOU CAN'T! THAT'S SO UNFAIR!
YOU HAVE TO AT LEAST GIVE US A CHANCE TO DO BETTER!
YOUNG LADY, YOU'RE IN NO POSITION TO SPEAK TO US THAT WAY!
IF WE DO NOTHING, BY THE TIME YOU GROW UP ON YOUR OWN, YOU'LL ALREADY BE IN PRISON—OR WORSE!
SOMEDAY YOU'LL THANK US FOR THIS.
YOU KNOW HOW GIFTED SAM IS WITH HIS MUSIC. HIS TALENT SHOULDN'T GO TO WASTE. HE COULD HAVE A FUTURE...
...YOU HAVEN'T FOUND YOUR TALENT YET, SHELBY, BUT MAYBE THIS WILL GIVE YOU THAT OPPORTUNITY.
SAM LOST HIS PARENTS, AND THAT'S BEEN HARD ON HIM. WE ALL MAKE MISTAKES WHEN WE'RE IN PAIN...
...BUT SHELBY, YOU HAVE NO EXCUSE FOR YOUR BEHAVIOR!
YOU SHOULD HAVE BEEN SUPPORTING HIM.
BUT INSTEAD...
...YOU ENCOURAGED HIS BAD BEHAVIOR!

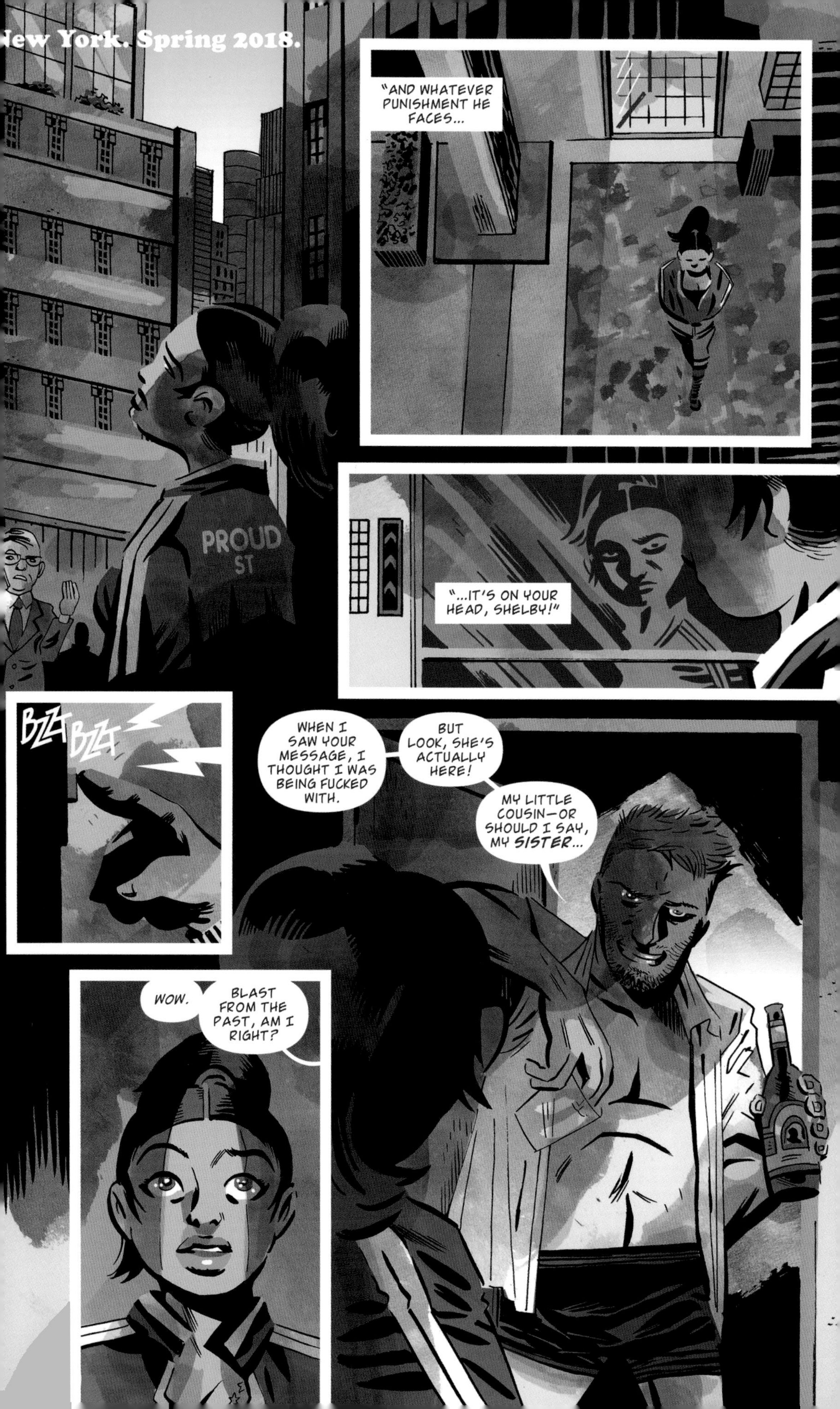
New York. Spring 2018.
PROUD
ST
"AND WHATEVER PUNISHMENT HE FACES...
"...IT'S ON YOUR HEAD, SHELBY!"
BZZT BZZT
WHEN I SAW YOUR MESSAGE, I THOUGHT I WAS BEING FUCKED WITH.
BUT LOOK, SHE'S ACTUALLY HERE!
MY LITTLE COUSIN—OR SHOULD I SAY, MY SISTER...
WOW.
BLAST FROM THE PAST, AM I RIGHT?

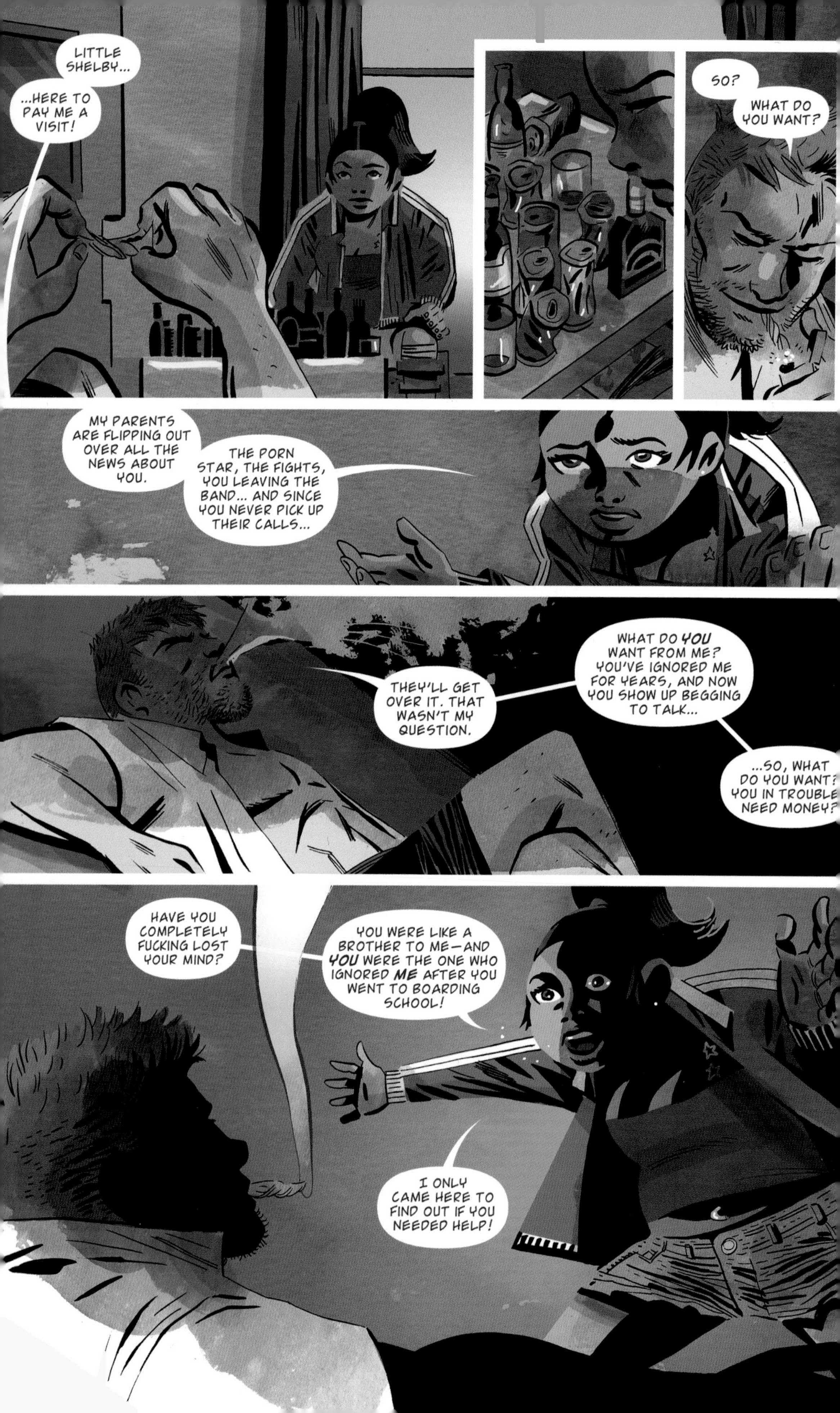

LITTLE SHELBY...
...HERE TO PAY ME A VISIT!
SO?
WHAT DO YOU WANT?
MY PARENTS ARE FLIPPING OUT OVER ALL THE NEWS ABOUT YOU.
THE PORN STAR, THE FIGHTS, YOU LEAVING THE BAND... AND SINCE YOU NEVER PICK UP THEIR CALLS...
THEY'LL GET OVER IT. THAT WASN'T MY QUESTION.
WHAT DO *YOU* WANT FROM ME? YOU'VE IGNORED ME FOR YEARS, AND NOW YOU SHOW UP BEGGING TO TALK...
...SO, WHAT DO YOU WANT? YOU IN TROUBLE NEED MONEY?
HAVE YOU COMPLETELY FUCKING LOST YOUR MIND?
YOU WERE LIKE A BROTHER TO ME—AND ***YOU*** WERE THE ONE WHO IGNORED ***ME*** AFTER YOU WENT TO BOARDING SCHOOL!
I ONLY CAME HERE TO FIND OUT IF YOU NEEDED HELP!

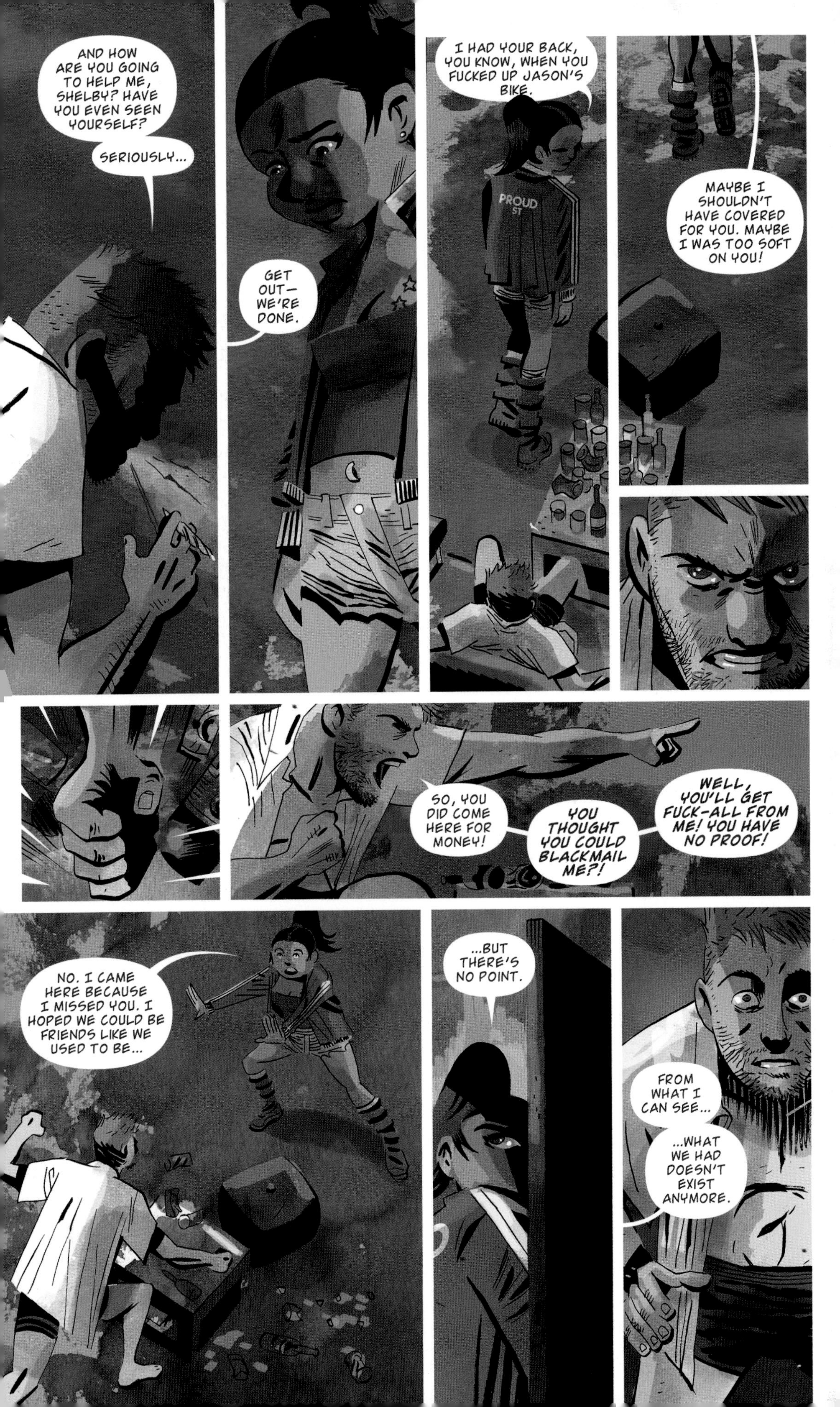
AND HOW ARE YOU GOING TO HELP ME, SHELBY? HAVE YOU EVEN SEEN YOURSELF?
SERIOUSLY...
GET OUT— WE'RE DONE.
I HAD YOUR BACK, YOU KNOW, WHEN YOU FUCKED UP JASON'S BIKE.
PROUD ST
MAYBE I SHOULDN'T HAVE COVERED FOR YOU. MAYBE I WAS TOO SOFT ON YOU!
SO, YOU DID COME HERE FOR MONEY!
YOU THOUGHT YOU COULD BLACKMAIL ME?!
WELL, YOU'LL GET FUCK-ALL FROM ME! YOU HAVE NO PROOF!
NO. I CAME HERE BECAUSE I MISSED YOU. I HOPED WE COULD BE FRIENDS LIKE WE USED TO BE...
...BUT THERE'S NO POINT.
FROM WHAT I CAN SEE...
...WHAT WE HAD DOESN'T EXIST ANYMORE.

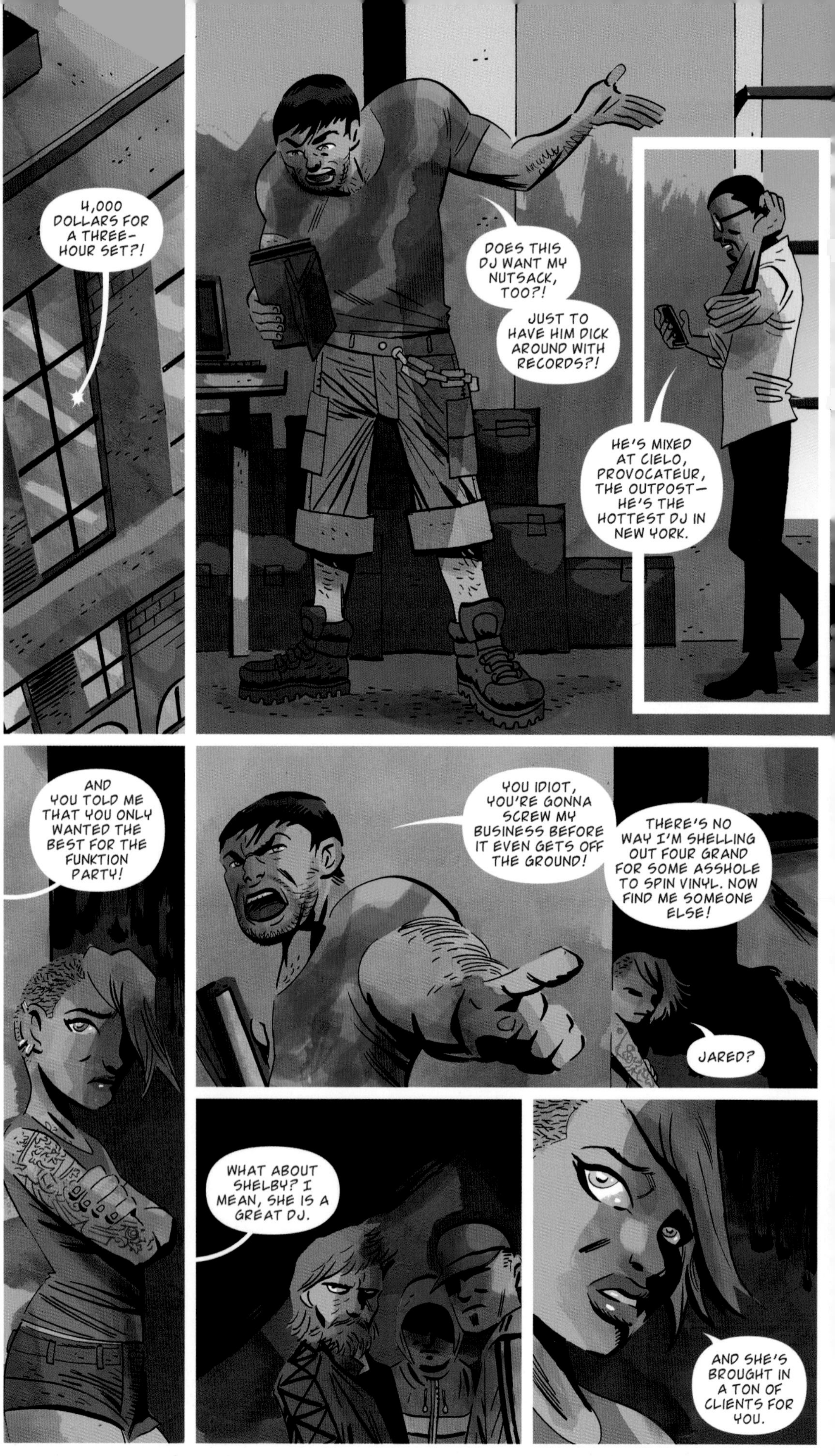
4,000 DOLLARS FOR A THREE-HOUR SET?!
DOES THIS DJ WANT MY NUTSACK, TOO?!
JUST TO HAVE HIM DICK AROUND WITH RECORDS?!
HE'S MIXED AT CIELO, PROVOCATEUR, THE OUTPOST—HE'S THE HOTTEST DJ IN NEW YORK.
AND YOU TOLD ME THAT YOU ONLY WANTED THE BEST FOR THE FUNKTION PARTY!
YOU IDIOT, YOU'RE GONNA SCREW MY BUSINESS BEFORE IT EVEN GETS OFF THE GROUND!
THERE'S NO WAY I'M SHELLING OUT FOUR GRAND FOR SOME ASSHOLE TO SPIN VINYL. NOW FIND ME SOMEONE ELSE!
JARED?
WHAT ABOUT SHELBY? I MEAN, SHE IS A GREAT DJ.
AND SHE'S BROUGHT IN A TON OF CLIENTS FOR YOU.

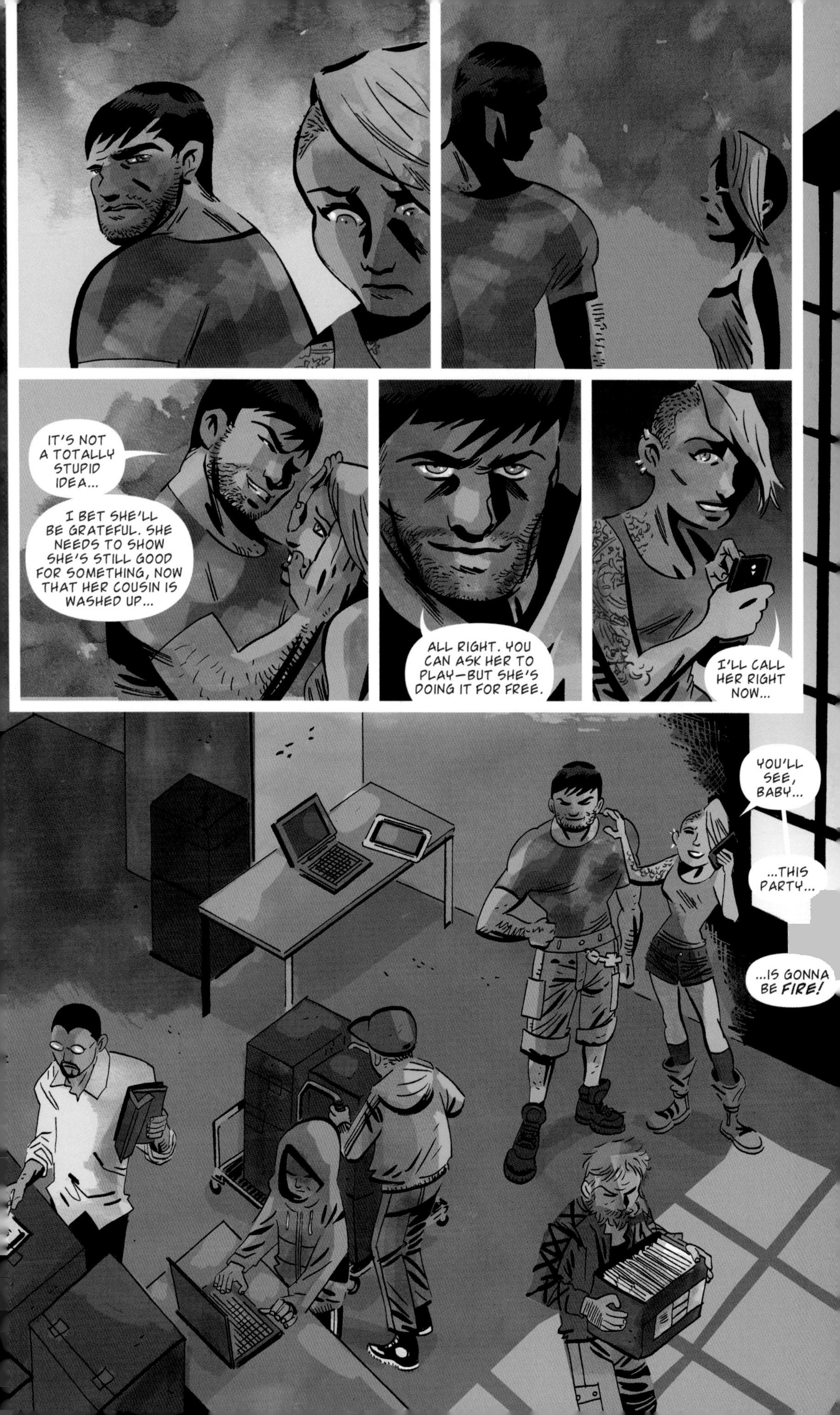
IT'S NOT A TOTALLY STUPID IDEA...
I BET SHE'LL BE GRATEFUL. SHE NEEDS TO SHOW SHE'S STILL GOOD FOR SOMETHING, NOW THAT HER COUSIN IS WASHED UP...
ALL RIGHT. YOU CAN ASK HER TO PLAY—BUT SHE'S DOING IT FOR FREE.
I'LL CALL HER RIGHT NOW...
YOU'LL SEE, BABY...
...THIS PARTY...
...IS GONNA BE ***FIRE!***

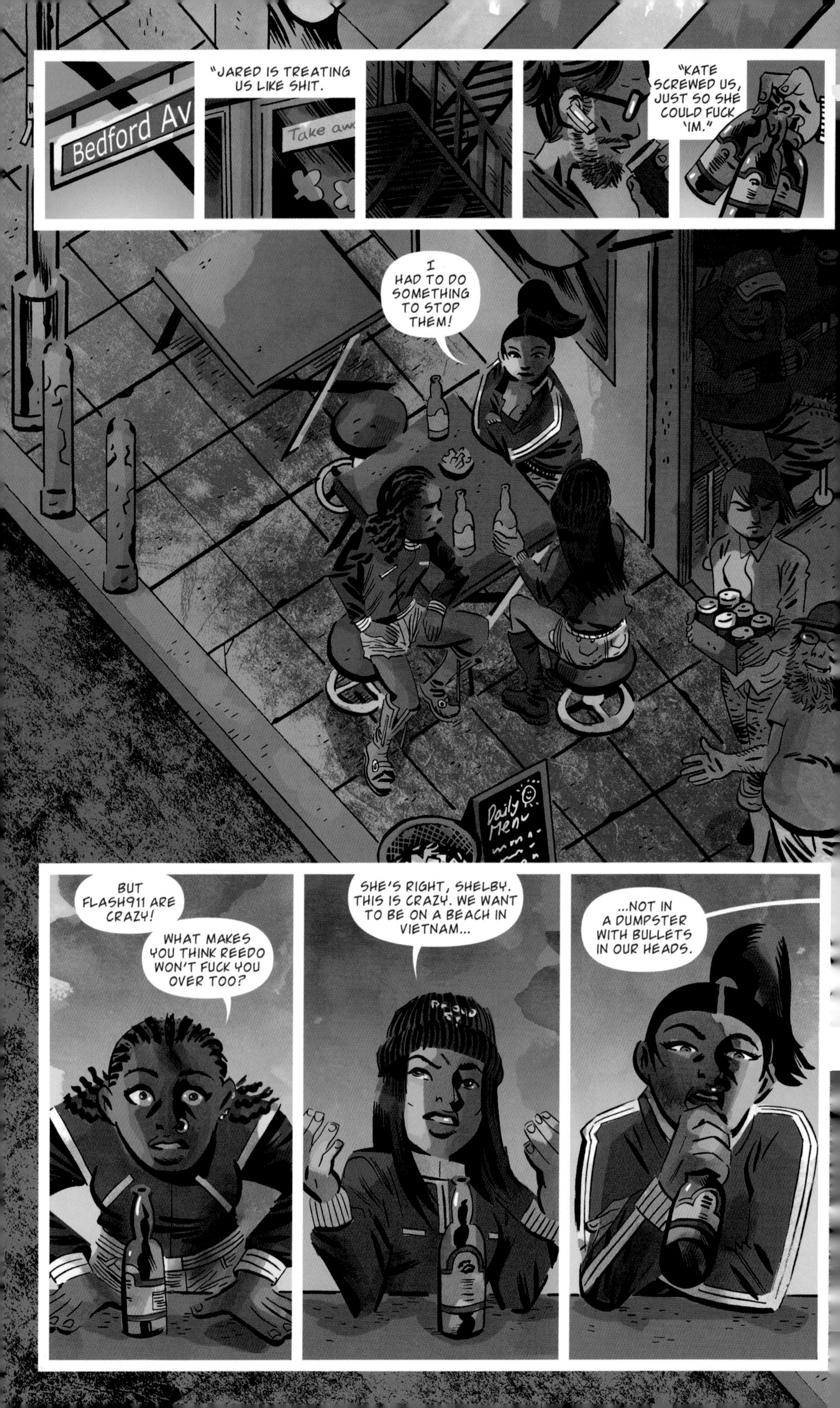

Bedford Av
"JARED IS TREATING US LIKE SHIT.
Take aw
"KATE SCREWED US, JUST SO SHE COULD FUCK 'IM."
I HAD TO DO SOMETHING TO STOP THEM!
Daily Menu
BUT FLASH911 ARE CRAZY!
WHAT MAKES YOU THINK REEDO WON'T FUCK YOU OVER TOO?
SHE'S RIGHT, SHELBY. THIS IS CRAZY. WE WANT TO BE ON A BEACH IN VIETNAM...
...NOT IN A DUMPSTER WITH BULLETS IN OUR HEADS.

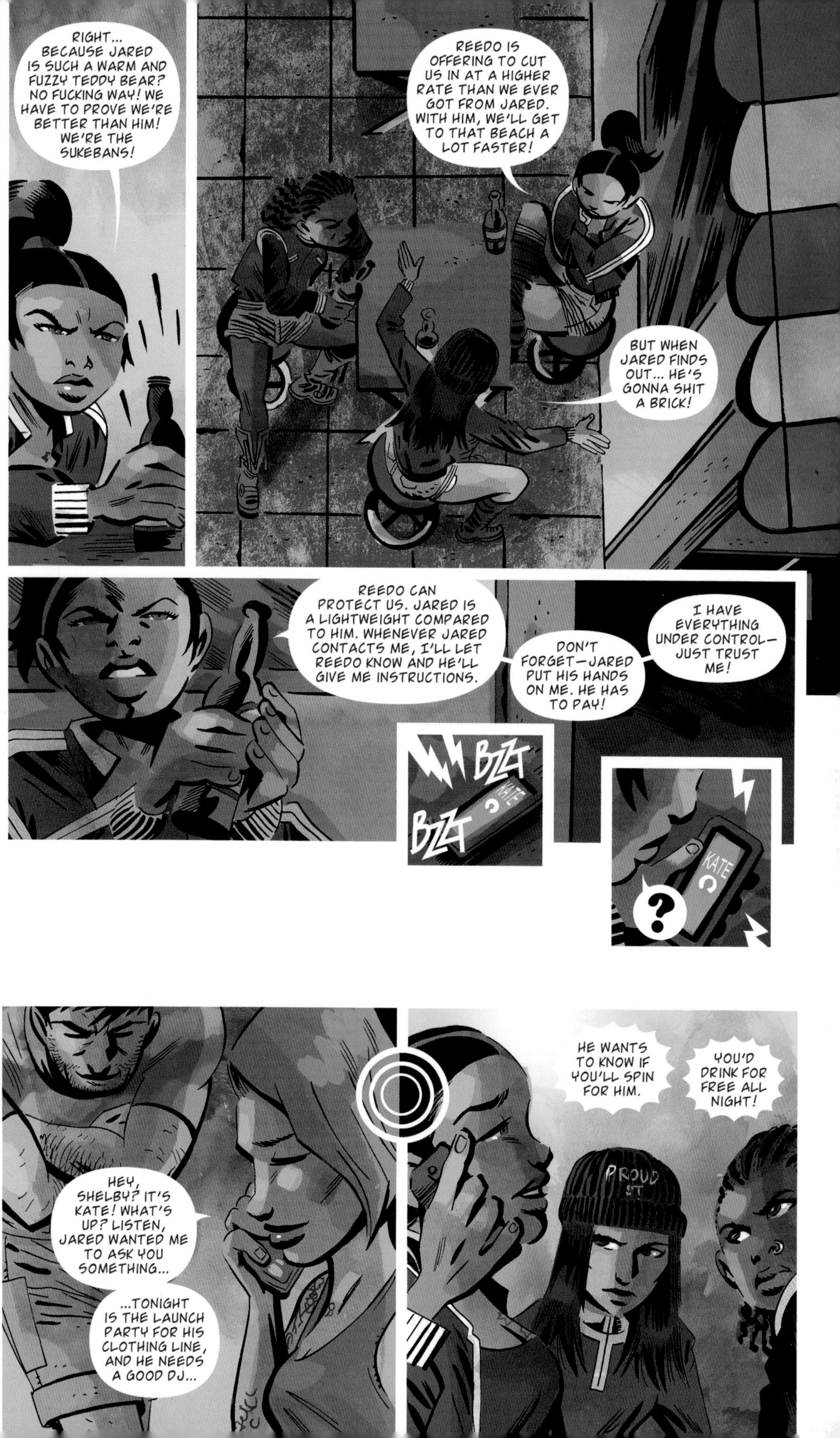

RIGHT... BECAUSE JARED IS SUCH A WARM AND FUZZY TEDDY BEAR? NO FUCKING WAY! WE HAVE TO PROVE WE'RE BETTER THAN HIM! WE'RE THE SUKEBANS!
REEDO IS OFFERING TO CUT US IN AT A HIGHER RATE THAN WE EVER GOT FROM JARED. WITH HIM, WE'LL GET TO THAT BEACH A LOT FASTER!
BUT WHEN JARED FINDS OUT... HE'S GONNA SHIT A BRICK!
REEDO CAN PROTECT US. JARED IS A LIGHTWEIGHT COMPARED TO HIM. WHENEVER JARED CONTACTS ME, I'LL LET REEDO KNOW AND HE'LL GIVE ME INSTRUCTIONS.
DON'T FORGET—JARED PUT HIS HANDS ON ME. HE HAS TO PAY!
I HAVE EVERYTHING UNDER CONTROL—JUST TRUST ME!
BZZT
BZZT
KATE
KATE
?
HEY, SHELBY? IT'S KATE! WHAT'S UP? LISTEN, JARED WANTED ME TO ASK YOU SOMETHING...
...TONIGHT IS THE LAUNCH PARTY FOR HIS CLOTHING LINE, AND HE NEEDS A GOOD DJ...
HE WANTS TO KNOW IF YOU'LL SPIN FOR HIM.
YOU'D DRINK FOR FREE ALL NIGHT!
PROUD

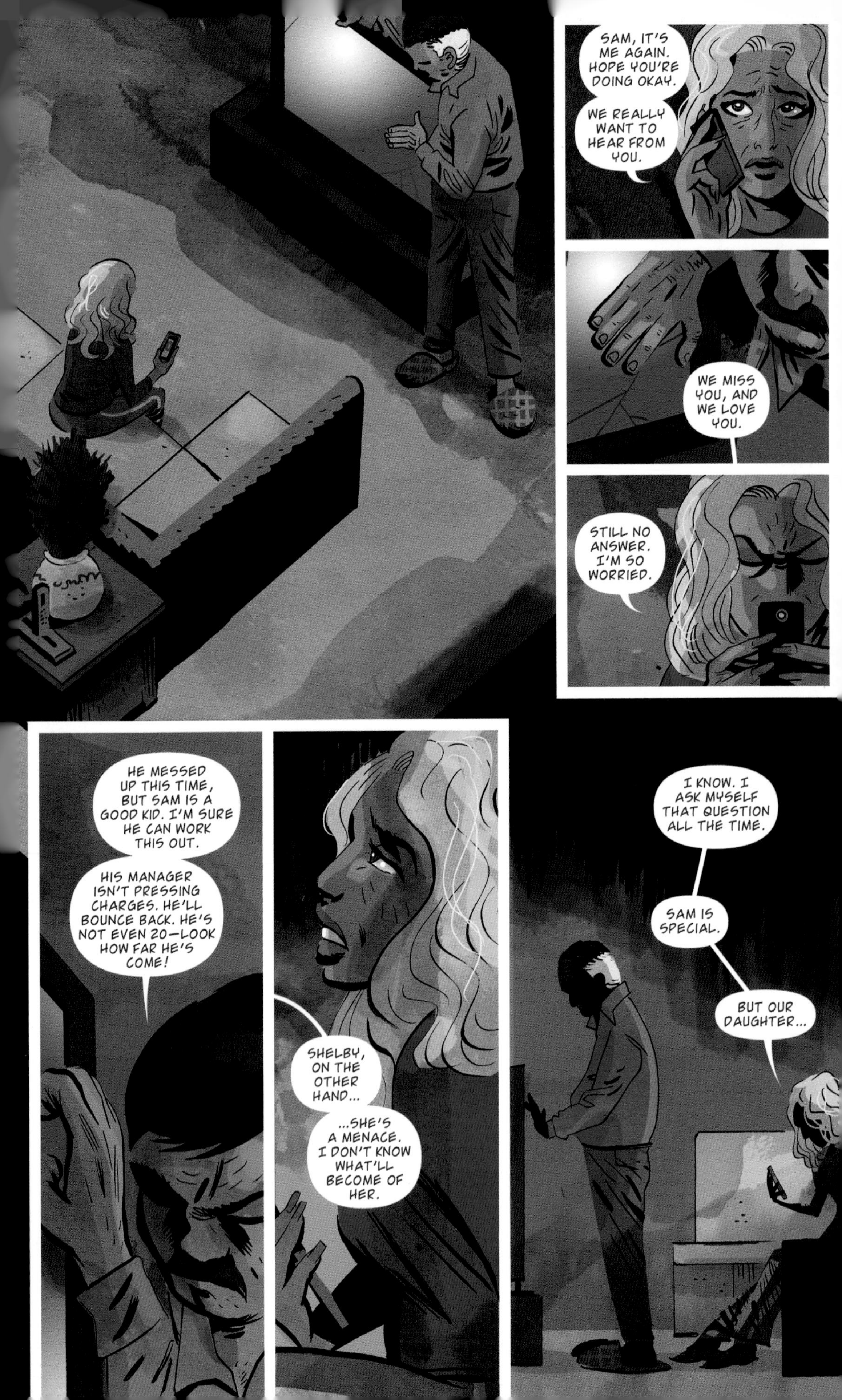
SAM, IT'S ME AGAIN. HOPE YOU'RE DOING OKAY.
WE REALLY WANT TO HEAR FROM YOU.
WE MISS YOU, AND WE LOVE YOU.
STILL NO ANSWER. I'M SO WORRIED.
HE MESSED UP THIS TIME, BUT SAM IS A GOOD KID. I'M SURE HE CAN WORK THIS OUT.
HIS MANAGER ISN'T PRESSING CHARGES. HE'LL BOUNCE BACK. HE'S NOT EVEN 20—LOOK HOW FAR HE'S COME!
SHELBY, ON THE OTHER HAND...
...SHE'S A MENACE. I DON'T KNOW WHAT'LL BECOME OF HER.
I KNOW. I ASK MYSELF THAT QUESTION ALL THE TIME.
SAM IS SPECIAL.
BUT OUR DAUGHTER...

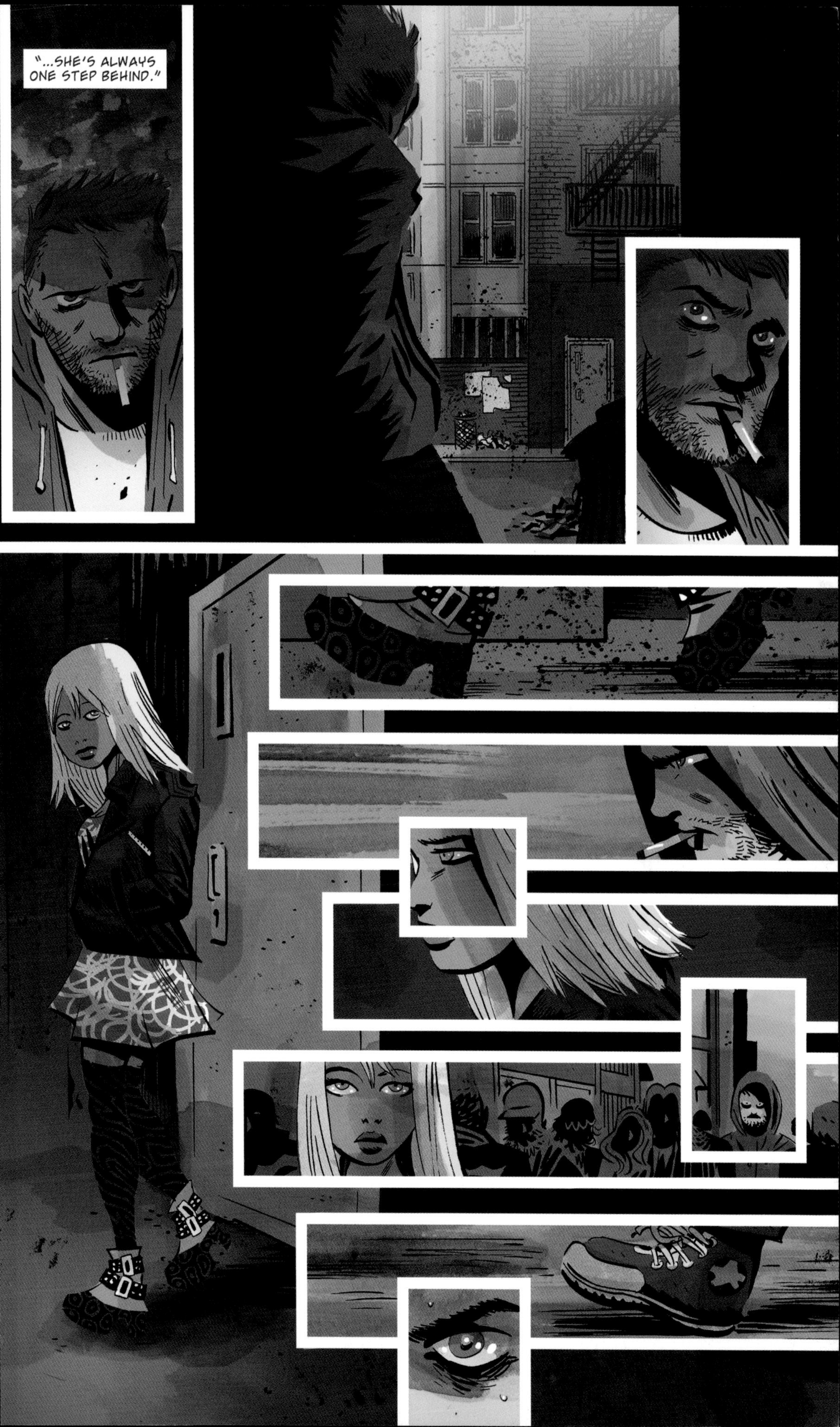
"...SHE'S ALWAYS ONE STEP BEHIND."

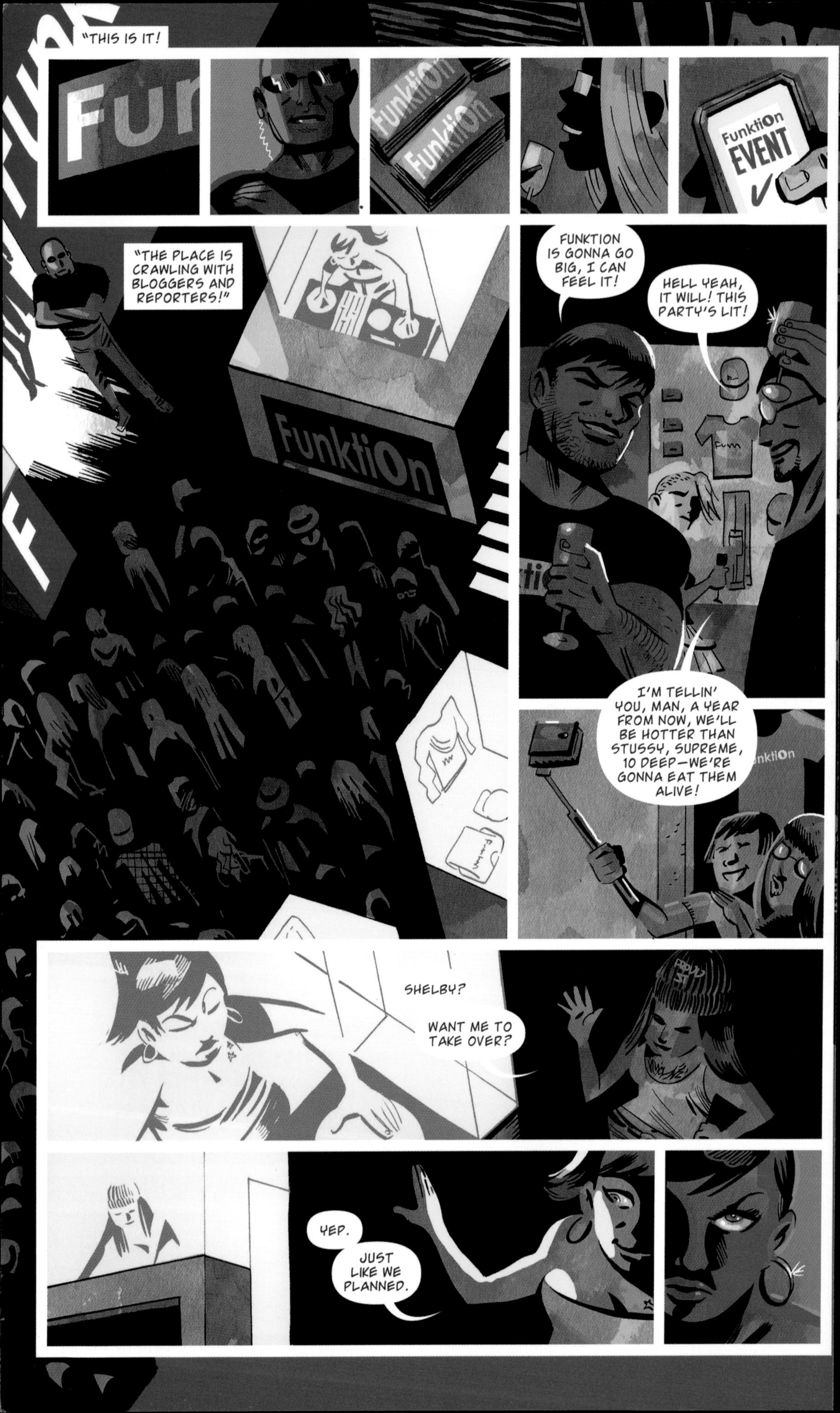
"THIS IS IT!
FunktiOn
FunktiOn EVENT
"THE PLACE IS CRAWLING WITH BLOGGERS AND REPORTERS!"
FunktiOn
FUNKTION IS GONNA GO BIG, I CAN FEEL IT!
HELL YEAH, IT WILL! THIS PARTY'S LIT!
I'M TELLIN' YOU, MAN, A YEAR FROM NOW, WE'LL BE HOTTER THAN STUSSY, SUPREME, 10 DEEP—WE'RE GONNA EAT THEM ALIVE!
SHELBY?
WANT ME TO TAKE OVER?
YEP.
JUST LIKE WE PLANNED.

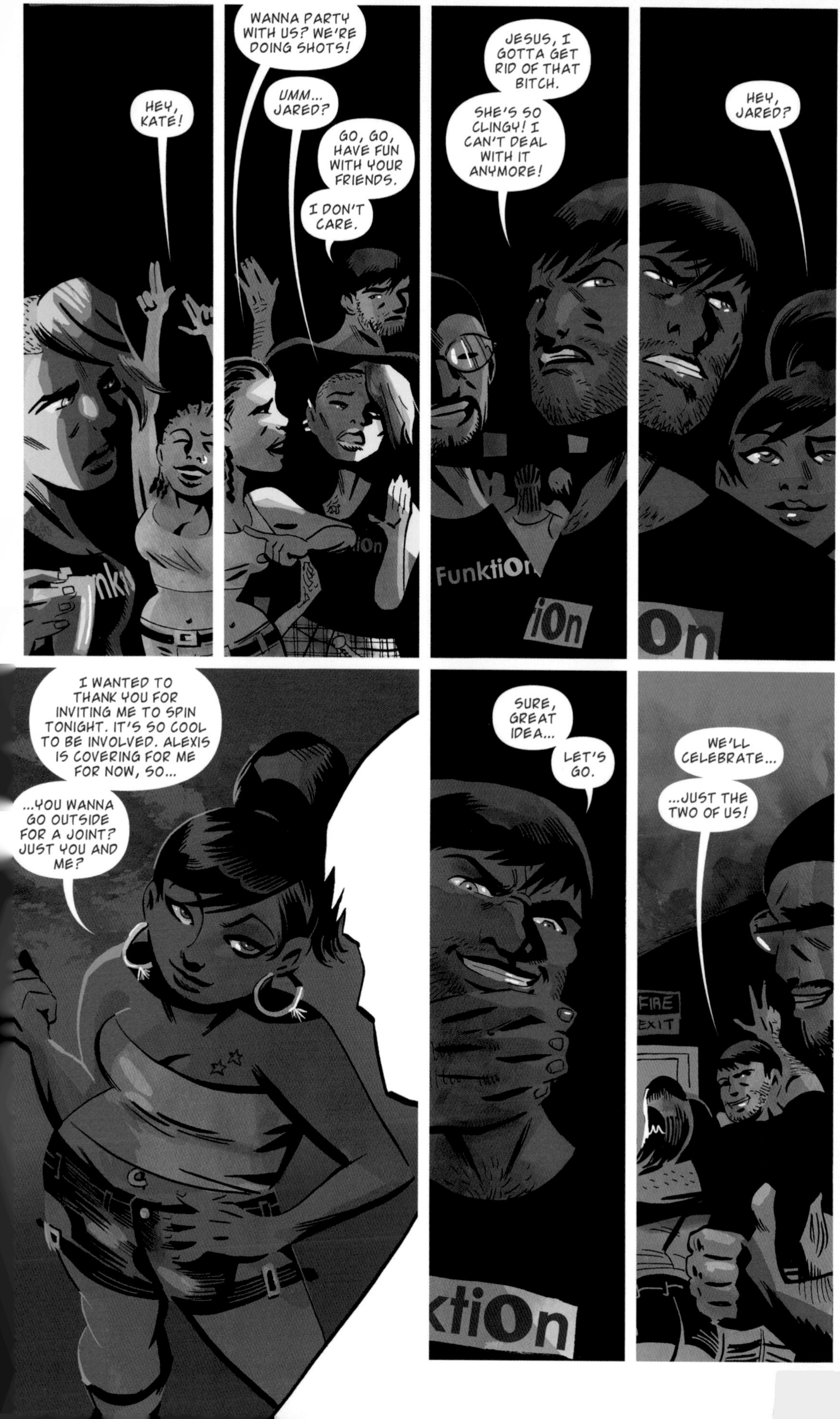
HEY, KATE!
WANNA PARTY WITH US? WE'RE DOING SHOTS!
UMM... JARED?
GO, GO, HAVE FUN WITH YOUR FRIENDS.
I DON'T CARE.
JESUS, I GOTTA GET RID OF THAT BITCH.
SHE'S SO CLINGY! I CAN'T DEAL WITH IT ANYMORE!
HEY, JARED?
I WANTED TO THANK YOU FOR INVITING ME TO SPIN TONIGHT. IT'S SO COOL TO BE INVOLVED. ALEXIS IS COVERING FOR ME FOR NOW, SO...
...YOU WANNA GO OUTSIDE FOR A JOINT? JUST YOU AND ME?
SURE, GREAT IDEA...
LET'S GO.
WE'LL CELEBRATE...
...JUST THE TWO OF US!
FIRE EXIT

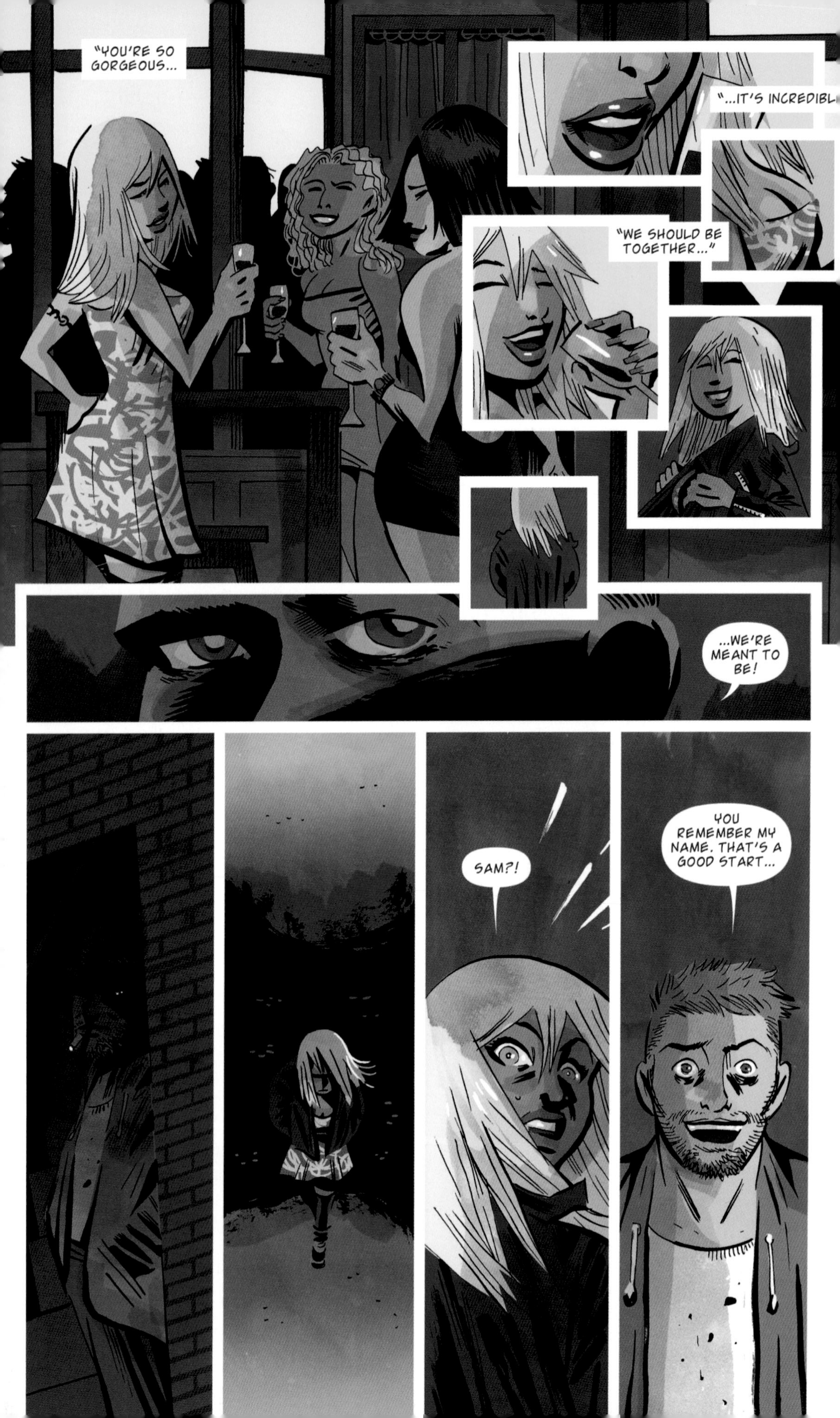
"YOU'RE SO GORGEOUS...
"...IT'S INCREDIBL
"WE SHOULD BE TOGETHER..."
...WE'RE MEANT TO BE!
SAM?!
YOU REMEMBER MY NAME. THAT'S A GOOD START...

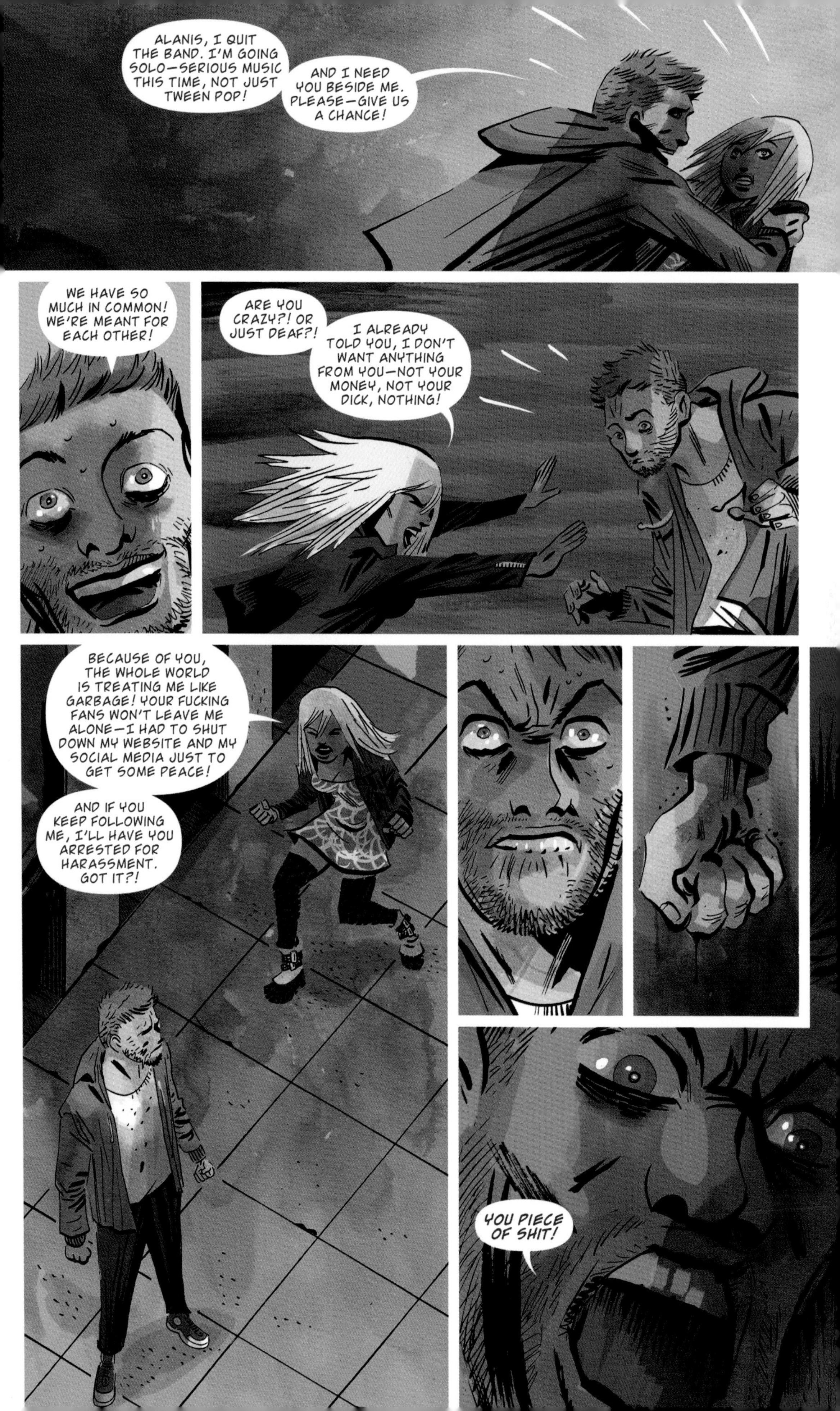
ALANIS, I QUIT THE BAND. I'M GOING SOLO—SERIOUS MUSIC THIS TIME, NOT JUST TWEEN POP!
AND I NEED YOU BESIDE ME. PLEASE—GIVE US A CHANCE!
WE HAVE SO MUCH IN COMMON! WE'RE MEANT FOR EACH OTHER!
ARE YOU CRAZY?! OR JUST DEAF?!
I ALREADY TOLD YOU, I DON'T WANT ANYTHING FROM YOU—NOT YOUR MONEY, NOT YOUR DICK, NOTHING!
BECAUSE OF YOU, THE WHOLE WORLD IS TREATING ME LIKE GARBAGE! YOUR FUCKING FANS WON'T LEAVE ME ALONE—I HAD TO SHUT DOWN MY WEBSITE AND MY SOCIAL MEDIA JUST TO GET SOME PEACE!
AND IF YOU KEEP FOLLOWING ME, I'LL HAVE YOU ARRESTED FOR HARASSMENT. GOT IT?!
YOU PIECE OF SHIT!

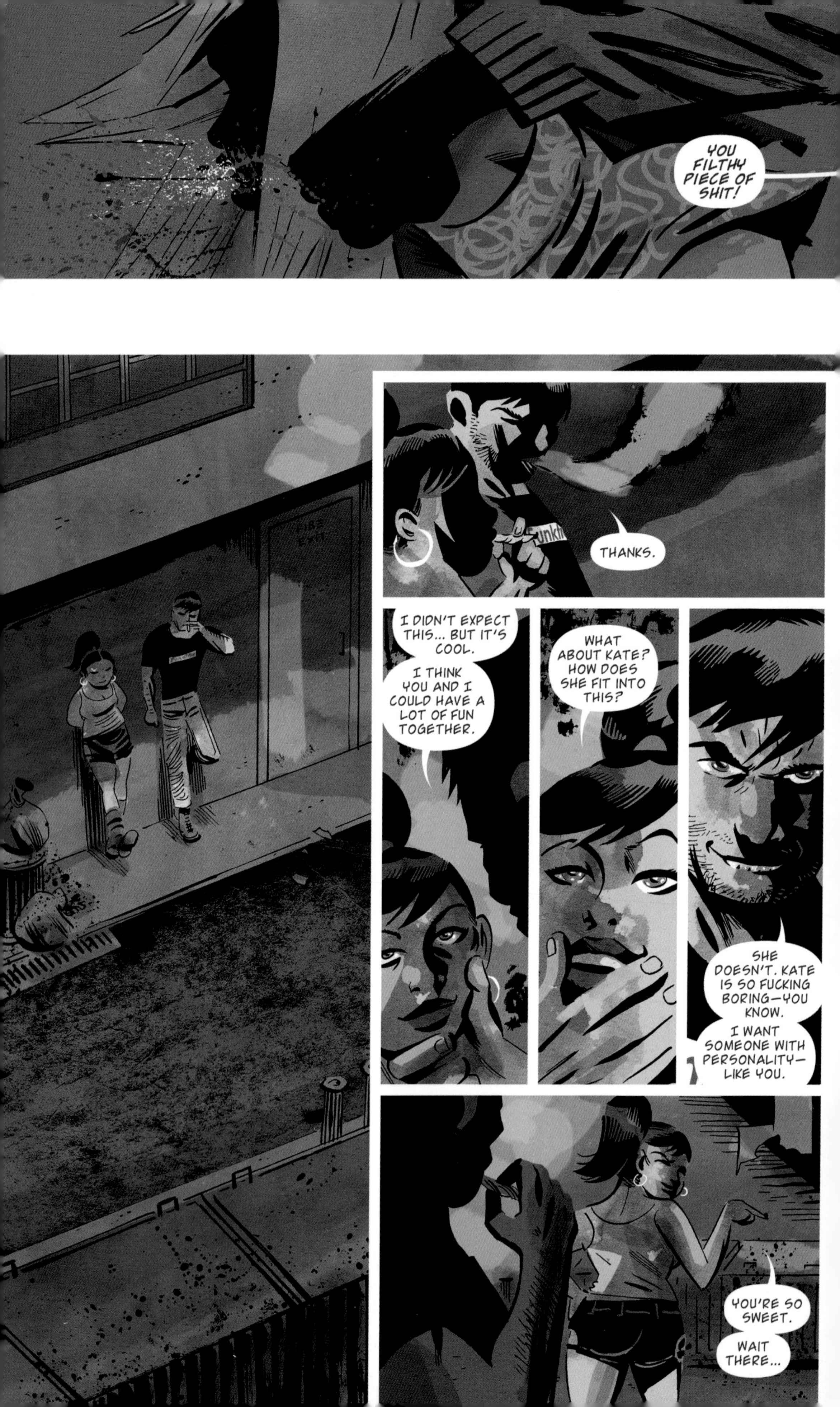
YOU FILTHY PIECE OF SHIT!
FIRE EXIT
THANKS.
I DIDN'T EXPECT THIS... BUT IT'S COOL.
I THINK YOU AND I COULD HAVE A LOT OF FUN TOGETHER.
WHAT ABOUT KATE? HOW DOES SHE FIT INTO THIS?
SHE DOESN'T. KATE IS SO FUCKING BORING—YOU KNOW.
I WANT SOMEONE WITH PERSONALITY—LIKE YOU.
YOU'RE SO SWEET.
WAIT THERE...

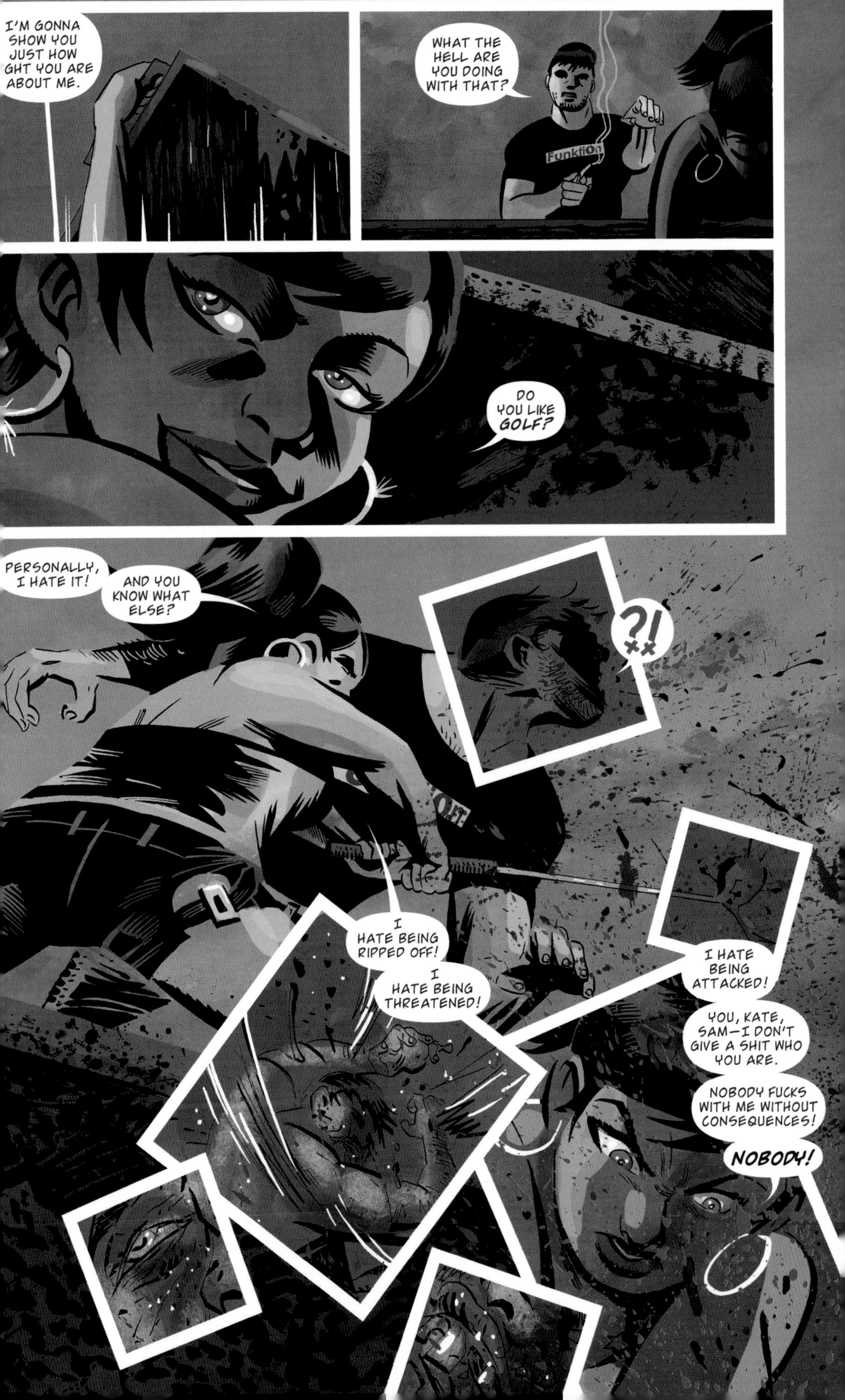
I'M GONNA SHOW YOU JUST HOW GHT YOU ARE ABOUT ME.
WHAT THE HELL ARE YOU DOING WITH THAT?
FunktiOn
DO YOU LIKE GOLF?
PERSONALLY, I HATE IT!
AND YOU KNOW WHAT ELSE?
?!
I HATE BEING RIPPED OFF!
I HATE BEING THREATENED!
I HATE BEING ATTACKED!
YOU, KATE, SAM—I DON'T GIVE A SHIT WHO YOU ARE.
NOBODY FUCKS WITH ME WITHOUT CONSEQUENCES!
NOBODY!

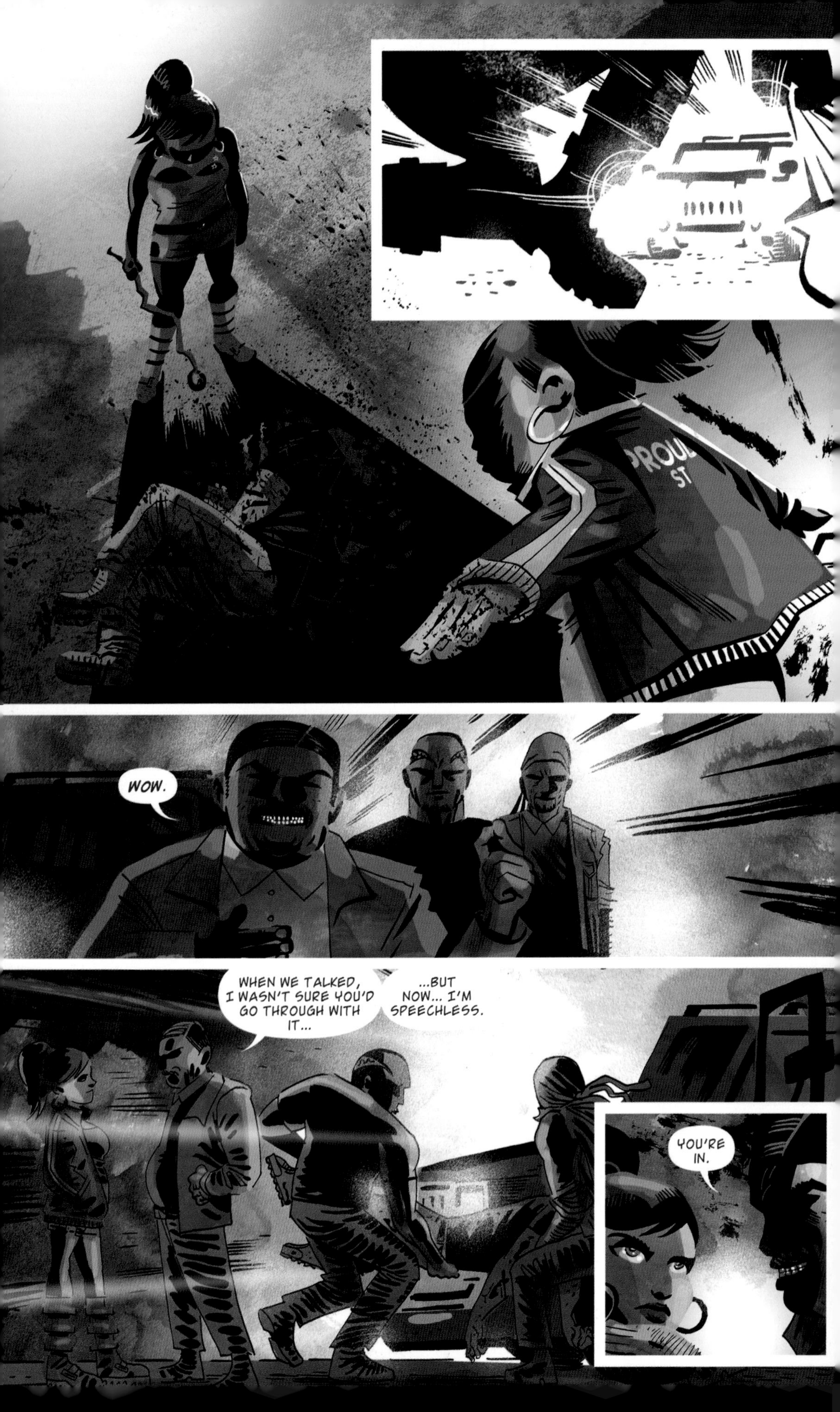
PROUD
ST
WOW.
WHEN WE TALKED, I WASN'T SURE YOU'D GO THROUGH WITH IT...
...BUT NOW... I'M SPEECHLESS.
YOU'RE IN.

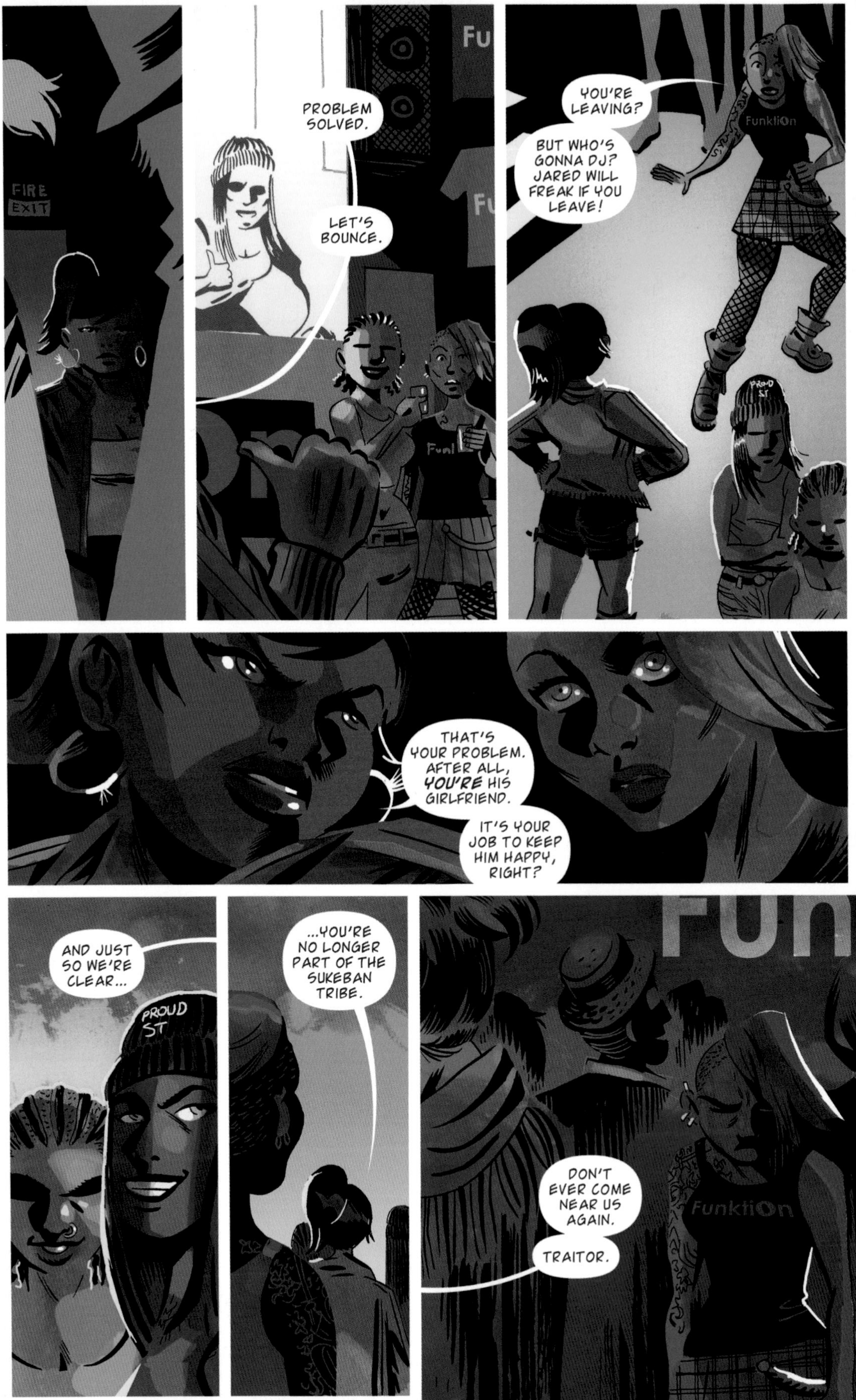
FIRE EXIT
Fu
PROBLEM SOLVED.
LET'S BOUNCE.
Fu
Funktion
YOU'RE LEAVING?
BUT WHO'S GONNA DJ? JARED WILL FREAK IF YOU LEAVE!
PROUD ST
THAT'S YOUR PROBLEM. AFTER ALL, ***YOU'RE*** HIS GIRLFRIEND.
IT'S YOUR JOB TO KEEP HIM HAPPY, RIGHT?
AND JUST SO WE'RE CLEAR...
PROUD ST
...YOU'RE NO LONGER PART OF THE SUKEBAN TRIBE.
FUN
DON'T EVER COME NEAR US AGAIN.
TRAITOR.
Funktion

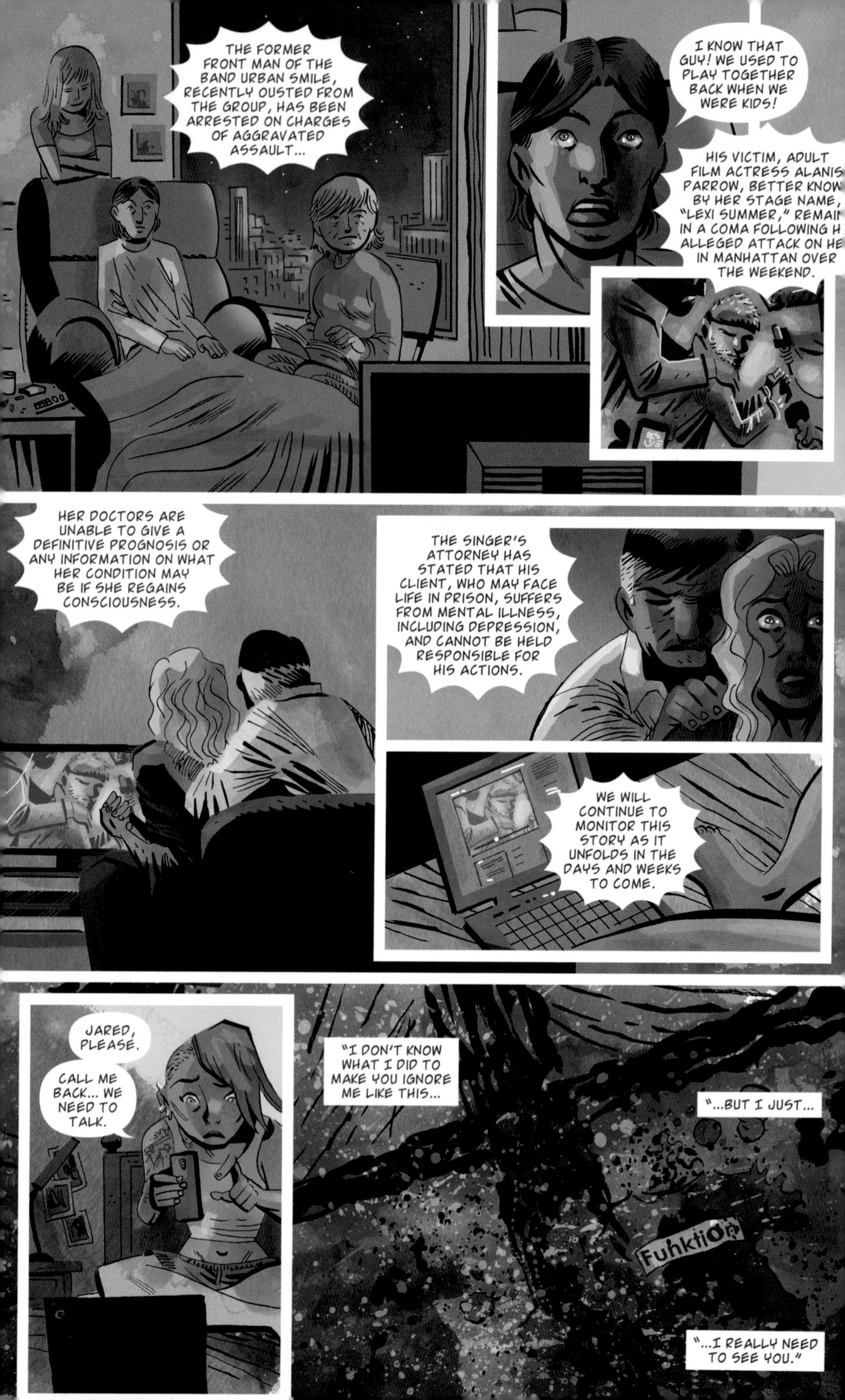
THE FORMER FRONT MAN OF THE BAND URBAN SMILE, RECENTLY OUSTED FROM THE GROUP, HAS BEEN ARRESTED ON CHARGES OF AGGRAVATED ASSAULT...
I KNOW THAT GUY! WE USED TO PLAY TOGETHER BACK WHEN WE WERE KIDS!
HIS VICTIM, ADULT FILM ACTRESS ALANIS PARROW, BETTER KNOW BY HER STAGE NAME, "LEXI SUMMER," REMAI IN A COMA FOLLOWING H ALLEGED ATTACK ON HE IN MANHATTAN OVER THE WEEKEND.
HER DOCTORS ARE UNABLE TO GIVE A DEFINITIVE PROGNOSIS OR ANY INFORMATION ON WHAT HER CONDITION MAY BE IF SHE REGAINS CONSCIOUSNESS.
THE SINGER'S ATTORNEY HAS STATED THAT HIS CLIENT, WHO MAY FACE LIFE IN PRISON, SUFFERS FROM MENTAL ILLNESS, INCLUDING DEPRESSION, AND CANNOT BE HELD RESPONSIBLE FOR HIS ACTIONS.
WE WILL CONTINUE TO MONITOR THIS STORY AS IT UNFOLDS IN THE DAYS AND WEEKS TO COME.
JARED, PLEASE.
CALL ME BACK... WE NEED TO TALK.
"I DON'T KNOW WHAT I DID TO MAKE YOU IGNORE ME LIKE THIS...
"...BUT I JUST...
FuhktiOn
"...I REALLY NEED TO SEE YOU."

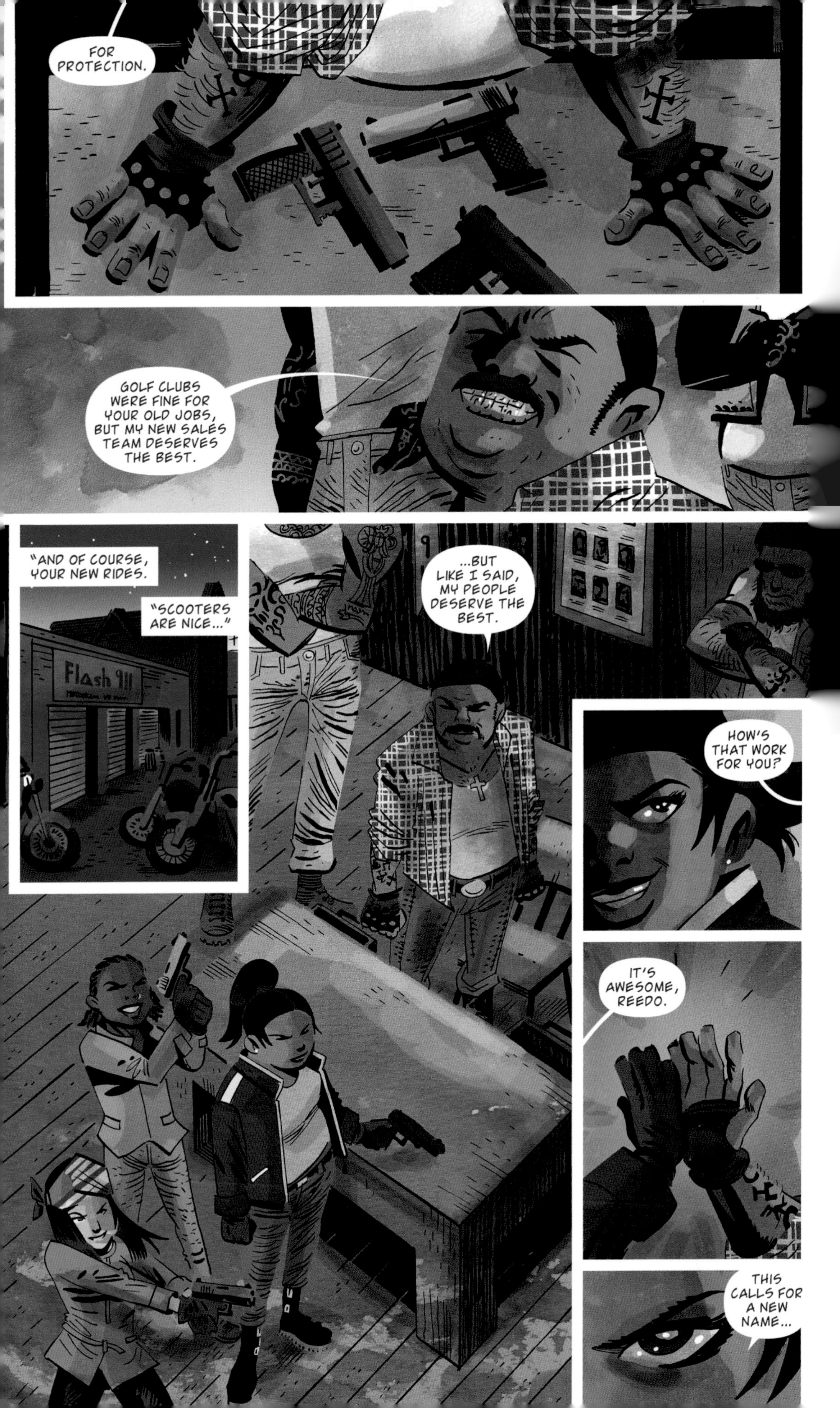
FOR PROTECTION.
GOLF CLUBS WERE FINE FOR YOUR OLD JOBS, BUT MY NEW SALES TEAM DESERVES THE BEST.
"AND OF COURSE, YOUR NEW RIDES.
"SCOOTERS ARE NICE..."
Flash 911
...BUT LIKE I SAID, MY PEOPLE DESERVE THE BEST.
HOW'S THAT WORK FOR YOU?
IT'S AWESOME, REEDO.
THIS CALLS FOR A NEW NAME...

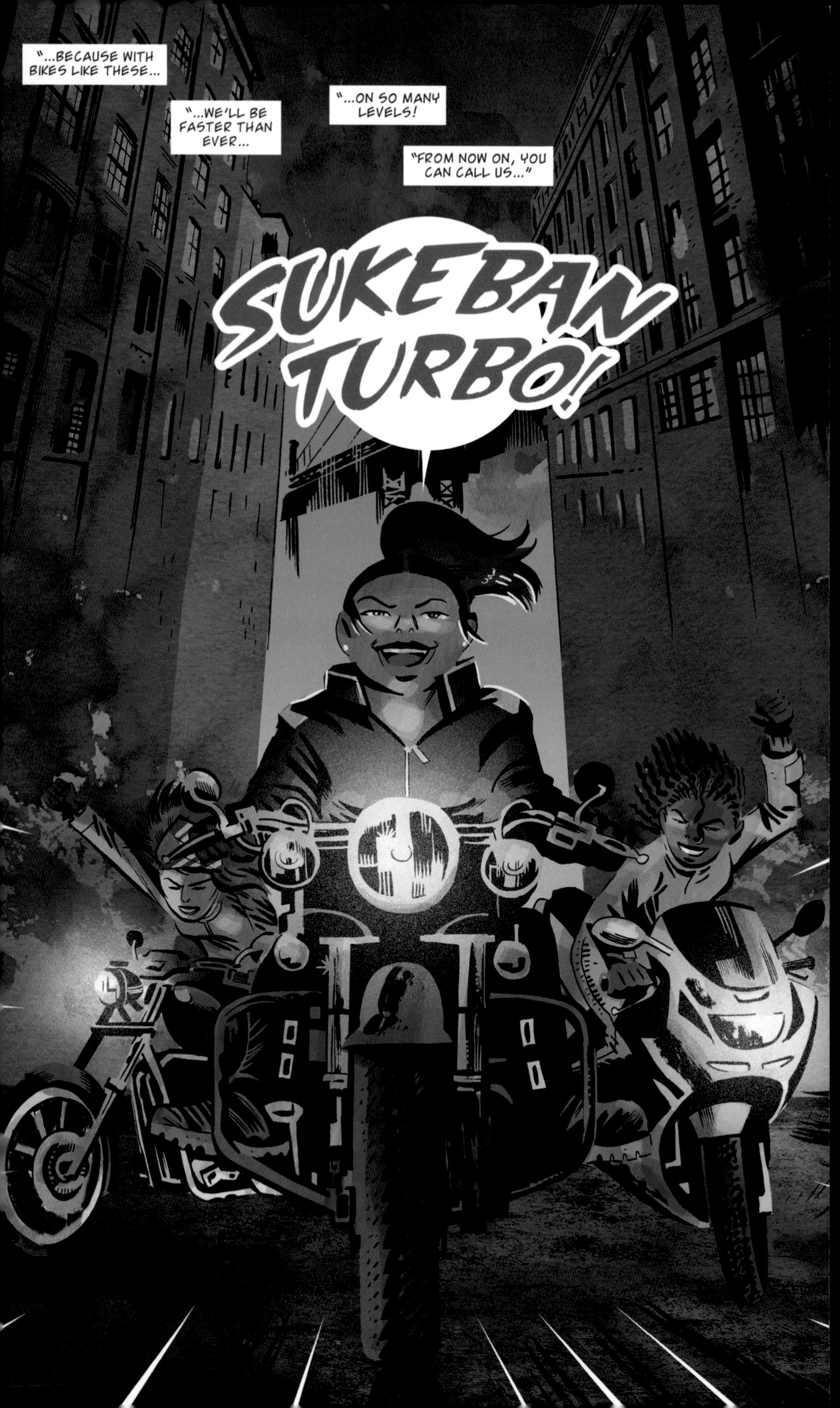
"...BECAUSE WITH BIKES LIKE THESE...
"...WE'LL BE FASTER THAN EVER...
"...ON SO MANY LEVELS!
"FROM NOW ON, YOU CAN CALL US..."
SUKEBAN TURBO!

FIN.

ART BY
CHAIRE ROE

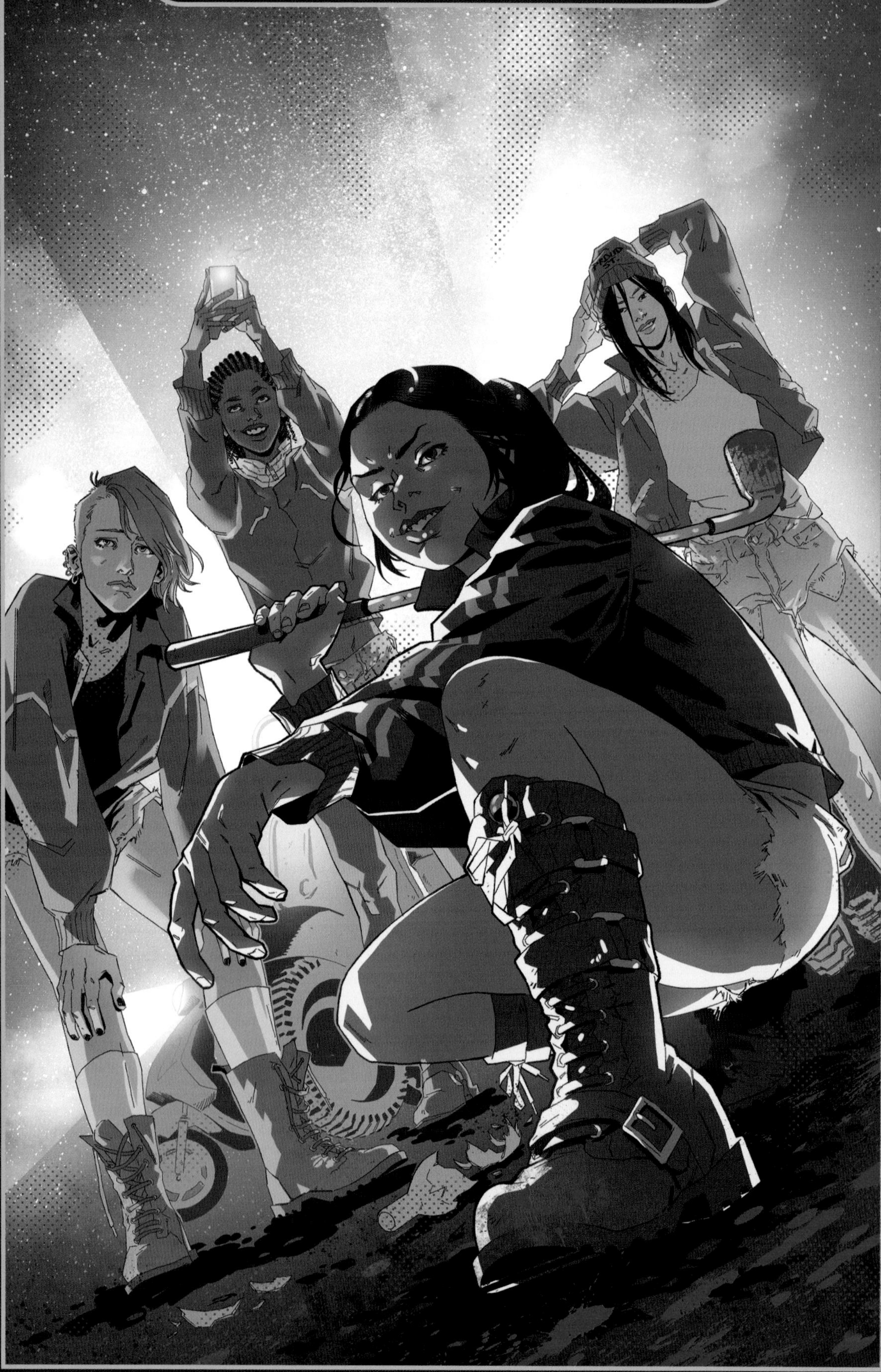

ART BY
CHAIRE ROE

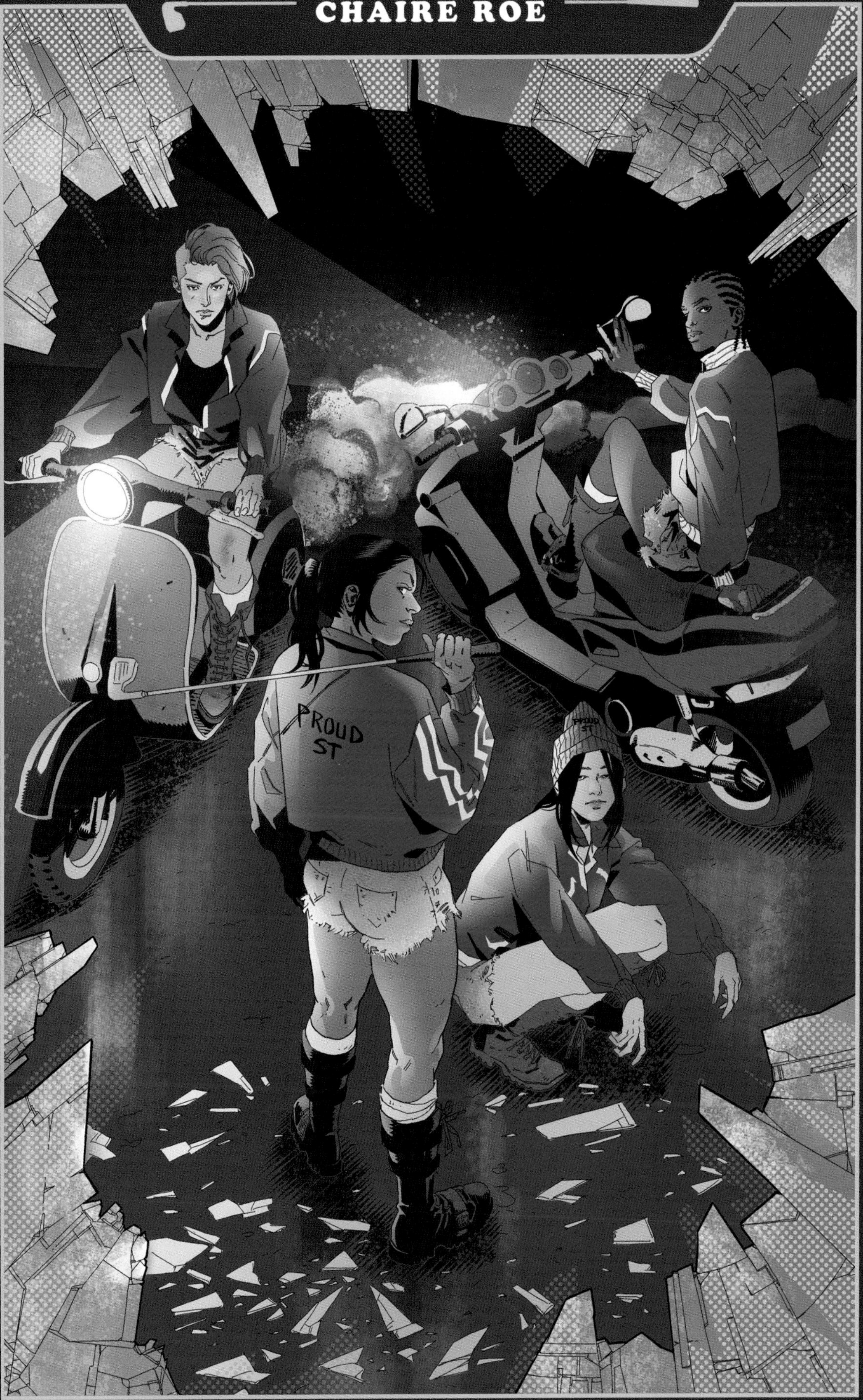
PROUD
ST
PROUD
ST

ART BY
CHAIRE ROE

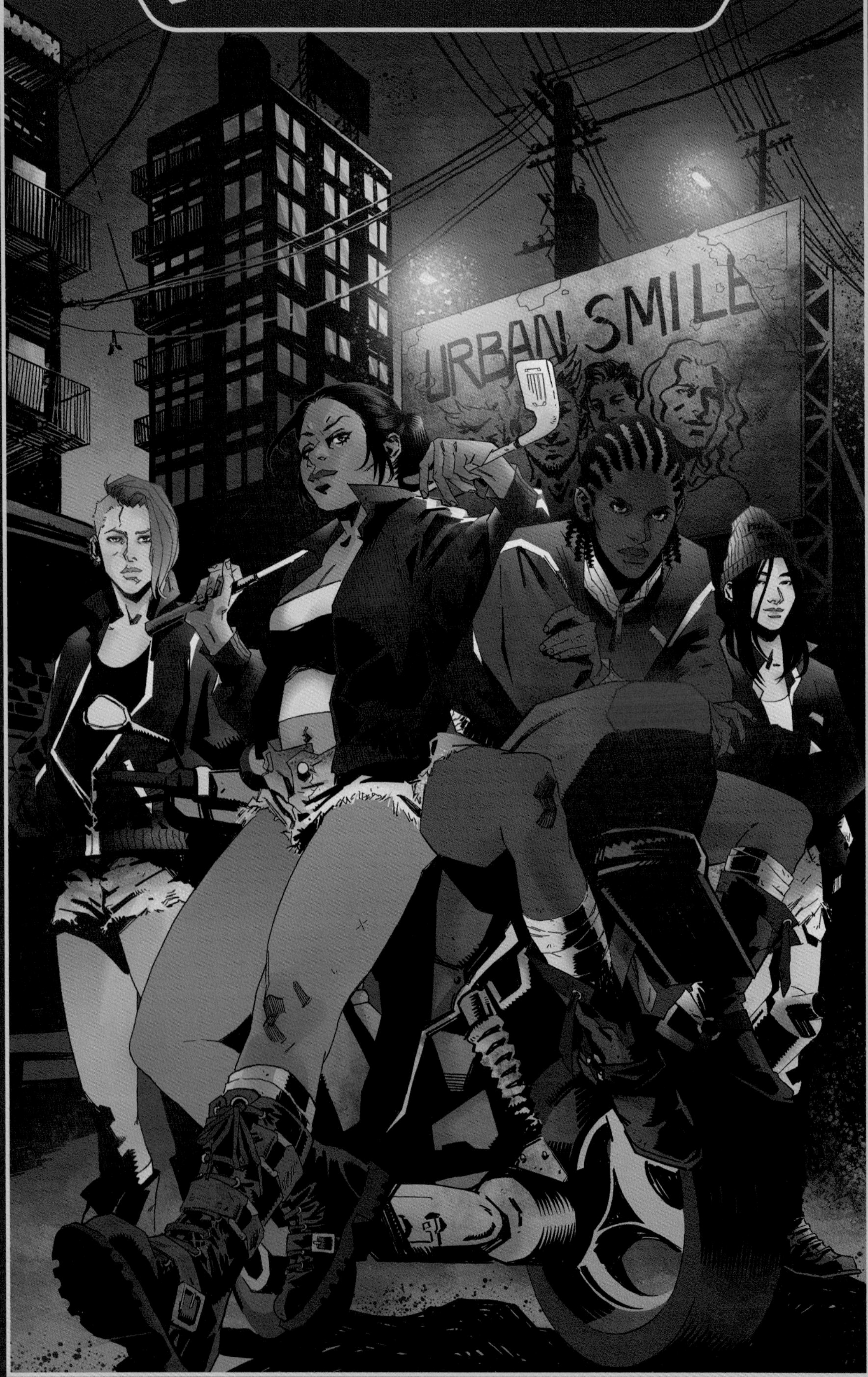
URBAN SMILE

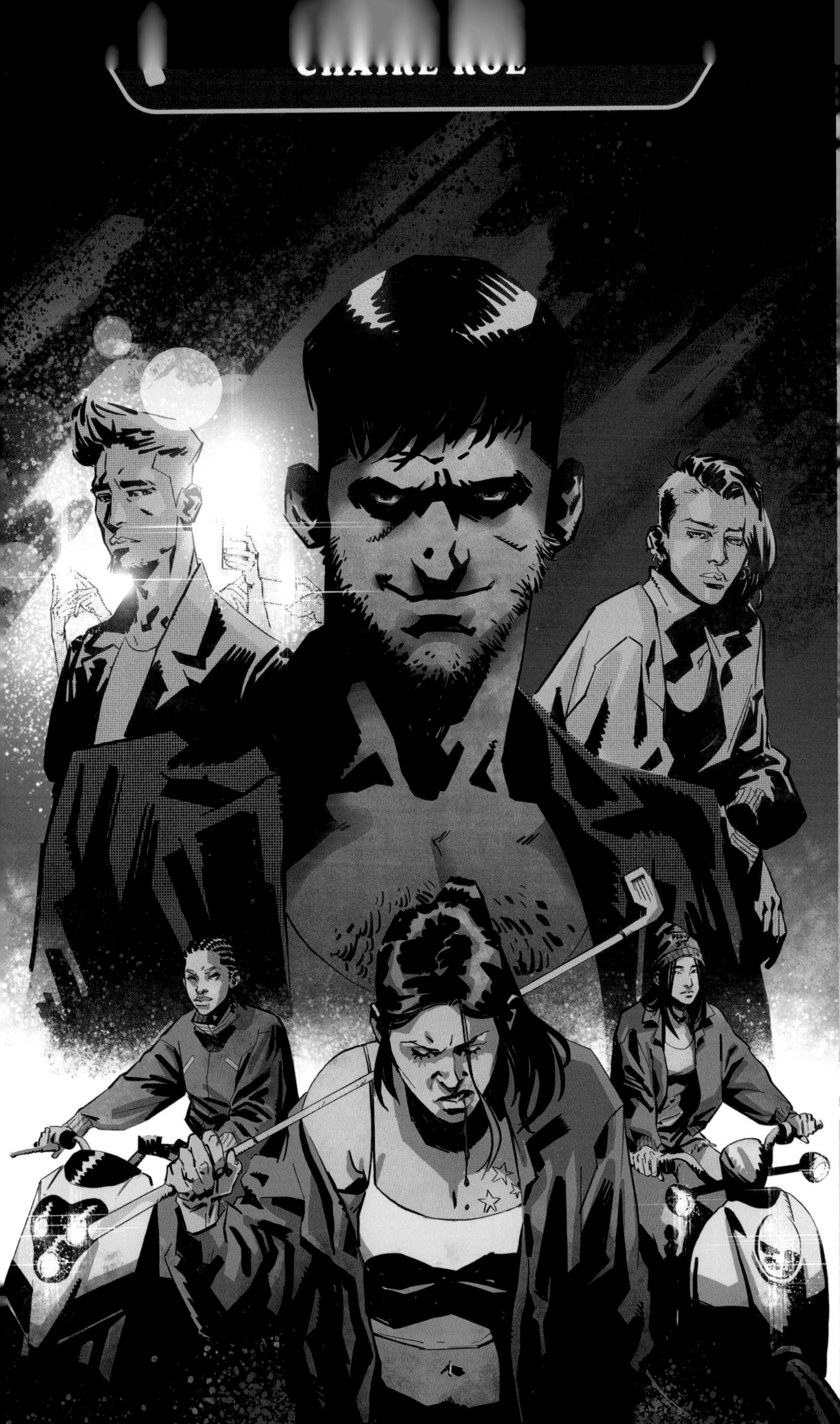

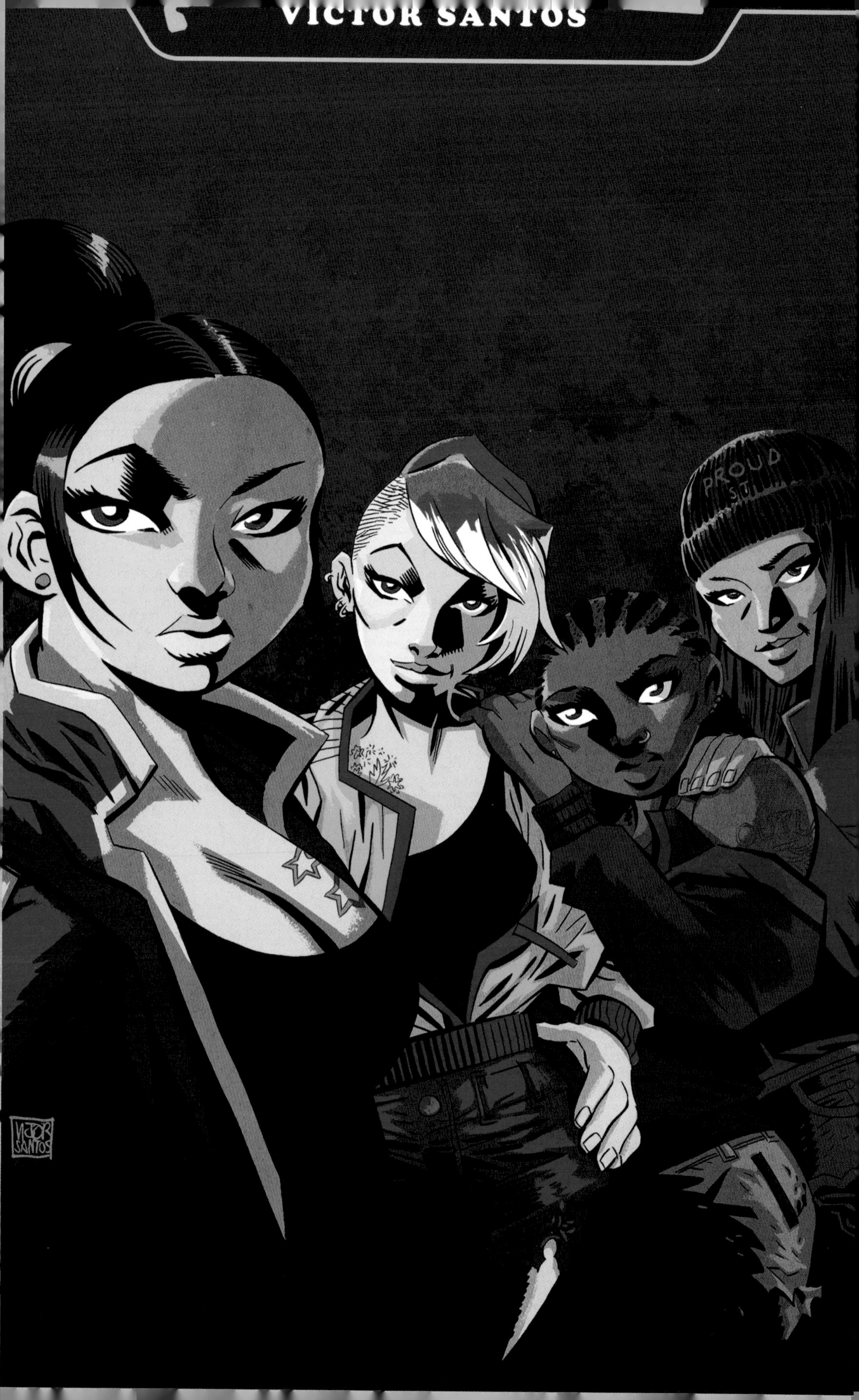
VICTOR SANTOS
PROUD
ST.
VICTOR SANTOS

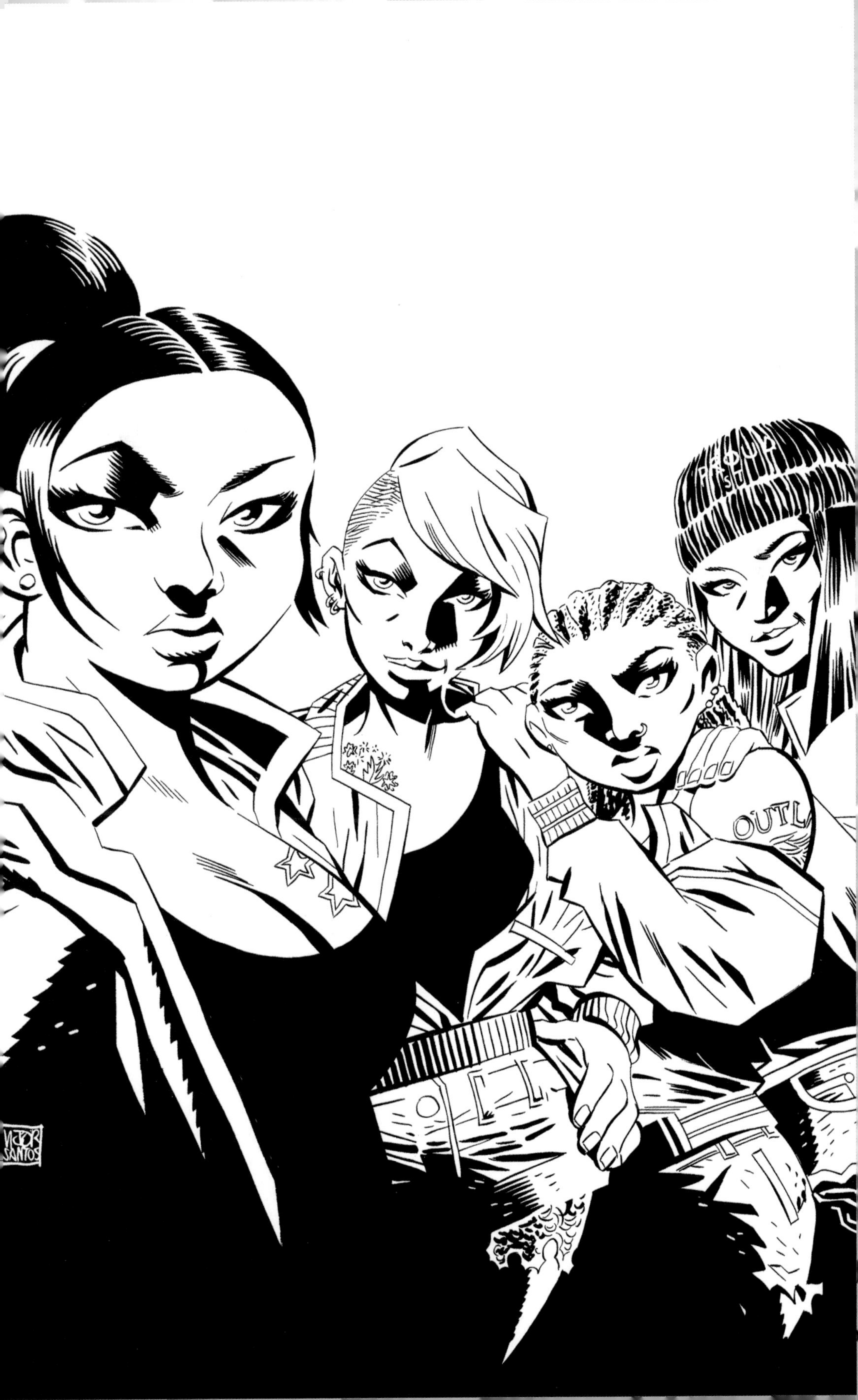
VICTOR SANTOS
OUTL

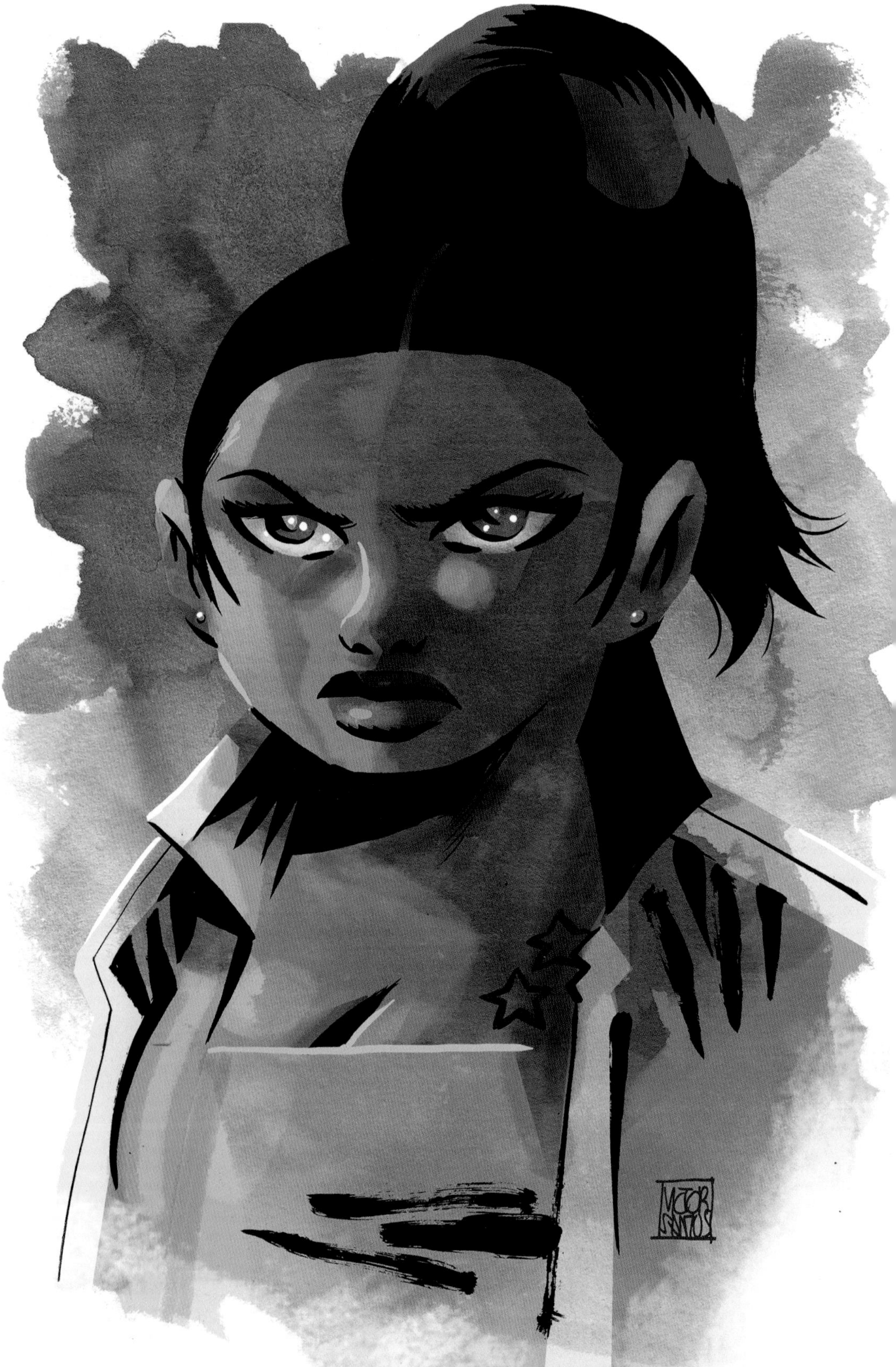

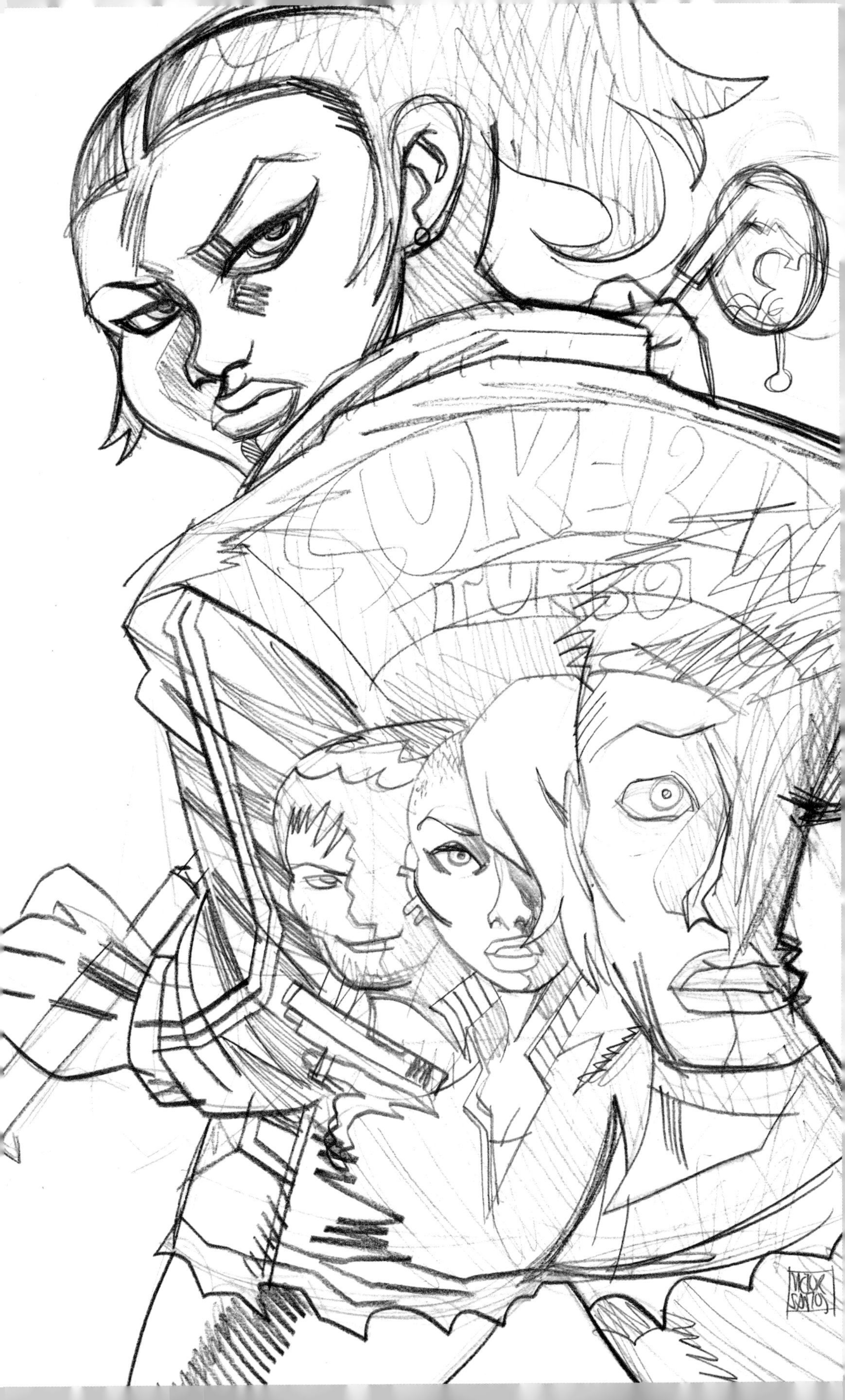
TURBO
VICTOR SANTOS

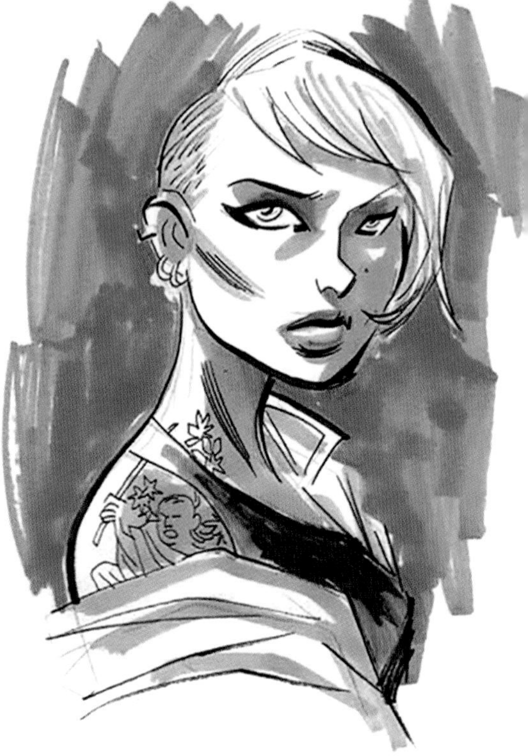

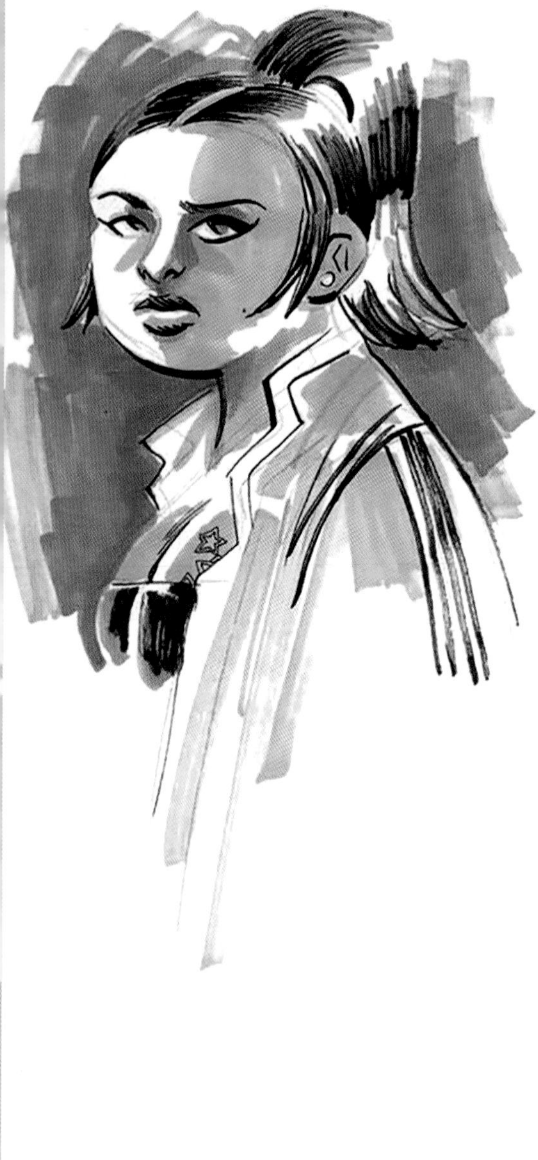

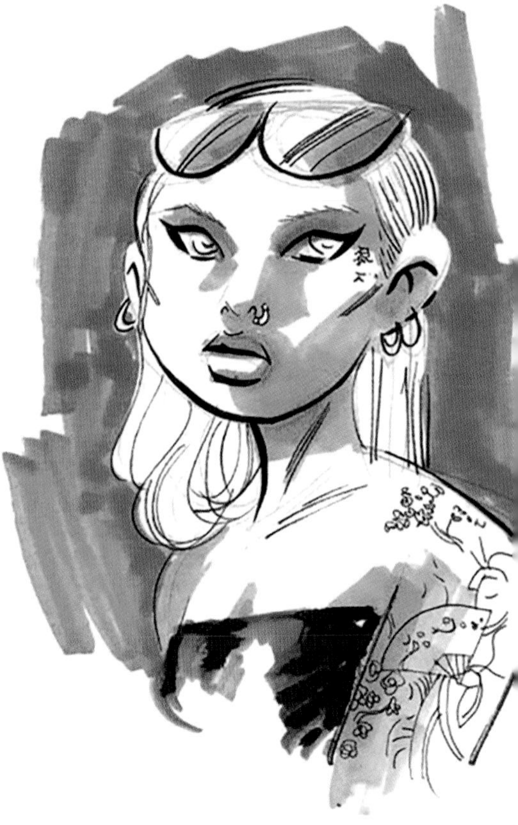

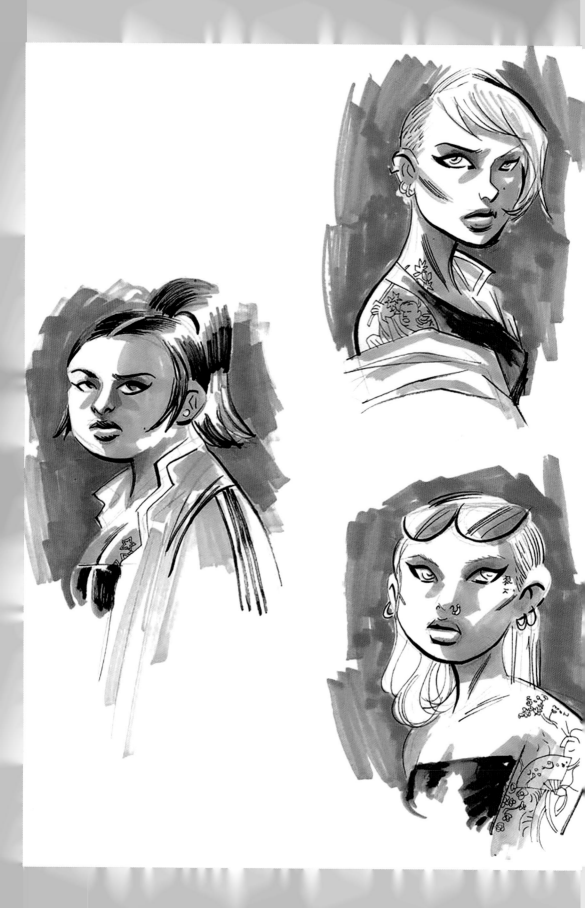

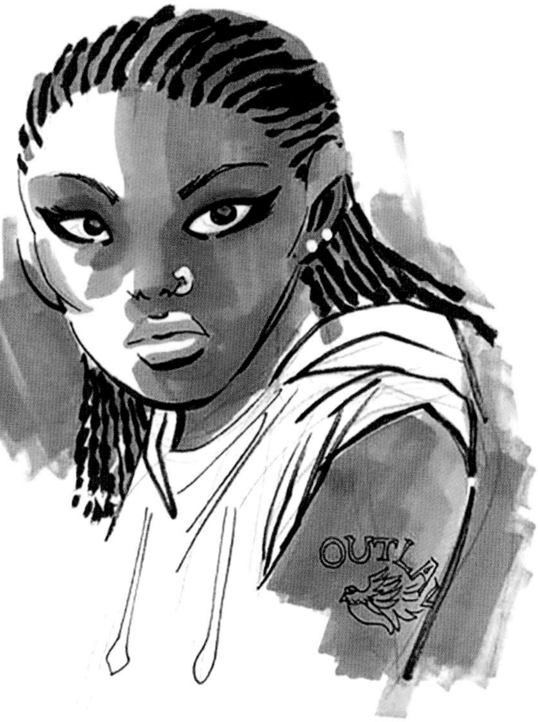
OUTLA

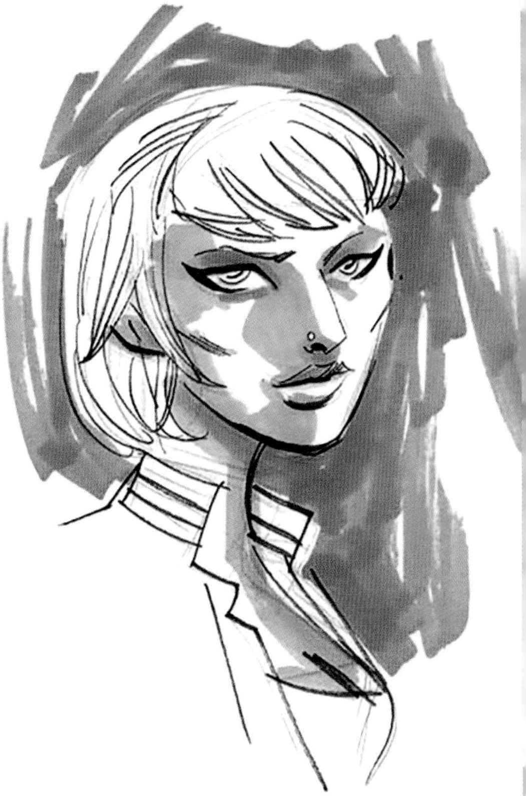

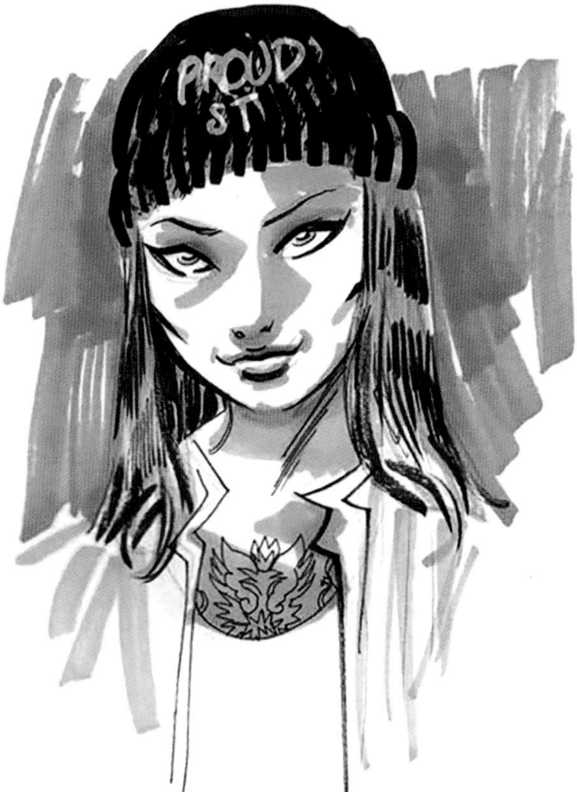
PROUD

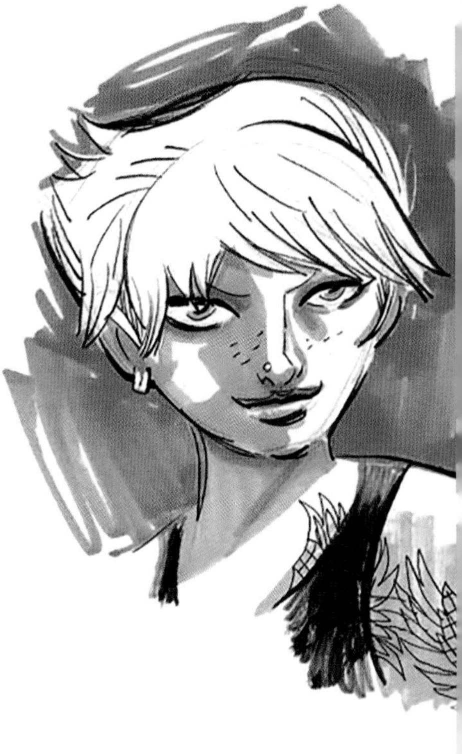

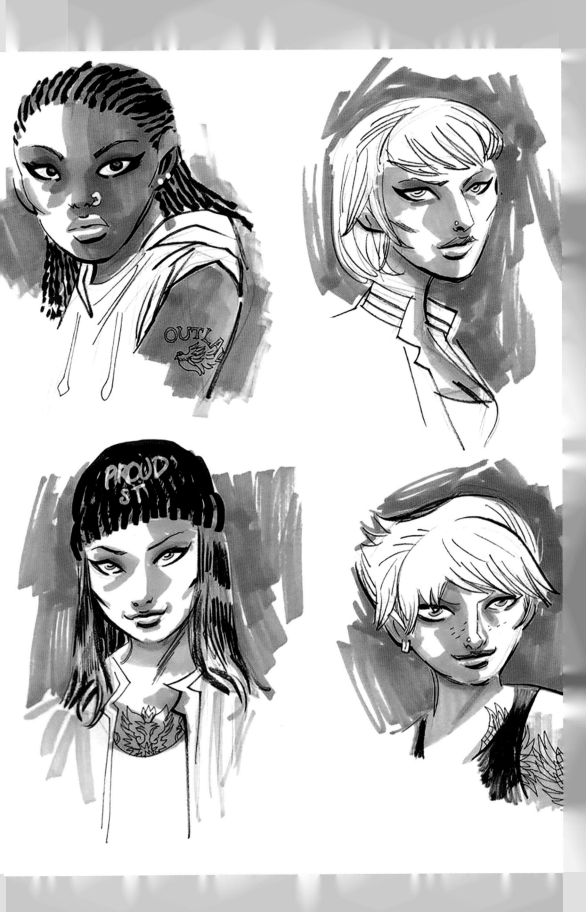

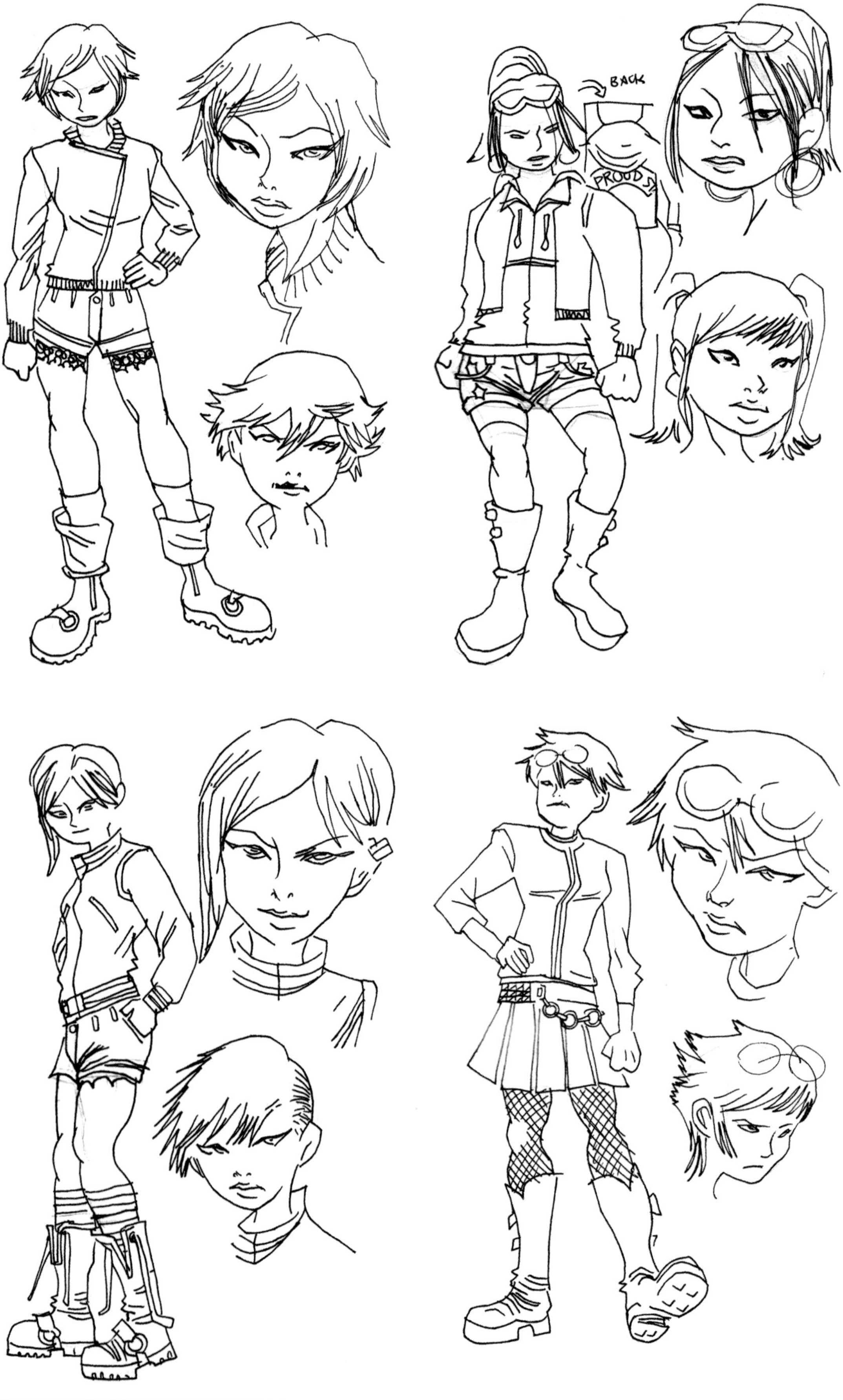
BACK

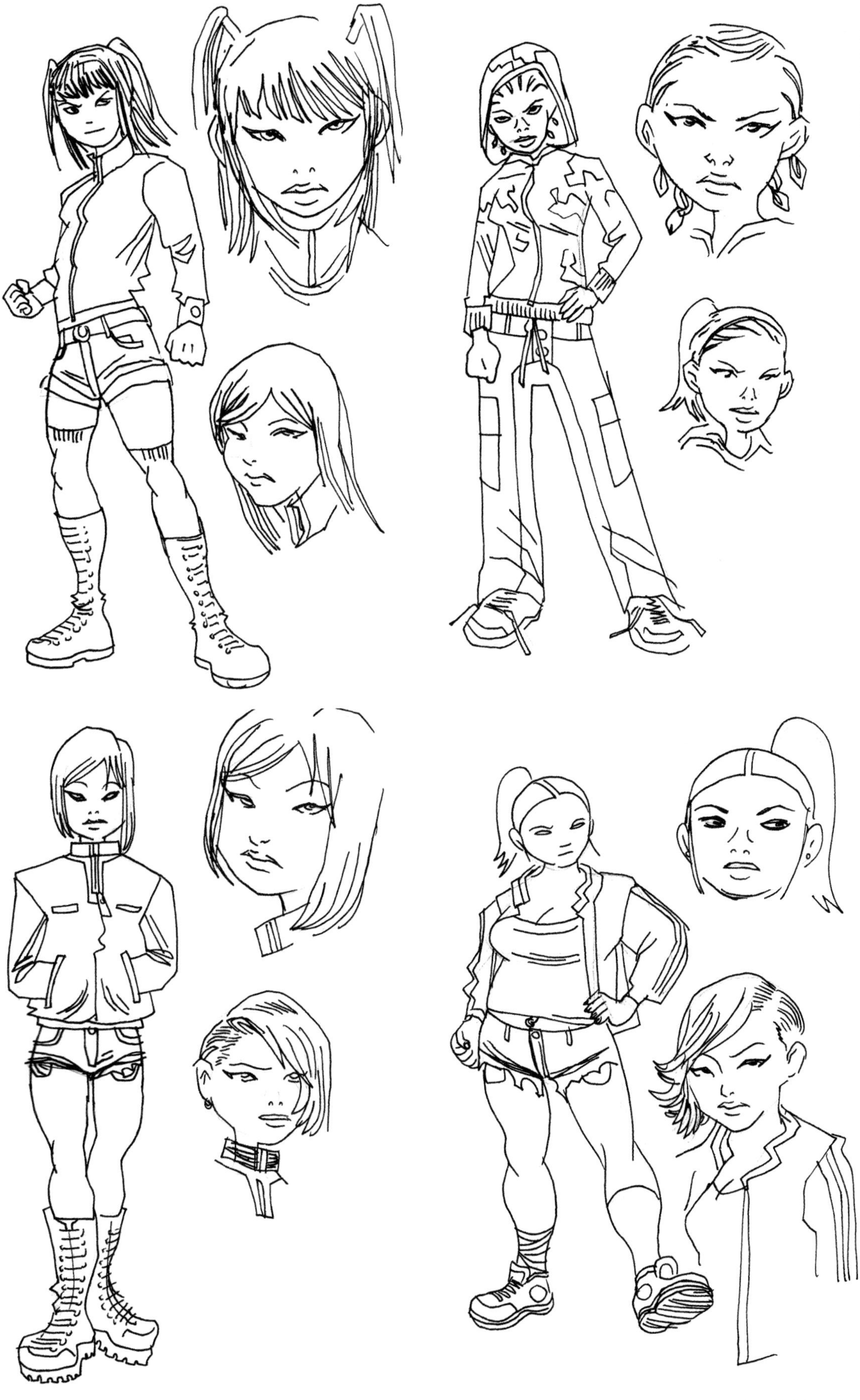

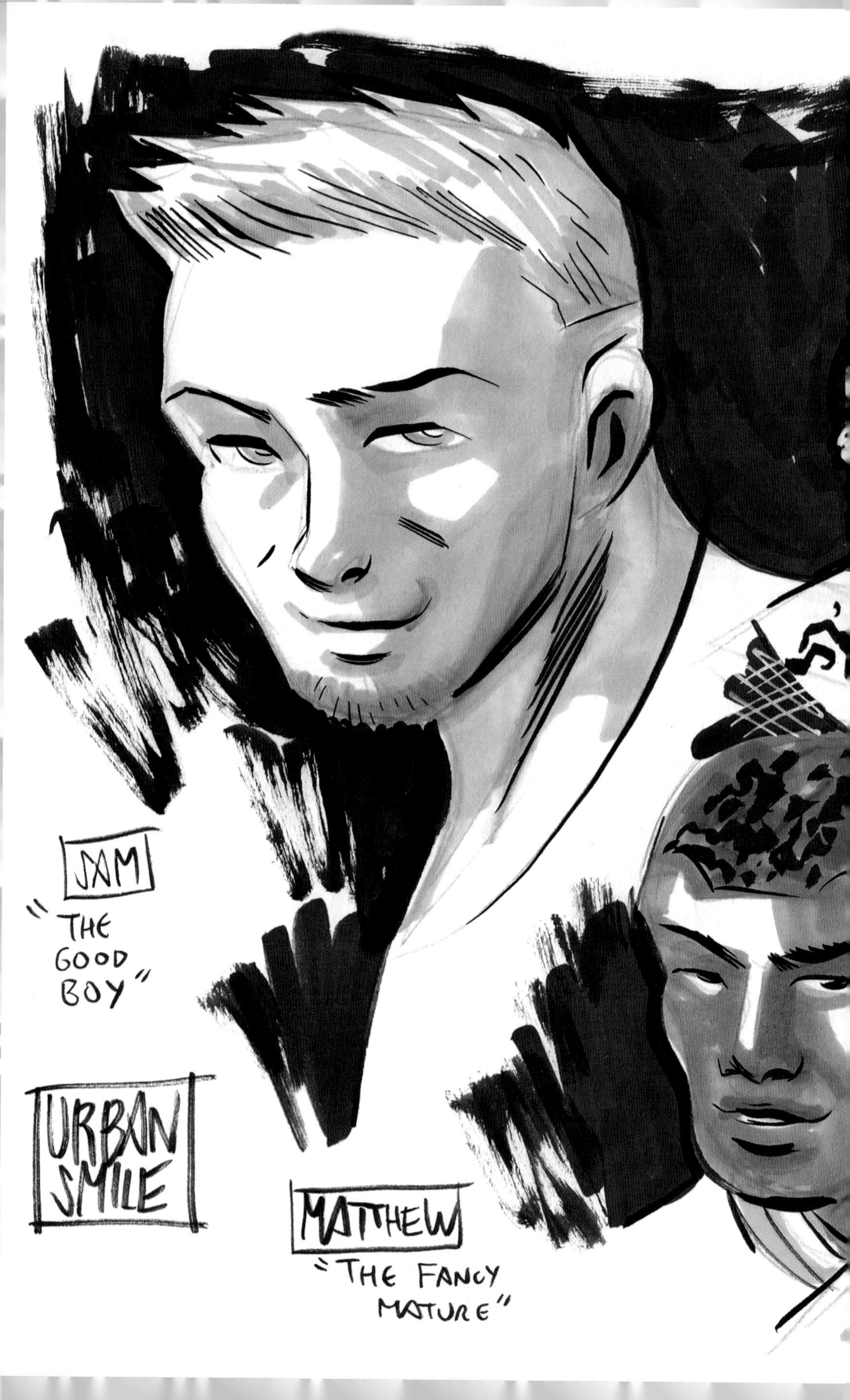
SAM
"THE GOOD BOY"
URBAN SMILE
MATTHEW
"THE FANCY MATURE"

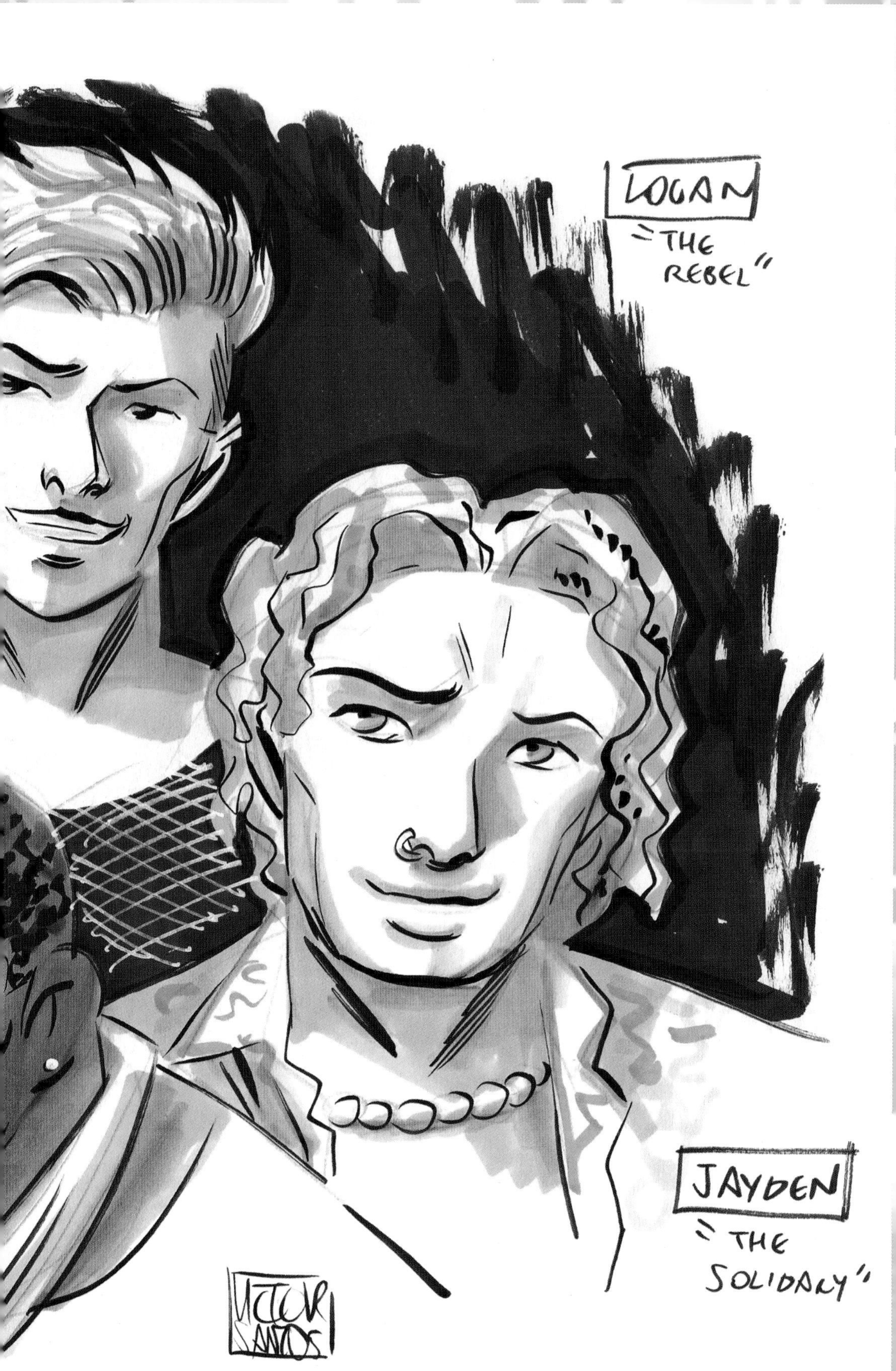
LOGAN
"THE REBEL"
JAYDEN
"THE SOLIDARY"
VICTOR SANTOS

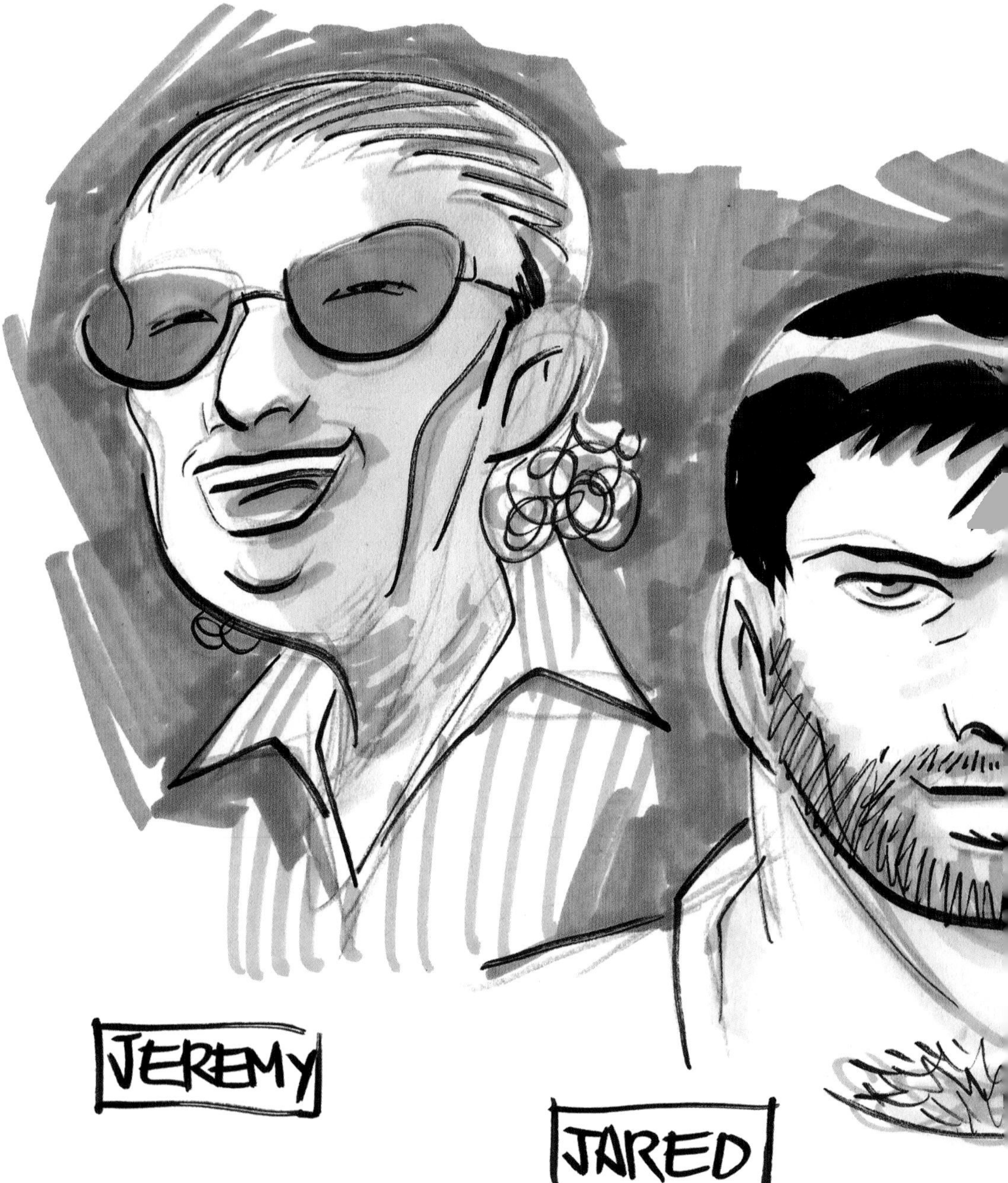
JEREMY
JARED

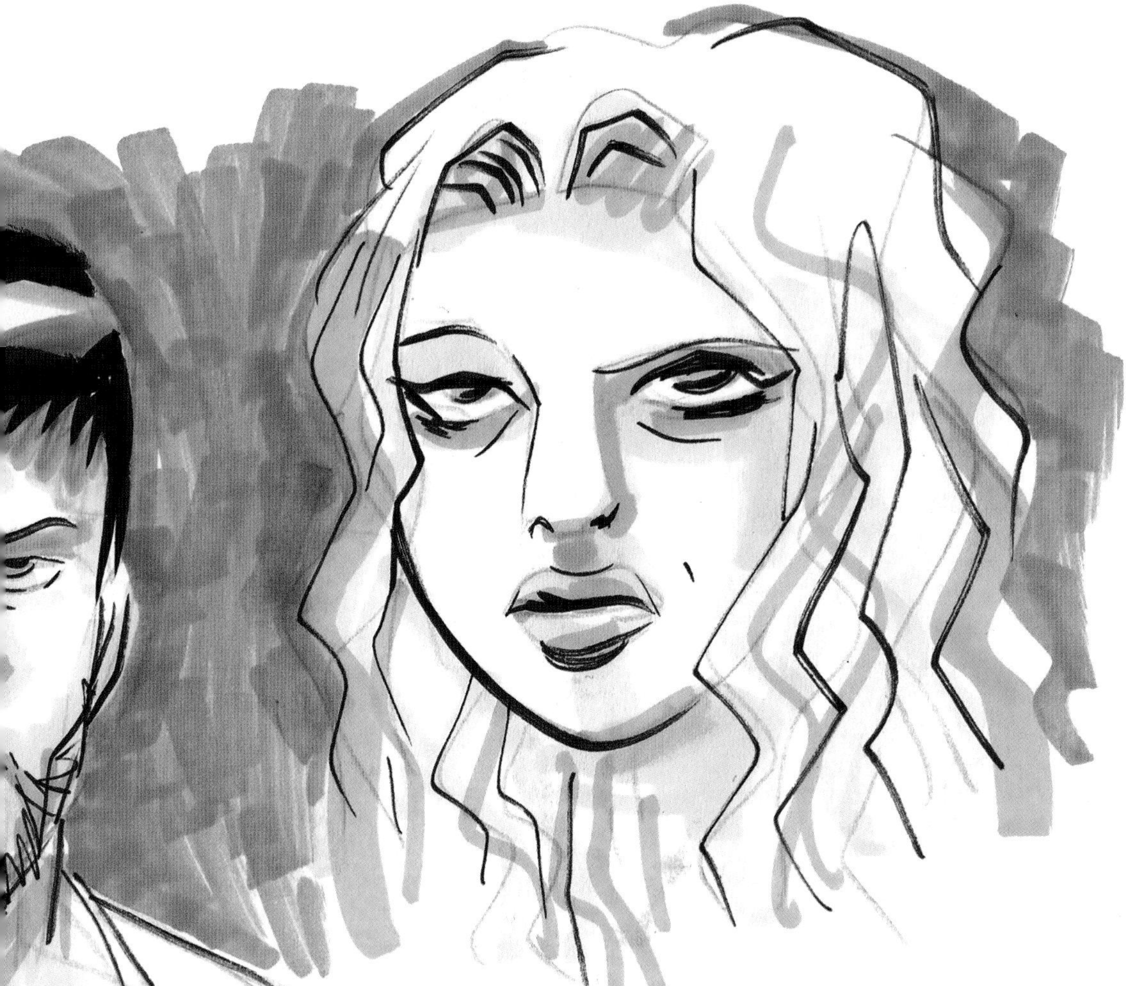
AMBER

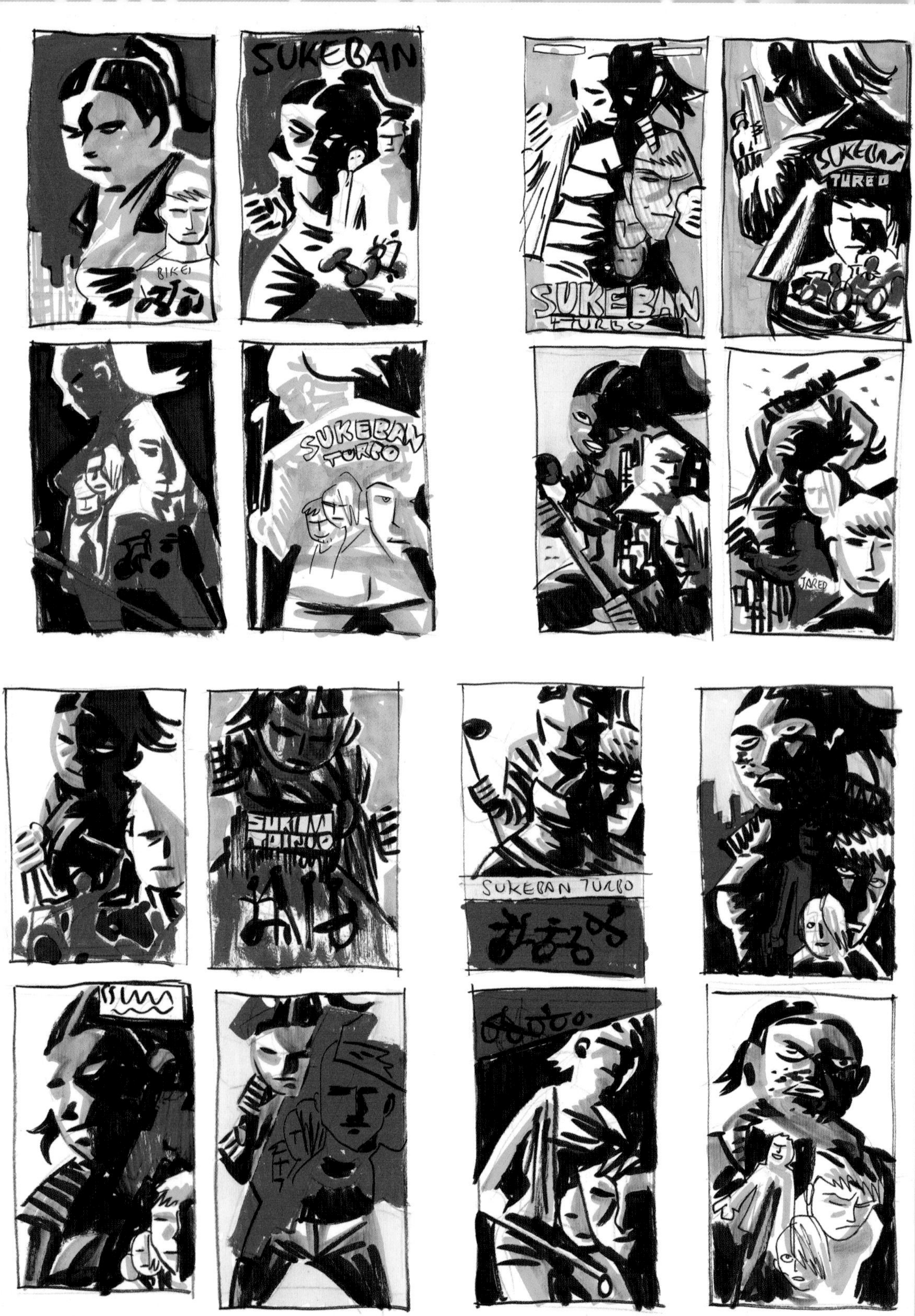
BIKEI
SUKEBAN
SUKEBAN
SUKEBAN
TURBO
SUKEBAN
TURBO
JARED
SUKEBAN TURBO

2
SUKEBAN
TURBO
3
SU
KE
BAN
TURBO
MOTOR CYCLES
SU
KE
BAN
TURBO
5
SUKEBAN TURBO
6

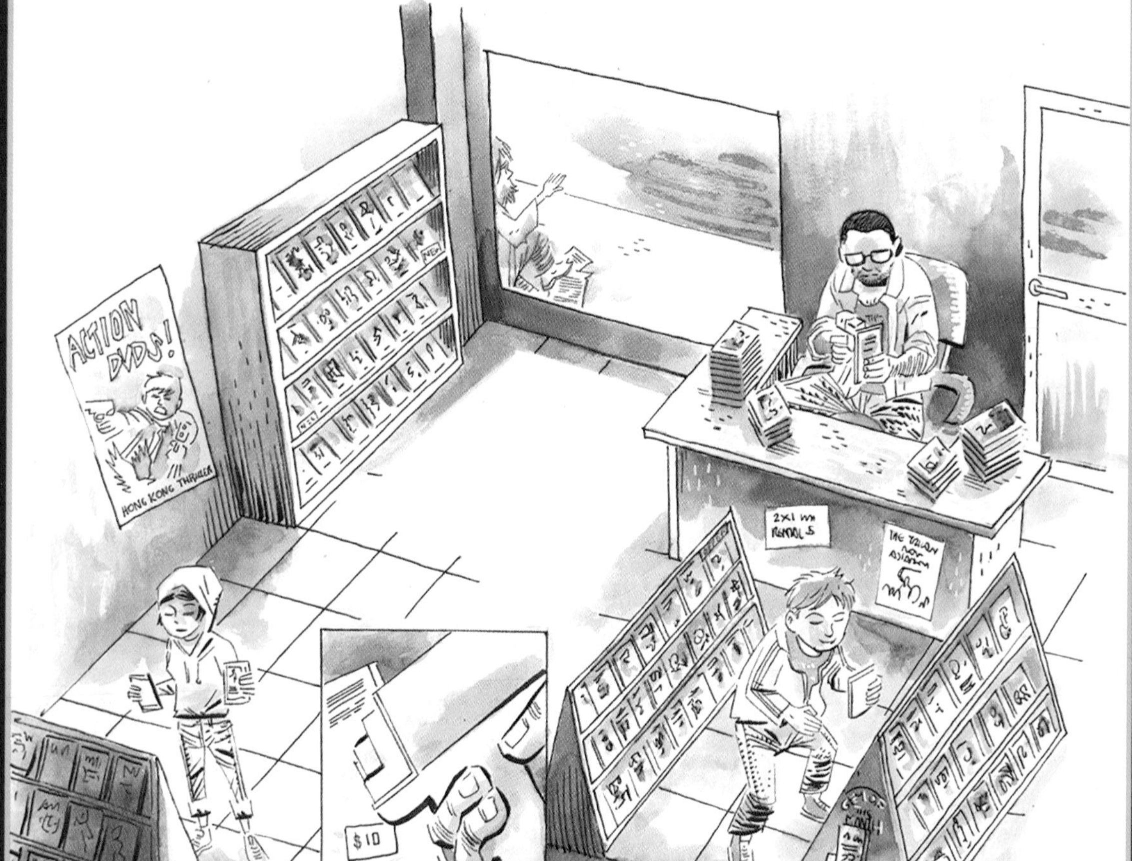
ACTION DVDS!
HONG KONG THRILLER
$10
DVD

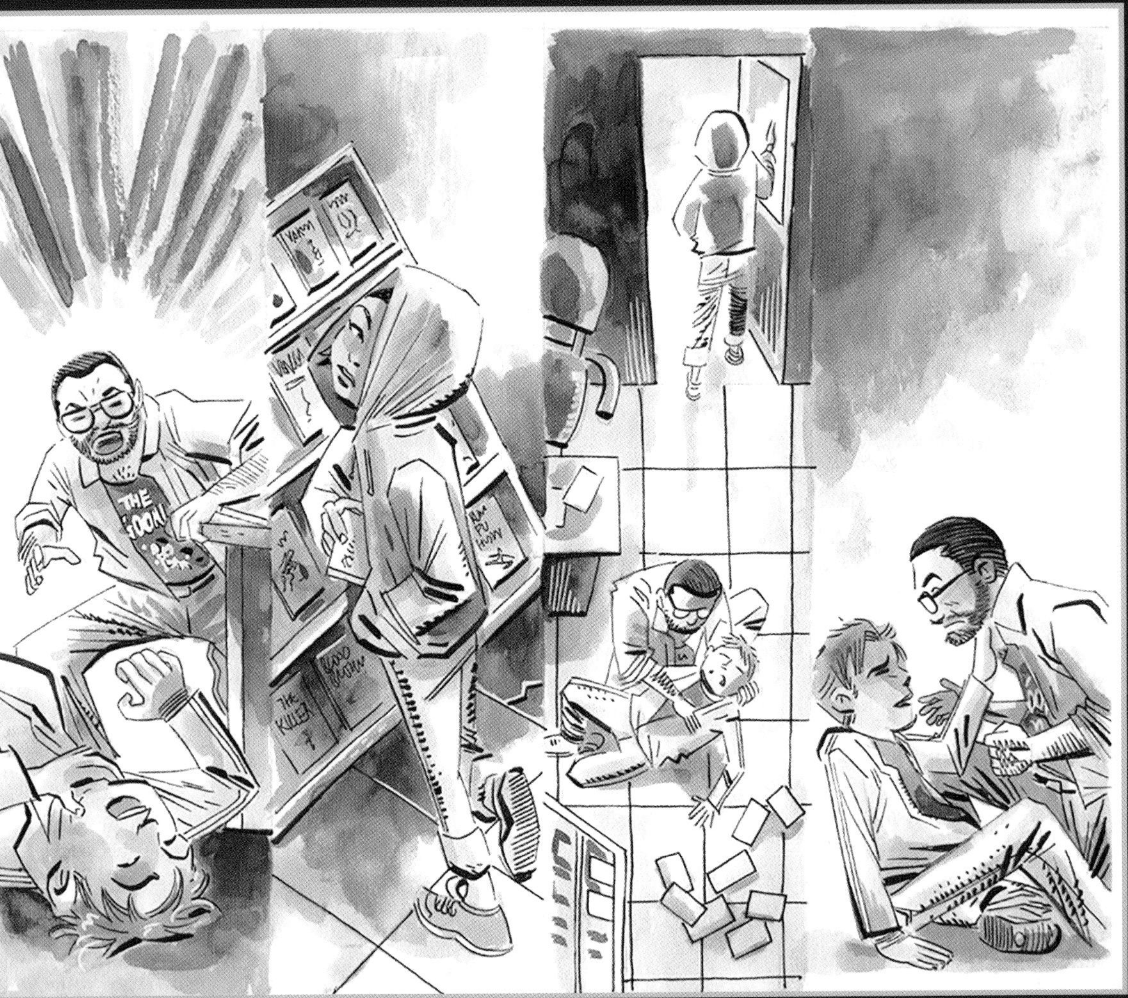
THE KILLER

スケバンターボ

PROUD
ST

EST.
2012

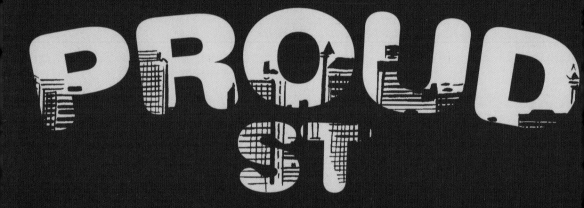

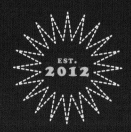